Underground

TOBIAS HILL

faber and faber

First published in 1999
by Faber and Faber Limited
3 Queen Square London WC1N 3AU
This paperback edition first published in 2000

Typeset by Faber and Faber Ltd
Printed in England by Mackays of Chatham plc, Chatham, Kent

A CIP record for this book
is available from the British Library

ISBN 0–571–20116–4

Quoted material from: 'All Along the Watchtower'
(Bob Dylan/Jimi Hendrix); 'Electric Ladyland' (Jimi Hendrix);
'Flash Gordon' (Queen, written by Freddie Mercury); 'Teclo' (P. J. Harvey,
written by Polly Jean Harvey, copyright Island Records Ltd); 'Down to the
River' (Bruce Springsteen); Lewis Carroll, *Alice Through the Looking-Glass*;
Zbigniew Herbert, 'Two Drops', *Selected Poems*

2 4 6 8 10 9 7 5 3 1

To my family, with much love.

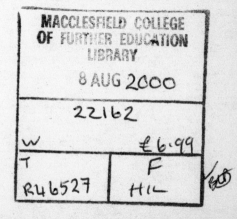

The apparition of these faces in the crowd;
Petals on a wet, black bough.

Ezra Pound, 'In a Station of the Metro'

Underground

Electric Ladyland

'Mind the gap. Please mind the gap. Please –'

The echo of closing doors goes along the Underground platform. The train creaks with stress as it begins to move. Its half-empty carriages fill with the sounds of motion, tunnel air loud against the dirt-streaked windows.

In the first carriage sits a large man in station worker's clothes. He rests with his eyes shut, arms crossed heavily, shoulders down. The skin of his face is tight against the cheekbones, smooth and reddened where he has shaved without water. The tunnel smells of car exhaust and human hair. It is familiar to him as the smell of his own rented room, which is the smell of himself.

First he is sleeping, then he is not sleeping. London passes overhead. He dreams briefly of catch pits, tunnels of white tiles, tunnels of dark grime. His hands lie twisted together in his lap, the tendons drawn clear towards the raw skin of the knuckles. Between his feet rest the black boxes of a cellular telephone, a track voltage tester and a waterproof torch. He keeps his feet and ankles touching them, like a cautious traveller in a foreign country. The groundwater on their scuffed rubber dampens his socks and working trousers.

The tunnel air sighs, open-mouthed: *Haaaah.* Where the structure widens or joins other tunnels, the sigh hollows out. Like water underground, the man thinks. He has not eaten or drunk this morning and the image of water makes him thirsty. He thinks of the city. Rain against shop windows. The smell of low tide near the river, in the plaster in the walls of his room on Lower Marsh. It makes his head hurt.

He knows the Underground line and that he will be awake when he arrives at work. It is not necessary for him to open his eyes. At each station, the rumble of the train doors cuts off fragments of platform announcements and the distant sounds of escalators in the miles of halls and concourses. Twice there is a movement of people in the carriage, their bulk blocking the light on his eyelids.

But it is early morning and there are few passengers. When he is asleep, the man still feels his hands against each other, the palm of the left slightly warmer than the heel of the right. When he is awake, he listens to the sound of the tunnel, how it deepens out at junctions and abandoned stations.

After some time he becomes aware of a voice. There is someone sitting to his right, singing. The voice rises and falls, loud for a moment and then quiet, humming against closed lips. He opens his eyes.

'There must be some kind of way out of here. Said the. Too much *confusion*. Can't get no.'

He has never liked music, the ways it changes what he feels. But the girl in the next seat is singing to her Walkman. Her voice is very young, musical even without the music. A beautiful voice, the man thinks. He tries to listen without being seen to do so. It is something to know about the girl, what music she likes.

She has her headphones turned up loud. He can hear the hiss of a beat over the Underground's roar. He listens with his head leant a little to one side, tie pulling tight against his throat. He keeps his eyes fixed on the yellowed strip lighting, the row of grey hand-grips swinging on their springs. *Cha, cha, uh-huh.* Her fingers beat on the armrest between them.

He wants to turn and look at her but does not. It is the same instinct which makes him cross the road at night if he is walking behind a woman. Because he is strong, he doesn't want to frighten people. He keeps to himself. But he has never heard a girl singing down here alone. Only the junkies. She doesn't sound junked-out. This is part of what interests him.

He looks along the carriage. This is the first up-train of the day, the 5.39 under the river and the West End, out towards the North Circular and the Green Belt. He can see two black men in tunnel-cleaner overalls, a boy dozing with a backpack on his knees, a woman reading the morning business sections.

There is no sound of people except for the girl's voice. Clear but out of tune. No one looks up at her. He watches her hand on the armrest, at the periphery of his vision.

'Have you ever been *have you ever been* to Electric Lady-land?'

She has been eating oranges while he slept. He can see the yellowish pith under her nails. Around her is a litter of peel, small bits torn off and thrown across the stained and corrugated wood floor. The sour smell of fruit mixes with those of rain and urine.

She smells of homelessness. He wonders how old she is and where she sleeps. He looks back at her hand.

There are ink marks where the prominent bones run to her index and middle fingers. A jumble of red and blue words and symbols in smudged print: UNDERWORLD, ΩHM. His eyes narrow as he tries to understand.

He looks down at her small boots. The left sole is coming away; she has tied it on with a second pair of shoelaces. He wants to tell her to use glue, glue would be better. The beat of her hand is regular as a pulse. He imagines what it would feel like, reaching out and covering that movement.

Instead he watches her in the window opposite. Against the dark of the tunnel walls, her skin and the scuts of her dreadlocks are white-blonde. The curve of the glass lengthens the angles of her cheekbones and chin. He doesn't remember seeing her on the first up-train before. But she is familiar from somewhere on the Underground. This also interests him. Her head is leant back, her eyes are closed, the eyebrows raised. She looks like she is dreaming. He wants to know if she dreams in colour.

She opens her eyes and looks back at him, first through the window's reflection and then directly, turning in her seat.

He thinks how dull they are, her eyes. Blue like blood seen through muscle. The shock of them makes him sit up. He is slow to register that she is talking to him.

'I forgot my Travelcard. I forgot it at home. It's for a month.'

Her voice is too loud, compensating for the Walkman. All the lilt of the music has gone out of her speech. When she sang she had an American accent; now she talks with the stopped-consonant voice of London or its satellite towns. For a moment he doesn't understand what she is saying. He turns to face her. She is looking at his uniform, not at him.

She has no ticket, he thinks. He shakes his head, tries to smile.

'I'm sorry. I'm not a ticket inspector. You don't have to –'

But she is looking away from him, eyes flickering across the windows. Outside the dirt-black tunnel gives way to a blur of posters, blue and white tiles, slowing past red-blue London Transport roundels and the station name, WARREN STREET. He turns back to her again.

She is no longer in her seat. He looks up and round, surprised at the quickness of her movement. She is by the door, staring back at him while the train brakes to a stop. He looks at her hands, balled into fists, the ink marks clear against the whitened skin.

He has a strong urge to get up and go to her, to tell her – what? That he finds it hard to look away from her or that he has seen her before? That he knows homelessness in himself, years old, still felt as if the bones are indelibly stained inside him? Instead he makes himself sit back. He wonders if he would be able to explain. The doors open and she steps out and begins to walk as they close behind her.

The train starts to move again. The man looks down at his large hands, thinking of hers. After a moment he turns quickly in his seat. The girl is walking along the platform, not hurrying. She has begun to sing again; he can see her lips moving. Her eyes are fixed ahead. She doesn't look up at him as the train carries him out of sight.

'So. Burton. Nice name. Where you from?'

'Mile End.'

'That's a way to come to Camden. What's that, thirty minutes' drive even this time of the morning, am I right?'

'Yeah.'

'Not to worry. Anyway, I'm Mick Adams. I'm Super. The bloody great foreign geezer over there, that's Cass. He's Assistant Super. You're trainee muck now, but one day all this could be yours. All you have to do is like being under six hundred square miles of London. OK? You must be a Hammers fan.'

'Oy. Don't diss my team, all right?'

'All right. I was only asking. I didn't say a word. Did I, Cass?'

He is by the escalators, down on his haunches. Something is caught in the machinery, he can hear it in the whirr and clank of parts as the steel-and-wood steps are carried round. Most likely it will be a plastic bag or a bag strap. Later he will check the maintenance chamber. The obstruction tears rhythmically, down in the works. He half-closes his eyes, trying to concentrate.

'Hey, Cass.'

For the most part he is not thinking of the escalator. He is remembering the girl on the morning train. The bones of her hands, marked with blue ink. The skin was very smooth, almost without lines, as if she might have no fingerprints.

The sense of having seen her before is still with him. He grinds his teeth gently, trying to remember.

'Casimir?'

'Yes.'

He straightens and turns. Adams is watching him, running fingertips across his side-combed scalp. A sharp, compact man, facial skin punctured with red pores and broken veins. The trainee is standing further off by the wall, very black against the white- and blue-glazed tiles. A pattern of stars is shaved into his hair.

'I was just asking him, wasn't I?'

'Of course. You are the supervisor.' He walks towards them across the tiled hall, which is also only a junction of corridors. Behind the station supervisor, dot-matrix boards begin to light up with the times of early trains to Morden and Bank.

'This is Burton. He's on Youth Training and he likes West Ham Football Club. Isn't that right, Burton?'

The younger man is looking down at his palms. Where he has touched the concourse wall tiles, a glittering grime has come away on his coat and skin. He swears, face wrinkling back from his teeth, narrowing his eyes. 'Look at this cack. It's all over everything.'

Adams tuts his tongue against his teeth. 'Force of gravity, Burton. All the dirt ends up down here. Don't knock it, though, it'll keep you in work for years. They should put it in government. Be like Cass here, he loves it. Still gets here an hour early for work, don't you, Cass?'

The younger man is looking away, up the escalator shaft. Weak dawn light reaches across the upper ceiling. Casimir thinks it will be a fine day outside. Sharp and bright. Adams goes on talking behind him.

'You're not worried by a bit of dirt, are you? A bit of hard work? No. Tell you what, since you've come all this way. Go back downstairs and tell Mister Oluwo to show you the old cross-passages. It's like the Cheddar Caves down there, all snickets and pope-holes. You can do a bit of cleaning, if you're feeling strong. All right? Remember the way?' A man in pin-stripes heads past them, walking hard towards the City platform. 'Chop chop.'

Casimir watches as the trainee goes, shoulders hunched angrily, rubbing his hand on his trousers. He remembers his own first few days on the Underground. The feeling of control in the tunnels and halls, their light and air and even life rationed out; and with that, the gradual calm of finding his own life under control. The darkness out in the open, all around him, so that although it could and can still bring him out in a cold sweat, he is always ready for it. The fear never takes him by surprise. The Underground's great extent and age were things he learned later, but the sense of order has never gone away, not yet. It is something he needs, the control.

Most of all, he remembers the Tube seeming like a hiding place. It felt as if he was coming to ground here, waiting for something to catch up with him. He doesn't know what he is waiting for. Casimir does not understand where this sense comes from.

A lorry goes past overhead, the crash of its load and fittings filtered down. He turns away. He finds the distance of the sound soothing. Like rain through windows. He leans back against the wall. 'He won't be back tomorrow.'

'Of course he won't. Why should he? There's nothing for him down here.' The supervisor hawks and spits away.

They go on towards the platforms. Overhead in the city Casimir walks stooped, shy of his own height. But here in the passages he moves more naturally, the scooped curve of the tunnel leaving him scant headroom. He is always aware that people can be threatened by him, and not only because of his looming, soft-footed bulk. He is disturbing, in the way someone who has been through deep fear is disturbing. He imagines it coming off him like an odour: not fear any more, but something to be frightened of.

Along the walls, layers of old advertisements have been ripped off, strips hanging down loose where the poster hangers have left their night-work unfinished. Casimir looks up at the shots of blue sky, water beading black skin, car tracks on white sand. The slogans: 'GET DOWN AT G-SPOT SNOOKER & BEER HALL!', 'MANY WHO PLAN to seek God at the eleventh hour DIE AT 10.30'.

The floor is uneven by the next junction of tunnels, scarred by heavy machinery. He stops and takes a spray can out of his work coat, then kneels to mark round the rough tiling. Later he'll get a warning sign from the storerooms.

'What's wrong with that? Eh?' Adams waits for him, impatient. Something of him is always moving, hands or mouth or eyes.

'It could be dangerous.'

'Dangerous! Did you hear what happened on the new line? The drum diggers went through into a cave. Eighty feet deep. So what they've done is, they've concreted over the top of it and gone and laid the track. What do you think of that? All those passengers thinking they're going underground, when really they're chuffing along eighty feet above it.'

The supervisor is looking up at the NO SMOKING sign bolted to the wall, the shine of black enamelled smoke. 'No, you're right to be careful. Good lad. Christ, I need a fag.' He puts his hands in his pockets, keeping them still. 'How are you, Cass? I haven't seen you much this week.'

He shrugs. 'We were on different turns. I'm well.'

'You don't look it. You look peaky. Cash flow all right, is it? No family trouble?'

'No.' He is surprised. Family is not something he and Adams have talked about since Casimir filled in his job application. *Next of Kin:* 'none', he wrote. Which was not true, although it is how Casimir lives his life. In eight years, the relationship of Casimir and the supervisor has never gone much beyond work. Casimir tries to remember if they have ever met above ground. He thinks not. Real friendship is never something he has wanted from the supervisor. He feels no need to be understood. He stands back up, clapping his hands clean. 'No trouble. I have no family.'

'That's right, isn't it? No offence meant, eh?'

Adams slows as they reach a flight of stairs. The steps are worn down at their centres, metal and stone uneven. He goes down with one hand on the ironwork banister. Two steps behind, Casimir tries to imagine him retired, in a room of his own. All he can see is Adams in the station office, leant forward over the stained plyboard consoles, face lit with closed-circuit monitor light.

At the bottom of the stairs, the poster hangers have put up a new film advertisement. The paper is still shiny with wallpaper paste. They stop together in front of the clean, blue-white image. A single figure stumbles through a field of snow. Smaller flyers have already been stuck over the poster diagonally, like steps through the white field: HAVE YOU SEEN THIS CHILD?, a picture, a number. Adams tuts and reaches for the flyers, then lets his hand drop to his side. An indecisive, anxious movement. 'What shift were you on yesterday, Cass?'

'Middle turn. With Sammons.'

'So you were. You missed the news, then.'

'What news?'

Another commuter passes them, a young woman reading a paperback as she walks, hair blown into her face, skirt blown back against her ankles. Adams follows her with his eyes as he talks quietly. 'There was a bit of fuss yesterday. An accident. Late turn, round about afternoon rush hour.'

'Here?'

Adams nods. They begin to walk again. It has been almost a year since the last accident at their station. A failed Bank Holiday suicide, a scrawl of explanation twenty pages long stuffed into his jacket pockets. Casimir remembers the man weeping, bloody and wretched. The hum of electricity trying to earth itself.

He requires the thoughts to be gone and they are. 'A suicide?'

Adams looks back at him, half-smiling. 'A suicide wouldn't be an accident now, would it? Line Management reckons it was a fall. The platforms were crowded up to the white lines. Most likely someone got too close, pushing and shoving and that. This girl went down into the catch pit like that –' He snaps his fingers. The retort echoes along the tiled corridor.

Casimir waits for him to go on. Adams adjusts his watch-strap, then looks down towards the platform. 'Clean fall, but she tried to climb up out on the negative rail. Caught a bit of current and a bit more off the signal line. The bruises were worse than the burns and no blood to speak of. They've kept her in overnight for, you know? Just in case. It looked worse than it was. The way she fell.'

'What was her name?'

'Her name?' Adams frowns, blue eyes staring. 'Is, not was. She's not dead, for Christ's sake. Doesn't matter anyway, does it?'

Casimir shakes his head, embarrassed by the other man's sudden irritation. It comes to him that this is the edge of something in Adams, some larger anxiety or hurt. The girl matters to him. Casimir wonders why.

'S something, Sarendon, Savallas, I don't know.' The supervisor has stopped again, still frowning. 'Nice girl, she looked. Done up nice. Training to be a foot doctor.' He grins at Casimir, suddenly relieved. 'I never knew there was doctors just for feet, you know?'

They go on out on to the platform. It stretches away from them, long like a church nave. The three entranceways are Victorian mock-classical, bas-relief architraves and columns curved round the tunnel's proportions like images seen through a fish-eye lens. Casimir feels a momentary familiar sense of dislocation at the subterranean space, its scale and lack of natural light. The black platform surface is reinforced with steel chipping and edged with white. Beyond that, the four track rails shine. Under them is the deep gutter of the catch pit. Casimir thinks of the Tube workers' slang: *suicide pit*.

He sees the gutter as that; the term feels accurate. Suicides are what it's made to catch.

The news of the accident touches him, but he is also relieved. He knows how bad accidents can be on the Underground and this is not a bad accident. The electricity in the negative rail is only as strong as the current in a household socket. And there was no train collision. A minimum of blood.

He blinks once, looking back at himself, feeling his own unease. It jars with him, the way Adams has told him the news. The supervisor has always been quick-witted and quick-tempered, but the nervousness is new to Casimir, the sense of strapped-down anger. As if the accident were more serious than it is. He feels a faint current of air along his left cheek and the broken line of his nose. A train is coming, still far off in the dark.

Casimir feels shifting motion around him. Not the tangible matter of air, but a moment of dizziness, more inside him than out. A perception of change, a loss of control. It is a kind of fear he has not felt for a long time, not for years. He goes on talking, willing it away.

'Did she call for help?'

'Oh yes. Plenty of noise.'

'You don't think she jumped?'

Now the train is audible, the sound of it warbling through the tracks. Like a stone thrown across ice.

Adams looks away northwards, the direction from which the train will come. After some time he shakes his head, no.

'That doesn't make it an accident. She could have been pushed.'

The supervisor looks back up at him. His reddened face and blue eyes are cocked like the head of some bright, sharp bird. 'It's an accident until Line Management says otherwise. D'you get me?'

'Yes.'

'That's good. Right then, son.' He slaps Casimir's arm. A friendly movement but also automatic, without affection. 'We should be going. Rush hour in no time.' He has to shout a little over the roar of the oncoming train.

He wakes up in the dark. The muscles of his shoulders ache from overwork. The window is open but the room is hot, and from outside comes the sound of a car alarm, streets away.

His left hand is raised on the mattress, next to his upturned face. He can hear the tick of his watch, separating the dark into measured time. He turns to see. On his wrist, the watch-face emits its faint, definite light.

His mouth is dry and he gets up for water, asleep but not asleep. The hallway carpet is a numb fur under his feet.

He was dreaming of the girl. Already he can't remember the colour of her eyes. He tries to picture her clearly, letting nothing else fade as he wakes. The muscles of his erection are still drawn out hard and aching, warmer than his inner thigh. He clicks on the bathroom light and the bulb goes with a dull *pock*.

The flash of light stays on his eyes. He turns back into the hall. The light switch is by the staircase, away from his rented room. There are no windows, only a square of pinkish London cloud through a skylight. He gets to the switch and the bulb is dead.

He can feel a familiar, drowsy panic rising in him and he stands, waiting for it to pass. Light bulbs go together, he tells himself, because they are bought together. He tries to think rationally. It is possible to control the fear this way, he has done it many times. The dark looms over him and he arches his bare shoulders forward against it. His hands cross at the wrists, holding on to the indistinct light source of the watch-face. It is no more than five feet to the staircase. He makes himself go forward and down.

Outside the car alarm stops, long after he has ceased to hear it. The silence jolts him fully awake and he misses a step, keeling forward in the stairwell. He reaches out for the banister and swings upright, breathing badly.

At the bottom of the stairs is the first-floor kitchen. The sweet smells of frying oil and raw chicken-meat seep up from the shop below. Casimir clicks on the light and stands in its abrupt illumination, the dark pushed back outside small windows. He puts his head back, glad of the glare on his eyes.

The wall clock ticks loudly towards four-thirty. He has

another hour before he will leave for Camden Town. He turns on the radio and sits down at the Formica table. The air is warm against his bare legs. After some time he closes his eyes and sleeps with his head on his folded arms. The news whispers behind him.

He closes the scuffed side-door and stands outside on the pavement. Taking a breath, getting his bearings. The plate glass next to him is smeared with rain and grease. Above its window, the shop's name is printed in red: DON'T FRY TONIGHT PHONE CHICKEN DELITE.

Casimir looks up, shading his eyes against the dull light. The early-morning sky is grey and clear and the moon is still rising, a northern summer crescent that reminds him of Poland; the flat, cropped fields of Silesia and the moon over them at midday, unnatural in the blue sky. The eye of a fish beached in the Russian waterlands. Out of place; out of its place. He looks down and starts to walk, up Lower Marsh towards Waterloo station.

The shops he passes – Tribalize Body Piercing, Honour Exclusive Ladywear – are unlit behind chain-links. Only the cafés are already open. Market stall-holders smoke and chat outside Olympic Sandwich and Maria's. Casimir walks between their vans, the scaffolds of half-erected stalls and the crates of jogging bottoms, dusty plastic geraniums, bruised green bunches of plantain. His work clothes chaff against the skin of his neck and thighs.

He has lived in this place for eight years. The smell of the weekday market is intimate to him; diesel and fried onions, like a fairground. The soot-black brick houses have become his mental neighbourhood. It is the nearest thing he has to a sense of home. He walks with his head down, uncurious, black hair hanging forward past his temples.

Outside the Fishcoteque Bar, a man with birds tattooed on each hand is unloading painted eggs in glass boxes. One of the boxes falls as Casimir passes. He turns to watch without stopping. The man carefully picks up pieces of red eggshell, glass and black lacquer in his faded-ink hands.

Casimir knows his face and his name, Weaver. His memory is good and he knows many of the people here, sellers and buyers. But few of them know him. He likes it that way. He turns left up the incline of Spur Road, towards the high arched windows of Waterloo terminus.

At the top of the road he stops to catch his breath. Tower blocks loom overhead, nearer the Thames. Already the sky is lighter; he can feel the changing warmth of it on his face. Below him, Lower Marsh is a row of sallow net curtains, extensions built in brick the colour of new skin. The rear views make him think of city hostels in Poland, cheap back rooms with windows looking out on to nothing but other windows. Casimir would watch people eating alone at small tables, old men brushing their teeth, young women walking up and down behind blown-in curtains. Humanity crammed in together; he always liked that, except when he caught people looking back at him.

He searches for the window of his own room, but there is nothing to mark it out and after a moment he turns away.

There are steps up to the terminus and he hunches forward as he climbs, too lanky for their measure, taking them in twos and threes. A dog skitters down past him, white with pink-rimmed eyes, quiet and alert. Casimir turns right along the foot of the terminus building. The side-entrance is a brick arch, small and ordinary as the house doorways of Lower Marsh.

He goes through, into the arched concourse. Pigeons whicker around the four-faced station clock, jostling for resting space. There is a young man by the W. H. Smith, slumped against newspaper bundles. His head rests on his T-shirted chest and one inert bluish arm lies outstretched, as if asking for something. Casimir can see no one else and there is no sound of people yet, only the hushed echoes of arrival boards and cooling engines. Casimir feels a need to shout, to fill the place with the sound of voices. He smiles at himself. The expression works against the drawn lines of his features.

He walks across the white-tiled hall to a descending shaft, over-lit and loud with machinery. There is a London Underground map on the entrance wall, a knotwork of tunnel lines, purple and brown and black: Metropolitan, Bakerloo, Northern. Casimir steps on to the down-escalator and stops walking. Behind him, a telephone starts to ring, faint but insistent in the huge interior space. Casimir turns to look back at it as he is carried down.

'All this time the guard was looking at her, first through a telescope, then through a microscope. At last he said, "You're travelling the wrong way," and shut up the window and went away. Look. Can you see the guard in the picture?'

'No. Lie, lie. Lie-lie-lie.'

He is sitting opposite a woman, a suitcase, a dog and a child. The woman is reading to the child. The dog tugs at the worn-down seats. Behind them is his own reflection in the Tube windows. Today the seat next to him is empty. His uniform jacket is open. He does it up.

'But the gentleman in white paper leant forwards and whispered in her ear, "Never mind what they all say, my dear, but take a return ticket every time the train stops."'

'Lie, lie. Mum, I'm tired.'

'Are you listening to this?'

'You did a lie.'

'What lie?'

'There ain't no gentleman in white paper.'

The boy is frowning across at him, dark irises under lowered brows. Casimir smiles back. He remembers the story, the soft Polish of his mother's voice. Now the woman looks up at him quickly. Not worried, just watching. Her eyes are shadowed, the skin bruised with lack of sleep. He thinks how early it is to be down here, with a suitcase and child and a dog.

He looks away at the tunnel going by. After some distance it opens out, losing definition. Through his own reflection, Casimir watches another train go past. Faces at the window turn slowly to look back. The boy cranes round in his seat, but the other train is already gone.

At Camden Town he gets out. The train pulls away beside him as he walks down the platform. The air today smells wet and warm. Casimir guesses it will rain, and he regrets that he won't see it. It'll be ten hours before he is outside again. He has always enjoyed summer rain.

Half-way down the platform, a black sphere hangs from the tunnel ceiling. Casimir can make out the shapes of closed-circuit cameras inside the translucent plastic. He nods at them, half-raises a hand.

At the southern end of the platform he turns down a side-passage. The lighting here is poorer, less public; signs point off to other platforms and the deep well of the emergency stairs. The right wall is lined with dirt-clogged grilles, 1930s panelled wooden doors and extractor fans from the Camden take-aways. There is a thick, sweet smell of junk food in the low-ceilinged hall. Casimir feels his stomach turn over with hunger.

At the corner of the passage is a blank modern door. Off to one side is a sign:

STATION SUPERVISOR: ASSISTANCE. PLEASE ENTER.
! FIRE DOOR: KEEP SHUT.

Casimir stands for a moment, unbuttoning his jacket. He can hear the sound of static and voices through the door, faint and serious.

An old woman comes round the passage corner. Two lean grey dogs strain ahead of her, tongues lolling out in the underground humidity. The woman's mess of dull hair has become tangled with the dog leashes knotted to her belt. She stares up at Casimir, at the door and then away. She is talking under her breath and Casimir has the impression she is asking him for help. He leans forward instinctively, trying to hear.

'Why are church roofs green? Because they're eyes because they're cheese because they're grass –' She looks up at Casimir, puzzled and urgent. 'Because they're sunglasses.'

She begins to move again, keeping to the far wall, away from the figure and the door. As if they are out of place or somehow dangerous. Casimir watches her go. His face shows almost no emotion. He turns back to the door and goes in.

'Casimir! Good morning. Are you well?'

Aebanyim grins down at him. She is standing on a swivel chair by the ventilation shaft with a black rubber torch in one small hand and a screwdriver in the other. The chair wobbles

[17]

and half-twists under her. Her teeth are stained bleach-white. Casimir grins back despite himself.

'Well, thank you. And you?'

'Oh, well, I am well too, of course.'

The office is a sparse, L-shaped room, cut in two by a plyboard counter. The paint on the walls was cream livery in the 1940s; now it is discoloured by decades to an uneven yellow. Casimir is always struck by the absence of windows here, the feeling of airlessness. Outside and above the walls there is nothing but water and power in pipes and shafts, and the density of London clay. The air smells of burnt coffee and the sour dirt of tunnel clothes.

Behind the counter Oluwo is leant back, watching the closed-circuit monitors. The screens flicker, as if their reception is almost lost. Oluwo's eyes are very white and unblinking in their dark sockets. Sweat silvers his face along the flat of his forehead and the angular three-scarred cheeks. He lowers his eyes to Casimir and nods once, without smiling.

From round the corner of the room, Casimir can hear Adams on the station-to-station telephone. Between bursts of static and distant conversation, his voice is harsh, losing patience. Casimir shrugs off his jacket and hangs it behind the door next to the racks of cellular phones, voltage testers and fluorescent waistcoats. He walks to the counter, opens it and edges through. Round the corner where Adams stands, the room is illuminated only by monitor screens. Adams's skin is lit the colour of newspapers.

'I don't care what they do on the Vic. Oy. Oy. Are you listening to me?' Adams is bent towards the wall phone so that his face almost touches the wall. One hand is leant out to support himself, the other grips the receiver. His face is screwed up with emotion. To Casimir he looks like a man in pain. He doesn't notice as Casimir finds a plastic chair and sits down.

'I don't care what they do on the fucking Vic or the fucking Pic. On this line you get your men off the track by switching-on time, all right? Because it's not even seven now and already the trains are ten minutes late because you and your lot were fucking around in the tunnels at five-thirty. All right? Have I made myself clear? That's good then, and you fuck off too.'

He shoves himself off the wall and back upright. For a moment he rocks on his heels, staring up into space. Casimir watches the anger going out of him or back into him.

'Adams.'

The supervisor flinches and turns. 'Cass.' He rubs his eyes with the knuckles of one hand. Smiling, tired. 'You're early.'

'So are you.'

'So I am, yes. We catch the worms. Who else is on today?'

'Sievwright and Leynes. Oluwo is on double shift.'

'Is Aebanyim leaving?'

'No. She is also early.'

He knows all this, Casimir thinks. He is just talking for the sake of it. It is not like him. Casimir watches as the supervisor eases himself into a seat.

'Really.' He looks over at Oluwo, then smiles at Casimir again. 'What you got for breakfast, Mister Oluwo?'

The black man stares balefully at Adams, clicks his tongue and looks away.

'No, really, what is it today? Pork pies? Jam tarts?'

Casimir shifts uncomfortably. Everybody knows about Oluwo's superstitions. He remembers the man's slow voice. *You eat underground, you stay underground.* Casimir has seen him drink black tea, and nothing else. The man consumes nothing here, as if being underground, the food will grow roots in his stomach.

Still, this is a delicate matter. He is surprised by Adams's teasing. After all, there are other beliefs about the Tubes. They all have superstitions. The supervisor is smiling, trying to catch Casimir's eye. He meets the man's gaze and tries not to frown. 'What needs doing?'

Adams sighs, reaches for a clipboard schedule. 'All right, all right. Take your pick. There's water getting into the sub-station again, the monitors have been on the blink all day, you could get on to Thames Water.' He leafs through pages of scrawled notes. 'What else? The vendor deliverers are coming with eight hundred units of Wispa, whatever that means; they'll need keys and that. There was a whacking great Rasta-farian fellow around yesterday, nearly as big as you – Leynes caught him painting coloured stripes on the platforms, he said it was to make the doors open. So if the station starts turning green and gold, that'll be why. And there's blue graffiti all over the old cross-tunnels. The stuff's like fucking mushrooms, it comes up by itself overnight. A couple of the new lads are down there cleaning up. Unsupervised. So if you've got a minute –'

'Of course.'

'Good. No hurry. Aebanyim!' His voice rises to a yell as he looks past Casimir.

'Yes, I am up here.' There is a clang of grille metal on concrete. 'No mice.'

'I heard them. Look again.' Adams has put the clipboard down. He is picking through a pile of *Traffic Circular* magazines, timetables and large photographs. Arranging them on the counter. His head is turned down to one side; Casimir can no longer see his face. Only the forehead, the deep frown lines. 'If I'm going to sit a hundred feet under the ground all day, I'm not going to breathe mouse shit too. Do you see them now?'

His voice is quick and sure but also flat, lacking the intonation of emotion. He has been drinking, thinks Casimir, and the thought surprises him. He has never seen Adams drunk. If he had been asked, Casimir would have guessed the supervisor drank often and alone. But not here. Not where he is seen and matters, on the Underground.

He runs his nails down the undersides of his thumbs. A small pain, to help him consider.

'No, I don't. No mice. I do not see no mice.'

'Bloody Jesus.'

Adams is on his feet quickly, pushing past Casimir and Oluwo. The black man follows Adams with his eyes. Then he looks back at Casimir, his head cocked, questioning. From beyond them comes the sound of Adams and Aebanyim arguing, the shrill clang of the ventilation-shaft cover as Adams climbs up on the chair and reaches out.

Casimir shakes his head and turns away. He hears the office door slam back as more workers come in, Sievwright and Leynes. Their London accents echo loudly, the sound trapped in the small room.

He leans forward on the counter. With his head down, the

sound of voices is diminished, cut off by the angle of walls. In this position he has some sense of privacy; the feeling of crowding is not so bad. The in-house circulars and papers are scattered where Adams left them. Casimir gathers them together, sorts them. After some time he stops. The photographs are in his hands. He remains bent forward while he looks.

There are only two shots. The first shows one of the four platforms at the station, Casimir can't be sure which. The other is of a woman in a street photo booth. He looks at the woman first.

She is leaning her head against the booth's orange background curtain. Light comes through the curtain and the pale weight of her hair. Her eyes are looking away from the camera and her smile is slight, distracted. She is wearing a man's pinstriped shirt. The collar is too big for her; it emphasizes the leanness of her throat. Everything is grainy and just out of focus, as if the image has been enlarged from a much smaller print. Written across the woman's shirt collar is a name in white developer's ink: REBECCA SAVILLE.

He puts down the picture of the woman. The other photo is a still from the station's closed-circuit cameras. Casimir recognizes the high angle of the black sphere, the slight curve of the tracks. Next to him, he knows, Oluwo will be looking at the same basic image. The freeze-framed tunnel is crowded with people, the tops of their heads packed up to the white edge of the platform. The still is grey-white, the quality too poor to enlarge.

A figure is falling from the crowd. Its arms reach out, instinctive, to stop the fall. The action is distant, sixty feet away or more; there is little facial detail, only the mouth's dark smudge. Hair spreads from the turning head, blurred by movement. In the camera's monotone it has become a startling white.

Something else extends from the mass of people at the platform's edge. It is hard to make out and Casimir narrows his eyes. The smudged shape resolves itself as his eyes adjust. There is a black sleeve, white skin, the suggestion of a hand behind the falling figure. Reaching out from the crowd.

'Cass. Casimir? Are you not gone yet? What's keeping you?'

The supervisor's voice jerks him back guiltily, as if he has pried into something private or illicit. With the sense of guilt comes an opposing impulse to go to Adams with the photographs, to ask him what they mean. The confusion of emotions disturbs him. He puts the photographs down where Adams left them, arranged on the dimly lit counter. Pushing the thoughts away.

'Nothing is keeping me.'

He stands up to go, and when he turns Oluwo is watching him, head still cocked a little to one side. In the other man's face Casimir sees how he must look himself. His threatening, looming tension. He makes himself smile, forces his shoulders down.

Oluwo smiles back. All his teeth are white metal, silver or cheap alloy. He has the shy grin of a child. Then the smile passes and the lines of his face settle back into their mask. Casimir steps behind him and past. When he blinks there is the image of the woman falling. The hand behind her, reaching out for her white-lit hair.

The graffiti are angular and intricate, like some violently debased Arabic script. Blue knotworks of writing have been sprayed on the yellowing tiles of the disused platform-to-platform tunnel. The tunnel itself is cluttered with stored materials. Boxes of pearl light bulbs, canvas-covered lengths of shining steel track. Casimir picks up a spray-paint can from a broken box of neon tubing. He turns it in his hands. Behind him, the two trainees work at the far wall with chemical sprays and sheets of green scouring fibre.

'Do you understand it, sir?'

Casimir looks round. One of the trainees is leering back at him. Hair the colour of rust, skin reddened with freckles. He nods at the graffiti. Casimir shakes his head.

The trainee puts down his scouring sheet and moves across the tunnel. He traces out the spray-painted writing without letting his fingers touch the waxy dirt of the wall tiles. Ian something, Casimir remembers. Weaver. Like the painted-egg man. He doubts they are related; London is too big for that. It is one of the reasons he likes cities. In this preference he is unlike most small-town Poles, he knows, with their sense of inferiority, suspicious of an order in the big cities beyond their comprehension.

'Look, see? That's an S. Then P, little I –'

The young man traces out a signature name. For a moment all Casimir sees are the shapes of snarling teeth, smiling faces, formed out of the lines like the ideograms in Chinese characters. Then the letters resolve themselves, curved backwards and into each other. Huddled together until it's difficult to tell them apart. Like the homeless, thinks Casimir. The canvas covering at his feet has been disturbed, pressed down. Casimir can see the indentation of a body, perhaps more than one. He looks around, narrowing his eyes to make out the graffitied names: SPIDER, JACK UNION, MISTER LEATHERS.

'What do they mean?'

'Mean?' The trainee shrugs, still grinning.

A rush of stale air and dust goes past them as a train arrives or leaves, somewhere up on the working platforms. The second trainee swears and covers his eyes, hunched over.

Weaver looks back at him, distracted. 'Nothing. They're just names.'

The second trainee stands upright, tall and angry. 'What are we cleaning down here for anyway? It's all locked up and that. No one comes down here.'

'It needs cleaning. We clean it. That's our job.' A length of rail has fallen off the stack near Casimir. He squats down and lifts the end back on to the pile. Quickly and easily, hand closed around the damp steel. The metal is cold and very heavy. There is the slight, good pain of work in the muscles of his arm. 'And you are wrong. Someone has been down here.'

He pulls the tarpaulin back over the stack of rails. The impression of a sleeping body vanishes as the canvas is straightened out. He stands up, puts the spray can in his jacket pocket, claps the tunnel dust clean from his hands.

Red is the Colour

Here. I am here. I am. My mother's voice comes calling, dipping through the trees.

There are my high places and this is my special place and his too with the black wet town road, horse carts, coal trucks, mud sleighs, a blue car coming to meet me with the flats over it like stone sky. I can see my flat with my head right back on my shoulders, I count up, eight nine ten floors and the winter coat collar wet against my hair. From here I can see almost everything.

My flat has green curtains, not orange. When I hide inside them they have green bits but also blue. I want blue cars and red meat so I am not hungry. I will eat fast to get it while I have the chance. I touch my face with my hands and my hands are colder. My face is nothing, I do not know it.

I can run away under the trees, which are white with the snow and blue with the snow in shadow and green and red-skinned and orange where the bark is broken, they are all the colours of traffic lights. I can run down my Strug C Block steps like flying, I go faster than snow when it falls from the wings of trees, I roll and laugh under it. I can press the snow in my hands and it shows I am here. There is proof of me in its shaped blue shadow.

Look at my hands! The cut short nails dig into the snow. The more you press snow the harder it gets. The skin is going red like meat but meat is only my outside. Inside I am Kazimierz Ariel Kazimierski. If I could choose I would be like the snow.

I have secret lists. There is the list of names and of frightening things, the list of loves and of trees. All are in my head except for the list of names. Today Piotr has written the names for me on thick dark rough ripped sack-paper from the farm.

For nothing he does this for me. It is because I am his friend. We do anything for each other.

This is my list of secret words:

People – *Ariel* my middle name is *Roman* it is Piotr's *Monika* who is a girl but with a rabbit's mouth *Tomek* who is Militia and the father of *Wladislaw* who has been into the burnt flat *Karol* whose brother found a German shell in the old coal mine. Something happened to him like to my balloon at the factory parade which went up into the sky and disappeared. *Boniek Lato Denya* they are footballers. I am the goalkeeper. As far as I can remember, I have only let in seven goals.

Places – *Poland Silesia Gliwice*, which is here. *America Russia Germany The English* we have beaten them all except the Yanks.

Machines – *Ursus* it is a tractor *Leyland* an engine *Berliet* the buses *Jones* the cranes in the shipyard, Father teaches me these names with his finger on the metal letters. *Polski Fiat* which Father will buy when he gets the big deal.

Kraut Cholera Blood Cock Gyp Damn Shit Fucking Devil Piss Yid Yank Balls Cunt Whore Slut Jew Arse Bastard Runt. All these were my father's. I have no words from my mother. It is because she speaks less. I list the sound of her voice but Piotr says that it isn't a name. *Black Market. Speculator. Underground.*

There are other names but they are not so important. I never forget because I have lists, it is the reason. I learn fast. I see everything.

In my fist the snow drips. All the colour has gone from it, even the white, it is no-colour. It takes time to run away. My hand hurts but I do not let go. I last, nothing of me has gone. I am stronger than the snow.

I listen. It is now that Mother is calling, her voice dipping through the trees. She does not know what I am doing. She does not call for me to stop. No one can see me, so no one will stop me. I breathe deep when I smile.

In the beginning there is Father and I remember he is happy.

My father travels for money. Now he is back and when he swings me up I watch him, to remember. He is frowning and

[25]

laughing. As if he doesn't understand me but he is happy to see me anyway. As if I am a pleasant surprise.

There are people waving around us. What are they waving? I watch and it is arms, hands, footballs, bottles, woolly hats, scarves, kitchen pots and radios. The room is full of noise. Outside the moon is out. I watch the words come out of my father's mouth.

'Poland beat the English. Poland beat the English! *Poland beat the English!*'

This was a while ago now but I remember it. It is the first thing.

My father has a gun from the war. It is small and has no bullets left. He shows it to me at the kitchen table. It comes apart like all machines.

'Russian guns are best. One day I'll get you a Russian gun, Kazio. When I get a big deal. Only the best for the best.'

I am four now. Not so small that I like being called Kazio. My real name is Kazimierz. Father doesn't smile when he puts the gun back together.

'Always shoot the German before the Russian. Remember that too. Business before pleasure.'

The Russians shot my father's mother. It was in the war and her name was Kasia. I love my father but he scares me. Only sometimes. My life is not ordinary, not good or bad. Sometimes he smiles with his mouth open and you can see his tongue. It is like watching a dog in June heat. It is when he smiles that I keep away from him.

Another time when I was very small, I was in a field of flowers with my mother and father. The flowers are yellow and white, scrambled together, spring flowers.

'Cut-upped egg,' I say. 'Like cut-upped egg.'

They laugh and laugh.

There is a sound above me. I look up and see an aeroplane and understand what it is. Father lifts me up on his shoulders. His hands are harder than my mother's. He is harder than her.

They are still laughing together. I put my head back. The aeroplane's shadow goes over us and is gone.

I ask Mother about the curtains. She does not tell me. I ask Piotr.

'Piotr, why do I have green curtains, not orange?'

He puts down the coal and wipes his fingers on the steps. Even so his hands stay black as if they are burnt. Our old flat was burnt; Mother did it. She cooked duck eggs and forgot about them. They split open as if they were hatching and out flew the flames. The smell was terrible, so we came here to Strug C Block. I don't remember this at all, but people tell me.

Piotr gives up cleaning his hands. 'I think it is to do with money. Green is in the middle. White net curtains mean they have less cash, and brown means they are old and rich. Red is for the people with Polski Fiats.'

'What colour do you have?'

He picks up the coal again. 'Mostly yellow. Yellow is for farms.'

He is writing on the steps of Strug C Block with the coal, I don't know what. I say, 'Black is for when there are dead people.'

I like it better when he draws. Sometimes he does tanks and we fight with them. Poland against the Germans and Russians, the Americans and English. Poland against the world. Most times I am Poland, so I win.

'Blue is for dirty Yids.'

I stand up and push him over. I am taller than Piotr, who is a year older than me. Now he looks at me and stays down.

'Why did you do that?'

I don't tell him. It makes me confused and angry, so I shout at him, 'Don't write when I don't like it. Now you must do drawings.'

'All right.'

He starts to draw something. I sit down to see. It is a ship with guns. There are people with hats and people with cats. There are black chimneys and flags. Some people are playing football.

'Does it go on canals?'

'Yes, it does.'

He draws the Gliwice canals. I keep quiet now. I do not tell him about my curtains, which are blue when I am close to them. I feel something like fear and it is shame.

Vodka hurts when you smell it. There are three bottles at home. One is in the guest room and it is Russian. One is in the kitchen on the high shelves with the glass doors and it is Father's. The third bottle is behind the stove. It's empty and flat, like it was made to be hidden. I think Mother forgot where she hid it.

When my mother was four she went to France. She told me there were fields of sunflowers, all in rows, all facing the sun. Only one sunflower was looking away from the sun and her father picked it for her.

Later she didn't remember that any more. I had to tell it to her. She forgets lots of things.

No one is here. I go into Mother's room. The beds are higher than mine and between them is a table made of glass. If you put your ear to the clock you can hear it tick. Like seeds falling.

There are wooden drawers painted white and I open the bottom one. My father's clothes are here, brown shirts and checked ones and socks. They smell of church, which is the mothballs. Of being dried on the balcony window in the sun and dust. Of Father. I press my face against the smell of him. When I am done with it I go.

Me and Piotr and Wladislaw, we go to the burnt flat. Everything is black, it looks like a picture Piotr has drawn with his coal. Sometimes there are other pictures in the black, just shapes. Wladislaw says it is from the fire moving. I can hear the loud-hailer cars, they are outside in the rain, they go round near and far loud-hailing about food.

'Dare you to go into the last room.'

'No.'

'Chicken.'

'You're chicken. Do the Choosing Song.'

Piotr does it, between the three of us. 'Ana Dua Likka Fakka Torba Borba Usmussmakka Deus Deus Cosmateus Imorella *Bugs*. It's you.'

It's me. I go into the last room, where there are no windows. The floor's burnt through to black wooden planks. I walk lightly. Piotr and Wladislaw stay in the first room, waiting for me to fall.

Me and Piotr, we have not been in the burnt flat before. It is a new thing. Before now there were Jews here, a man and a woman and three babies, two boy babies and a girl baby. I never talked to them or anything. I don't know where they have gone now.

There is black glass in the last room. It is round at the edges and quite smooth. Black for dead people. I put it in my pockets and go back to the first room.

'What's in there?'

'Nothing. Just the burning.'

I don't show them the black glass. It is my secret. I deserve it because I didn't fall. Later I will look at it again, when I am alone, and see how beautiful it is.

Today Father is home and with him there is blood.

It is dark like cod liver on the floor then red on the white bowl. Red for people with cars. The iron smell of it fills the kitchen. I stand away from him across the table.

I stop breathing to keep the smell of him out of me. I can make it so I am not breathing at all.

'We've no iodine. I'll go and ask the Sommers to –'

'Stay here.'

'But, love, it needs to be clean.'

'Make do. We can look after ourselves.'

She brings hot water in a white bowl. He smiles when his hands go under the water and smiles again when he takes them out. It is nothing to smile about because he is still bleeding. His teeth are yellow in the kitchen light. Quickly Mother cleans all the blood off his hands. She has white cloth and she puts it round and round. First the blood comes through a lot then a little then not at all.

We all go quiet, waiting to see if the blood is gone. It is. I can hear Monika who lives next door, she is singing play songs. I hear her through the wall.

'I'm not going back down. The shipyard was better than this.'

'We need the money.'

'Eh?'

'We need the money, love.'

'Money again! Money is all you think about. And why should I be surprised?'

My mother moves around the kitchen and says nothing. Her dress has flowers the colour of new leaves. It makes her look pale. It is usual, her not talking, Father talking. This is an ordinary night. My life is not good, not bad.

'As if you've got nothing stashed away. Such a good little miser. I know, *love*, we'll get you a job, how about that? How would it be if you got your hands bloody for a change? Your precious white hands. I'd like to see that. *Blood!* I need more cigarettes.'

Father looks at me and he sees me. *Blood* is the worst curse, the most secret. Sometimes he looks at me and doesn't see but now he smiles again. I take a step back, nearer the door.

'Where's your grandfather, son?'

'In his room.'

'See if he's got any cigarettes.'

'OK.'

I go out. In the hall I sit down like I am playing and I listen. It is not hard.

'They won't have me back anyway. The Black Trout Shaft foreman said so. Says I'm a danger with the machinery, so that's that. I'll travel again.'

'No.'

'What's wrong with you? Didn't you hear about Latek? Three months ago all he could buy was soap, now he's selling leather jackets. Do you know what he gets on those?'

'You could find other work.'

'And the Party worker in Katowice, didn't you hear that? A

million dollars from nothing worse than tractors, and now he's disappeared to Cuba! Cuba. It drives me mad, Anna, watching them. I feel stuck here.'

'Don't go.'

'I didn't say that.'

'Don't leave us.'

'I didn't say that, did I? Why, would you miss me?'

'Yes. I don't know. I don't.'

'Ah. You look so much better when you're sad. Say it again. Nicely.'

'Don't.'

They stop talking. Now there is only sound and movement. It is stupid and I am bored. I can hear Monika in the hall now. If I tell her about her mouth she will run away. I think I will do it. I run.

Karol has a red Brando. Monika has a green one. They click them in their mouths. *Clickety-click*. I have no Brando but I see everything, I watch the day happen. The Chorzelski brothers have a motorbike but there are four of them so they take turns. The sky is yellow at the ends and blue on the top and the grassy dust is warm. It's a good day. It would be better with a Brando.

This is the list of frightening things. It is still in my head. I am not scared of so much as Piotr or Monika but more than Wladislaw.

Piotr doesn't write the list for me. He is at school now. I am alone.

- The statues at the Hall of Local Government which are devils, they have horns and no cocks and their knees go backwards.
- Wallpaper flowers.
- Lighting cigarettes from candles because it means you'll die at sea.
- My father's blood.
- Writing.
- Meat tokens. Mother got liver for a month.

[31]

- Wax dropped in water which tells fortunes.
- Turning lights.
- The burnt flat.

It happened at night and we went down and stood on the steps in rows, all of the neighbours in Strug C Block, hundreds all big and small and fat in coats and blankets and pyjamas and sometimes nothing, just pink. The firemen's ladder went up five floors and they waved.

I never saw this myself but Mother tells me it was so. I was mostly asleep. I only remember stairs and turning lights.

My father drinks winiak brandy at breakfast. It is to thin his blood. He went on an aeroplane and brought me back three lemon wipes. I keep them wrapped up in brown paper with red writing on it. The first wipe stopped smelling, so now I'm on the second wipe. It smells better than real lemons.

Games are good. I play the Anywhere Game with my mother. We do it on the bicycle.

'Now where?'

'Left.'

'Here?'

'Yes. Faster.'

'All right. There, this is pretty. And now?'

'Left. No. Right. *Right.*'

'Leave the – Sit back! Back. Or we stop.'

One time we came to a road with no other roads at the end, only sunlight striped down a wall and big crows eating from rubbish bins. In the wall was a door and we went through and there was a garden. It was beautiful. There were trees and water.

'Can I play here?'

'Of course. It's for everyone.'

Her face was all ripply with light from the water. I laughed back at her like an echo. I ran into the trees, where I could be her echo.

[32]

Or there were riddles. They can be done anywhere.

In the cheese and shoes shop: 'Why are birches white?'

'Because they're whitewashed, like apple trees?'

'No.'

'Because they're hiding in the snow?'

'Yes.' She's quite good at riddles. In the bath: 'What is red the colour of?'

'I don't know. Mind your eyes. Here it comes.'

'People with cars. Why does Dad go away from us?'

'I'm not sure.'

'To get money?'

'Maybe he just likes going away. Careful. Ariel –'

My mother sneezes when she gets wet. Three times, then a breath, then the fourth. She always sneezes the same way.

When she cries it is like coughing, like something breaking. It is small sticks breaking under the trees when I run. When I dream of running under the trees I know this, that Mother has been crying while I sleep.

I hate music. It gets in the way of thinking. There is a hole in the radio's back where a button came off and I get a little stone and push it inside to stop the music but it doesn't.

I go to the road where the new flats are going up, high and hollow. There are loads of little orange stones and I take them home. I put more little stones in through the hole in the radio. It takes 226 stones to stop the music. I go and smell my lemon wipes. It is quiet in my room and the sun comes in through the open window, bright and sharp like the smell of lemons.

Now Father is at the kitchen table with the radio and a winiak brandy and Grandfather's tool box. There is nothing to show it was me with the stones. I stay with him anyway. I stand close and talk fast.

'Did you eat food on the aeroplane?'

'Sure. Food, drink, cigarettes.' He frowns. When he lifts up the radio, the stones go shuffling around inside.

'Can you fix it?' Mother comes in with her hands up to her blue-black hair, winding it around itself.

'Damn thing sounds like a concrete mixer. I don't know what's wrong with it.' Now he opens out Grandfather's tool kit. I play the Question Game to slow him down even more.

'Did everyone have lemon wipes?'

'Eh? Everyone did, yes.'

'Why?'

'To clean their hands with. There –' He notches the driver into a screw. The first one comes out straight away.

'Why?'

'Mm? I don't know. Because they were dirty people.' There are only three screws. The second one is in hard. Father grunts through his teeth and it gets loose.

'Why?'

He swings his face round at me and away. The third screw rolls off and he catches it in his hand and grins. 'Why? Because they were on dirty business, that's why.' He takes the back off the radio and lifts it up to look inside.

'*Borja!*'

Little orange stones come rattling out over Father and the kitchen table. He drops the radio and jumps backwards. The glass of winiak cracks like ice on a waterbutt. I watch it drip gold before I run.

We went to Krakow to see soldiers. It was the first time. On the train there was a tunnel and my father said we had to hold our breath, it is the Breathing Game. I held my breath as long as I could, but when I opened my eyes we were still under the ground. My father held his breath right out into the light.

When I came back my town was different because I could smell it. The smell of my town is of coal. I like it. Coal smells like under the pine trees in summer, but sweeter.

We are making supper but I am thinking of the names of trees I have learned. Birch, larch, sycamore. I stand on the stool and she is behind me. We are four hands. Our hands clean the potatoes. Our hands take them out of the sink. The potato skins are grey and shiny, like aluminium.

'You're quiet.'

'Yes. I'm making secret lists.'

I can feel my mother laugh through my back. Laughing is a feeling.

'Are they good secrets or bad?'

It's not a clever question. How can I tell her? If I did I wouldn't have secrets any more. We go on cleaning. The big windows are open and the blue-green curtains are open and the net curtains belly inwards, full of light. Outside children are screaming. I wonder if they are hurt or playing.

'Do you have secrets?'

'Yes.'

'Do you make lists with them?'

'No.'

'What do you do with them?'

She lifts out the potatoes. They are drained and almost dry but they still shine.

'What do you do with them?'

'I try never to think of them, or say them. That way I forget. Then I have no secrets. Arms out.'

She dries our hands on the blue towel. Next I will go and play.

'Like middle names.'

Her hands stop drying. Her arms go hard round me. I look up with my head right back.

'Like Ariel. No one says it so they forget.'

Her face is upside-down and I smile at it. I can't work out if she smiles back. She puts her wet hands on the sides of my face and she leans down to me.

'That's right. It was your grandfather's name.'

'No, it isn't.' Grandfather's name is Pavel. I heard him say it to a Militia man.

'Your other grandfather. Mine. Now it's our secret, yes? It belongs to both of us.'

'Yes. And to Father. Your hands are wet.'

'Not to Father. Just us.'

She kisses my face. Breathes in my ear, *Shhhh*. It feels nice.

'Do it again.'

Laughter. *Shhhh*.

'Again.'
She bends low. Darkness. *Haaaah*.

Winter. I am watching at my window. The world is black and white with snow. Down there I see my mother. Her footsteps go small and black down the centre of the white path. In the distance she stops. She has forgotten which way she is going. For a long time she stops. Then she goes on again.

I turn back from the high place. The trees are all quiet and listening. One, I put my head right back on the flat of my shoulders. Two, I open my mouth back over the teeth to shout and, three, I breathe right in. It will be so loud this shout, it will be like the whole trees breaking. Here it comes.

Roses

It is a day before he sees her again and then it is twice in the space of hours. As if she is a new word in his life, something he has never known and so never seen. He catches sight of her bent by a platform drinks machine through a crocodile of day-trip schoolchildren, gone when the crowd separates. Then again, that afternoon.

He recognizes her before he has seen her face. It's the end of middle turn, three o'clock. Sievwright's cracked voice echoes through from the office toilets, singing one line of pop music again and again over the hiss of a basin tap. Casimir looks up absently at the monitor screens. Smile lines crease around his eyes. The irises are near black, red-black only in the strongest light. Now they stop, pupils narrowing to focus.

'Flash! Ah-hah. Save every one of us. Flash! Ah-hah –'

The Underground girl is walking down the platform, quick among the loose mid-afternoon crowd. A train pulls away next to her, black roof curving close to the fish-eye camera. Casimir can't see her face and she is wearing different clothes – a man's chinos and a pale cord jacket. It is the way she moves that he recognizes. Faster than the crowd but not pushing. Just faster, as if her blood is circulating at a different rate.

He sees that her hair has changed, the dreadlocks washed out. She still has her headphones on. Once she turns and he sees her face smiling, lips moving. Then she is taken in by the crowd and he can't see her face any more.

'Ah-hah. Flash! –'

The screen blinks with interference, then clears again. Casimir wonders how many times he has seen her before, or looked at her without seeing. How long can it have it taken him to notice her? He tries to place the earlier sense of familiar-ity, but there are so many people and places on the Underground. The grey thickness of the monitor screens, slow parades of rush-hour crowds. Solitary figures in the halls or wells, shafts or concourses.

Even so, he is surprised to have seen her twice in a day. She has not been commuting, he thinks. Not in transit, but here in a less temporary way. Again, he wonders where she sleeps.

'Flash! – Hello, Cass. You look like the cat what got the Mogadon.' Sievwright peers past him at the screens. 'What's up?'

'Nothing. I saw someone I knew.'

The pace of the crowd slows as they reach the exit. Casimir narrows his eyes, trying to keep track of the Underground girl, but it's impossible. She is becoming lost in the crowd. He is losing her for a third time.

'I didn't know you knew anyone. Who was it, comrade, Mikhail Gorbachov? Your mum, was it? Oy –'

He is on his feet, the swivel chair clanking back against the control-room wall. Weaver and Aebanyim are by the door, shrugging off orange visibility vests. Casimir pushes past and out into the Underground, Sievwright's laughter echoing after him.

The passage is still crowded with people. Casimir stands back, waiting, his eyes going from face to face. He sees a man built like a darts player, the nails of one hand broken down past the quicks. A woman with blue-rinse hair and matching blue jogging shorts. A tall Chinese man, shirt loose over his hollow ribcage. Children kick up against wall posters as they run by.

He waits until they are almost gone, checking that the girl is not among them. Then he turns up the empty passage towards the southbound platform, quick but not yet breaking into a run. There are two side-passages before the platform entrance and he stops at each, listening. There is no sound except the whirr of ventilation outlets and the sound of a busker's music from one of the distant tunnels; the engine growl of a didgeri-doo, becoming indistinct against the subterranean roar of trains.

Casimir tries to think what he will say if he catches up with her. The English in his head seems to condense, becoming inexpressively hard. He thinks of what he felt when he saw her on the morning train, the sense of shared experience and the physical desire: simple things. But he knows he'll say none of this. If he tells her anything it will be to remind her of the train, of her own song. He remembers the words of it. *Have you ever been to Electric Ladyland?* He wonders if she will remember him at all.

At the point where the passage opens on to the southbound platform he stops. The crowd has thinned out, filtering up to the surface or through to other platforms. On the nearest bench an old couple are eating white-bread sandwiches, greaseproof paper spread on their knees. They don't look up at Casimir.

He turns back. Twenty feet down the corridor a figure is turning into the first side-tunnel. Small steps and a woman's fine long hair, blown back bright. Moving fast, already out of sight.

'Wait! Miss, I need –'

He doesn't know what he needs. He begins to run fast, too fast to speak. Air filling his mouth, the sound of his own feet clattering around him. There is a sign on the side-tunnel wall, NUMBER OF STEPS TO EXIT 100, the enamel lettering dull with dirt. Casimir swings into the emergency stairwell and goes up the spiral of steps, taking them three at a time.

'Wait! Please –'

It is hard to make out the footsteps ahead of him, but they are there. Casimir gauges they are not far ahead, but quickening. He feels a momentary shame, that the girl should be running from him.

He goes up fast, large but carrying his bulk easily. In his mind the Underground's levels and rooms are laid out, clear and certain. He feels a trembling in his arms which has nothing to do with exhaustion, which is instead the adrenalin brought on by excitement. He visualizes the emergency stairwell, its spiralled length. There are no exits except those at the top and base. There is time, he thinks. I have time to catch her.

The metal stairway smells of dry shit and dust around him. He is near to the top before his heart rate starts to quicken. He remembers a church tower in Poland; Pentecost, laughter, the bell-tower floor strewn with blue irises. In the sides of the shaft are painted-over doors, entrances to bricked-off levels and storerooms, wartime tunnels and deep shelters.

He comes out into the surface concourse and stops, not understanding. The Underground girl is gone. Up ahead he can see one of the trainees on the ticket barriers, bored and inattentive as the passengers mill around him.

Casimir pushes past, out of the eastern exit into the Kentish Town Road. On the pavement the crowd is thick and slow, spilling into the gutters, where a hot-dog salesman has set up his stall. Steam rises in the warm air. Bike couriers brake and hoot at the market jaywalkers. For some minutes he looks around, knowing it is useless. His breath tastes of iron and he gulps it back, breathing slower now.

I was wrong, he thinks. With the thought comes the dizziness he felt yesterday, the sensation of the Underground shifting around him. As if he is losing control. He pictures the staircase again, going over his mental blueprint, trying to imagine if any of the old doors could have been unsealed. He tries to remember which lead to storerooms, and the blueprint in his mind fades and falters. Casimir realizes he does not know where all the doorways go. The feeling of dizziness rises in him again and he groans softly, clenching his teeth.

A double-decker bus goes past, a wall of red metal briefly cutting off the light. Then it changes gears, accelerating north towards Kentish Town and Holloway. The afternoon glare catches Casimir full in the face. He frowns against it, raises a hand to shade his eyes. A stubborn man, still looking, still looking although he knows that she is gone.

'Do you want a Neon Nerd?'

The shop is full of children and the smell of chip vats. Mrs Navratil is behind the scoured-chrome counter, ruddy-faced as she shovels out fried meat. She sees Casimir as the door swings shut behind him. Calls to him without looking up, 'It's Friday. Your rent is late again. Help me with these.'

He looks down. There is a small black girl beside him, her hair braided, the braids curled flat with red ladybird ties. She is cradling a paper parcel of chips in one hand. With the other she is holding out a packet of sweets. Casimir shakes his head. 'No. You must not offer sweets to strangers.'

'Mister Casimir?'

He looks up. Mrs Navratil stares at him. Eyes wide, brows raised, almost aggressive. 'I need these portions served now.'

'Yes.' He nods and tries to make his way to the counter. Something is holding him back. The girl with the sweets is tugging his uniform jacket. He looks down at her again.

'Are you an Underground man?'

He smiles. It makes him look older, the skin at the ends of his eyes creasing. 'Yes. Yes, I am.' He pulls gently and moves through to the counter.

There are six chicken parts on the hotplate, their skins yellowed and thickened with oil. He scrubs the grime from his hands with green soap, then works with an efficient minimum of movement, folding the thighs and breasts on clean squares of newspaper. Wrapping the corners in, rolling the paper tight.

'There was a letter for you.'

'What did you do with it?'

She snorts laughter, leaning one shoulder down as she lifts a metal basket of fish from the oil. 'You think I do what? Fry them up and sell them?'

She looks over at him, still smiling. He is not embarrassed. He looks away because it is not possible to meet her stare. He would have to leave, and he cannot afford to leave. Navratil's rooms are cheaper than the hostels. The extra work he does here is not unpleasant, is easier than paying more. These are the facts of their relationship.

'It's in your room. Under the door. I didn't go in.'

He wraps the final portion of chicken. Gives it to the stretched-out hands of the last two children. A tall boy with a scar denting the skin of his forehead. A smaller boy with the same eyes, angry and eager. The shop is almost empty. He looks round at Mrs Navratil. 'Thank you.'

She is already turned away, wetting a cleaning cloth in the sink. 'I need the rent by tomorrow, please.'

'Yes.'

He wipes his hands, drops the kitchen paper into the bin

and then takes out the black rubbish sack, knotting it as he holds it up.

Outside in the street someone screams, high-pitched. He looks round quickly.

Through the plate window he can see the children fighting. One of them is hunched in the gutter between two cars. Lightly built, younger or just smaller than the children bunched round it.

There is a bag of fish and chips split open on the pavement. One of the bigger children picks up a piece of fish, lobs it at the child between the cars. The window is frosted with condensation, Casimir can't make out faces or details. He can hear other children, jeering and swearing. One of them pushes forward to kick at the smaller child.

It sprawls against a car and the alarm goes off. The sound is loud and panicky in the narrow street. The children scatter. After a moment the child in the gutter stands up. It wipes its face once, steps out between the cars and begins to run.

He turns away. Mrs Navratil is doubled over the hotplates, scrubbing at the chrome. She stops to wring out the cloth over the sink, her teeth bared with the effort. The door to the back rooms is unlocked and he goes through and closes it behind him.

His room is not tidy or cluttered, just bare. There is a grey metal bed with a plastic-covered mattress. A wardrobe hanging open and half-empty, a mirror on the inside of the door reflecting back the room's darkness and linoleum. On the wall beside the wardrobe are the thick, black lumps of gas and electricity meters. There is the small click of their mechanisms, and the faint sound of radio music from the tenants on the floor below.

There is no desk, no chair. On the floor by the bed are three books piled together: the *London A—Z*, a book of Zbigniew Herbert's poetry in Polish and a copy of the same book translated into English. There are other belongings in the room, but not many. Casimir does not lose things here because there is little to lose. He likes it that way. He has lived here for eight years.

The letter is against the wall, pushed back by the open door.

He shuts the door, picks up the letter, walks to the window.

The net curtains are closed and he opens them and sits down on the floor with his back against the wall. The feel of a day's work is good in his shoulders. The last daylight filters in across his hands.

The envelope is small and cheap, the blue-grey colour of soap and water. The light air-mail paper has been sealed tight, there is no room to open it with a nail or knife. The postmark has been stamped twice, each black circle skewed across the Polish three-zloty stamps. Casimir can make out the town name 'Gliwice' only because it is what he expects.

The handwritten address is unsteady but not difficult to read. An effort has been made to make it legible. It is the way people write on the Underground, when the train is moving around them. Or when they are old or weak, hands travelling uneasily across the paper. Casimir taps the contents down, tears the envelope across the top.

There is a note and a Polaroid photograph, the colours run where someone has touched the surface too soon after exposure. Casimir turns the snapshot over in his hands, looking for a date or time. But there is nothing except the familiar image, a view of the Labedy steelworks far off towards Gliwice town. Factory smoke rises in the distance, straight lines of it in a windless sky. Nearer in are trees, a back road. Meadow scrub, the rough weeds that grow quickly over wasteland.

In the foreground an old man is smiling hard into the camera. He looks anxious, as if he is trying to say something. He is drunk; Casimir recognizes it in the way he stands. Arms folded, holding himself together.

The man is wearing a quilted check shirt, a cardigan and dark trousers, all discoloured by the Polaroid's over-exposure. His hair is almost gone now, the last white strands combed across the reddened scalp. Nothing in him shows that he is a cruel man, or that he has killed. That he makes money from death. In this sense his appearance lies. This is how Casimir thinks of it.

He leans forward, hand supporting head, fingers combed under his own black hair. There is very little expression on his face. The anger he feels is internal, a private thing. He opens the note and reads it once, his eyes moving quickly along the uneven lines:

Wittlin Farm, 22 August 1996

Happy Birthday – Happy returns.
Twenty-eight you are now. Good for you! Like you are, I am learning English. Can you read this? I want to know. Now it is the Wittlins go into Gliwice – Tomek and small Eliza and Zofia. Eliza and Zofia to the watering place. Tomek to the Laboratory of Haematology. And then to the post. When will you come home? Here is Piotr. For you he has taken this photo of me.
Yours sincerely,
Father

When he has finished, Casimir puts the note and the photograph back in the envelope. He stands up, opens the window and looks out. The daylight is fading quickly as the sun goes down behind the glasswork of Waterloo station. From here Casimir can see the Houses of Parliament upriver. In the low light, the stonework of St Steven's Tower is the colour of rust.

Below his window are the Lower Marsh backyards. Oil drums and piles of rubbish, white in the deep shadow. The sound of radio music is clearer now, coming up from the first-floor rooms. It is like the music the Underground girl was singing on the train. Like, but not the same.

He leans out, forearms crossed on the windowsill. The letter is in his hands. He tears it in half again and again. Then he opens his hands. The pieces catch the sun as they turn and separate. He loses sight of them as they fall below the level of light.

He closes the window, goes to the bed and sits down. The room is almost dark now. He picks up the books of poetry and opens them. The rough pages hiss against his fingers as he reads, head down, not minding the dark. First the Polish, his old language, then the English. Making the words his own.

> *People ran to the shelters —*
> *he said his wife had hair*
> *in whose depths one could hide.*

*

'Will the passenger who's lost a five-litre container of salad cream please come to the ticket office? Customers are advised to take care of their belongings. This is a platform announcement.'

Overhead the tannoy is distorted, as a voice heard through water. Casimir moves in a low ape-slouch down the platform crawl-space. A yard above him is a thick glass manhole cover, set flush into the southbound platform. Light flits across his face as passengers walk above him.

He is checking for signs of trespass – graffiti, the smell of urine. There is nothing except the stench of lime and clay. Cave-like, as if the concrete is reverting to natural stone. His radio phone coughs and stutters as he shifts sacks of Blue Diamond concrete, set hard into their slumped, bent shapes.

Somewhere down here, people have lived, he thinks. Not people in transit, but people sleeping and eating. Living. The idea disturbs Casimir and he stops, frowning, trying to work out why.

He thinks of people hiding in the station, from the cold or the police. Casimir can sympathize with that. What disturbs him is what the Underground will do to people. It is where Casimir has come to ground, but he knows it can be an unsafe hiding place. Things are less mundane down here, more precarious. There is always the way the Underground can contain things, trapping them in its corners, hiding them, making them stronger.

Adam's voice comes through on the cellular. 'Anything, Cass?'

He unclips the receiver, holds it nearer his face. 'Nothing. No one has been here. There are more chambers to check.'

'You check them then. You do that.'

He frowns. The supervisor's voice comes through again. Faint, weakened. 'Always careful, that's the ticket. Good lad.'

'Adams? Is anything wrong?'

'I'm out of fags, Cass, that's what's wrong. Look after the office for me, will you? I'm just going upstairs.'

There is a clunk as Adams's transmitter is laid down. The line is left open and Casimir waits, only curious, listening for the sound of Adams's voice or movements. There is nothing except the manic chatter of the other workers, a shriek of laughter. He can hear Sievwright and Weaver, their voices tinny and childlike with distance. The frown eases from his face as he goes forward again, listening as he checks the last yards of crawl-space.

'I'm telling you, it's the dog's bollocks. All bikes, no dykes. Five minutes in Bar Rumba and you're sorted. We should get up there tonight. Have an interfere.'

'What are you like? Dykes and bikes. You sad old man.'

'I'm not sad. I'm not sad, mate. 'Cos tonight I'm getting my ride, you know what I mean?'

Wires spill from the wall next to him, a tangle of colour like a map of the Underground itself. Casimir touches them carefully with the tips of his fingers, wary of loose current. He reaches down for the radio again.

'Sievwright. Mister Sievwright?' His raised voice ricochets along the narrow space. There is a clatter of movement from the far end of the line.

'Depends who's asking.'

'Casimir. There is loose wiring in the crawl-space under platform three.'

'Is there? Blow me.' Sievwright's voice is amused, barely tolerant.

'Yes. Do you know why?'

'Maybe it felt uptight, you know? I reckon it just wanted to loosen up a bit. You should try it.'

'Sievwright, I need to know if people have been down here.'

'No one's been down there in months, mate.' The worker's amusement is already fading to boredom. A hint of aggression. 'Anything else you want to know? Football score, price of fish?'

'No.'

'Good.'

The line clicks shut. Casimir looks over the wiring one more time, then clambers on to the chamber's far end. There is a second manhole cover here, old hobnailed wood, and Casimir opens it and goes up into a room full of ranked fuse boxes, power switches and bulbous glass insulators. He opens the fuse-room door and walks out along the public platform.

It is nearly noon and the air from the ventilation shafts is sweet and damp like old leaves, the smell of surface weather carried down through the intervening clay. People turn to look at him as he passes. Their expressions are startled and guilty, or half-smiling as if with recognition. He knows it is the uniform they see, not him. A kind of invisibility. *Are you an Underground man?* he remembers, and he smiles as he reaches the control-room door.

Adams is no longer there. Sievwright and Weaver the trainee are still arguing, leaning by the rack of orange visibility suits, the suits leaning back towards them like an audience. Casimir nods to them, goes past, sits down. Beside him at the counter Oluwo is bent over paperwork, face lined with concentration.

He looks up at the monitor screens. Two cameras cover each of the four platforms, the crossroads of northbound and southbound lines. There are elevated shots of the escalator shaft, the cross-tunnels, the surface and subterranean concourses. The monitors are the office's windows, full of flickering light.

Crowds pass from screen to screen. A tattooed man with no shirt, belly huge and mottled in the camera's abrupt light. A group of Japanese girls, black-haired, walking close. Travellers, not commuters.

Casimir is almost certain he will never see them again. He likes that about London, the way it keeps people apart. It simplifies things, like a room bare of belongings. Except there is the girl, he thinks. The Underground girl. Sievwright and Weaver chatter behind him.

'How much is it then, Bar Rumba?'

'Don't worry about it.'

'Are you sure?'

'No problem. First Saturday of the month, isn't it? I'm well wedged. All I need now is Claudia Schiffer and five pints of Grolsch. Two double shifts I did this week. You weren't in on Tuesday, were you?'

'I only started Wednesday.'

'You're lucky. You missed the accident. It's been nine, ten years since we got one that bad. Some Care in the Community bloke pushing people off platforms. Ten years at least. It's the worst thing about the job. The accidents.'

The crowds are like water, Casimir thinks. Huge and quick and mindless. They collect along the platforms and then empty out into trains and cross-tunnels. He tries to imagine what would happen if the momentum went wrong somehow, the crowd failing to drain away. He thinks of how many people have travelled through the station since it was dug, a hundred years ago. Whole populations hardly touching in the Tube's huge interior, its warren of halls and stairwells. It seems like a fragile apparatus. One accident could break it.

He checks each screen in turn, half-listening to the other men. Workers in ash-grey suits are crammed in on the Moorgate line, running late for their Saturday overtime. By the platform telephones there is an area of space, as if the crowd is pressing against some invisible obstruction. At the centre of the vacuum stands a woman dressed completely in white.

Casimir sighs and sits back as he recognizes her. The woman's black face and hair are whitened with flour or paint. Her hands are covered in long pale gloves. Her mouth is moving, but even from this distance Casimir can see she is mumbling, not really talking. On the monotone screen she shines, surreally bright.

Casimir raises his voice, loud enough for Oluwo to hear, not loud enough for the other workers. 'Rose is back.'

Oluwo's chair creaks as he stands up, comes over. 'She looks older. Shall I go to her?'

'No.' Casimir watches the woman. It has been a year since he has seen Rose in the station. Then she was on the platforms every day. Leaner, more threatening. Eating on the platform benches; white meats, white milk. He wonders where she has been for a year, to make her look so old. 'No, leave her. She is doing no harm.'

He looks up at Oluwo, smiles. He remembers the worker carrying Rose out of the station, his scarred face emotionless. Then, Rose had trapped two Asian children in a deserted side-passage. She had covered them with white flour. Rubbing it into their hands and faces.

Oluwo nods at Casimir, not smiling, already turning away.

He looks back at the Moorgate screen. Blocked out behind Rose is another figure. Now Rose begins to move away, Casimir can make out a fat man in a logo T-shirt, jeans and backpack. One person at least who is not scared of the woman in white.

'Cheers anyway, for the club entry. We should get a crowd together, like an Underground night out. Oy, Olly! Casimir! Are you up for a bit of clubbing tonight? Cass – What's his other name?'

Laughter. Sievwright's voice is quiet, jeering. 'Mikhail, probably. Rasputin or something. I don't know. No one uses it anyway.'

The fat man is smoothing something out against the telephones with one hand; political posters, Casimir guesses, *Keep Britain White With Dynamite* or worse. There will be time to go down there later and take them down. He looks back at Rose. She is still singing as she moves away, staring people down. Avid but furtive, like the Underground trainspotters and the platform missionaries – Jews for Jesus, Nation of Islam. The Underground is full of Roses, Casimir thinks. Anyone with enough to hide from. Like me.

The poster hanger turns away from the kiosks and moves through the nearest commuters, suddenly graceful. Casimir thinks how fast he is. Big in the bone but muscular, the weight seeming to count for nothing. Already he is almost out of sight. Taken back into the crowd.

'Hey, Casimir. You coming to Bar Rumba tonight?' Weaver jostles against Casimir's chair as he moves past.

'No.' He looks down from the screens, sits back.

Weaver's shadow flickers and looms against the yellowed office walls. 'It's Saturday night, man. Come on.'

Casimir doesn't reply.

The trainee's voice is childlike, disappointed and enthusiastic at the same time. There is the track noise of tap-water as he fills the kettle, plugs it in. 'Saturday night. Olly's going to come, aren't you, Oll? What's your first name, Cass?'

'Casimir.'

'Eh? What's your last name?'

'Casimir.'

'Piss off. What, Casimir Casimir?'

'My name is Kazimierz Ariel Kazimierski. You can call me Cass. It is easier.'

'Fair enough. *Ariel?*'

'Yes.'

'What, like the washing powder?'

The station-to-station telephone rings once and Casimir leans back, ignoring Weaver, reaching for the receiver. The trainee mutters behind him.

'Camden Town.'

'Who is this?'

He doesn't recognize the voice. It seems to him over-measured, as if English is not the speaker's first language. He can hear no accent.

'This is Assistant Station Supervisor Casimir.'

'Where is Adams?'

'He's working. Can I help?'

'This is Line Management.'

The voice makes Casimir think of teachers and politicians. Low-pitched, made calm. Deceptive. Immediately he is on edge, not wanting to say more than he has to. He tries to place the voice as masculine or feminine. It is hard to be certain.

From round the corner comes Sievwright's loud voice and laughter. The voice on the line is still talking. Casimir cranes over the receiver.

'I'm sorry. I couldn't hear what you were saying.'

There is a pause. Not long, patient but suggesting impatience. 'I know Adams is working this shift. It is very important that I talk to him.'

The accident, he thinks. He remembers Adams's voice on the radio. The ashen tone and broken sentences. *I'm just going out for a minute.*

'The station is a big place. He may be working anywhere. I can give him a message as soon as I talk to him.'

'Can you see him on the monitors?'

There is an edge to the voice, almost musical. Feminine. She knows the control room and where I am sitting, Casimir thinks, and then: be careful. There is more than you understand here. Be careful if you lie.

[50]

He turns round, looks up at the screens. The crowds thicken and come apart. Monotone sunlight comes in through the east–west entrances of the surface concourse. Two children run along one of the platforms with a kite, racing to get it airborne in the tunnel wind. It batters along the ground behind them.

'Assistant Casimir –'

'I can't see him. I can give him a message. By radio or when I see him.'

The line goes quiet again. Casimir can hear no background office noise, no breathing. When the Line Manager's voice cuts in again it is more tentative, less sure of itself.

'This is confidential. It is about Rebecca Saville. The accident. It is unfortunate.'

He waits, not saying anything. He remembers the photographs. The woman's neck exposed, lean and beautiful. Her hands reaching out towards the track.

'Adams may not have told you. The doctors say she was born with a heart defect. She had a pacemaker. Any large electric shock would –'

'Is she dead?'

'Yes.' The Line Manager sounds surprised. As if Casimir should have known all along. 'She died late last night. The police are coming to talk to Adams this afternoon. Between two and three. Just for the facts. It was an accident, of course. We just want him to give the facts. Can you tell him to be ready?'

'Yes, I can do that.'

He puts the phone down. Stops with his hand out, head down. He doesn't want to hear any more. After some time he looks round at the monitors.

He can see Adams now. He is in the surface concourse, leaning by the east exit, the noon light slanting in around him. Almost lost in the public crowd. He might have been standing there all the time, Casimir can't be sure. He is quite still, looking out across the streets and midday traffic. As if he's waiting for something.

His jacket is hanging on the wall and he takes it down, looks up.

On the monitor screen Adams is watching the Camden

streets. The light coming in parches his features and simplifies them. From here it looks as if he is grinning.

He walks through the late summer rain to the river and sits, a lone figure under the trees, while the embankment pavement begins to darken and shine with water. He is hunched forward on the iron bench with his elbows on his knees, supporting himself. His head is bent and his hands are clasped loosely together, so that from a distance it looks as if he is praying. The rain plasters rat's-tails of hair against his scalp and runs down his cheeks and back.

He is not praying, only thinking. He thinks of how scared Rebecca Saville must have been as she fell, knowing the weakness of her own heart. He thinks of the Underground girl, the smell of rain on her and the acid odour of oranges on her hands. The vividness of her being alive.

A cyclist goes past and he looks up at the hiss of tyres on the wet ground. The shadows under Casimir's eyes and the hollows of his cheekbones make his face look bruised. He will not sleep until morning tomorrow as he prepares for the night shifts. But he is surprised at how alert he feels, as if the closeness of death has shaken him awake. He looks down at his watch, stands up quickly and begins to walk back up past Westminster Bridge and the grey hulk of County Hall, shoulders raised against the rain.

By the time he reaches Lower Marsh the sky is already lightening, the afternoon sun breaking through as it falls below the level of clouds. Mrs Navratil's shop is crowded with people, their jacketed shoulders pressed against the steamed-up window as they queue for Saturday night fish. Casimir can see Navratil's weekend workers behind the vats, Den and Merrick, their faces shiny with sweat and oil just as his own is slicked with rain.

He opens the door and edges through the crowd to the chrome and glass counter. The smell of cooking meat makes him hungry and he tries to remember how long it is since he's eaten. Den nods at him from the cash till, hands still working while he smiles.

'All right? How's the Tube?'

Casimir shakes his head, tries to smile back. He doesn't know how to answer. He opens the counter, goes through and locks it behind him. The vats hiss and spit as Merrick drops in fishcakes one by one.

'Cushty little job, that is. Isn't it, Merrick?' The younger man laughs and nods. 'All those strikes, feet up on the picket lines. Cushty. Desk work, is it? You're not down in the tunnels, are you?'

'Not today.' He opens the rear door. 'Is Mrs Navratil here?'

'Upstairs with her loverboy, heh. Laters, yeah?'

'Yes.' He closes the door behind him.

The rear staircase is narrow and walled-off between shop floor and storerooms. Casimir has to turn his shoulders to walk up, the bare steps creaking under him. On the first floor is the lodgers' kitchen, four o'clock light streaming in across the empty surfaces. The hallway light bulb has still not been replaced and Casimir goes on up carefully, past his own second-floor room to a last flight of stairs at the back of the building.

There is a small door at the top, thickly repainted, the yellow gloss already chipped in layered patterns of brown and red. Through the door Casimir can hear the low monologue of a radio or television. He knocks and waits, knocks again.

'Who is that?' Mrs Navratil's voice is close to the door, waiting before opening. Casimir takes a step back down before he answers.

'It's me. I have the rent.'

He is looking down, reaching into his jacket as the landlady opens the door. He hands the money up to her and waits while she counts the notes. Her hair is down and she is wearing good clothes: a long skirt and blue-grey silk blouse, old-fashioned but well kept. Casimir hasn't noticed Mrs Navratil's hair before. It is tarnished like old silver.

'Good.' She is looking at him again. 'You seem tired.'

'There was an accident at work.'

'A bad one?'

He nods. 'A death. It has never happened before at my station, in my time.' When he looks up to meet her eyes, Mrs

Navratil is already glancing away, back into her room. 'I'm sorry, you're busy –'

'Yes. Can you work the chicken vats tonight?'

'I have to go out first. I can try and be –'

'No. It doesn't matter.'

She is already closing the door. He turns and goes back down the stairs, thinking of the lodgers' stories of Mrs Navratil: that she loves a television newsreader; that she sits in her best clothes, waiting for him to notice her. Behind him the television monologue is turned up, a deadpan masculine voice against a background of theme music.

He goes into his room and locks the door. The net curtains are drawn and he opens them and then the window, letting in light and air. He sits down on the bed and then lies back on the cheap mattress.

He is still wearing his uniform jacket and he takes out the rest of his month's pay, smooth brown and blue banknotes in a white packet. The pocket is full of material, neatly folded and arranged: a notebook, a staff list, a dozen International Registered envelopes, stamps and pen. Sitting up, he unfolds £250 and puts the money in an envelope, then tears a page from the notebook.

The *London A—Z* is on the floor beside him and he picks it up, flattens the notepaper against it, holding the book's spine to keep it taut. He writes quickly. Each letter is joined but distinct.

131b Lower Marsh
London SE1 7AD, England
Saturday 7 Sept.

Dear Piotr

Here is money for September. Write to me if Tomek's treatment becomes more expensive.

I hope you are all well. Summer is almost finished here. Tonight is not so warm and the leaves are falling. Even in London there are trees.

I do not want my father to write to me. Please do not post his letters again.

Love,
Ariel

When he is finished he goes to the window, closes and locks it. Upriver, the faces of Big Ben read ten to five. He goes out of the room and downstairs to the lodgers' side-door. The queue for fish has lengthened into the street. Casimir walks without hurrying. Taking long steps, covering the ground.

He looks up at the railway bridges and high-rises, enjoying the feel of sun on his face where the clouds have broken. High up the nearest high-rise an office has been burnt out. He slows as he passses its blackened, hollow space. The windows above it have been dulled and warped by the fire's intensity.

The road ends at the south bank of the Thames, three streets of all-day rush-hour traffic meeting at Waterloo Bridge. At the hub of the crossroads is the Bull Ring, subways opening into its half-underground space. Casimir can see the tops of lamp-posts and a warning sign on the far concrete wall, FIRES ARE PROHIBITED. In the mouth of the northern underpass he can make out figures moving and the bare, skewed shapes of card-board shelters. Signs are already up, warning of new construction work: a multiplex. Casimir wonders where the homeless will go, forced out of the old shanty town.

The post office on the corner of Stamford Street is still open and he hands in the registered letter and leaves quickly, heading towards an empty phone box, crossing the street between grid-locked cars. He swings open the phone-box door and picks up the receiver. It has been smashed open, the mouth-piece trailing like a lid from a nest of red and yellow wires. Casimir holds the receiver to his ear. There is still a dial tone, only slightly muffled by the parts twisted out of alignment.

He takes the staff list out of his jacket, folds it out on the wall and leafs through the pages of names – Weaver, Sievwright, Aebanyim. Under Adams's name are a telephone number and address: 215 Coppermill Lane, an Outer London area code. Casimir feeds in a pound and dials the number. He leans back against the booth door as he waits. The smell of urine in the box is overpowering. The windows are scrawled with graffiti, purple and green ciphers like those in the Under-ground cross-tunnel.

Casimir closes his eyes while the telephone rings and rings. He is trespassing here already. He has no place in Adams's private life, knows nothing about it. He imagines the supervisor drinking alone in a dark room. Thinking of the day.

The connection clicks open. For a moment there is no voice, only a sense of distance. Casimir can hear gulls.

'Hello?'

'It's Casimir.' He waits uncomfortably. The breathing on the other end of the line is Adams but not Adams. Hoarse and weak, like an old man. 'Casimir from the Underground.'

Again there is the sound of seagulls. Now he cannot hear Adams at all, not even his breathing. The gulls and the silence make him think of waterlands, or the sea. 'Adams, are you there?'

'Yes. What do you – What can I do for you?' There is irritation in the other man's voice.

'The girl who fell, Rebecca Saville. I want to talk about it.'

'There's nothing to say. She's dead.'

He feels anger start up in himself at the quickness of Adams's answer. He waits, letting himself become calm again. 'You knew about her heart.'

'Not to start with, no. Not when I told you.'

'But you knew she was pushed. You had the photographs.'

There is no reply. An ambulance goes past outside, siren loud in the built-up streets, moving slowly through the five o'clock traffic. Casimir leans forward, trying to hear his own voice or Adams's.

'You must have –'

'Yes, I knew.'

He remembers Adams telling him about the fall, three days ago. The half-smile. *A suicide wouldn't be an accident now, would it?* Now he holds the receiver carefully against his ear and mouth, trying not to loosen the smashed parts.

'What did you tell the police?'

'I left them the photos.'

'You didn't see them?'

'I don't know anything, Cass. Nothing to speak of. They've got the photos, they can make up their own minds. I don't want nothing to do with it.'

He is surprised at the levelness of the other man's voice. Not deadpan, only tired.

'I'm on sick-leave from today, for two months. That's my notice. I'm not going back down there again. I've had done with it, Cass, and if you've sense you'll do the same.'

'Who pushed her?'

'How the fuck should I know?'

Adams's shout is distorted by the telephone. Casimir pulls his ear away from the harsh, ragged sound. The supervisor is still talking, fast and loud. Casimir puts his ear back against the broken mechanism, holding it together with both hands.

'– rotten about this whole business. Something brewing. You're a careful lad, Cass, why don't you just take care of yourself? That's all I'm doing, taking care. Looking out for myself, it's what I've always done. When I'm down there now, I keep wanting to look over my shoulder and I don't, but the feeling's that strong. I trust my feelings. I've been down there a long time, you should remember that –'

'How long?'

'Eh?'

'You know more than me. About the Underground and about Rebecca Saville. I want to know. I only want to have things clear, to understand. All you have to do is talk. Then I will leave you alone.'

When Adams speaks again his voice is softer. As if the feeling has been allowed back into it. 'Leave it, Casimir. You can't help her now. Just let it be.'

The line goes dead in his hands.

He needs to walk, and London is good for walking. Casimir crosses Waterloo Bridge with his head down, then loses himself in a mare's-nest of back streets and hotel service entrances with their smell of kitchens and clean, steaming laundry. His thoughts feel packed tight, as if the day with its death leaves him no room to think of anything else.

When he looks up again he is by Embankment station. He climbs the steps to the Hungerford footbridge, heading back south. Night trains clank past him, moving slowly over the river, out towards the suburban stations of Eden Park, Clock House and Summer Hill.

He stops to lean on the metal railing, breathing easily. The anger towards Adams is dull, walked out. Downriver the city lights are laid out along the curves of roads and the lines of towers. They remind Casimir of the bright watch-work mechanisms on his grandfather's black repairer's cloth. Cogs and teeth and springs. The dome of St Paul's is lit up, grey against the brighter illumination of Docklands. He goes on towards Lower Marsh, down concrete steps, under railway arches to the Waterloo subways.

This is a different kind of underground – more open to the sky and weather, less enclosed in itself. Unlit where the Tube station passages would be barred with light. There are graffiti on the concrete walls, high rambling letters. Casimir can read them only where there is light from staircases and entrance ramps: HOT WIRES. LITTLE LEGS LOVES MIDGET.

There are figures sitting against the walls, on damp mats of cardboard or newspaper. Casimir looks at faces as he walks carefully between their hunched forms. It is an old habit, the looking for someone familiar in these lost places. Casimir has done it for as long as people have been lost to him. It is longer than he cares to remember.

The subway opens out into the concrete arena of the Bull Ring. The place is empty except for a ring of metal benches at its centre, arranged like a barricade around one tall halogen lamppost. A small child is standing on the benches, peering downwards, her back to Casimir. From her height he guesses her to be no more than three years old; an inhabitant of the cardboard city. From overhead, he can hear the evening traffic on the roundabout, the slow groan of lorries and the late rush-hour tailback.

It comes to him that she could have been here, the Underground girl. In the dark he is almost convinced that he remembers seeing her here. She sits cross-legged in one of the subways, pulling the white dreadlocks back from her profiled face. The bones of her cheeks and the small, neat hook of her nose.

He walks towards the benches, trying to remember more. But already the vividness is gone and he is unsure. He has walked home this way many times, and the images of the homeless are dulled by familiarity. The memory seems uncertain now, or imagined. The face of the girl becomes blurred with that of Rebecca Saville. For a moment he thinks of going up to the child standing on the benches, asking her – what? She would have nothing to say to him.

He is nearer to the benches now. The child is still standing, pale and unmoving. From here Casimir can see there is something wrong with her neck, the shoulders hunched forward. He steps towards her. A gentle man, needing to help.

The child's neck stretches out as it turns to look at him, white and long as an arm. In the gloom Casimir stops, the fear jerking him back before he can understand what he sees. The figure is a heron, not a child. It angles its head away again and bends at the knees and leaps, opening out, colourless in the half-light. Casimir watches the slow beat of its wings, east-wards along the river.

He waits for the fear to pass. Then he turns towards the southern exit, away from the subway. In his pocket he can feel the watch on his wrist, small and hard and certain. He walks on towards Waterloo Road.

'Casimir. It's a nice name. Is it Polish?'

'It's just a name.'

Crunch of boots on ballast stones. Echo of voices in miles of tunnels, a city under the city. Casimir makes himself go on talking. It is good to talk, in the tunnels at night.

'My middle name is Ariel. It means Lion.'

'Polish lions?'

'No. Hebrew.'

'You don't look Jewish.'

'No.'

'Are there many Jews in Poland?'

Aebanyim walks ahead of him, bulky in her bright orange overalls. Between the rough gravel are track sleepers, wood flush with the tunnel floor. There is the smell of damp and cre-osote. The white bowls of track insulators gleam in the line-lights.

'No. It's not a good place to be Jewish.'

The tunnel walls are riveted plates of iron, crusted with

grime. Their raised edges arch overhead, like ribs, and the grime itself is creased and ridged, layer on layer of coal dust, exhaust and limestone glittering black. Cables run along the wall at shoulder height, thick as Casimir's arms. Parallel to the cables are two thin lengths of copper, clean and bright: the old clip-on telephone wires, still kept live for emergencies. On Casimir's belt his cellular coughs and mutters on its open radio line. Garbled snatches of conversation. Interference from other lines and works.

'You must miss it. Poland.'

'Sometimes.' He thinks of zúr soup, its taste of hot rye bread and soured cream and garlic. The forest, pine trees intersecting like helices. Birches, their pattern repeated again and again; spindles of some pale and cold organism. The forest's dark, which he almost loved. 'Not often.'

'Oh, there's always something. Not your family?'

'No.' Watered light against his mother's drawn features. Just the two of them, playing. He tries to recall where and cannot. 'Aebanyim is also a good name. Where is it from?'

'Nigeria. But my first name is Sarah, you know? You forgot. I told you before.'

Her voice is full of gentle laughter. They trudge on, measuring distance by the ten-foot space between light brackets. What colour there is down here stands out, vibrant against the coal-pit background. There is a single apple-green wall cable, spiralling between grey wires. The red headlines of a tabloid front page, blowing from station to station.

'What is it like? Nigeria.'

'Oh –' She laughs. 'Well. There are lions there.'

'What about Oluwo? Where is he from?'

'Nigeria.'

'The same? Did you come here together?'

Short laughter between closed teeth. 'No. Nigeria is big. Not like Great Britain.'

Casimir thinks of the staff list, the eclectic muddle of names from Africa and East Europe. The Underground has always been a place for immigrant workers. There are never enough people willing to work the tunnels. It is part of the reason he is here himself.

'Oluwo is Yoruba.'

'What are you?'

'Not Yoruba.'

He smiles. The air is warm and stale under the weight of earth, streets and buildings. Between the harsh illumination of line-lights are bands of dark, curving around the ceiling and walls. There is always darkness waiting, underground. He tries not to think of it, to concentrate on their talk. Their voices are a thread of sound against the background hush of air.

'Just a moment.'

Aebanyim stops by a track join, squinting in the bad light. She kneels, reaching out with her hands. The long lines of metal are eroded where they meet. She reaches into her jacket, takes out a can, shakes it to loosen the spray paint. The can hisses as she marks the fault for the engineers. A circle of fluorescent yellow on the discoloured steel. They walk on.

'Are you married, Casimir?'

'No.'

'Why not?'

The tunnel walls shine with water. The cell phones crackle again, in unison. Casimir slows to turn his receiver down. Taking careful steps even now, when the track is dead. The black box of the voltage tester bangs against his thigh.

'Why aren't you married, Casimir? I am. Don't you want to be with someone?'

'Yes, I want to.'

He can hear the care in his own voice. A careful man, the way his mother took care. He tries to say something, a real answer, but it is impossible. He shakes his head, three steps behind Aebanyim. The next line light shines up ahead. The runners curve away north-west, four gleaming steel parallels.

It is what he likes best about night shifts, the tunnel-walking. If he can, he comes down here alone. Not because the proximity of the dark doesn't scare him. Once, he has been here when the lights have gone for less than a minute. The fear was so strong it felt as if his breath no longer reached to his brain. Then, he stopped, bent double, taking in great ragged lungfuls of the black air. But only if he is alone; sometimes it's better for him to be alone here.

[61]

He walks in the tunnels because he can. They are the place he has taken on the dark. He has been trying for eight years and the fear is still with him. But he has learned to manage it. Now he walks against it, leaning slightly, as if into a slight gradient.

It is why he came here, to the Underground; one of the reasons. Not because he needed a job – there was other work he might have done, on building sites, or the seasonal farm work undertaken by many immigrants. He remembers the first time he travelled on the Underground, in from the Heathrow air terminals. Besides the spread-map view from the aeroplane, the train was his first image of Britain. The suburban surface stations, plant-pots hung in a grey mizzle of rain. Then the shock of descent, under Hammersmith and the West End. He couldn't take his eyes away from the windows. The pressure of air rattling against them, the tunnel roaring past outside.

For Casimir the dark is the Underground. It is a place where light has no real place. He is here because the dark is here, because he will not run away from it. He has never turned away from what scares him. Because the fear is too great for him to ever turn his back.

'Listen. Can you hear?'

He stops. From up ahead comes the sound of voices. Laughter, raucous and high-pitched.

He shrugs. 'Cleaners. Or the Camden engineers. Maybe they are lost.'

'Yes.'

Aebanyim's voice sounds uncertain. Down here the laughter sounds eerie, hollowed out by the tunnels' acoustics. He thinks of children's stories in Poland, the frightening ones. The Ohyn, babies stillborn with cauls and teeth, who came back at night to eat their grieving parents. Voices speaking from underground.

They wait by the track side, listening as the sounds come closer. Casimir can make out a female voice, an Australasian accent.

'So I told him New Zealand, and he said, Oh, sheep country, ha ha. I said, Right, ha ha. And then I said, Actually I do have a sheep, and he said, Really? I said, Yeah, it's like a house-pet sheep, lots of folks back home have them. He says, *Really?*'

Four figures appear around the next corner, bent double under giant plastic sacks. A cleaning team, Casimir thinks. Aebanyim looks back at him, smiles. He sees her teeth catch the light, their bleached whiteness.

'I said, Yeah, they're kind of like dogs back home. People walk them around the city centres. And the guy keeps nodding and going, Oh right, right. I mean, Jesus, I felt sorry for him. Hello, who's that? Is that gorgeous Mick Adams from Camden?'

'No. Mick Adams is absent tonight.'

The cleaners stop talking at the sound of Aebanyim's voice. The odd choice of words, textbook English spoken out loud. Casimir can see them properly now. Four women, none of them young. Their hands and forearms are covered by thick rubber gloves. He recognizes the New Zealander, a stocky woman, her frizz of red hair tied back with a metal hair-grip. Her name is Muir, Anne or Anna. She doesn't recognize him.

'Mick? He's never off. What's wrong with him?'

The cleaner is looking past Aebanyim at Casimir. As if the black woman isn't there. After a moment he answers, not stepping forward, 'Adams is not well. Supervisor Leynes will be on his shifts for a few months.'

'A few months? Shit. Tell him to get well, will you?'

'Of course.'

The cleaners move past, stepping across the track to make room. The last woman's rubbish sack bumps against her side, half-open. Inside Casimir can see the mass of tunnel refuse. Neon-yellow crisp packets, bundles of human hair, torn scratchcards, golden credit cards.

As she passes him, the woman grins and thrusts her hand out. Something clacks between her fingers and Casimir steps back. She is holding a pair of false teeth, yellowed and dusty.

'Look what I found!' She turns away, small and anxious. The other cleaners have already gone on southwards. She grins again and then hurries after them.

They walk on. Now there is no sound except the crunch of their feet. Two rhythms, not quite in time.

The wall beside him gives way to space. Casimir steps sideways, ducking under the loops of cables and the line-telephone

[63]

wires. Beyond is another track, an adjoining tunnel curling away. He looks up and down, checking for damage to the walls, track, signals. Moisture shines on the tunnel's curvature, so that it looks like a giant sewer.

'Why was Mick Adams sick? Was it because of the woman who fell?'

The woman who fell. He turns back to Aebanyim, frowning at her choice of words. Not an accident, or a suicide. Just the woman, falling out from the crowd. He shakes his head.

'I don't know. Does it matter?'

'Maybe.' She turns to walk on northwards and Casimir follows, two steps behind. 'He is a careful man. Maybe it matters, if he leaves. Once I was with him down here. The line was not working, because there was water coming in from the big sewers, the old rivers. We came to the break – I was in front. I saw black things moving in the water. They were – fish like snakes.'

'Eels.'

'Yes. From the underground rivers. Like snakes. I wanted to move them but Mick said they bite. He said they were dirty inside, like rats. He was very careful of them. We went back to the station, and cleared the lines, and he turned the power on –'

There is a rattle of loose stones as Aebanyim stumbles. She falls over towards the track, her hands going out, twisting down. Casimir bends and reaches out, instinctively quick, so that she falls into his arms. She is heavy but surprisingly thin, the uniform flapping around her torso. Casimir lifts her upright, stands back.

'Are you hurt?'

'No, thank you.'

He watches the worker feeling her hands and left arm, checking for blood or broken skin.

'Not another accident.' She smiles up at Casimir, teeth very white in the dark between lights. 'Thank you.' Then she turns away, walking on more slowly. She doesn't talk again.

Casimir follows her, moving carefully on the wet ballast stones. They come to another junction, their northbound tunnel opening briefly into a southbound. The line-light has shorted out here. There is the sound of water everywhere in the near-dark. Casimir listens to its musical drip-drop, trying to place the source of the leak.

'I was working when it happened. The accident.'

He stops and looks round. It is impossible to make out the other worker's face properly, to see what she is thinking.

'In the control room?'

'Yes.'

'You saw it on the monitors? When Rebecca Saville fell?'

'Yes.' Aebanyim steps closer. Now Casimir can see her eyes, their whites, staring. She talks quickly, the accent making it hard for Casimir to understand. 'They are video cameras. So it is all recorded.'

'Photographs. I saw.'

'No. Not photographs. They are video cameras.' She is nodding, as if agreeing with Casimir.

'There are videos, of course. Where are they kept?'

'The police took them.'

Casimir feels the urgency go out of him. 'The ones who tried to talk to Adams?'

'Yes. One police. A policewoman. She took all the tapes from that day.'

He swears in Polish: *Cholera*. Aebanyim's cellular crackles into life and she unclips it from her belt, talking into it between bursts of static.

'Yes? Aebanyim. Yes. I will come back. Casimir . . . I will come now.' She clicks off the radio, looks up.

'Go. I can manage here.'

The black woman smiles. 'See you soon.'

Casimir watches her walk back along the tunnel towards the Camden Town platforms. Long after she is out of sight there is the sound of her footsteps, echoing back along the empty line.

He looks down at his watch. It is past three-thirty, less than an hour before he has to be clear of the track. He can hear the soft tick of the mechanism as the watch-hands move imperceptibly, thin and black against the luminous dial.

He holds the small light up ahead of him briefly, like a beacon. Then he lowers it, curls up his hand. The next line-light is close; he can see illumination diffused around the gradual north-east curve. He is almost at the midpoint between stations now. Somewhere ahead are the disused platforms of South Kentish Town, where he can turn back towards Camden. He knows the distance in line-lights; there are a hundred more. His radio volume is turned down and he switches it back up before he starts to walk.

When he reaches the next light he stops in its bluish illumination, breathing a little fast. It is very warm here; he can feel sweat running down the sides of his torso. There is the sound of water too, the drip and echo of it.

The line is straight here and he keeps his eyes on the patches of illumination, measuring off the steps. The ballast stones have been scattered away and his rubber-soled boots slap on the bare concrete.

He has been hearing the music for some time before he registers it. It is very faint – a voice, guitars, echoes. Out of place among the hushed sounds of the tunnel. Casimir feels for his radio, lifts it to his ear. There is no sound from the receiver now except the soft hiss of static.

The sound is coming from up ahead. Turned down low or played softly or simply distant, echoing back along the tunnel. They are playing music at the next station, Casimir thinks, but as the idea comes to him he already knows it is wrong. The Kentish Town platforms are nearly half a mile away. If I am hearing music from there, he thinks, I should be hearing the engineers working at Camden.

He starts walking again, trying to tread without sound. He is closer now and the music is perceptibly louder. He frowns, trying to remember if there are any ventilation shafts from the surface here, anything that might carry the sound of music down from an all-night restaurant or dance hall.

It is at South Kentish Town, he thinks. There is someone at the abandoned station. Briefly he can make out sung words and a female voice, clear and low.

'Let me ride . . . Let me . . . ride on your grace for a while . . .'

Then the sound is carried away again. He moves forward and immediately there are ballast stones under his boots. He is not ready for them. Gravel clacks and skitters against the track metal. There is an echo of movement ahead and then the music stops abruptly. Another sound, regular, almost too soft for footsteps.

Casimir breaks into a run, through the last barred sections of light and dark. Then the tunnel walls widen around him and he is at South Kentish Town. The derelict platform is almost chest high beside him. Rows of tiny stalactites are forming from the platform's lip, gleaming grey. Broken equipment is piled against the far wall. Sixty feet away a single light bulb shines in the platform's only side-tunnel, swinging slightly on its flex.

He puts his hands out on to the platform, vaults up and stops still, listening, dirt cool on his palms. There is no sound now except his own breathing. The light from the side-tunnel fans out across the platform, filtering away between the crates of equipment.

The smell of limestone is strong here. Sweet and damp, like church stone. Casimir tries to remember how long ago the station was abandoned; seventy or eighty years, sometime between the wars. Now it feels more like a great natural cave than a place dug and built. He kneels down, looking away across the black platform grime. Deposited in thick ridges, it is too uneven to keep much sign of movement.

He moves forward along the platform, stopping to look between teetering stacks of wrought-iron benches, fourteen cracked-faced platform clocks, enamelled cigarette sand-trays, great rotting scrolls of posters for THE UNDERGROUND: ALWAYS WARM AND BRIGHT and MASKELYNE'S MYSTERIES – ST GEORGE'S HALL. Letting his eyes adjust to the empty dark between objects.

At the side-tunnel he stops. The bare bulb shines off the tiled walls. Casimir can make out old serif lettering, EXIT THIS WAY, the words defaced by graffiti. Down the passage he knows there must be other platforms and tunnels, staircases, an old cage-lift. He remembers that a worker was once trapped in the lift shaft for three days; he wonders if there is still a surface exit. On the floor by the corner of the wall, something catches the light.

He stoops down. Against the platform wall are metal electricity cables and emergency power points. Pushed back against them is a small square of glass. Casimir picks it up, turns it in both hands, wipes it clean.

It is the lid of a box, chipped but not cracked. Small enough to lie flat in the palm of his hand. There is a faded picture on the glass. A man in military uniform next to a burning match. Casimir narrows his eyes. 'LIGHT A LIGHT FOR IKE!' is written under the picture in curving script.

He smiles. Around him the deserted platform and the memory of music suddenly seem fantastical, half-imagined. He closes his fingers on the box lid and tucks it carefully into his jacket pocket.

There is a cough of static from his cellular and then an alarm tone. He looks at his watch. It is four-thirty; already he should be out of the tunnels. In an hour the track current will be switched back on. The alarm tone blares again. Once, twice.

He looks up. The graffiti are directly in front of him, stark black on the cracked tiles. The pattern of letters is familiar. He can resolve the shapes into words: JACK UNION. The spray paint shines and he reaches out, touching the motif.

His fingers come away clean. The cellular repeats its warning. He stares back up at the graffiti for a moment longer, as if he is waiting for something to happen. Then he turns back towards the tunnel mouth.

After the Candle

'Either the well was very deep or she fell very slowly, because she had plenty of time as she went down to look around her, and to wonder what was going to happen next.'

'I know what happens.'

'Because you're so smart.' The page chuffs like a kitchen match. *'She tried to look down and make out what she was coming to, but it was too dark to see anything.'*

This is mother reading to me. Before she came in I was in the mirror. In the mirror I was the second-shortest thing. The tallest was the wardrobe, then the picture of London Piccadilly England from a magazine, the white CaPamoB Russian refrigerator, the black Singer in its hood, the desk with the green candle on it, then me. Then the bed. Over the bed is Jesus Christ. He is nailed to the wallpaper with its greenish flowers which used to frighten me and now they're ordinary. The nail only goes through his cross. Altogether there are four nails.

'She found herself in a long, low hall, which was lit by a row of lamps hanging from the roof. Go on then, what happens next?'

'There were doors.'

'There were doors all round the hall, but they were locked.'

I waved at the mirror. It was my left hand but the mirror's right. It was my west hand and the mirror's west too. I know why it happens. Left and right are inside, like blood and liver. West is outside, like London Piccadilly England. West is the best. It stays still.

'"Oh, how I wish I could shut up like a telescope! I think I could, if I only knew how to begin —"'

Outside will be dark soon. The town is already dark because the lights have gone down. My candle is square and green, and in the mirror my skin was green in its light. I felt my chest, knuckly ribs, belly, cock. My cock is much smaller than Dad's in the swimming changing rooms, but my belly is pretty big. It's all because we had zakashka blood sausage for breakfast and there was one left in the CaPamoB on a white plate with blue spots and I ate it. I was hungry. My dad swore and put down his mug so hard the handle broke off. He didn't touch me, but I am going to bed without supper.

Supper was only liver anyway and I still get a story. I lie with my eyes shut. I can taste the oiled spiced sweetness of zakashka in my mouth.

'*And she tried to fancy what the flame of a candle looks like after the candle is blown out, for she could not remember ever having seen such a thing.* Have you ever seen that?'

'No.'

'There, enough. Tomorrow we'll do Pippi Longstocking.'

'No. More Alice now.'

'Not tonight. Only when you're good.'

'One page.'

'No.'

'Up to the next picture.'

'*No.*'

I don't mind so much. My eyes are shut. The candlelight is green through my eyelids. Sometimes I am awake and then not. I dream something about water, light on it and under it. I hear Mother shuffle around. She is looking for the cigarettes, which are on the desk. In a minute she'll find them.

'Listen, Casimir. Ariel, love. I'm sorry if you're hungry, but you mustn't steal food, not ever. I know it's hard.'

'Why?' I'll play the Question Game to keep her here. I try to open my eyes but it's difficult, part of me is not trying hard enough.

'Why? Because things are hard for us.'

'Why?'

'Just because. Because life is hard. We have to learn to find ways through. Sometimes they are the right ways. If we are good rats.'

The bed creaks as she leans away. Everything is quiet and slow because I am asleep, and then the cigarette crackles. I open my eyes and Mother is leant over the candle and her face lit up green and white like a face under water. Her breath hisses, *sss*, through the cigarette. I jump up shrieking.

'Mum – Mum, *no! Mum!*'

I pull the cigarette out of her mouth and throw it across the bedroom. It hits the dark blue of the window and scatters red. Mother pulls away from me.

'Oh, *Borja!*' She stamps around and shakes the curtains, putting out bits of cigarette. I sit on the bed with my knees up, hard on my hard ribs. The air is cold on my skin. In a dream it wouldn't be so cold. I don't cry yet, not on my face.

She stops. 'What the hell were you doing? What's wrong with you tonight?'

'You lit it from the candle. You'll die at sea.'

My voice is small. It makes her sit down. It is the smallest thing in the room.

'Ariel! It's just a story. A stupid story, like Alice. Don't cry. Shh.'

Later she blows out the candle and goes. I look for the flame but there is only the smoke. It twirls up for a bit and then stops.

Alice is right about the flame. She is right. The story is right, it is not stupid. I cry without making noise. In the morning I open my eyes and I can still smell candlewax and burning.

Now and from now there is school. The steps are clever. They have wavy thin iron up over them to keep the rain off; it is like an umbrella. The walls have little patterns in them like biscuit. I have seen it all before.

It is the Strug Estate school, with the blocks all around it like a great stone fence. I am surprised because I do not recognize the children, even though they are from my home.

Mother goes. It is like usual. I am all here in my arms, legs, heart, teeth which taste of breakfast, it was oiled salt herrings; I run my tongue against them to get the taste of it. I put my hands in my coat pockets to be together and strong.

Someone screams but it is just girls. I am ready for it. There is sand and a slide and the sun is out.

In the classroom I am next to a girl and her hair is red. I do not know her or anyone. Piotr, Monika, Wladislaw and Karol are all in other classrooms. All the children have their own friends here, so they can talk.

It is a bit worrying, so I keep looking down. I have a desk; it is grey metal like an Ursus. I try and wrap my legs around its legs. The legs of the desk are very much colder than mine.

If I were not in school I could play with the desk. I would drive to Russia with it. Already I want to be out of here. I make the desk move with my legs and it bangs on the next desk. The girl with red hair looks at me. She has a little case with lots of long pencils. I have only one pencil and it is not so long.

A woman walks in. I look up quick to see how big she is. She is quite big and she has a black shiny necklace; it is very pretty. Everyone stands up, so I stand up, and then everyone sits down again.

I am left standing up. It is so strange, now I am swaying, I don't know why. Someone laughs and then I can make myself sit. I hate them already. I will be careful. They will not laugh at me again.

The woman doesn't say anything; she turns her back on us. She is writing with chalk and suddenly everyone is writing too, but with pencils. How do they know what to do? I know. Their mothers and fathers have told them. I am angry that Mother did not tell me this.

There is my small pencil on my desk. Next to me the girl with red hair is writing. I copy her with my small pencil. It is not so hard.

I am writing! It is this: MY NAME IS MRS NALKOWSKA. YOU ARE CLASS 1C. TODAY IS MONDAY 4 AUGUST 1974. THE TIME IS 09.06. THIS IS POLAND. WELCOME.

It looks clever.

Wedel bonbons are good. With three you can make a door. With four you can make a wall. With two you can do nothing but eat them. If you only have two it's best if you can get red and green. Together they taste like blood. The taste is exact.

Only once. My father hurt me only once. It was because of the little bottles. My life is not good, not bad. We are ordinary, like anyone.

Once he was in a fight at the shipyard. He hit a Czech with a long hammer. It was because of foreigners, expecting us to roll out the bloody red carpet. The Militia men came and talked with him. There was no blood on him that time. They all bowed and clicked heels and the Militia went away.

Once he was home from travelling. I went into the room where he sleeps with my mother. His suitcase was empty on the floor, a big loose mouth with small bright teeth. I went to the white drawers, to touch his clothes.

In his winter coat were two bottles full of powder. They were small and glass, white and green. They had labels with writing, like the bottles in the story of Alice: *Drink Me.* Mother bought the story of Alice from France. Every time she drinks from a bottle, the whole world changes. Caterpillars as big as cows.

I took the bottles out. They were small, like things made for children. You could tell they were for booze from the labels, all gold and great colours. On one was a smiling man in a red suit and red hat, and on the other two dogs, black and white. There was English but my father had written over it, to show what was inside.

I held the bottles up. It took me a long time to read the words right. The first one said *Water*. I unscrewed the top but there was nothing to drink, just the white powder. It had almost no smell, like water. Maybe it was powdered water though. Afterwards snot came out of my nose and I couldn't stop it, and the blacks of my eyes went small as millimetres. I could pinch my nose and cheeks and not feel them, it was pretty good.

The second bottle said *Flour*. It was the same inside, only green glass. I opened it to make sure the powder was flour, but it was different. It hurt my eyes, so I closed the bottle again. I touched the bottles together, a toast: *To the name of Jozef Stalin, Na zdrowie, Na zdrowie.* The bottle glass clicked; a clean, fine sound. I did it again, then harder, *clack.* It echoed in my mother's room and I laughed.

Then I was hit. I dropped the bottles and above me was my

father's voice, roaring and swearing. I never heard him come in because of the noise of the bottles clacking. He tried to get me but I ran out around him and out, out of the room and the apartment, down the concrete stair flights, to my special places. Later I came back and he was OK, he hugged me and told me never to look in his things. I asked him about the little bottles but he said they were gone. He asked me if I touched the powders and I said no.

I don't know what he did with the little bottles. Maybe he made bread. Flour and water make bread. I don't know.

It hurt when he hit me. I didn't cry at all. It only hurt because he is so strong. When I am as strong as my father, I will never hit anyone.

When I grow up I will make time.

'The wheels have teeth, you see? They bite together. And here I wind the spring, the spring turns the little wheels, the little wheels turn the big wheels and the big wheels turn the hands, so we make time! All because of the little wheels.'

When Grandfather speaks, it sounds like the new houses where the road ends. It is the noise of machines mixing concrete and it means he will die. He spits snot the way Wladislaw can do it. Christ knows it is the cigarettes. Sometimes I don't understand what he says, it is bad as foreigners on the radio.

He is eighty-three years old and that is the second oldest on the list of ages. Father is fifty-one, Mother is forty-six, Piotr's father is thirty-one and his mother is thirty-one and Monika is almost seven, Piotr and Wladislaw are six and as for me, I am five. King Casimir the Great is 365. I have no grandfather from Mother, no grandmother and no uncles and no aunts. They all died in the war.

First he lived a way away and then he lived in Butcher's Square, but for most of the time he has lived with me. This is Grandfather. He smells like Father except more and older. Older cigarettes, older meat. His room smells of it and even the carpet in the hall outside his room all the way down to the kitchen.

Sometimes I stay with him. Only to watch the watch-works.

'There. And the face, so.'

He holds it up next to his big grey brown white face. The hands of the watch make a V. Two faces smiling. 'What time is it, Casimir?'

I don't know. There are lots of things I don't know; it is quite worrying. However, I can lie.

'It is too late.'

Grandfather laughs. 'Too late for what?'

I hate him laughing. It makes me speak up loud. 'Too late for old people. Too late to kill the Germans because they killed us first. Too late because we did the pleasure before the business. Too late to kill all the Yids because they went away –'

'Enough, Kazio. Quiet now.'

He is not laughing any more. His big face turns away, looking out of the window. 'Remember that every man is a variation of yourself.' What he says makes no sense. Now he is not moving at all. It is like the watch when it is not put together right.

While he is still not looking I touch the watch-works. With my fingertips I stroke the cloth, which is soft and black like cat skin. I pick up the wheels and put them down quickly.

They are so precious. Shiny and sharp bits of time.

I can lie. It is good; sometimes I believe it myself.

I tell Monika that Grandfather is dead. Blood came out of his mouth because of the cigarettes. She cries. I cry too.

Now I don't let Monika come to play in my flat. If she does she will see Grandfather and how alive he is, coughing snot and smelling up the carpet.

I wish he would die and then Monika cannot believe I am a liar. If he dies I won't cry. I will have his cloth, which is like black cat skin.

Me and Father, we go into town in a taxi. We are going to find Mother, who is queuing for meat, and we have things to give her: presents. They belong to us now but soon they will belong to her. Father will give her cigarettes and me, I have sweet tea in a thermos. It is big on the outside but it only makes one cup.

The taxi driver has a flat hat on backwards. You can feel the engine through your legs. It is a Fiat of course. Outside it is late and everything is the same dark colour as the sky, first fir trees then flats then houses. Only the birch trees are not dark; they are cold, white, thin. It makes me tired and I sleep a bit until Father speaks.

'What will you say to her?'

'Dad's sorry. Will you forgive him?'

It is because she was crying in the night. I heard her crying and his shouting. It doesn't happen so often, not so often. Sometimes she has to stay in bed afterwards. I always say sorry for him.

It is Zwyciestwa Street and there are light bulbs on strings between the houses. One of the light bulbs is dead; I watch it as it goes over. The shops are still open, Kapelusze the clothes shop and the grocery which only sells stockings and canned ham and the queues of people, all women standing in the dark. There are nuns there too, queuing for stockings.

The Fiat taxi stops and we get out and Father doesn't pay; the taxi man owes him. Outside the air is freezing, tasting of firs. I wake up fast. I look around for Mother but it is hard to see, there are so many women here.

'Casimir!'

It is her. We go. She gathers me up and she whispers my other name, *Ariel*, our secret. Her face is hot and red raw. It isn't just the cold. I think of Dad's face, grinning. Soon he will go away again. It is ordinary, his going; both good and bad.

'Dad's sorry.'

'Shh.'

She has two pairs of Miss Marilyn and all the meat she had tokens for. Father takes out the cigarettes. I give her the one cup of tea.

'Will you forgive him?'

'What for?' Father lights the cigarette for her and she smokes it, watching him, smiling at him. 'I've forgotten already.' We pass round the tea. The nuns go off into the dark. All you can see is their white headscarves floating away.

On the register I'm Kazimierz Kazimierski. The middle name stays mine. My favourite class is Military Studies. We do the Nazis. I am the youngest in 1C and the second biggest. Wladislaw is bigger. He is a different Wladislaw. He has eighty-four stitches; they are in his belly. He shows them to his friends. I have not seen them. He is older than me so he will die first.

The girl with red hair is clever in class. Everyone knows it's a stupid thing to do. Whoever shows they are smartest is the one everybody hates, and it is her. Her name is Hanna.

I push her up against the wall of school, which is grey like the wall of home. She hits me in the mouth and I feel her knuckles get wet on my teeth. I am bigger than her so she only does it once. Instead of hitting she talks and her voice is strange.

'Please leave me alone.'

When she says the words they sound wrong. It is because she does not come from here.

'*Leave me alone.*' I copy the way she says it and she starts to cry.

I pull up her dress. Her pants are dirty and baggy, like mine. I hold them by the edge and pull them down.

It's true what Piotr said. She has no cock, just the skin and a hole. It's terrible. I shout and let go because I'm surprised to see it.

When I start shouting, she stops crying; now she is just looking at me. Something has happened and I cannot understand. I go away from her three steps. She's putting her dress down straight, not even looking at me; she isn't scared of me now. I turn back from her and run.

I look for her again. She is sitting on the ground. She has little stones from the asphalt. She is making patterns of black stones on the white sand.

Will I talk to her? Yes, I will.

'Do you forgive me?' She says nothing. I sit down. 'Do you have a Polski Fiat? Because your hair is red. Red is for people with cars.'

Hanna looks up at me very quick, with her eyes and nose screwed up.

'You're stupid, Casimir. Red is for Communists.'

I don't hit her when she calls me stupid. Everybody hates her so I don't bother. I ask her, 'What is Communists?'

She shrugs. 'Communists have cars. Like my father.'

Now she goes back to her stones. She is making words, black on white. I can read it pretty well now. She showed me how to do it. The stones make HANNA.

It is Mother's birthday and so we go to the Restaurant Diamont. There are red curtains, red carpets, red walls, red cloths on the tables. There is a piano but it isn't red. A restaurant man comes with a list of food. He has a red tie clipped on his white collar.

It can only mean two things. Either the Restaurant Diamont is all Communists or the restaurant man has brilliant cars. I ask him when he brings the food but everyone is talking and he doesn't hear me. I get cherry soup with stones in it and then pork. Father asks for steak tartare, but they don't have it, and caviare, but they don't have it either; the man's list is quite wrong.

Mother drinks vodka with bison grass. They have that. Her dress is made in London and the buttons shine. It's so beautiful, it makes her look tired. Father never looks tired.

He puts his food away fast and I do too. When it's all gone, he wipes his mouth three times on a red napkin. 'Heh. Why not play the piano?'

'Michal. No.'

'Go on. Play. Play!' He's smiling. She is too.

Mother goes to the piano. Everyone looks at her but she looks at no one. The waiter opens it for her but she doesn't notice. What is she doing? She just sits there with her hands on her knees and her head down. Then all at the same time she breathes out and looks up and starts to play.

She makes beautiful music. I didn't know she could do that. When she has finished, everyone claps for her. When Mother smiles her lips stop against her teeth. Not like Father. When he smiles you can see his gums and the insides of his mouth and the gold dog teeth.

Once I had lots of lists but now there is only one. It's the list of trees. Some is from the radio programme *Poland: Forest, Lake & Mountain* and some is mine. I keep it all in my head. I say it to myself before sleep.

Larch. Interestingly, in the coldest climes it is the deciduous trees that flourish. Take the larch. Tall and handsome, it conserves water by shedding its leaves, and so it thrives where evergreens cannot.

Larches look dead. They go near death and trick it. It takes patience.

Poplar. They are twisted and black like balcony metal. When you break branches they're the colour of rust.

Firs go up in green heaps. The biggest heap at the bottom. At Christmas we put lights on one while we wait for the first evening star, when we can eat. Last Christmas the Gypsies came with a thing blown up and we jumped on it.

Pines. From the Krakow train they are all one green height, like soldiers. Inside they are like a cage. The cage has no inside or outside. It moves with you.

Birch. Snow goes blue in shadow but birches don't, so birches are whiter than snow. You can peel the skin off like white sunburn. On Piotr's farm there are fat old birches and we peeled one and wrapped up Monika and she looked like an Extra Mocne cigarette.

They are white against the sky. All other trees are dark. Inside birch forests the darkness is broken up with white lines. Ice weighs down the saplings and they make doorways in and out.

At night they are so white and clear, straight and arched and leaning, it must mean something. It looks like writing. If it was English I would never know. I look hard to read the language of trees.

I walk to the forest. The land goes away in lines: a picket fence, a long dirt path, then railway rusted up orange. A woman is on the path, walking balanced with buckets of potatoes.

Now the forest. The soft ground smells sweet as coal. The orange railway goes on, east towards Oswiecim. Sometimes there are pylons like tall grey climbing frames. There is nothing else, nothing made. Only me. The forest is dark and safe and in it I know everything.

'Casimir's got a Yid girl!'

Wladislaw says it. We are in class and waiting for Mrs Nalkowska. He is smiling and his eyes shine, as if he has found out a wonderful joke.

No one laughs, not yet. As for me, I say nothing. I don't look at Hanna for the whole lesson, not at anything, I just sit here with my eyes on the desk. Grey metal, like Russian guns. Hanna keeps looking at me; I see her doing it. I hate her for it. I wish she would look away.

I wait until the lesson is over and we are in the playground. Out here it is just children and for the moment it is better like this. Wladislaw is with all his friends by the back wall and I am alone.

I go up to him. They're eating Nuscaat bars from the Strug Estate shop. I knew that one day I would have to fight Wladislaw anyway. My pockets are heavy because they are full of sand from the pit. His friends all lean around against the wall.

'Why did you say that lie about me?' I meant my voice to be loud, but it comes out soft. It's still clear, though. Wladislaw takes his hands out of his pockets.

'Piss off, Casimir. You've got no friends round here.' His eyes are narrow and blue. It makes him look worried, even though he is bigger than me. It is not so good always having friends, because now he can't run away.

He comes up to me, close. I can smell candy in his mouth. Brandos, warm and sweet like animals breathing. 'Go fuck your Jewish girl.' He smiles around the candy and starts to say something else.

I push the sand up into his face, into his eyes and mouth with the heel of my hand. He groans and bends over. Green drool and sand come out between his teeth but I keep pushing. I am good with my hands, like my father. I hold on to his hair with one hand and his face with the other. Then I throw his head back into the wall. It makes a noise like a hoofbeat on cobbles.

After the fight no one talks to me much. I stay away from Hanna. She plays by herself at the edge of the yard, making words with stones.

Me and Mother and Father, we are listening to the radio. It is the Thirtieth Anniversary of the People's Republic. Even the music is better than this. I look at Mother's hands on the kitchen table. Her fingers are big, red, hard on the sides of them. The nails are dotty with old bits of red paint. I turn the hands in my hands. Back, front, back.

'What are you doing?'

Nothing. There is nothing wrong with them. They are just my mother's hands.

'What's your name, son?'

'Casimir Ariel.'

'Ariel? Ariel what?' This is the Militia man who is talking. He has a big moustache. I am by the Ikarus Street cheese shop, waiting for my mum to come out. Why did I tell him my other name? It just came out. But he is Militia, he must know all my names.

'Kazimierski.' He is looking at me hard and straight.

'Kazimierski. What does your father do, Ariel?'

I shrug. 'Lots of things.' I wish he wouldn't look at me so hard. He smiles.

'What is his job?'

I can't remember. My dad goes to Russia for money. I shrug again; I try and hide down between my shoulders. 'He's my dad. That's all.'

'Where is he from, your father?'

'Casimir?'

The Militia man and me look round. It is my mum.

'Mum!'

It's great to see her. She gives the Militia man a hell of a look. He stands up straight and tries to say something but it comes out soft and jumbled; it is half one thing and half the other. He clicks his heels and bows and goes. I sit close to Mum on the tram home. I would hold her hand if I could, but people are there.

He is my dad. That's all.

It's the night of St Andrew's Day. In my grandad's room there are:

Eight big cans of Russian fish with pictures on.

Two boxes of Russian vodka. There were three until tonight.

The gun of a cosmonaut in a wooden box.

Fish eggs in little jars. Lots of them.

Furs. Smooth black and grey curly. The smell of them is so strong I can't smell Grandfather any more. I don't know how he stands it. The gun is small and ordinary with Russian on it. Dad says it was in case the cosmonaut came down in a jungle. It was a present to Dad from colleagues. It has a red star on it too.

St Andrew's Day. The guest room is full of people. I go round counting cigarettes. Elzbieta and Eva smoke Carmen. Mr Wittlin and Mr Chorzelski smoke Caro. Grandfather smokes Extra Mocne and coughs black spit. My father smokes the fastest and it is Marlboro. Once he offers them round. Everybody takes one except Mother.

'Casimir! Oh, sweet little big child. Come here. Hup.' It is Eva. She is Father's friend, like everyone. She is old and her hair is purple. 'Look what your Auntie Elzbieta is doing, see?'

Elzbieta isn't my aunt. I look anyway. On the table she has my green candle, our door key and the washing-up bowl. The bowl is purple plastic with black bits and full of water. Wax drips from the candle, through the key's hole, into the bowl.

'You see? She's telling her fortune.'

'I know what she's doing.' Eva's breath feels wet against my ear. I don't like her breath or the fortune-telling either. It is better not to know. I try to get down but Eva holds me tight. 'I'm tired.'

'Poor little big boy. Look, look! It's a palace!'

Everyone looks. There is wax on the water and Eva says it looks like a palace, so Elzbieta will get rich. I lean over the bowl to see, but there is no palace; the wax is just wax. Dad comes round with more vodka. His face is red with drinking, burnt with it around the eyes. His eyes are shiny and clear, like the vodka. He shouts and waves to Mother.

'You see what Elzbieta has got? Palaces. Palaces, Anna, wife. Come here and we'll find our future, eh? Maybe we'll find my big deal.'

My mother shakes her head. She is standing in the guest room doorway. The air comes in cold behind her.

'Dear wife, come.'

My mother turns back, out of the doorway. She didn't smile.

Eva shouts after her, 'Anna! What are you afraid of, eh? An unhappy marriage?'

Everyone goes quiet. I get away from Eva and go. Mother is in the kitchen, making beetroot soup and cabbage pasties. The stove flame makes her face blue and calm. She is singing to herself, words I can't understand. Sometimes she does that. When she sees me she smiles but not until.

'Hello, love. Are you having a good time?'

'Yes. Are you?'

She laughs in the stove light. 'Me?' She picks me up. She is thin but strong, my mother. 'Thank you for asking, Casimir. Sometimes I worry about your father, that's all. About what he plans to do for work. Bedtime, yes? I'll ask them to be quieter.'

'And get my candle back.'

'And the candle.'

I try to sleep. The light comes in, long flowers of it through the net curtains. Gold from the streets and grey from the moon.

I know why my mother is afraid. It is not because of my dad. I go to the window and stand. There is a coal train going east. I count the trucks up to thirty-one. Past the train are the railway's blue lights. Then birch forest, the line of its edge like writing. I screw up my eyes to read what it says. My mother will die at sea, but if there is a way to save her I'll find it. Like a good rat, finding the way.

Alice on the Underground

He is woken by the flash of sunlight between houses. The Underground carriage has come out of the dark, on to the surface tracks north of Tottenham. Casimir looks out at the rows of pebbledash houses, disoriented for a moment. Terraces stop dead where the railway runs through them.

At Blackhorse Road he gets off, takes Adams's address from his pocket, then walks towards Coppermill Lane. After a few blocks the buildings begin to separate out. High metal fences run on towards the Walthamstow marshes. The wind comes in over open country, whining in the razor wire. The air smells of water and Casimir feels something shift inside him, a sense of loneliness as he looks at the last houses, their peeling clapboard and isolation.

Number 215 is the last before the road ends. There is a sign on the fence behind Adams's house: DANGER DEEP WATER. RESERVOIR NO. 5. Through the fencing Casimir can see electricity pylons marching off eastwards between colossal stretches of water, railway sidings and dump-hills of sand and gravel. Miles away is the pyramid summit of Canary Wharf tower, already illuminated in the early evening light.

The windows of the house are dark and uncurtained. Casimir walks up towards them between soft white beds of pansy and cyclamen. From the door he can see Adams, hunched forward in a front-room armchair.

He rings the bell and the supervisor turns his head. His face is round and moon-like in the dark room. He raises a hand to Casimir and stands, supporting himself on the arms of the chair. Casimir turns and looks out across the reservoirs while he waits. A flock of birds is settling over the water, silhouetted against the sky.

'I told you not to come.'

'I'm sorry. I need to –' he searches for the English phrase – 'to sort things out. About what is happening, underground. It's important to me.'

'I'm not even talking to the police. Why d'you think I'll see you?'

'I'm sorry.'

'Why? You haven't done anything yet. Come in.' The supervisor goes back into the front room and Casimir follows him through.

'I can do you tea or coffee, if you like.'

He sees that he was wrong; the room is not dark but full of mobile light. It is reflected from the water outside, then again off the polished wooden surfaces of furniture, so that the room is filled with an oddly beautiful lucidity. There is the tick of a carriage clock from the mantelpiece. Photographs of smiling faces. The sweet musty smell of old cigarettes and English food.

He goes to an armchair, sits down. 'I would prefer alcohol.'

'I don't drink.'

Adams is still standing, so that Casimir can't make out his face. Only his voice, the tightening of it. The edge of what might be anger or a lie. But he has seen Adams angry before and his anger is not quiet like this. He waits, head slightly to one side, not looking at the other man or away.

After a moment the supervisor walks towards the mantelpiece. In the half-dark there is the sound of a screw-top on the lip of a bottle, the clink of tumblers and liquid. He turns back without speaking, hands a glass to Casimir. Then he sits down in the second armchair with his back to the window, takes a drink, bares his teeth as he swallows. Casimir can smell the whisky in his own glass, cheap and harsh.

'You have a nice home. Close to the water.'

'Tell me what you want, Casimir.'

'What do you think happened?'

'To the girl?' Adams barks laughter. A nervous, unhappy sound, without humour. 'She fell, that's all. It might be she was pushed or it might not. If it's an accident it's bad, if it wasn't it's worse than bad. I don't think it was an accident. I think there's someone down there who gives me the frights. I

[85]

can't tell you anything you haven't thought for yourself.'

Casimir sits forward in the armchair, the glass held in both hands. He waits patiently for the supervisor to go on. A car goes past outside, high beams wheeling light across the far wall. Adams looks up at the window, eyes narrow. When he talks again his voice is soft, an amazed whisper.

'Thirty-seven years I worked down there. Quite a time.'

'You think she was pushed.' He watches Adams's slight nod. 'Sievwright was talking about another killing. Someone else who was pushed, years ago.'

'Was he now? Sievwright doesn't half talk, eh? It wasn't just one person pushed. Three died. The last one was at my station. Ours, Camden. That was the first time I thought, maybe I don't like it down here any more. Underground. Maybe it's changing down here, I thought. And I was right.' Adams screws up his eyes, presses his fingers gently against the eyelids. 'It was a few years before you came. One day after the general election, so I remember it – 12 June 1987. That's when they caught him. His name was Thomas Gray. They kicked him out of hospital, so he was living down in side-passages. Got away with it for months, staying down there all night, out of the way of the cameras. Not that we watch, half the time, or know half the tunnels there are any more.'

'Where did he hide?'

'I don't know, do I? Maybe he was in the old cross-tunnels, like you thought someone was the other day. There's all kinds of places down there. Snickets and pope-holes, you know that. He probably knew it better than we did. You'll not guess how we caught him. All the men he pushed looked just like him. Only men, spitting images. He just waited in the crowds for someone to come along. Six million people a day. All he had to do was wait.'

Adams's voice has gone soft and rapid. Private, no longer meant for Casimir. 'I caught him, as it happens. I was the one who recognized him. I thought I was stopping something then, I really did, but he wasn't the only one. You see? He was just the first one I noticed. And this one's going to be the last, because I've fucking well had it up to here.'

Casimir hears the chink of ice. As if the older man is

swirling his glass, or as if his hands are shaking.

'I used to love it down there, really I did. It has been my life. I've had precious little enough of it up here. I loved being inside the system, like being in the pipes of a whacking great engine. It scares me now – enough to leave. And I trust myself on that. I dreamed about the Tube the other night, and it was like Joe Stalin's railway, where one bloody worker died for each sleeper. That's how it was in the dream: dead bodies and sleepers. What gets me is the line between it happening and not. What does it take for somebody to push someone? And all I can think is, it could be anything. Anything at all. Who's to say what? In a place the size of London, there's somebody pushing all the time.'

'What about this time?'

'Eh?'

He looks up, distracted. Even in the bad light, Casimir can see how grey the skin of Adams's cheeks and forehead has become. This is not the face of a well man. He wonders if the supervisor's sick-leave is necessary or if it will become so. How Adams will look out for himself, alone in the last house by the water.

'How do you know Saville was pushed?'

'There's the photograph. Anyway, she told me. She said it. She wasn't talking to me by then.'

Casimir drinks. The alcohol settles in his gut, warm and oily. 'You knew her?'

Adams stands up, goes back to the mantelpiece. 'No. I went to see her, in hospital. Just to see how she was doing. They took her up to the Royal Free. She was full of pipes and junk. Past noticing.' There is the chink of glass as he refills his tumbler. 'But she was muttering all the time. This was Wednesday night. I went back the next day and she'd gone quiet. The doctors couldn't keep her going long.'

'What else did she say?'

'She didn't know him – she kept asking who he was. Like the men who Gray pushed, they wouldn't have known him either. Strangers in the night, eh?' Adams sits back down. 'I thought I might get him then. She might have said something then. But she didn't really, and I was getting the frights. I wanted to keep off it, even then. I only went to see how she was doing.'

'It was a man?'

'It was.'

'Will you help me find him?'

'No.' Adams knocks back his drink. Bares his teeth again, hisses against the burn of it.

'Don't you want to find him?'

'I want to be left alone.' He stands up. Puts down his empty glass. 'And I want you to do me a favour. Keep the police away from me. Will you do that?'

Casimir stands. He shakes his head. 'I can't. I want him found.'

'I know.' For a moment they stand in the dark, watching each other. Then Adams moves past, into the hall. 'It's time you were leaving.'

Casimir hears the front door click open. His glass is still half-full. He puts it down and turns to go.

It is the third day of night shifts. There is time to kill before work begins. He walks up Spur Road in the early evening, through Waterloo terminus, down towards the Thames embankment. An elderly busker sits on a fishing stool by the Hungerford footbridge, playing ragtime clarinet into an echoey amplifier. Casimir goes past him up the steps, over the river.

The tide is strong today. He watches it as he crosses, the way the sea currents churn the green river water back against itself, forcing it upstream. He enjoys walking in London, the simple rhythm of movement. The way his thoughts become clear and deep, skimmed of consciousness.

Near the north bank a small man in a grey winter coat stands by the footbridge railing, an oversized spool of kite string in both hands. Casimir follows the cord with his eyes, out and up over Cleopatra's Needle and the white stone of the Inns of Court. The kite is a glittering silver edge in the dusk, almost imperceptible above the Thames mud flats.

'Nice evening for it.'

It takes Casimir a moment to register that he is being spoken to. The kite man is talking to him.

'Nice evening. You work round here?' The man doesn't look away from the sky.

'No. Not so near.'

His own voice is still sleep-rough and he coughs to clear his throat, leaning forward. When he straightens, the kite man has turned to look at him. His eyes are keen and intensely blue. It makes Casimir think of the sky from the aeroplane when he came to Britain, the colour of sky light at high altitude. Beautiful eyes in a wrecked grey face.

'Office?'

'No. Underground.' The man looks at him, expressionless, as if not understanding. 'The Underground. I am a Tube worker.'

The kite man turns away. 'You poor cunt.' His voice has gone quiet. Casimir can still see his eyes as he looks back up, the pupils narrowing to pinpoints. He steps back and walks on.

The footbridge goes on overland, a raised walkway above Embankment station and the left-hand side of Villiers Street. The riverside plane trees are already beginning to lose their leaves, late seed-balls hanging from the bare branches like winter decorations. There is the smell of frying food from the take-away cafés below, sweet and rank and familiar.

He is following the Underground line northwards and as he realizes this he smiles, looks down. There is nothing to see, although he can track the direction of the tunnels with his eyes. The Tube system is like the city's bricked-over tributary rivers, he thinks; the Tyburn and Fleet, other names he has never learned. A network hidden under the surface and visible only sometimes, like the blue of veins where they lie near the skin.

By the entrance to Charing Cross terminus a small market has been set up. The stall-holders stand hunched forward, hands shoved in pockets while they wait for custom. Casimir goes on between the trestles of second-hand books, cheap cut-glass figurines and used telephone cards.

The station concourse is crowded with people, faces upturned as they wait for the departure boards to change. Casimir finds his way through the commuters and out across the Strand. A car blares past on the red light and he moves forward out of its way. His reactions are quick and he is in control of the instinct. Not falling. Not like Rebecca Saville.

The thought of Saville has been with him for days now; since before he knew she was dead, he realizes. Since Adams told him about the accident, the day he saw the Underground girl.

He thinks of the supervisor, his fear. *Keep the police away from me.* He has never spoken to the British police before. He keeps away from authorities, when he can. In Poland he would do the same; even in his own town, Gliwice, with its canals and looming garrison church. It is the way he is with control. He doesn't like to be authorized or unauthorized. Still, he thinks of going to them, to tell them he can help. That he knows the Tube, the ways people think and behave underground. The ones who feel trapped and those who feel hidden.

There is a Chinese pharmacy at the top of Adelaide Street, windows full of ginseng roots and medicine jars. Casimir ducks through an arch next to it, then down into the passage of Brydge's Place. Security lights click on over the back doors of pubs and concert halls. The grime-black walls are high and narrowing towards their end, creating a trick of perspective, the vertical line of yellowing sky seeming far distant. Casimir's jacketed shoulders scrape against the bricks as he steps out on to the busy pavement of St Martin's Lane.

There are taxis double-parked outside the London Coliseum, the traffic hardly moving around them. The road is filled with the smell and light and noise of traffic brought to a standstill. Casimir crosses carefully between two orange-striped *Evening Standard* vans, then goes on down the paved side-streets towards Leicester Square.

He walks almost without looking where he is going, a large man alone, passing easily through the crowds. There is no one thing that makes him look not English, only the combination of details. The colours of his clothes, they way they hang on his prominent bones. The bones themselves, the angular cut of his cheeks and hands that suggests an experience of hunger. The black of his hair and eyes, which is revealed as red-black only in the strongest light.

His face is slackened and set in its natural half-frown. His thoughts are disconnected but also seamless, passing from thought to thoughtlessness and back without intention.

He is thinking of his home. Of his and Piotr's mothers on the canal bridge, selling fruit and herbs. Fennel laid out on newspaper like pale green ox-hearts. Bilberries measured out in a chipped white enamel mug. Then later, in the curtained dark of the kitchen, his father's hands cupping his mother's face, holding up its heart shape. His father's voice, its undercurrent of laughter cold and dangerous. *Better. You look so much better when you're sad.*

He is thinking of the platform photograph. The hand in the crowd, stretching out from the mass of bodies. He cannot tell if it is pushing Rebecca Saville away or reaching to save her.

Then he is thinking of nothing again. He looks up to find he is in Piccadilly Circus. He has walked more than a mile from his lodgings. Electric light twinkles cleanly on the high circle of buildings. He remembers a picture of exactly this scene in his childhood bedroom, something his mother cut out of a magazine. The memory is painfully sharp. Tourists mill around the statue of Eros, posing for photographs. The fountain is blocked with rubbish and water spills over on to the steps, staining the grey stone black.

A neon hoarding flashes up Coca-Cola slogans, the temperature and time. It is past nine o'clock. Casimir turns away. Tomorrow night he has a double shift, three in the afternoon until seven the next morning. Then for fifty-six hours he will be free, on his own time. The entrance to Piccadilly station is yards from where he stands, steps curving out of sight between wrought-iron palings.

He takes a last breath of the stale city air, then goes down to the underground concourse. The ticket barriers at this station are mechanized, filling the hall with the clank of their opening and closure. Entrances lead off like spokes from a wheel, some of them continuing on into underground shopping malls. Casimir takes the escalator down to the Piccadilly Line platforms, an anonymous figure in his everyday clothes, work bag slung over one shoulder.

The train is hot and packed with people. There are no seats

and Casimir stands, head touching the curved carriage roof, held motionless by the crowd. At the next stop he gets out and walks across to the Northern Line platforms. The tiled cross-passage becomes yellowed and uneven as he passes into the Tube's oldest excavations. Across each wall poster someone has stencilled SUBCIRCUS in crimson or bright green. It is senseless to Casimir, just another thing he doesn't understand about the Tube. He wonders how much he has ever understood of the system. What proportion of it he still has to learn.

The northbound train is half-empty. The windows between carriages are open, and the air is warm and damp, as if the weather underground has no relation to that above. Casimir watches the passengers around him. A Rasta girl with silver platform shoes and blue sunglasses, an old Asian man reading a worn Koran, lips moving silently, stations passing behind him. The Rastafarian makes him think of Adams again. *If the station starts turning green and gold, that'll be why*. He realizes he misses the supervisor and is surprised.

The stations give Casimir a sense of motionlessness. Each platform is the same blur of crowds, tiles and hoardings under London's great squares and malls. A woman sits down next to him. Tweed jacket, wire spectacles. She picks a magazine off the carriage's wooden floor, snaps it flat, folds it and begins to read. Casimir can see fragments of headlines like incoherent snatches of conversation: 'BLIP GIRL', 'MAD COW', 'ANY MINUTE I'LL JUST START SINGING'.

When he looks up again, the Camden Town roundels are flashing past the windows opposite. He stands up as the train slows, reaching for a hand-grip. The woman looks up at him. Smiles widely, too wide, light opaque against her spectacles. It blinds him and he looks away.

'Cass! All right?'

'Cass, you're early, ain't you?'

'Casimir, come here. Look at this.'

The control room is crowded with the last of the late-turn crew and the first of the night-shift workers. It takes a moment for Casimir to get through to the counter. Supervisor Leynes,

Sievwright and Weaver are standing under the monitor screens, staring up at them. Casimir ducks through, looks up.

'There. You see her?' Leynes is pointing up at one of the southbound platforms.

Casimir frowns, eyes moving quickly. A train is just pulling away towards the camera, under it. The evening crowd moves slowly along the platform, making its way out towards Camden's bars and restaurants.

He watches the passengers. They are wearing night clothes now, the colours and cuts of fabrics darker and more varied than in the daytime. On the train in, Casimir could smell the make-up and perfumes on women, sometimes on men. Now he can see the shine of jewellery and accessories in the stark light of neon tubing.

The current of the crowd is uniform, moving towards the exit. A few people stand still, waiting for the next train southbound. Now he sees that there is only one figure walking against the current, down towards the side-tunnel passage. The woman stoops down, one hand moving out of sight. It is a moment before Casimir makes sense of the scene. As she moves on the woman's hand comes back up, out of the shoulder bag of the person next to her.

It is an old woman, hair long and frayed, a great grey rope of it down her back. She walks with a sluggish wide-shouldered roll, one hand tugged ahead of her by dog leashes, the dogs themselves out of sight in the crowd. The woman's other hand is stuffed in her coat pocket as she turns back down the platform. Behind her a tall, elderly woman in black reaches into her handbag. Stops walking, looks down at the platform floor.

'I have seen her before. The woman with the dogs.'

'I was just saying that. Didn't I say that? I seen her hanging around weeks ago. Did she talk to you? She's ape, man.'

'Obviously not that ape, Mister Sievwright.' Leynes turns away and snaps the counter back, raising his voice. 'Weaver? Call the Transport Police – no, ring Kentish Town Met, they'll get here faster – then get up to the barriers. Casimir, wait down by the side-tunnel. Apeman will be with me. We'll come on to the platform from the escalators in two minutes, then shepherd her down to you. All right? Let's go.'

Casimir runs out after the others, into the public tunnels. Weaver is already going up the emergency stairs, the echo of his footsteps pounding back. Leynes and Sievwright turn left, running hard. Casimir goes right, stopping at the mouth of the southbound platform.

There is a circular mirror on the corner wall, a convex metal plate placed so as to make the platform visible. Reflected in it, Casimir can see the crowd emptying out, the dog woman left behind. She is not coming towards him. Instead she sits down on a bench near the public telephones, clicking her tongue at the lean grey dogs until they have curled up at her feet. She stretches her legs out straight, sighs with satisfaction. The platform starts to fill up again with new passengers, waiting for a West End late train.

The dog woman goes still, head cocked sideways. Casimir follows her gaze. Leynes is at the main concourse entrance, looking up and down the platform. The woman has seen him long before he notices her. Sievwright appears behind the supervisor, still slowing down from a running pace.

She turns her face away from them. Casimir can see her features creasing up into habitual lines. Bitterness and disappointment, but also something harder, tougher. She keeps her head turned like that while the men in uniform walk quickly down the platform towards her. They are yards away when she yells out in her cracked voice.

'*Kill'm*, girls!' She stands up and begins to run.

Behind her the dogs uncoil with their heads raised, skin peeling back from the teeth as they bark. The sound is savagely loud and rapid in the enclosed space. Casimir hears Sievwright shout out in pain, his voice high-pitched, almost a scream. Other screams, passengers moving away from the scene. The woman looms up fast in the metal mirror, not looking back.

He catches her as she comes around the corner, then he holds on tight. She cries out once and tries to bite him, but her face is against his chest and her hands are trapped between them, pushing to get free.

She begins to kick out at his legs. Taking her time, the blows slow and hard with her weight behind them. He listens to her

[94]

boots thudding off his bones. For a moment he is detached, waiting for the pain to come.

It is bearable. He staggers back at the force of one kick, feeling blood on his legs, hot and then quickly cold. She struggles again, heavy-built but not muscular under the layers of coats and shirts. He tries to keep her still, his face against her hair. She smells of dogs, sweaty and sweet.

She goes loose in his arms, then he feels her begin to cry, the sobs rocking through her. He waits a few seconds longer to be sure, then stands back. Immediately she begins to slump against the passage wall and he catches her, holds her up.

'Ah, you bastards. Why can't you never just leave me alone?'

'It is our job.'

She looks up at him, calm and sad. 'What will you do with my lurching girls?'

He shakes his head, not understanding. Leynes comes round the corner, his eyes jittering from the woman to Casimir, taking everything in. He nods at Casimir as he takes half the woman's weight. His voice when he talks to her is smooth and fast. Part-parent and part-interrogator.

'There we go. Easy. OK? This way, please.'

The woman looks round at Leynes, eyes wide. 'Will you give me back my lurching girls?'

The supervisor grins. A cold expression, bone-hard. 'Your dogs? Lurchers, are they? Well, we'll see about them a little later. Right now we're going to sit you down in the ticket office. See the stairs? Off we go.'

By the time they reach the surface concourse the dog woman is a dead weight between them. They carry her out to the ticket office, but at the door she wails and pulls back. 'No! I'm not sitting in a room. I never sit in rooms.'

'It's all right, love. Mister Casimir here's going to wait with you, and I'm going to get you a chair. All right?'

It is a cold night. The concourse is crowded with people, waiting in the light and the warmth until the station closes. Casimir can feel them watching the woman, their interest and detachment.

The dog woman begins to pull things out of her coat, piling

the objects in her lap. A green canvas wallet and a black leather purse. A Knickerbox plastic bag, small and unrumpled. A full hip bottle of Rebel Yell bourbon. A necklace of garnets, tiny and bright and blood-black.

'Tell me something.'

He looks up. The dog woman is leaning towards him. Hissing, owl-eyed. 'What's behind the doors? All the doors underground. They all go somewhere. There's something on the other side. You know, don't you?'

'The doors?'

She picks up the Knickerbox bag, distracted. Smiles, sweet-faced. 'The last time I wore these, I was invisible for six months.'

Blue light flashes in across the oxblood tiles of the concourse walls. The dog woman stands unsteadily. Two policewomen come in from the western entrance. They nod at Casimir and he steps back.

'Right then. Are you coming with us?'

'Yes, I am.' The dog woman looks back at Casimir, still smiling. 'Goodbye, then, Abyssinia.'

'Goodbye.'

He watches them go, the voices of the police hushed, the crackle of their radios loud as they hustle through the crowd. He feels a sudden sense of regret and guilt, wishing that he had let the woman go.

'You're bleeding.'

He turns round. The Underground girl is standing by the emergency stairs, against the wall. Watching him.

He looks down. The uniform trousers are short on him, and the skin of his ankles is bare and startlingly red. His feet are cold. He realizes his socks are soaked through with blood. But the Underground girl is talking to him again. He stares back up.

'I said I've seen you before. What's your name?'

'Casimir.'

She meets his eyes without blinking. Not aggressive, just considering. 'I saw you on the train.'

'Yes.'

'You're very tall. How tall are you?'

'I don't know. I haven't –'

'Do you work here?' Her eyes stare through him, making their own private calculations.

'At the station, yes. I've worked here for years.'

'I thought you were a ticket man.'

'No.'

'Because you were watching me on the train.'

He stops. Her gaze stops him. It is the way crowds sometimes look at those outside themselves: without expression, with no need to communicate. He thinks of it as almost inhuman and, briefly, he wonders what she wants from him.

She is waiting for him to answer. He moves a hand inexpresssively. 'Yes. I thought you were beautiful. I think I have also seen you here before.'

'Maybe.'

She is wearing the same clothes he saw her in last week, chinos and jacket. They look clean and he wonders where she washes them. There are ink marks on the back of her hands, like the first time. Her hair is loose except for two rat's-tail braids, tucked back behind her ears.

'It makes me think of blood, "Casimir".'

'Why?'

She shrugs. 'It just does. What's your first name?'

He sees that her skin is freckled. Even now, in autumn, when the sun is weak. 'How do you know Casimir isn't my first name?'

She shrugs again. It comes to him that she looks a little like Rebecca Saville. There is a similarity in the leanness of her neck and cheeks. Her skin is paler than Saville's, even her lips lacking redness; a face without colour, except for the freckles and eyes. It makes her look cold.

'My first names are Casimir Ariel.'

'Ariel.' She repeats it carefully, the first vowel long and open. *Ah*, like a sigh. It shocks him, a physical feeling like static; the sound of her voice, saying his name. He sees that there is expression in her eyes, but that it is kept back; the way she smiles without it going beyond her eyes.

He takes one step towards her. She doesn't move.

'Casimir! You there?'

'Yes.' He looks round. Leynes is at the door of the ticket office, silhouetted in the bright light.

[97]

'There's an ambulance coming for Sievwright and a van for the dogs.'

'Is he in pain?'

'He's not in pleasure anyway. He needs shots and stitches. The police are coming back for a statement. You OK talking to them?'

'Of course.'

He expects her to be gone when he turns back, but she is still there, waiting for him. He tries to think of something else to say. Anything that will keep her there. It is hard, knowing so little about her.

'You have writing on your hands.'

She looks down, then back up at him. 'From clubs. Don't you know?'

When he shakes his head, she smiles properly. Eyes narrowing, head cocked fractionally to one side. It brings warmth to her face, he thinks. A car goes past outside, stereo bass echoing through the concourse. The girl looks away towards it and then at the western entrance, where the police came from. He can see her thinking, the alertness of her.

The smile is already gone when she looks back at Casimir. 'Nightclubs, concerts, parties. Sometimes they stamp your hand, it's like a ticket. If I know people, I get in free. It's somewhere to go at nights. To keep warm.'

'What's your name?'

'Alice. Jacqueline. Lin.'

'All of them?'

'Yes. I use them all, and others too. You can choose, if you like. I have trouble with names.'

Trouble with names. He turns the phrase over in his mind. 'Jacqueline is your family name?'

'I don't have a family.'

She doesn't smile. He wants to apologize, or to make her smile again. He feels so slow, and speechless, as if English is a new language again and every sentence an effort.

She squints up at the lights and the station clock. It is almost twelve o'clock, closing time. 'I have to go now.'

'Why now?'

She shrugs. 'Places to go, people to see.' Already she is distracted, buttoning up her jacket. 'You should clean up the blood. Get some antiseptic.'

'I would like to see you again.'

'I know. Here.' She holds something out to him. It is a glass tray, smaller than her palm, cracked and dusty. 'You forgot this.'

He takes it, turns it in his own hands. There is a ridge around the top, where a lid would fit. On the bottom a brand-name is embossed in tiny letters: VICTORY SULPHUR MATCHES.

'I'll see you there.'

'Wait –'

He looks up. Alice is walking down the emergency stairs, out of sight. She doesn't look back. Casimir thinks of the abandoned station, the echo of singing. JACK UNION on the age-cracked walls. He stands quite still, waiting until she is gone.

'Mister Kazimierski, is it?'

'Casimir. I prefer Casimir.'

They are in the back of the ticket office, pressed together on rickety Formica chairs. The policewoman is almost as large as Casimir himself, broad-shouldered and masculine. She sits with a notepad open on her nyloned knees.

'That's not the name on your Polish passport. At least according to London Transport.' He sees that her eyes are grey and quite beautiful. She doesn't seem to blink, although she looks away from him often. Down at her pen, up at the clock. 'Have you anglicized your name recently?'

'This is irrelevant.'

'Fine. Mister Casimir. My name is Detective Inspector Phelps.' She frowns, not offering her hand. 'Is this a bad time to talk? You look busy.'

'No.'

He shifts on the small chair. In his jacket pocket he can feel the glass matchbox, cool against his chest but becoming warmer. He thinks of her eyes, the smile held in. Alice, or Jacqueline. Jack Union. Watching him from some corner of the derelict station, with its preserved glitter of antique equipment and tiny stalactites. He shakes his head, trying to concentrate.

'Yes. I am busy, of course. It isn't a problem. You want to talk about the woman with the dogs.'

She stops writing, puts down her notebook. 'Actually, no. I know what happened tonight. It's a dangerous job, working on the Tube, isn't it? I hear about attacks on staff all the time.'

Casimir nods. 'All the time.'

'What happened last week was more unusual. The accident.'

He looks at her again, gauging her. Waits for her to go on. She smiles. It is a hard, bright expression, without humour.

'I haven't been able to meet the supervisor who was on duty that night, Michael Adams. So until I get hold of him, I was wondering if I might talk to some of the other senior staff here. A bit of a surprise visit, in case you all turn out to be as reluctant as Adams. I've talked to Leynes and Sanusi already tonight. Do you mind?'

'No.'

'Good. Why won't Adams meet me?'

Casimir sits back. Taking a breath, trying to focus his mind. He is caught off guard by the policewoman's sharpness.

'Because he doesn't want to talk about it.' Now it is Phelps who waits until he goes on. 'Adams thought the woman was pushed. Rebecca Saville. He believed it could happen again. He didn't want to be here when it does.'

From outside comes the rattle of the entrance grilles closing. The main concourse lights go out, darkening the ticket windows. The policewoman sits thinking, watching Casimir as she does so, not registering his gaze.

'I see.' She sits up, puts her pen down. 'Were you on duty that night?' He shakes his head. 'How do you know her name? The woman who fell.'

'There were photographs. I saw them.'

'You shouldn't have. What do you think?'

'I think the platform photograph shows she was –'

She interrupts. 'Your general feelings. I've seen the photographs.'

He makes himself think before he speaks. 'The Underground attracts strange people. Even ordinary people are different. Less social, more isolated. It only takes one person to push her. It happened before, about ten years ago.'

'Yes, I know.' Phelps is writing again, the chrome pen delicate in her large hand.

'I don't want it to happen again. I could help. I could look at the security videos you have from that day.'

'Could you?' The policewoman stops and looks at him again, thin eyebrows pulled together in a slight frown. 'You know a lot about this, don't you? Why is that?'

He sits forward, searching for words. 'I don't think it was an accident. I feel the same as Adams.' I can feel it in the Underground, he wants to say. In the tension of crowds and empty platforms. He doesn't say this. 'I think a woman has been killed.'

Phelps is still frowning. 'I'm afraid that's my job.'

'I know the Underground. You don't. Let me help.'

'No.' Phelps sits back. Now the eyebrows are raised, in surprise or regret. 'I'm sorry. The videos are police property now. Was there anything else?'

He feels anger building up in him and he pauses, requiring himself to be calm. 'Yes. There are signs that people have been in the station at night. Maybe the homeless –'

'Yes, Mister Leynes told me. Fine. Call me if you think of anything else.' Phelps stands, puts out her hand. 'Thank you for your help. Will you show me out?'

After she is gone he locks the grille behind her then stops still in the empty hall, listening. The sounds of his station are different at night. During the day there is the repetition of footsteps, layer on layer of echoes, a kind of human white noise. Hundreds of millions of people a year; a city under the city. He remembers his first night shift. Hearing the station by itself, the hollowness of it. There are less than a hundred people in the complex now. The tunnels magnify every noise, like a cave or a shell. Some nights, Casimir can hear the trapped air sigh against his ears: *Aaah*. Like the trains. Like his name.

There is work to be done. He digs in his pockets for keys as he crosses to the far side of the concourse. There is a single metal door at the top of a short flight of steps. He opens it and steps through into the storerooms. Feels along the wall, clicks on a switch. Dusty fluorescent light gutters over stacks of boxes. Yellow paint peels off the walls in yard-long skeins. At the far side of the room steps lead down to other levels of storerooms, and from there to stairwells, locked rooms and offices. Further, blacked-out platforms and lines. Down to deep shelters and abandoned stations. Dozens of them, under the capital. He thinks of their names, beautiful and redundant. Down Street and Waterloo Necropolis. Snow Hill and British Museum. South Kentish Town.

Outside a police car goes by and Casimir stops, listening to the howl of its siren. He closes the door, cutting off the sound. Locks it behind him.

He lies still in the rented room. Waiting for morning to come, when he can let himself sleep properly before the next long night shift. There is nothing to see except the bare bulb's light on the damp-stained ceiling. The sky outside, square and black against the window.

He is too long for the bed, so that even lying diagonally his head is tilted back on the pillow. He takes it out and lays it on the floor. Lies back flat on the sheets. Their fabric is worn soft as down.

There is pain in the muscles of his legs, where the skin has been broken. Sleep comes at him in soft waves, natural as the ache of physical exhaustion in his limbs. Usually even the action of thinking helps him sleep, but not tonight. The day runs through his mind, uneasy and uncalled for. He thinks of Adams and the falling woman. The disused station and the Underground girl. Alice. Already he wants to see her again, just to hear her voice. He listens to the sounds in the small room. There is the sigh of his own breathing, harsh against his teeth. The tick of the electricity meter in its black box. The echoed clank of goods trains from the terminus.

The electricity meter runs out. He has no more money to feed it. The dark is solid, set like amber. When he looks at the window, the sky outside has altered by comparison. Now he can see the reflected illumination of the city; a fantastic orange glow, as if the whole of London is on fire. After a while, he can make out the faintest hint of first light.

The disused station. He recollects the echo of music and the graffiti, JACK UNION. A strange name, he thinks. Political, the

British flag reversed. Rhythmical, like something from a children's story. Tomorrow he will go and ask Alice why she chose it. Tomorrow he can go to her, at the abandoned station. *I'll see you there.* The Underground girl with freckled skin and the eyes that shock him out of himself.

Sleep nags at him. He thinks of amber. His mother's voice. Clear, as if he is dreaming it. *The green ones are the rarest, see? Green, from the pine.*

She is laying out objects on a checked tablecloth. He is very small and the objects look like congealed honey, clear and dark and opaque. His mouth fills with saliva.

Baltic ambers. He remembers them with the vividness of early childhood. The way his mother laid them out, like a story. Always the smallest droplet first. It was yellow with ancient pollen, the rich colour of calving cream. Then others, a small red amber from Persia. The one which was flat, like his tongue. The yellow pebble he once found which wasn't amber at all, just a stone he gave his mother, valued only for that. Last of all the largest, green like canal water the day he fell through the ice. Bigger than his father's fist, bigger than a duck egg. Charred and cracked along one side. It was full of trapped things: round stress-cracks like little coins, prehistoric seeds, an insect crushed in on itself by the resin's dead weight.

There were more before the war. My father had to sell them.

What for?

For me. I was so hungry. For potatoes.

And he remembers not understanding, only turning the ambers against his fingers, the refined smoothness of them. His mother's hands are larger than his, and red from work. She is the woman who chooses to forget her past. And Casimir is the one who remembers for her, even when the remembering hunts him down. Catches him in the dark, presses over him like the weight of London clay.

He is a child again and it is five years before she leaves him. She smiles and holds the last amber for him, up to the light. A window of sky wobbles through it. It is summer, early morning, and quite warm.

He wakes. Outside there are pigeons roosting around the vents and guttering. The sound of their crooning is vivid as memories. Of his mother sobbing softly in a nearby room. Of lovemaking, and the faces of women. The shock of Alice's eyes meeting his. Waking dreams muddled together.

The room is full of grey dawn light. For a moment he thinks he is back in Poland, that there is snow on the way. Then he realizes he is thinking in English and he remembers everything.

Squirrel Cage

'Now?'

'Wait.'

'*Cholera*, this is a bad idea. Now?'

'No. I'll tell you when.'

It's the end of spring. The sky is all blue except for five puffs of factory smoke, orange like clouds at sunset. St Barbary and the Garrison Church and the Cathedral are all ringing for Pentecost, and in the streets are stalls with Pentecost irises. In Old Square is Mr Susicka's stall with its long green tables and tall white pots and the pavement dark where Susicka has washed it down. He's got tattery bunches of yellow broom and willow buds, but most of the stall is irises. A high deep blue wall of flowers.

We have no money to buy Pentecost irises. Until Dad comes back we have no money. Mother said so, on the telephone to the telephone man. I heard it. She said other things too, about money. It was just after Piotr's birthday. He is nine now. I'm still eight, but I've got more muscles. On the classroom door my mark is the highest.

'We could get flax. That's blue too. There's still a field of them over near the state pig farm. Casimir? Casimir?'

Piotr reaches out for my arm. It still hurts from when Dad went away. He held me so hard the skin has gone blue and yellow. Like irises. He has got a big deal now. It makes him smile more. I shake Piotr off.

'It's Pentecost. You can't use flax. It has to be irises.'

'Why bother? Only old people have the irises now. Broom is much prettier. I know where there's wild broom –'

'Shh!' Two old women are at Susicka's stall. He wraps their flowers slowly because of his stumpy hand, with the bouquets on his knee. He did the hand in the Memory of Jozef Stalin steel factory and now he sells flowers. He can drive too, even going fast.

Now the old women are going off down Zwyciestwa Street with their arms full of irises. There are only the three of us in the square. It's quiet except for the churches.

'Now!'

I push Piotr out. He goes because he's my friend. I'd do the same for him. The colonnades are flat arches of sun between shadow. I run through them as Piotr walks across the open.

'Hello, Mister Susicka.'

'Hello. It's cold weather, isn't it?'

Susicka always says that. It's not cold. His big soft face is always smiling except when he drinks; then he never smiles. I come round into the southern colonnade. The stall is up against the far end. There are collared doves in the square, they sing *coal, coal*. I run in the shadows so they won't fly away.

'Yes, sir. Can I have some irises? Just three of them.'

'Just three? You know, it's only sixty for a bouquet. Don't you have sixty? Three's no use.'

I come in close and low. Susicka is wrapping the three irises, holding them lengthways on his knee. I'm so close I can smell him, like two-days-old milk. I crawl between the green tables. Susicka's shoes are home-made and rimmed black where water has stained them. His socks are worn thin between their ribs. I can see the skin of his fat ankles. It is blue-grey, like the insides of raw fish.

'All done! I put in one extra for you. Three's no use.'

'Thanks. Could I have them unwrapped?'

'Unwrapped?' He laughs from his belly. 'Unwrapped flowers are for lovers. Have you got a lover already?'

'No. I do. Yes, sir.'

He goes on laughing and unwrapping. A soft, slow man. I come up behind him, diving upwards from the push of my arms, lifting the irises out of two white pots. They squeak together, wet in my arms and smelling of onions.

'All done!'

All done. I jump back between the tables, light and strong, down through the sun and shadow. The excitement fizzes in me like bottled Fanta, bubbling up sweet. I try to laugh but the flowers keep hitting me in the face. The air is full of sweetness and church bells. I run until I have to stop and then I stop.

Piotr comes belting up. He's laughing too now, his red face happy under the grey-brown hair. He still has the four unwrapped irises. We go on towards the Strug flats, up to my place. The stairwell lights have gone and we hold the irises up ahead, the yellows of them like candles. It seems like they make the dark lighter. Piotr says they can't but it seems they do.

For Pentecost you cover the floor with irises. We do it in the kitchen and Mother's room. There are plenty of flowers and two left for Mother's bed and Dad's. It takes ages; our hands go yellow with iris dust. When we're done, the sunlight is still coming in the windows. It falls on the flowers and takes their colour, like light off water. The stove and refrigerator and white kitchen cupboards take their colour. The rooms have all gone blue and golden.

We go and wait in my room. We play with my AH-18 Combat Helicopter. Piotr is the secret police and I'm the speculator with Russian vodka and American cigarettes.

'Casimir?' It's Mum. We jump up, remembering. What do we do now? She goes into the kitchen and cries out, so we run into the kitchen.

'We got them! Do you like them? It was me and Piotr together.' Mother is smiling with both hands to her mouth. It makes her look young. Then the smile begins to go.

'Where did you get them? Casimir?'

I shrug. 'We got them. For Pentecost.' I'm still smiling. I can't make it go. It starts to hurt. 'For you. We both got them.' Her eyes are hurt. It's the same look as when Dad has hurt her. The shame begins. It's a shaking in my belly and legs, then my chest. 'For you. For Pentecost.'

I turn and run. I go into the trees and don't come out until Piotr stops calling and goes home.

I open the door and the house smells of flowers, but the irises have gone. The rooms are back to their ordinary colours. Even the golden dust is dusted away. We have chopped-ham salad and beetroot soup and cabbage pasties for supper. We don't talk because the radio is on.

She said other things, my mother. Not to the telephone man but to herself. She has no friends, my mother, no one to talk to. It was night and she was drinking, alone in the kitchen. I heard her rattling the glass and cursing, I heard her say blood. She was arguing about blood money. She wouldn't have it in her home. It sounded like she was arguing and that scared me, because it was just her there, and me listening. It was my father she was talking about. His mother, who was killed by the Russians. And blood money.

I got them without any money. And I liked the rooms being blue and gold; I never saw rooms like that before. It made me feel empty and good inside. But blue is the colour of shame.

'Ariel? Have you done your Human Philosophy?'

'Don't call me that.'

'I knew you didn't. How do you like my hair?'

'It's OK.'

'It's only hair anyway. What's wrong with it?'

'It's OK. I said it was. It's fine.'

'I don't care. It's not important. Yours is much more manageable. I can help you with your homework, you know.'

We walk home. I like it better when she doesn't talk. Once she taught me to write and I wrote my middle name and now she uses it all the time. She knows what my name means and she won't tell me. She could be lying though. She makes me nervous.

'My parents have new jobs in Warsaw. Party jobs.'

'I heard.'

'We'll move soon. In Warsaw no one knows anyone. What do you want to do when you grow up?'

It's a stupid question. I wish I hadn't told her my middle name. I try and look at her without her seeing. So I can remember her. From the side she looks proud. From the front she just looks skinny.

'Grow a beard.'

She stops. Crows cough and clatter by the foot of B Block. She throws a stone. 'Don't be stupid. I know you're not.'

'What about you? What do you want?'

A car horn. It is her father, waiting for her. The sun is ahead of us. A little boy on a tricycle comes out of the light. His shoulders rock and the wheels creak, creak.

Hanna stops. Red hair and blue eyes. No one has hair like hers. It is the colour of squirrel fur. Beautiful. 'I've got to go.'

'I want to be like snow.'

'Why?'

'The more you press it, the harder it becomes. In the end it's ice.'

I give her her geography books. She takes them without saying thanks. She looks at me again with her thin eyes.

'I want to go somewhere where no one knows I am Jewish. Then I can just be me. Don't get like ice, Ariel.'

She turns away without saying goodbye. In three days I will never see her again. I shout goodbye after her but the car's already going.

'I told you. Look at it. It goes mad.'

In my mouth the spit tastes sweet and rich as blood. I hawk into the silo dust. I hurt from running hard.

He is right; Piotr is usually right. He takes off his gloves, which are dark where the squirrel bit him, and he sits down between Monika and me. It is spring and cold in the silo. The blood hardens fast.

The squirrel goes round and round without falling; there is no up and down in its head. Its red fingers flutter in the chicken wire and Maria tries to stroke them, but she is only four and slow with it.

'Leave it alone.'

'I want to stroke it.'

'No –' Monika pulls her sister away. 'Stupid *Ohyn*.'

Maria starts to cry. Not making any noise, just crying down her cheeks. The squirrel chatters and the cage shakes; it is just sheet chicken-wire pulled up into a ball, messy at the top where I bunched it together. Maria stops crying to watch. Now the squirrel jumps hard to one side. The cage tips over and begins to roll. It goes towards Monika and she screams and kicks at it.

'No, oh no! Get it away from me!'

No one wants to touch the cage because we know the squirrel will bite. It has gone mad, as Piotr said it would. We would bite, if it was us.

Her hands are quite red from work, and the ambers red in them or gold or black, like lumps of tar on the new town roads.

I watch her face. She holds an amber up to the light. The blacks of her eyes go small; they are smaller than a millimetre. She smiles and frowns at the same time.

'Where's that one from?' It's the red amber, from Persia. It's too big for millimetres, it is in centimetres. The light moves slowly inside it.

'You know where.'

'Tell me,' I whine at her. We're at home, no one can hear.

She picks it up, turns it in her hands.

'This is from Persia. Your grandfather bought it from the Gypsies. They came to Kielce every spring and harvest. Their king was richer than almost anyone then, but we were not so poor either. Do you know what your grandfather did, Ariel?'

'He bought amber from Persia.'

She laughs. 'Do you know what his work was?'

'A miller.'

'I never saw him with flour on his skin, not once outside the mill. He was a clean man. He liked everything in its place. You have that from him. And the size of you, and your name. I know it's not much.'

She puts the Persian amber down and I take it. It is smoother than my skin. Smoother than my mother's skin.

'Was he rich?'

'I wouldn't say so. We weren't allowed to own the mill, so he rented it. It belonged to a German called Wagner. He was the only German in town and quite friendly. We weren't rich. Comfortable. My father rented the mill for forty years –'

I look up. She is frowning down at the ambers. 'There were more before the war. He had to sell them.'

'What for?' I keep my voice quiet, like hers. Like church.

'For me. I was so hungry then. For potatoes.'

I look down at the amber and think of potatoes. All the beautiful colours of honey and green water, changed into grey. 'Lots of potatoes.' It is half question and half not. She shakes her head. Her eyes don't move to me.

'No, no. One for each amber. One potato, one egg. The taste of one egg!' Her eyes close. 'Pushing his hands through the wire, my father. Everybody's hands and all their jewellery, the gold worth less than potatoes. And the people outside, who were our old neighbours. Wagner and the rest, taking all they could. I still remember everything. If I am not careful, I remember it all. It is so much better, to just forget –'

She shakes her head. It means she won't talk any more. Already it is more than ever. I don't understand, but I remember for later.

'Why wasn't it his mill, if he was the miller?'

She takes the amber out of my hands. 'It doesn't matter why. It's time for your homework. What do you have?'

'Human Philosophy.'

We go to do the Human Philosophy. It's boring for me and boring for her. Then Dad is home, smiling, with two big handfuls of broken biscuits and poppy-seed cake, and we kiss and laugh with him. First things first.

It was Piotr's idea but I caught it. The Wittlin farm is three fields, three pigs, the duck Archangel and the chickens for eggs and carp in the pond for Christmas, fat as pigs. The barns and the silo, white paint and red rust.

We were in the woods by the top field, where the pines are old and fat at the roots like spring onions. The red squirrel sat quite still. Not looking at us but away to one side, as if it was listening to music.

'Catch it!' hissed Maria.

I leaned forward into my run and pushed hard with my thighs and feet, arms and shoulders, curling my feet into the pine earth. Then I was on to it and it came alive, biting at the sleeves of my winter coat. Piotr said take it to the silo and we did.

In the cage the squirrel stops upside-down, holding the bars. It is a beautiful thing, but it scares us too. A rich little man in a red fur. A speculator, loan shark, Party member. It has hands, face, heart and eyes, just like me.

'What do we do now?' says Monika, and I say, 'We can do anything we want. We are alone.'

'Hey, is that your dad's car?'
   'Yes.'
   'That's brilliant, that is. A Polonez. When did he get it?'
   'Casimir! Is that your car?'
   'Yes, it is. He got it yesterday from Katowice.'
   'Hey, mister! Can we touch it?'
   'Mister Kazimierski, sir? How much was it?'
   'No. Four hundred. Oy! Hands off, you.'
The price comes out with Dad's smoke. He has an American cigarette, a Marlboro. The smoke is like a speech balloon in a cartoon, silvery-white.

   'Four hundred thousand zloty? Bloody hell. Did you hear, Boleslaw? Four hundred.'
   'Thousand? Bloody hell. What colour is it, sir?'
   'You ponce, are you blind? It's blue.'
   'Hey – watch your language. And it's not blue. It's navy.'
They all crowd round outside the school gates, kids and teachers too at the back, Mr Kruczkowski, the Human Philosophy master, and Mr Grudzinski, who does Arithmetic and PE. Dad doesn't smile, but I know he wants to. It's good that he doesn't. Being too happy is like being the smartest in class. It's better to keep quiet about it.

Ours is the biggest car on the street. It's got a boot and four doors. This morning it took eleven tries to start; it would have been quicker to walk to school but we drove anyway. I'm the second one in school to have a Polonez but it is the first to be navy.

We go on a car trip to see my Uncle Jan. He is a guard at the Russian border. Mother says he met me when I was baptized.

   'Be polite to him, love. He can get very angry, your uncle. It is just his temper. Are you ready?'

'Yes.'

'Let's go then!'

She is as excited as me. The car starts first time. It's a March Saturday, and the sunshine comes down between the houses and at street corners, through trees and leant long down hill-sides.

We have Marlboro for my uncle. Dad brings an emergency oil can so if we run out of benzene, we can stop at garages and fill the can for free. He does it even when we already have a full tank. Mum says it's dishonest. Dad says it's the law and he didn't make it. Their voices get louder, softer. Wind comes hush-ing in the window. Mum sings, not out loud, just humming.

For a time I sleep in the back seat, where the plastic is warm in the sun. Then I wake up and look out of the window. The coalfields have gone and instead of them I see fields of flax, twisted walnut trees, apple orchards in long bony rows with their whitewashed trunks.

'When do we get there?'

'Soon. Go to sleep, love.'

I'm not tired now. I sit up. 'What is it called, the place he lives?'

Mum turns round in her seat. I wait for her to tell me. She turns back again. She talks without looking at me. 'Where are your gloves?'

'Here.' I hold them up drooping from my coat. They are on elastic through the arms. She isn't looking anyway.

'Just sit still. We'll be there soon.'

It sounds like what she said makes no sense, but it does. It means she forgot where we were going too. It happens more and more often, her forgetting. Dad makes a joke of it. He says one day she'll go shopping and forget where she lives. It's not much of a joke.

One time, I was waiting for her in Pieronek's shoe shop and she left without me. I was in the back with the mirrors with pictures of French women, measuring my feet on the foot-measuring stool. When Mr Pieronek saw I was still there he called my flat but no one was home. Then he locked up the shop and took me back on the tram. My mum went back to the shop later and there was a note, so it worked out fine.

When Mum forgets, it's different from the way I do. It's something to be scared of, you can feel it. I don't ask Mum about it because if I do, she'll tell me and then it will be true. My mother's eyes are blue and the brows are thick and the nose is small and hooked. I think she is probably beautiful but I don't know. She is just my mother.

Mother and Father. I look at their heads in the front seats. Their hair is the same colour, black and bright. They grew up together in Kielce. Kielce is at the heart of Poland. Where did I learn this? In school I learn that Silesian anthracite is the richest coal source in the world. My parents' hair is the colour of anthracite. My hair is a different kind of black, more like road-tar. From behind, my parents look like the same person.

Uncle Jan is different. The veins in his face are the road-map across Poland, from Gliwice in the west to Terespol in the east. His hair is white like a grandfather, although he is not even a father, not even married. He is my father's brother and in the Militia Border Guards. His uniform is green and itchy and he has to carry a satchel with a book of the names of all travellers.

He won't show me his gun and he shakes my hand without smiling. He smells hot and sour, like zúr soup. Not like my dad, who smells of his imported aftershaves, sometimes like firs and sometimes salt.

'Casimir? You're getting big. God knows you don't get it from my family. When are you going to start helping Michal with his work, eh? It's a long haul he does now, to Astrakhan. Hard work. Do you know where that is, eh? Astrakhan?'

'No, sir. In Russia.' I stay polite with him, for now.

'In Russia. Go off and play.'

The smell of him is ugly and dangerous. Now he brings out winiak brandy in a brown bottle and I go away while the two of them drink. Mother is standing at the window but she doesn't see me go past. Outside it is not cold at all; I could do without the gloves.

Terespol is two towns with the border through it. In Russia it's called Brest and it looks bigger. It's not dark yet but there are no kids around, only border guards. I play by myself, as far as I can go. There are oak trees here with rook nests in them, big balls of twigs like mistletoe.

I come to a pair of wide-open doors. I look inside and there is flour everywhere, on the machines and shelves. It is a flour mill, like my mother's father's. His mill, which was not his mill. I get some of the flour and put it in my mouth but it doesn't taste of much. I clap my hands to get rid of it.

Outside I can see the railways, lines going away silvery, crossing and separating. There are queues of cars at the border. One lot waiting to go into Russia, one lot queuing to come out. Some of them will wait for days to go through, but when Dad goes he doesn't have to wait long. Uncle Jan gets him through. They work together on the speculations.

I see glasshouses long as trains with giant doors. Sunlight in Russia but not here yet, it moves across the flat fields towards me. On the far side of the glasshouses is where Russia begins. It looks ordinary. There are chimneys steaming in the light. Houses with roofs built heavy for snow. The land white with snow and black with thaw.

'America is the land of milk and honey, but Russia is the land of champagne and caviare.' Dad says that. He tried to give me golden caviare one time. It smelt like cod liver. He sold it to the Finns for dollars. They're welcome to it. I like tinned sardines better.

It starts to rain. I stand by the flour mill, watching the rain in Poland and the rain in Russia. The asphalt smells of sourdough. It makes me hungry. I go back to Uncle Jan's house to see what I can find.

The woods are my special place. I never get lost or forget my way, like my mother.

It makes me angry that she forgets. I know she does it on purpose, because she told me. Forgetting is what she does with secrets. That's what she told me. I think about her at night, under the ceiling cracks. There are new cracks, one like East Germany, one like Great Britain.

The woods start after the allotments with their woodsheds and fruit trees. The allotments start after the factories with their red-topped chimneys. Sometimes there is woodsmoke through the trees and sun through the smoke and what happens is, the trees and the shadows of trees are both bars of dark cutting through the light, you can't tell which is which. I like it.

Today there is food in the kitchen, dried peas soaking in water for the soup and potato pancakes with cheese and eggs from our friends the Wittlins. I am alone. I take one pancake wrapped in newspaper. I take an egg too. I leave a note, so it isn't stealing.

I go westwards into the woods, away from the big towns of Katowice. First I pass the Wittlin farm, round the bottom field. Then I come to a rubbish dump, its bitter smoke catching in the trees. There are fewer firs here in the deep wood; the trees are naked inside and thick at the tops, stands of pine and larch and birch. The bare pine earth rolls up and down where the Germans hid tanks in the war. I see squirrels and I find boar shit. In the deep woods there are bison, they are red and they eat bison grass. Grandad told me that before he died. I don't know if it's true, because sometimes he lied.

Now I go south, then west, then north-west. Walking a circle is more interesting than a there-and-back. It's past noon now and raining. I'm looking for somewhere dry to eat and just when I turn, the ground falls through.

There is no time to scream. The darkness comes down around me and I hit the ground blind and go over on one side. My legs hurt and I cry out, not moving. There is cold black water coming through my coat. The underground place smells sweet and oily. It's the smell of coal, the smell of my town.

I open my eyes. There is light from the hole; it isn't so far up. I sit up and look at my hands and they are black, steeped in coal dust.

I stand up, the water echoing off me in slow drips. I breathe softly, listening. The shaft sounds big. First I look up and there are big tree-roots round the sky. I can climb out; it doesn't look so hard. Then I look around.

In school Mrs Nalkowska told us about the old mines. Some of them are a hundred years old, or hundreds. They were the most dangerous things, more than gun shelters or strangers. But here I am. It's too late to stay away.

The coal shaft goes away westwards and downwards. When

I was small, my friend Karol's brother went into an old mine and found a German shell and died. Still, now I know where I am my legs don't hurt so much. I climb out to make sure I can. I get a birch stick and then I climb in again.

My feet slap against the mine bottom. I tap ahead with the white stick, like the blind. The shaft smells of coal and earth and the trees above my head. I have a good look round for bullets but there's nothing. The shaft is getting bigger and I stop, listening to it.

I look down. There is no reflection off the black water. I tap ahead with the white stick and the ground has gone. The darkness is flat black, without sound. I can't tell how far ahead it goes or how far down. Up above, a blackbird goes singing away in fear.

My breathing starts to go fast and I wait, making it slow again. Then I take a step back, more steps. When I'm sure of the ground, I kneel down, feeling for a piece of loose coal or stone. When I find one I throw it forwards, into the down-shaft.

The darkness makes no sound.

I go back to the mine entrance. My eyes are used to the underground now; I can see the walls, shining rough blue-black. I get another loose stone and scratch my name zigzag across the walls, KAZIMIERZ. Now it is mine, a secret place in the deep woods.

I climb back out. The rain has stopped. I eat my pancake and my egg. It all tastes good but it makes me thirsty. I go back home the way I came.

Her hair is tied back in tight red lines, like the copper wire in machines. Her shoulders are goat-thin even though she is tall for a girl. Her hips too. Her father and mother both work in the Office for the Control of Press, Publications and Public Spectacles. Dad says they are high up. He calls them leftover Yids. I also heard Mrs Nalkowska talk about them in the vodka and meat shop. She said it's not their fault the Jews killed Jesus, after all. They had a Fiat before anyone in school but Hanna didn't tell us.

It's not the colour of copper exactly. Sometimes there are goods trains which take old iron cable from the factories. Twisted and tough and rusted. This is the colour of Hanna's hair.

When I was small we were friends and sometimes we still are. When we are not I still dream of Hanna. In the dreams I made love to her. We are underground in the deep woods and naked and I lie flat on top of her in the cold black water. Lips on lips, belly on belly, legs on legs, down to the simple feet.

After three days the squirrel stops moving and watches us. Waiting with its head on one side, the way it did in the forest to begin with.

We take it to the abandoned mine and throw it in. This time you can hear the bottom. The cage clatters once. Then there is silence again and then it splashes. The Black Trout Shaft is called that because sometimes fish swim into the flooded chambers and the miners catch them and eat them. The cooked flesh is black and sweet. Maybe the trout will eat the squirrel, down underground. Maybe the cage came open when it clattered and the squirrel got out in time.

When I was small I thought there was nothing else in the dark except myself, so I knew everything and I loved it. Now there are questions and dangers. The squirrel drowned white in its cage. I don't know the darkness any more. It's my own fault. Piotr takes his father's torch, so we can see where we're going.

In Hanna's house there are white patches where the stove and pictures were. They are the only Jews I know in town, the only ones I have talked to. Hanna says there are more in Warsaw, but not so many. Not since the war.

There was a hole in the door where they kept Jewish things, and candles like trees on the mantelpiece. Her guest room was always dark and smelling of oil and turpentine, but now it's plain, the net curtains blowing outwards, white and ordinary. Her mother sits in the car with their cat in her arms and the bread bin on one side of her and a green glass lamp on the other. I wave at her as we go past and she waves back.

'Where are we going?'

'The woods.'

'How far?'

'They'll wait for you.'

She follows me. A #5 tram goes past us into town and the wire fittings ring together like sleigh bells, long after the carriage has gone.

We pass the last tram lines, then the last houses. There are yellow cranes dropping four-fingered hands, lifting trees. Thin chimneys and fat chimneys. The thin chimneys are red brick with red and white stripes at the top to stop aeroplanes going into them. The fat chimneys have no stripes. If the aeroplanes can't see the fat chimneys coming they must be blind.

Factories, allotments, woods. Hanna walks ahead, then beside me. There have been deer here; you can see where they scratch their backs on the pine trees.

Our hands are close; the knuckles knock together and the fingers catch. No one can see us here, where the light stops in the wings of firs. We can do whatever we want.

It's a long way to the mine but she doesn't talk. When we get there I help her down, then along in the dark.

She laughs. In the dark it is a wild sound. 'What a place. Did you find it yourself? I want to see it. Do you have a light?'

'Yes.'

Now we're at the mouth of the down-shaft. I got matches from the kitchen and tore rough paper from the box. She looks around in their flare. The shaft is round at the end, like the inside of the rabbit's skull in the glass cabinets in room c2 at school. The down-shaft drops away in front of us. Its darkness begins again, ten or fifteen metres down. Hanna doesn't make a sound. She puts out a hand towards the drop, palm out. Steps back into me.

The match goes out. I find her face with my hands, then her mouth with my mouth. I feel her fingers link at the back of my head, where the bone is thinner. Her lips are soft against her hard teeth and I can taste her breath.

'Light another match. I want to see.'

I strike two at the same time. There are two more matches

[119]

left. Hanna looks around for a stone to throw. I go back for some birch twigs because they'll show up in the dark.

We throw in the pebbles and twigs. Sometimes the pebbles click. The twigs make no sound at all. Hanna comes up close to me again. She puts something into my hand.

'I got you this, look. Light another.'

In the match-light I see it's a little amber, still warm from her jeans pocket. The thin yellow of honey strung down from a spoon. The edges are not smooth, but carved. There is a face in it. Grinning, full of teeth.

'I got it in Warsaw, when we went to see my new house. It's a lion, you see? For your name, Ariel. It means "Lion" in Hebrew. Do you like it? Who chose it for you, your name? Was it your mother?'

I have time to look at her before the match goes out. Then there is a sound from outside, a pheasant. It chatters like machine-guns. Then it stops.

'When you asked me what I wanted to be when I grew up and I asked you, you said you wanted to go somewhere where no one knew you were Jewish.'

'Yes.'

'Then why tell me this?'

'I don't –'

'Now someone knows. I know.'

'I thought you knew already. Didn't your mother –' She's feeling for my hand, but I step away from her. The down-shaft is close, somewhere beside me. I make myself stop.

'Ariel?'

The amber is still warm from her. Her body must be warmer than mine. I throw the carving out over the down-shaft. It clicks once, twice. Now it's gone where no one will know.

'Ariel?'

Unless the trout eat it. Then the miners will catch the trout. When they cut it open the lion will be there, its yellowed teeth on the cooked black flesh.

'Ariel!'

'Don't call me that.'

'Light the last one.'

'Why?'

'I want to see. Because I want to see your face. Please?'

I do it. Her own face is thin and white. She runs up too fast and I reach out to stop her falling. I hold her for a minute or two. It's true; her body is warmer than mine. It must be that her heart is stronger. Then I let her go.

'Let's go back.'

We get out. Her hands and face are smudged but I brought newspaper to wipe them clean and she does that. We don't say anything now. Underground in the secret place we could say anything, but not here.

She walks ahead of me. Fast, so I have to keep up. We come into sight of the town, yellowed coal smoke rising from all the house chimneys. At the beginning of the tram lines she begins to run. I call her name three times but she doesn't turn round. I called for her three times.

Undertakings

'What's up, sir?' Weaver shouts to be heard over the roar of machinery. 'Oy, Cass, what's the problem?'

Casimir glances around. The movement makes him look surprised, lining his forehead, making him old. 'With what?'

'With everyone. The geezer that left.'

'Adams.'

'Him. And you.'

'Me? Nothing is a problem with me.'

Above them the dark ceiling moves and roars. Great tank-tracks of escalator machinery, an armour of steps flattening as they turn.

'Yeah? Well then, I reckon you should all talk more, all the old workers. Get out a bit. If you don't mind me saying. 'Cos some days you're all so quiet down here, it feels like Lenin's Tomb. You know what I mean?'

He smiles. 'Yes, I know what you mean. Do you want to leave?'

'No.' There is a question in the trainee's tone. It is gone when he speaks again. 'No. A job's a job, even if it's underground. I just wish you'd all talk a bit more.'

'I'm sorry. I'm glad you will stay.'

They are in the escalator-machinery chamber, waiting for closing time. To the south, the ceiling slopes upwards over two engines, all steel and axle grease. The engines are surprisingly large, barrelled sides curving above the heads of the two workers. At the southern end of the chamber there is room for two doors; to the north, the glittering movement of escalators almost reaches the floor. There is the fat smell of grease. The sour odour of metal and rust.

He is thinking of Alice. For the time being, nothing is wrong. It is twenty minutes until closing time. Ten minutes along the lines to South Kentish Town. He has left the glass matchbox in Lower Marsh and now he wishes he had it with him. A souvenir of the abandoned station, he thinks; something to be remembered, by which to remember something. He remembers her skin, fine and freckled in late summer, and feels the fierce excitement of attraction. It is not unpleasant or unexpected. Not a problem. In this sense he is not lying to Weaver.

Caterpillar belts and gear chains grind together overhead. When he looks up Casimir can see graffiti on the leathery hand-grips, electric-blue spray paint scrolling out on the escalators' underside. He is too far down to read the ciphers, to see if Alice's name is there. He thinks about running to the chamber's shallow end to look again.

The smell of the escalators reminds him of Polish churches, their black metal and turpentine. A Madonna outside the nunnery in Katowice with a tubular neon halo. Circular, like an insectocutor. The religion of an industrial town.

'Are we finished, sir? Closing time soon.'

'Yes. Almost finished.'

They work for a few minutes more in easy silence, checking for obstructions until each belt of steps has circulated. At the chamber's higher end Casimir stands upright, stretching his arms and shoulders. Weaver stops by the doors, wiping axle grease off his hands, reading the signs: ENTRANCE C, ENTRANCE D.

'That's good, that is. "Entrance-d". Do you reckon they thought of that when they did it? What's down there?'

'You can see. We can go to the platforms that way.'

Casimir unlocks the door and leads the way down one flight of stairs, out into a larger hall. It looms around them, damp and smelling of ozone. Like a sea-cave, thinks Casimir. The walls are cracked with subsidence.

'What do you call this?'

'The substation.'

'That'll be because it's under the station then. It's a bloody maze down here, isn't it, sir? All hidden away. Gothic. Like in that film with the cannibals. You know what I mean?'

'No.'

'Doesn't matter. I mean you could get lost for days down here. Does it happen, people getting lost?'

'I don't know. It could happen. The Underground is old. Older than the states of Germany or Italy. Bigger than London. The deepest subway ever made.'

'Is that right? Is there anything further down than this?'

'Yes. In the war they built deep levels. Shelters. They were never used. The bombs became rockets, and the rockets were too fast to shelter from.'

'Have you been down there?'

'Not often.'

Casimir imagines the deep shelters under him; their massive, locked silences. Around the two workers, panels of red lights flicker on domed ranks of back-up generators.

'There isn't anything living down here, is there?'

Weaver wanders past him, into the dark, looking around. Casimir sees that he hasn't shaved. Stubble emphasizes the teenager's hollow cheeks and the nervous eyes. Fox-like.

'Mice.' He starts to walk, stepping around hooped ends of orange cable, the broken bowls of ceramic insulators. 'Rats from the sewers; they are only small and brown. Much comes in from the sewers.' Five more steps. A pile of emergency torches, a stack of decaying magazines with their sour smell of old perfume samples. 'Once I saw a tunnel wall covered with white crabs. There are plants, mosses, where there is any light. And in the deep shelters there are moles.'

'Bollocks!'

'Bollocks, yes.'

'Oh, right. Nice one. Hold up.'

Casimir realizes he has been walking fast. Trying to get through the dark. Just ahead, steps lead up to a plain grey-metal door. Limestone salts glitter on the raised concrete. Casimir makes himself stop and wait.

'Cheers. What's all that noise?'

He listens. Off to one side of the steps are wooden racks of fuses, bright and intricate as the trays of a beehive. Casimir hears the clatter and spit of electricity coming loose. He turns his head and shoulder, allowing light past his bulk. Water runs down the corner walls in slow, flat sheets. He unbelts his radio, clicks it on.

'Leynes?'

'Cass? You're late. What's up? You struck gold or something?'

'There is water in the substation again. By the fuse boxes.'

'Aha. That'll be why the bog lights are buggered. The monitors are down too. I'll call the Water Board to check the mains, OK? Out.' The radio line goes dead. Casimir turns and goes up the steps, walking between pools of groundwater.

'Sir? Did you get to talk to that policewoman?'

He digs in his overall pockets for keys, looks round. 'Stay out of the water. Inspector Phelps, yes.'

'All right, wasn't she? Bit built, though. Built for the beat. I wouldn't want to walk into her on a dark night.' Weaver is kneading the small of his back, massaging the spine. He screws his face tight, a quick expression of pain. 'Do they reckon she was pushed, then? That woman who fell.'

'They don't know.' He unlocks the heavy door, steps through. 'No one does.'

The door clicks shut behind them. They have come out into the warren of side-passages by the emergency stairwell. The sounds of the Underground change abruptly, from the humanless hum of generators to the commotion of the midnight trains: footsteps, voices. The rumble of train doors closing, the rising whine of acceleration.

'That's weird, down there.' Weaver walks over to the far wall, looks left and right to the platforms, then leans back on the cracked blue tiles. 'Being behind the scenes. I've got a friend, he's Aladdin at EuroDisney every summer, good money but a bit hot. He said it was weird behind the scenes there too. All the characters sitting around with their heads off, drinking tea. Last year he got off with Goofy. She was from Poland. Isn't that where you're from, sir?'

'Yes.' Casimir looks down the tunnel, towards one of the West End- and City-bound platforms. On the corner is a convex mirror and he remembers the dog woman. Now there is only the sound of the crowd, coming closer. 'Stand up. There are people coming.'

Weaver elbows himself upright. An old man with a folding bicycle hurries by, flat cap pushed back on his head. Most of the passengers go slowly, though, making for home at the end

[125]

of their days and evenings. No one looks at the uniformed workers as they pass by. Weaver grins across at Casimir, rolls his eyes.

The crowd peters out to three girls in purple puffa jackets, the first girl pulling off gloves with her teeth as she walks and talks.

'It's all babies with her now, it's boring as fuck. I don't care if she's my sister, I just feel like leaning over and turning the volume down.' They swagger towards the stairs, laughter carrying back.

Weaver follows them with his eyes. 'They make me feel old. I know I'm not, but still. How old are you, Cass?'

He looks at his watch as he answers. 'I am twenty-eight.'

It is ten minutes until the last train, out north to the depots and yards. Casimir imagines he can feel it approaching through the tunnels and passages, a fractional pressure of air against his face. But then there is wind all the time down here. The air rushes and falters, always in motion. Sometimes if he closes his eyes, the Underground feels like open land. The coalfields of Silesia, anthracite dust blown against his hair and skin. Blue-black, the colour of his parents' hair.

'Is that all? Jesus. Sorry. What time is it?'

He smiles at the other man, amused despite himself. 'Past midnight. We have to check the platforms now, to see they are clear of people and belongings before we close. If you could check Three and Four, I will do the other two. Wait for the last train on Three.'

'No sweat. I'll see you back at the control room, will I?' Weaver is already walking away, looking over his shoulder as he goes.

Casimir watches him reach the Barnet platform, then turns away. In the fish-eye mirror Platform Two looks deserted already, its motionless strip of bright track and black bitumen curving to a vanishing point in the pocked metal surface.

He walks out on to the platform, to be sure. Posters line the opposite wall, massive rectangles of gaudy reds and golds advertising suspenderless stockings and Japanese beer. Small flyers have been stuck across the Japanese beer and Casimir recognizes them from days ago: HAVE YOU SEEN THIS CHILD?

He wonders how the posterer got across the live tracks, shakes his head to clear the crazed image.

The far end of the hall looks hazy and for a moment Casimir thinks it is his eyes before he smells the peppery odour of smog, dust pooled from the streets above. He walks the platform's length, checking the catch pit beside him, remembering other closing times. Umbrellas and cashmere coats left on benches, underwear and used condoms on the track. A broken branch of blossom one spring, laid neatly on the platform's edge. He hadn't recognized what kind. Black bark, and the buds plush and almost blue, the colour of cigarette smoke. Startlingly beautiful.

There are no people sleeping on the benches, no belongings left behind or abandoned. All around is the sound of the station closing down, echoes of movement draining away. A good sound, Casimir thinks. He tries to remember who else will be line-walking tonight. How long he will have to get to Alice, if she is there. If she is waiting.

He turns back, takes the stairs up to Platform One, and comes out of the side-passage beside the southern tunnel mouth. He looks up at the great keystone of its archway. A pair of closed-circuit monitors is bolted to the platform ceiling, placed for train drivers to check their rear view as they leave. Casimir stops under them, looking along the empty hall and then up. The screens are dead, a flat grey-green.

The air here is also hazy, the far tunnel mouth shadowed with dust. Machinery lines the near wall: wall telephones, chilled chocolate dispensers. Casimir screws up his eyes and nose at the harsh smell, trying to see clearly. A crimson plastic bag fishtails in an air current, floats out across the catch pits.

There is something at the platform's main entrance, a hundred feet away. Casimir looks up at the monitors then down, frowning at the lack of a closer image. Something protrudes from the entrance arch, a shining vertical bar and the edge of a small, black wheel. From where he stands, Casimir thinks it looks like the front end of a shopping trolley.

He walks up the platform towards it, the slow steps of his long stride echoing in the bright, empty place. Now he can see that the front of the object is no more than four feet high with a horizontal bar at the top, padded black. An armrest. Casimir breaks into a run.

At the entrance he stops. The wheelchair sits abandoned in the side-passage, skewed slightly to one side. Casimir reaches out to touch the armrest but the brakes have not been set and the apparatus jitters away from him, down the empty corridor. He takes two steps towards it, to halt its movement, then stops. Turns round and begins to move, slowly at first then running, back on to the platform. He sprints north, towards the far tunnel mouth, its circle of dark encompassed by the end wall of the platform hall.

He is still some distance away when he sees the body. It has slumped down, half-hidden by the walls of the catch pit. Casimir backs away, not crying out. After three steps he is able to make himself stop.

It is a woman, slight and blonde. She has been wearing a transparent plastic watch, cheap and gimmicky. Through it Casimir can see blood. The watch-works are still moving, tiny and regular, over the blood. For a moment he can't understand how the watch is still moving, now the woman is dead. The detail pulls at his vision, nagging at him.

The smell of burning and electricity is sour in the air. Under the woman a crumpled mass of litter is charred black and glowing, ready to catch. As Casimir scrabbles at his radio a strand of blonde hair lights, burns and shrivels back towards the turned head.

He covers his mouth with one hand, breathing shallowly. There is a lot of blood, more than he would expect. It is still bright red, oxygenated, staining the piles of trash, the skin and clothes. The radio has become stubborn, banging against his clumsy fingers.

He can't take his eyes off the catch pit. The suicide pit. The watch-face, the tiny wavering mechanism. On the woman's arms veins have broken, a hatchwork of violet exposed in the white skin.

Casimir remembers that the wheelchair is behind him and he looks round quickly, then back at the body. He sees how its nails are painted reddish brown. Sepia. There is blood on the hands too, but that isn't sepia. The nail varnish is cracked – no;

the nails themselves are cracked, like the skin. Casimir's mind races and stumbles. White-blonde hair is jumbled over and through the stained catch-pit litter.

He unclips the radio from his belt. It almost falls on to the track but he catches it, hands held out together.

He can feel the terror rising in him and he makes himself close his eyes and wait, shaking. Clicks the transmitter on.

'Leynes.' His voice is too soft. He tries again. 'Leynes. Aebanyim.' He cannot raise his voice beside the body. The names whisper around him.

'Cass? Cass, is that you?'

He opens his eyes as a shiver runs through him, rocking him forward towards the platform's edge. Abruptly he realizes how close he is to falling himself. He stands slowly, finding his balance. 'Leynes. Turn off the tracks.'

'You what? Cass, where – Is that you on One?'

He sees that behind the watch-face the blood is still moving and gathering. As if the blood, like the watch, has somehow survived. 'Someone is dead. In the catch pit.'

'Oh no, Christ. Jesus Christ. Oh, Jesus.' The supervisor's voice has become a whine, almost blaming. Like a child, Casimir thinks. He closes his eyes again.

'Leynes. Please turn the tracks off.'

A large man standing alone. The wheelchair, skewed and empty. His voice whispering on the silent platform.

'Please. Turn off the tracks.'

'Mister Kazimierski?'

He blinks. Someone is bent over him, silhouetted against bare bulb-light. There is a hand near his face, too close. The first two fingers and thumb are extended in a curious gesture. Like a priest, he thinks.

'How are you feeling?'

He remembers the sound of fingers snapping. The figure draws back, into the light. It is the policewoman, Phelps. He tries to remember what she is doing here, then realizes he doesn't know where here is. He focuses beyond the inspector, taking in the control room. Leynes and Sievwright are there, other people he doesn't recognize. Voices, low and urgent. There are the smells of sweet tea and work-clothes sweat. He breathes deeply, once, twice. The odours become overpowering, like the smell of burning. Of rank fish and caviare in a Russian market, his father's footsteps ahead of him.

He closes his eyes again. 'No. My name is Ariel Casimir.'

'Good for you. Up you come –'

Blinks. The world has altered again. Ahead of him is a street at night, its junctions dark and deserted. The chuff of windscreen wipers. Acceleration tugs him back into the warmth of a passenger seat. It is raining hard, shimmering on the road ahead. Car alarms whicker, disturbed by the downpour.

Fast. Everything is moving past him before he can react. Then he breathes deeply and time slows down.

He turns his head. Phelps is driving. Streetlight passes across her calm face.

'Where are we going?'

His voice is quiet, an accompanying calm. The police officer glances at him, looks back at the road.

'The station. Mine, not yours.'

'Am I under arrest?'

'No.'

Her intonation is level, inconclusive. The police radio stutters news of other accidents, other deaths. She clicks it off. 'I just want to ask you some questions.'

He looks out of the side-window, into the rain. 'What was her name?'

'Asher. Marion Asher.'

They pass between low walls, a view downwards to flat, hazed water. Casimir recognizes the Grand Union Canal and then their route, heading north on the Kentish Town Road.

Phelps's voice is dry and level, used to its undertone. 'She suffered from multiple sclerosis. Recently it was getting worse. She was twenty-four.'

The traffic lights are red by Castle Road. They wait without talking. Outside the rain begins to ease. Neon winks over shop entrances. Casimir sits back, eyes running across the bright names: AL ARAF SAUNAS, CASH CONVERTERS, VENUS OFF-LICENCE NO. 5.

'Sad. She had a Filofax, which helps us. Role Models Islington comes up regularly – it's a fashion agency. We can't get hold of anyone there tonight, but from the diary entries it sounds as if she modelled one day a week. Catalogue clothes. A year ago she was working double that. Remarkable, don't you think? To go on modelling. Beautiful girl.'

Beautiful. He thinks of her hair, thrown out by the impact. Burning white strands. 'I need to see a picture of her.'

The lights change to amber. Phelps turns in her seat, not releasing the handbrake. 'Why?'

He shakes his head. Green-lit rain ribbons the glass beside him. A young man comes out of Al Araf Saunas. Shakes open an umbrella under the doorway's black plastic awning. 'How long were the cameras dead?'

Headlights shine in from the car behind, stark and colourless. Phelps releases the handbrake and accelerates.

'Too long. Hours. How often does that happen?'

He raises one hand, the gesture meant to explain something of the Underground's age and decrepitude. Lets the hand drop back. 'Often. What happened? After I found her.'

'You were in shock. I'd be surprised if you remembered nothing.'

'What time did she die?'

'Not sure yet. The tracks didn't kill her, though. There were stab wounds. In her back. The shock stunned her, but she bled to death. I think the knife was just to make sure, don't you think?'

'Yes.' His own voice sounds brittle.

Phelps clicks on the left indicator, voice rising as she turns the wheel. 'You sound angry with yourself, Mister Casimir. Why is that?'

He allows his eyes to close again. The sense of disorientation grows and fades. 'I would like to have been stronger.'

'Really. Welcome to the human race.' She pulls up, switches off. 'Can you get out by yourself?'

They cross the pavement and go on, under the blue light of a Metropolitan Police lamp. Casimir has never been inside a police station. He imagines the institutional chipped-paint walls, cracked plastic chairs, the smell of antiseptic and linoleum. Then they are inside and it is too late.

A drinks machine hums against the far wall. The cropped office carpet smells of old tea. Casimir is surprised; the room carries no sense of threat, or authority. It feels more like a bank waiting room than a place of law. Posters are arranged on two large pinboards: MISSING PERSON: HAVE YOU SEEN THIS MAN?, TERRORISM: SUBSTANTIAL REWARDS, KNOW YOUR COLORADO BEETLE. Only the lighting suggests any potential for strength or violence, the neon dimmed fractionally behind metal grilles. A desk officer watches them through cash-till glass.

'Hello, missus. Who's this?'

'Inspector missus to you.'

'Inspector missus, ma'am.'

'He's from Camden Tube. Any problems?'

'The Noise Pollution unit clocked off three hours early. We've had eleven complaints . . . Mrs Trueblood of Lady Somerset Road is not happy. That's about the worst of it. Quiet night.'

'Here. Photocopy this lot, will you? I'll be back for it in a minute.' Phelps passes a green card folder through to the policeman, then turns back to Casimir. 'Right. Are you tired? Coffee any help, no? Good.'

She is already walking away. Her heels echo along the unlit corridors.

Casimir follows the policewoman slowly, trying to gauge his own state of mind. His head feels very clear, as if he has recently woken from a long night of sleep. Only the memory of Asher disturbs him. His thoughts slide away from the event, forgetful even when he tries to remember. He thinks of Alice at the abandoned station and wonders if she is waiting for him. He wants her to be waiting.

'Here. Sorry about the walls.'

Phelps opens a door, clicks on a light. The interview room has been painted pastel-pink, the catalogue colour wildly out of place in the institutional building.

There are chairs, a TV. Casimir sits down. 'She must have been able to stand, a little.'

'Why must?'

'It is regulations. Passengers must be able to stand on the escalators. So if there is an accident, a fire –'

'Leynes says you're not supposed to help, is that right?' She half-turns in the doorway, light cutting across her face as she studies him.

'Yes.' He thinks how hard it would be, at his station in a wheelchair. The fear of being trapped underground. 'Did she have no one with her?'

'No one. Leynes remembers seeing her before. He says she made a point of asking the staff for help every time. A one-woman access campaign. Take a seat. I'll be with you in a minute.'

He waits. The rain has eased, he can hardly hear it. Sirens go past outside, heading south. A wall clock clicks towards four a.m.

'I want you to go over the Saville tapes with me, tell me what you see, all right?' Phelps comes back in with folders and a video, its casing marked with the London Transport insignia. Red ring, blue bar.

'Why are you asking me now?'

Phelps passes him the folders, kneels down by the television. 'Why do you think?' The video display lights up. 'Two people are dead.' She unpacks a cassette, pushes it into its slot. An image of a deserted Underground platform appears on the screen, marked with white digits: PLAT 4 CAM TN. 03/09/96. 13:10:26. Eight days ago. The seconds accumulate as he watches.

The recorded picture is linked up to one of the end-wall cameras, so that the whole platform is covered. The far tunnel mouth is tiny with distance. The nearest advertising poster looms up, a giant image of a woman's throat and teeth.

'We're a few hours early.' She looks back over her shoulder. He is struck again by the contrast of her face and eyes. The hard lines of her forehead, the gentleness of her gaze. 'I'll fast-forward, shall I?'

He nods, wondering which is real and which instilled. Looks back at the screen. A Tube train careers towards the camera and stops dead. Crowds flood out of the carriages and disperse. Speeded up, the platform movements make Casimir think of time-delayed nature films – flowers bustling towards light, the circular flight paths of stars. On screen the Underground crowds are reduced to a pattern, simple as breathing.

The image clicks back to normal speed. Two children stand on tiptoes by a chocolate-vending machine, tugging at the wall brackets. Another walks round and round a laughing couple, tying them up with elasticated gloves. The screen readout shows 16:54.

Phelps sits down in the chair next to him. 'Are you ready?'

He nods again, not taking his eyes off the screen. The rush-hour crowd is building up, pushing itself closer to the platform's edge – an ordinary, everyday kind of danger. Casimir remembers the photograph of Saville, days ago in the control room. Now a tall man in anonymous City pinstripe steps closer to the platform's edge and becomes familiar, part of a set background. Casimir searches the mass of people behind him. It is an odd sensation, he thinks, to watch the photograph falling into place. Knowing the future.

A young woman is moving through the crowd. Her hair drapes against shirts and jackets as she turns her shoulders to get past. Faces turn to follow her. From the camera's-eye view they are expressionless with distance.

Casimir leans forward, intent on the recording. For a moment he thinks the woman is Alice, but the similarity is superficial; this woman's movements and attitude are different. More elegant, less quirky.

Rebecca Saville looks down at her wristwatch, then puts her head back, stretching the shoulder muscles. Her neck is startlingly thin, as it was in the photo-booth picture. Figures move in the crush behind her, almost indistinguishable, like forms under water. There is a monotone flash of clothing as someone steps through a gap, back into shadow. A black woman reaches up to adjust her headphones, nodding to their rhythm. Casimir stares, trying to take in everything.

It happens in the space of seconds. Rebecca Saville twists at the white platform edge, toppling forward. The crowd moves back from her as she falls, like water from the impact of a stone. There is a flash of electricity as Saville's arm grazes the negative live rail. Concussively bright.

[134]

Motion ripples back through the crowd, as if it is they who have been pushed away. The pinstripe man turns, shoving. The black woman half-kneels, both hands going out. Black skin, pale blouse sleeves.

'It was not her hand. In the photograph.'

'Watch again.'

The tape whirrs. Saville flails back up on to the platform, ungainly and unchangeable. Phelps clicks the remote. Saville stands at the front of the crowd with her head back, eyes closed, stretching her thin shoulders. Inexorably, the sequence begins again.

The woman falls. Every part of Saville is in motion, her face, arms and body turning as she goes down. Behind her the hand is drawn back into the crowd, its outline already lost in shadow.

'What do you see?'

'Nothing. Just the hand.'

He searches the packed faces of the crowd, looking for intent. But the passengers are a grainy blur of movement. The only expression visible is in their motion. The panic of bystanders, fighting clear of violence.

After a moment Casimir looks at Phelps. She is waiting, studying his face. 'I'd have seen you in this crowd. If it was you. But it isn't.' She is thoughtful, her voice quieter.

'I'm sorry. I thought I could help.'

Casimir begins to stand up but the policewoman doesn't move. 'Not yet.'

He sits down again. In his mind he can still see Rebecca Saville, so like Alice from a distance. The body in the catch pit, its hair paler than yellow.

'The photograph of Marion Asher. Do you have it?'

'In a minute. Tell me about the Tube first. What's it like, working down there?'

He sits back, requiring himself to be patient. 'Like anywhere. No.' He is thinking, so that when he talks his English will be clear, precise as his thinking. 'The Underground starts out perfect. At first it isn't like the city above it because it is conceived all at once. Everything must be created, heat and the passage of air. For the engineers and architects it begins as a perfect technical form. Then years go by – decades. Cross-tunnels are found to be unnecessary, so they are bricked up. Deeper tunnels are added by the government, then closed down. Limestone comes through the concrete as if it were muslin. Up above, communities die out. Stations are abandoned.'

He looks up and she nods for him to go on.

'The Underground becomes a reflection of the city above – organic, not perfect. Full of small animals and weak plants. Good hiding places, and places that are dangerous. Some people – Adams – he felt it was becoming more dangerous.'

'Why?'

He shrugs. 'I don't know, but I also feel it. The first Underground trains had no windows. They were padded, to keep people safe. Now there are children who ride flat on top of carriages. They call it Tube-surfing. Dangerous, you see? Muggings, killings. People end up on the Underground who are –'

Force of gravity, Burton. All the dirt ends up down here. The voice comes at him out of nowhere. He shakes it away.

'– needing to shelter. Sometimes weak people, sometimes not. It is not only victims who need to hide. You see?'

'I don't know. It sounds like you care about it. Still, you haven't answered my question. What's it like, for you?'

He shrugs. 'It is safe.' Hesitates. 'Most of the time, it feels safe.'

The policewoman sits back from him, as if she is still waiting for something. When Casimir doesn't go on, she reaches down for the files. Opens the newest, leafs through for a sheet of paper. 'Thank you. Here. You asked for this.'

He takes the paper. It is a photocopied snapshot, shades reduced to stark black and white. Two girls sitting on a low wall under broad trees. Looking down as they laugh. Sunlight coming through their hair.

'From her Filofax. The one on the left's Asher.'

He turns the page in his hands, as if he could see more of the photograph in that way. Marion Asher leans forward slightly as she laughs, supporting herself on the flats of her hands. Her hair is much lighter than the other girl's, the photocopy reducing it to page-white. Light is reflected up on to her face. Casimir is struck by the long cut of her cheekbones. The nose curved outwards towards the bridge, not quite aquiline. A small, neat hook.

[136]

'Remind you of anyone?'

He looks up fast. Phelps is turned away from him, clicking the video back into its case. 'Like Saville. Don't you think? A little, anyway. Enough for it to matter.'

'Of course.'

Casimir looks down again. Collecting his thoughts. The urge to run is stronger now, to get to the abandoned station and ask Alice – what? At least to see her, to see she is safe. The picture lies on his open hands, almost weightless. He is aware of the policewoman moving around him, clearing things away. When he looks up Phelps is standing in front of him, the folders in her hands.

'That was what you wanted, wasn't it?'

'What ?'

'To see what she looked like.'

'Yes. Thank you.' He stands and stretches, an automatic movement. Rolling the shoulders back, feeling the circulation quicken. He screws his eyes closed for a second and Asher's image flares and fades. He glances up at the wall clock; it is long past five. And there is someone else he has to see. He thinks it is not too late. 'I'm sorry I was no help.'

'You tried. It's more unusual than you might think. You must be tired. I'll get one of the officers to drive you home.' She is already turning towards the door.

'No. I would like to walk.'

'To Lower Marsh?' She opens the door, looking back at him.

'No.' She remembers his address so quickly. He wonders how long she has considered him as a suspect, and if the consideration is over now. 'Just to walk.'

Phelps raises her eyebrows, shrugs. 'Whatever gets you through the night. Just remember you've been through a traumatic experience. I wouldn't advise walking along the canals, or down to any King's Cross nightspots. Not tonight.'

'Thank you for the advice.'

Together they walk back, past the desk officer to the station doors. Outside, Casimir can see the sky beginning to lighten. Over the rooftops, the dark is faintly hazed with blue, like dust.

'I may need to talk to you again. And call me, if you think of anything.'

'Of course,' he says. He lies. He has never liked authority and he doesn't need its help now. Casimir opens the doors, steps out. The air is cool, still smelling of rain. It makes him feel alert. And he likes to be alert.

Phelps waits in the doorway behind him. 'Thanks again. Remember you're in London. It can be dangerous here, even if you're big and strong. Especially then, Mister Casimir.'

'Yes. Thank you.' He walks down the steps without looking back.

On the Kentish Town Road he turns south, heading back towards his station. The streets are still almost deserted. When cars pass Casimir can hear them coming from far off, tyres hissing against the wet asphalt.

It feels colder now he is outside and alone, and he presses his hands down inside the pockets of his uniform jacket. Somewhere behind him a burglar alarm begins to ring, the sound going on and on over the Victorian terraced streets and railway arches.

The Castle Road junction is empty, traffic lights clicking through their sequences, red and green reflected across the wet ground. Casimir crosses over and stops, breathing slowly, feeling the gentle adrenalin of walking go through him. Outside a row of shops he stops.

He looks up at the shop signs: 'Cash Converters' on a white Perspex lightbox, 'Al Araf Saunas' in pale green neon, the tubular letters looped together like graffiti. Both shops are housed in the same two-storey building. From where he stands Casimir can see the whole façade. Rain against plate-glass shop fronts. Oxblood tiles, gabled and patterned with old lettering. The second-floor windows are flat and arched, like tunnel mouths.

The design is familiar to Casimir as the warren of his own station. Above the arch windows, foot-high letters are moulded into the ceramic tiles. Even in the streetlight they are faint, the colour weathered away. Casimir moves his head so that the illumination catches the raised characters. Narrows his eyes against the rain as he reads: SOUTH KENTISH TOWN STATION. Lower down, UNDERGROUND.

He drops his head and looks around, but the street is

empty. Casimir is breathing faster, already nervous at what he is about to do. Exhilarated to have got something right; the concrete fact of the abandoned station, here in front of him. At the side of the building an alley leads off towards high blocks of post-war flats. Casimir ducks down past the Al Araf Saunas plastic awning, following the old station wall back out of the streetlight.

The side of the building is untiled, bare brick covered slapdash with mortar. There are no doors or windows, only wild screeds of graffiti in bright silver spray paint, towering over Casimir's head: SEX IS GOOD, TIME FLIES BUT AEROPLANES CRASH.

The back of the building is surrounded by a rambling fence of corrugated iron. A small door has been blowtorched into the fence and padlocked shut, and Casimir puts his face up to the wet iron edge, looking through the gaps. Beyond are a few yards of wasteground, old carpets and empty boxes half-lit by the lampposts on Castle Road.

Casimir reaches down for the padlock. The bar is clamped down over the latch. He pulls hard. Harder. The bar chafes open, stubborn but unrusted. He wonders how many times someone has come here, at night, unnoticed. Whether it is always Alice, or Alice alone. Carefully, he lifts the door open and goes through.

The yard is uneven, with piles of rug ends and carpet stair-lengths. The ground is covered with their waterlogged patterns: mottled purple flowers, yellowed kilim abstracts, a deep greenish design of branches and birds. The back of the station is windowless, cracks opening in its damp brickwork. A peeling wooden door has been propped open with a sagging roll of blue linoleum. The doorway itself is blocked off with a jumble of barbed wire and red-white striped emergency tape.

He squats down. The carpets are heavy and very cold in his hands, slippery with an accumulation of grease and dirt. Casimir shoulders them away layer by layer, working down until he finds a piece small enough to make use of. He wraps it around both hands like a muffler and goes up to the doorway.

The barbed wire scratches against his forearms as he gets a grip. When he pulls it comes out easily, bouncing and skittering against the walls of the doorway. The warning tape flutters its writing into his face: LONDON TRANSPORT PROPERTY. KEEP OUT. Beyond the obstruction is a straight unlit staircase, leading down.

The mass of metal is surprisingly heavy. He turns at the waist and drops in on to the carpets. Their fabric oozes groundwater. In the streetlight Casimir can make out one flight of descending steps. More faintly, light from behind him illuminates a square white patch of floor further down. It is hard to tell how far down the stairwell goes.

He thinks of Phelps. Her voice measured, like hard footsteps. Something about strength and danger. It reminds him of childhood, the time he went through spring ice on the canal. The sour taste of ice and the feel of it against his face, coming up under a frozen surface. Something behind him in the dark green water, beautiful and monstrous.

He pushes the thoughts away. For now there is only Alice, the killings, and the dark stairwell in the abandoned station yard. Casimir looks back at the lampposts behind him, blinking in their glare, grateful for the after-images of light. Then he goes through the doorway. Edges forward, feeling the ground with his feet.

At the third step he stumbles and again at the ninth. He makes himself stop at the first landing, waiting impatiently until his eyes adjust. The staircase is not truly dark, but his pupils are still narrowed to the strength of surface light. Mica flecks glitter in the stone under his feet. Illumination comes down from the street above but also dimly from below, filtering up the shaft of a spiral staircase. A huge worm-like ventilator extends from the vertical well, segments curving upwards to its silver turbine mouth.

Sound carries up from the tunnels underground, faint as the light. There is a rumbling gust of air as a train passes, north or southwards. An irregular musical banging, metal against metal. Casimir stands entirely still, listening. He can make out voices, high and childlike. Like something out of *Alice in Wonderland*, but more real. Down to earth.

'Kevin would strip your hide, man.'

'Yeah. But I'd slap him though. I'd kick him with six legs though.'

'He'd strip your hide.'

'Yeah.'

The core of the spiral stairs is iron mesh, furred with dirt. Casimir can see lift cables and pulleys inside, moving in the air from the doorway above. He puts his face up close to the wire, then pulls back. There is a door in the mesh and next to it a palm-sized red button on a flat metal panel.

He presses the button. There is a jerk of machinery from above his head and voices below cut off abruptly. Casimir steps back as engine machinery clatters into life, shockingly close to his face.

The lift cables loop and wind. A red cage-work lift rocks up into place and Casimir pulls at the door. It has been wired shut, but his movement breaks the wire cleanly. A bundle of tunnel workers' clothes is slumped in the far corner. On top of the bundle someone has propped a London Transport sign: THIS LIFT IS NOT IN USE. PLEASE WALK DOWN.

He swears softly and turns away, going on down the spiral staircase. Carefully, staying close to the outer wall, where the steps are at their widest. At the bottom a metal door leans open in the staircase's core and a pair of archways lead off through the stairwell's curved walls. Casimir reaches out and carefully opens the heavy door. From experience he knows that this must be the entrance to South Kentish Town's substation. But he can see nothing, not even the steps that will lead on down. He can hear the soft lapping of floodwater, and against his face the darkness is solid and cool. He steps backwards towards the nearest archway and through it, breathing fast. Turns round.

He is in an Underground cross-tunnel, a long low hall, lit by a row of light bulbs hanging from the roof. There is the church crypt smell of damp and sweet dust that he remembers from the abandoned platform. The harsher smell of urine fermenting in closed-off rooms. There is writing all over the ceiling in neat black charcoal, and Casimir cranes his head back to read the nearest message: *'Royal Lincoln bound for Malaya 1955. RSM Brown is a fat ugly barrel-gutsed bastard.'*

He looks down again. At one end the tunnel stops dead at two public lift doors, their square apertures bricked up with breeze-blocks and sloppy mortar. At the other, the corridor turns away out of sight. Casimir walks down towards the corner, quiet and alert. Here the cream-and-oxblood-patterned walls shine with damp, wet as bathroom tiles. There are wooden storeroom doors along the walls, but when he tries them they are all locked up.

There is the sound of running water, and Casimir stops again to listen. The voices have gone quiet but the metallic hammering is still audible. Casimir bends forward, frowning, trying to make out where the sounds are coming from. But it's hard to tell; the tunnels and chambers trap the sound, echo it, turning it back on itself.

Ahead of him is another flights of steps. There are no lights here, but stuck to the walls are long strips of luminous tape. They cast a faint, greenish radiance around Casimir as he walks down. A narrow arched cross-tunnel leads off left and right. In the wall ahead are two enamelled Underground maps, South Kentish Town circled in red and black like a bull's-eye. Between the maps is a high, thin wooden door. Light shows under it. Without letting himself stop to think, Casimir turns the handle. Steps in.

'Did you put it back?'

He blinks and stares, trying to take in everything at once. The room is long as a train carriage. Near the end where Casimir stands are a tall wooden lampshade and a bar heater, wires trailing away. The Underground air is uncomfortably humid. There is someone humped asleep under a pile of blankets, grey rat's-tails spilling out across the floor. A man sitting against the near wall, broad head shining with sweat, staring back at Casimir.

'I said, did you put it back?'

'What?'

The man turns his face away, expelling smoky breath through clenched teeth. There is a cigarette in his hand, burning down into a horn of ash.

'He means the barbed wire. In the yard.'

Casimir turns around. Alice has come in behind him. She is

standing so close they almost touch. Her hair is tied back, and Casimir can see the collarbone under her skin. Like wings, he thinks. She reaches out and takes his hand. Turning it, feeling for the pulse with her forefingers.

'Your pressure's really low. I like your watch. Who's the head?'

He looks down. A tiny profile is embossed on the white face. 'Lenin. The watch is from Russia.'

'I like it. Two faces. I've got one too.' She holds it up fast and close. He doesn't jerk back. 'It's only digital. I set the alarm for 2.12 p.m. Not because I have to be anywhere. It's just to see what I'm doing each day, at 2.12. It's never the same, unless I'm sleeping. I'm glad you came back.'

'Why?'

She smiles. 'I'm just glad. Why do you think?'

The hammering starts up beyond the door at the far end of the long room. From here it sounds like an anvil being worked. When Casimir looks back at the Underground girl, she is still half-smiling, waiting for him to talk.

He reaches out with his free hand, takes her hair, as if he is weighing its smooth mass. Lets it fall. 'A woman died at my station. Did you know?'

'Yes.'

'Another died last night.'

Behind Casimir the man begins to cough; a hacking rhythm, three times.

'I want to know why.'

She watches him, sharp and feral. Gauging him with her quick eyes. She is so quiet he wonders if she is holding her breath. Then she is reaching out, putting her hands on his shoulders. He can smell food on her breath, warm and salty.

'If we kissed, I'd have to stand on tiptoes.' She leans on him, pushes herself away. 'I've got to go. OK? I'll be back soon. Wait for me.'

'Where are you going?'

She doesn't answer. He goes to the door in time to see her run down the cross-tunnel, out of the staircase's green luminescence.

He turns back. The man in still watching him. He is big,

shaven-headed like a wrestler. When he speaks again his voice is thick with phlegm.

'You're a worker, ain't you?'

Casimir walks over and sits down. From here he can watch the greenish darkness of the doorway as he waits.

'Yes, I work. On the Underground.'

'A worker. Bloody hell. Congratulations.'

The man smells of Elastoplast. His thick neck is wound round and round with skin-pink lengths of it.

'Where did she go?'

'Alice? Got to see a man about a god. No, that's not right, is it? Spit meth, she's gone for. Are you comfy? There's blankets, if you want. Alice got them in a launderette.'

'What is spit meth?'

He leans towards Casimir, whispering and grinning. His nose is flattened out against broad cheekbones. 'She's good at getting things, she was in the papers for it. Blip Girl, the one-woman juvenile crime wave. That's what they said. Spit meth? Some of the people on methadone want the stronger stuff and some of the people get a taste for methadone, so the people with methadone puke it back up and sell it. That's spit meth. Everyone gets their poison. What's yours?'

'I don't know.' He checks his watch, then looks back up at the doorway. It's long past dawn. He feels wide awake. 'Not spit meth.'

'You didn't take the lift down then?'

'No. Why?'

'It's out of order. There was a worker like you, got stuck in there for three days. Well out of order.'

'I heard the story.'

'It's true. Have you got anything to eat?'

'No.'

'Fuck and buggery. There's nothing here either. Last thing I had was from that bloody Chan's Kitchen, some Chinese crap, crispy arthritic duck. That's a joke. Laugh like a drain, why don't you? I used to live in a park, but that was crap too. It was crap spelled backwards, that's why it was so shit.' Something else juts into the man's brain and he looks back at Casimir. 'Are you wearing working underwear? Do you understand underground underwear, Mister Worker?'

'My name is Casimir.'

'Nice name. I'm Bill. That's my wife, Hilary.' He shakes Casimir's hand and begins to talk rapidly, still holding on to Casimir's fingertips. 'Bill Aeaeae. That's a nice name too. Like Circe, that was her other name you see. Names are important, aren't they? Miss Circe Aeaeae – Miz of course, Miz nowadays, Circe was some time ago now. It's all a matter of time. A stopped clock never boils – no, that's not right, is it? Even a stopped clock tells the right time twice a day. That's it. That's me, you see; a stopped clock. Not like you, poor you, always running, Mister Worker with your shiny watch. Always watch-watching, always running fast. You see? A fast clock never tells the right time at all. Better off stopping than window-shopping. You should come down here more often, sweetheart. Take a break, take a knick-knack. Like this.'

He pulls out a hip-flask bottle from his parka. It is half-full of a gritty, brownish liquid. 'Do you want it?'

'What is it?'

'Spit meth. I told you. You can have it.'

He shakes his head. Sits back from the man's leering face. 'Is Alice her real name?'

'Alice? Why not? It's very nice.'

Casimir stands up, walks to the open door. Outside there is no sound except the hushed movement of air. Another train is coming, still far off.

Bill yells after him as he walks aways down the cross-passage, 'Are you going? Not out there? Ooh, how low can you go?'

There is yellowed light ahead. Casimir turns a corner and finds himself at the end of the cross-tunnel, a bare light bulb hanging down from the arched, tiled ceiling. Three steps lead down to the southbound platform, and Casimir ducks under the bulb and walks out and stops in the centre of the ruined space. The echoes of his footsteps fade around him.

The darkness is more substantial here. Casimir's breathing comes quicker. He forces it slow. Across the tracks, the hall's curved panels have been removed. An intestinal mass of pipes, cables and iron ridges has been exposed, their shiny lengths and knots running off towards the distant tunnel mouths. From the south come the sounds of trains, the whine-down of deceleration carried along the miles from other lines or stations.

'It's like that film. When they go into the mother ship and the walls get alien.'

He turns round. Alice is further up the platform, sitting on an old ironwork bench. Her hands lie on her knees. Like a pianist waiting to play, he thinks. The tunnel wind is picking up, and it tugs against her open coat and hair.

He walks over, sits down beside her. 'I don't see many films.'

'You wouldn't like it.' She turns to him, pushing back her hair. 'No films, no clubs. What do you do at nights, Casimir?'

'I work. When I am free, I go walking. I learn English.'

'Do you like England, then?'

He shrugs. 'When I came my life was very bad. Now it is not so bad. I made my own life here. Yes, I like it.'

Alice is smiling, lips pulled back against her gappy teeth. 'I like sitting here, watching the trains. All the people inside them. No one ever looks out of the windows. You can run around and scream at them but they never notice. It's like being invisible. When I was little I always wanted to be. And now I am.'

'Why did you want to be invisible?'

She stops smiling. 'Don't do that. You sound like a social worker. Everyone wants to be invisible sometimes. You do. Don't you?'

The wind is stronger now. He sits thinking, face lowered against it. Shakes his head.

'Liar. Why did you come here tonight? Because of me or because of those women?'

'They looked like you. I thought you might be in trouble –'

'You came because of them.'

'No.' He meets her eyes and holds them. They are too close for the contact to be anything except aggression or desire. 'I came because you are here.' He feels no aggression. He needs to know what she feels.

'Someone is following me.'

'Are they here?' He forces his words to be heard, eyes narrowed against the wind.

She has been watching the northern tunnel mouth but now she looks round at him again, unsmiling. 'No. No one finds me here, unless I want them to.'

'Who is it?'

'I don't know. Just someone. I've never seen him.'

'How do you know it's a man?'

She shrugs and looks away. 'I've heard him breathing. There's a train coming.'

The air pressure is rising to a roar, louder and more violent than at an active station. Behind the bench, a storeroom door begins to rattle in its frame.

The air hammers against them as a train goes through at full speed. Windows flicker past, crowded bodies and profiles lit up and instantly gone.

He looks back round at Alice. 'Their names were Marion Asher and Rebecca Saville. Someone killed them.'

She is still watching him. The roar of the train fades to a thread of sound. He leans towards her. 'It was you, wasn't it?'

'No.' She looks past Casimir. Eyes unfocused, giving away nothing. 'I was sleeping in your station. Then that woman died. I started hearing someone, in the station at night, and then all my stuff got stolen. My blanket and everything. So I came here. I ran along the tunnels and this is where I came out. Do you believe me?'

'Yes.' She is sitting so close they touch. He can't feel her body's warmth or coolness against his own. As if they are too similar, or as if she doesn't exist. Invisible. 'You were sleeping in the old cross-tunnel. By the railway sleepers?'

'Yes.'

'You must have seen him.'

'I don't know. I wasn't sure. There are so many people there. Once I heard him in the cross-tunnel, in the dark. I kept still and he went past me. I came here a couple of days after that.'

Casimir leans his head back. Takes a breath and lets it out, a long sigh. Mostly he feels relief, to be here with Alice, to hear her talk. But there are other feelings too, disturbances. She has always disturbed him.

'You don't need to stay down here. I have a room. You could stay with me.'

[147]

She grins and tuts, kissing the back of her teeth with her tongue. 'No one's going to find me. I like it down here. There's plugs for music and lights, room for my friends, and it's warm. It's safe down here, don't you feel that? We don't die if the bomb falls. It's a good place. And I've got you now. You're on my side.'

'How long has he been following you?'

She shrugs. 'I don't know. A long time. It doesn't matter now.'

She leans over him and presses her hand against his chest. Hard, so that Casimir can feel his ribs and sternum against his lungs and heart. He isn't surprised by her strength. She kneels up, close to his face, staring. Her eyes jitter, as if she is trying to see round his own, to get inside him.

Then she kneels back, letting him go. 'You can stay with me, if you like.'

'I can find out who is following you. There are places I can go.'

'Good. Stay anyway. As long as you can.'

She takes his hand as he stands. Her fingers are bony and cold and too small to reach across his palm. He follows her up the half-lit platform, past rusting escalator steps, their vertebrae of chainwork laid out flat. There is another side-tunnel here, another staircase. The darkness makes him blind and he closes his eyes against it, one hand on the worn wooden balustrade and the other around hers. At the top of the stairs is a door and she unlocks it in the dark and pulls him in and kisses him, reaching up against him. Pulls him down.

There is bedding under them as he kneels, a thick pile of unzipped sleeping bags and blankets. Alice sits back from him, silhouetted dark against the dark as she pulls her skirt loose over her head. Her hair catches in the collar and he lifts it out. Lies back as she undresses him. He closes his eyes, feeling her hands and kisses against his chest. Her skin is very smooth, colourless in the dark. The cold lines of sleeping bag zips press against his back. Their lining is smooth as her skin.

She makes almost no sound, nothing except the breath forced out of her by their movement. When he enters her she holds on tight to his arms, gripping the sides of his biceps, eyes

[148]

open and watching. He lifts her under him, her smaller body moving against his, his hand around the small of her back.

Even when she comes he can't tell whether she is about to embrace him or push him away. Then she shoves him off, reaching down to strip off his condom, throwing it away. Curls up into herself, instantly asleep.

For hours he watches her, naked against the arch of her spine. She mutters and laughs in her sleep. It surprises him that she gives away anything. Once – when he is on the verge of sleep, still raised up on one elbow – she begins to sing in a small, private voice.

White scars run up from the curve of her hip to the hollow, angled blades of her upper back. Casimir counts their seams. There are seventeen, wrinkled and ugly, a patchwork of old violence. He doesn't touch them. He thinks of knives. The movement of watch-works over blood.

He kisses the backs of her thighs. The skin there is hot and still damp and salty, as if she is feverish. Her body has the rank smell of honey. He kisses her lips and temples and the thin back of her skull, at the roots of her wet hair. Her movements move his heart.

He stands up. If he is to try and help Alice, then it is time to go. For a moment he waits, planning his route upwards through the dark.

'Don't look back.'

She speaks without turning over. Casimir curses himself for waking her. Only as he bends and kisses her shoulder does he wonder how long she has been awake.

'I have to go. Sleep well.'

Her mutter is thick and anxious, running over itself. A voice out of dreams. 'Don't look back though.'

'Why?'

'You just mustn't.' She is whispering now, subsiding back into sleep. 'You just mustn't.'

He kisses her again. Then he goes. The streets outside are crowded with people and bright under a clear white sky.

The Feeling of Sight and the Feeling of Sliding

I'm tall as my father. I am twelve and he is old.

One time I was with my class in the school bus and I saw my father drunk. He was wearing a check suit. He was leaning on the windowsill of Kapelusze the clothes shop. The window is very big, with stone around it, so Dad looked smaller. Like a kid. His name is Michal.

No one else saw him; they were shouting about Kozuck, the blind champion runner. I turned my back on the window and shouted too. My dad didn't see me either because he was looking down, with his legs apart to steady himself. It was only me who saw what happened there.

This was a while ago. It was easy to tell when Dad was drunk round then, because everything got more. More radio music to dance to. More happy, more angry. Nowadays it's even easier. The only hard thing nowadays is finding him when he is sober.

My mother forgot the morning of my birthday. It was only for a few seconds. I went in and she was reading at the glass table. I waited for her to say something and she didn't know why, I saw it in her eyes. Then she remembered and she kissed me and we went to open the presents.

My life is ordinary. Not good, not bad. Sometimes it feels as if it's getting worse. I dream of it as a feeling of sliding. My life sliding down a steep, dark hill, going under the ground. I can't stop the slide, it is out of my control. It is my worst dream, but just a dream. I do not think my life is so different from anyone else's.

I got zúr soup the way I like it best, with horseradish and two eggs and a whole garlic sausage in, and I got marble cake and blue track-suit bottoms and blue trainers with white stripes. The trainers are imports, Made in the UK.

I go running down through the Old Town. Smoke goes up from the apartment chimneys straight and brown as dead grass. When I get back I clean the dust off the trainers and put them neat together in my cupboard. There's the smell of mushroom and cabbage dumplings frying for supper. Starlings outside, arguing for somewhere to sleep. The sound of my parents' voices through the wall, high and low.

'More than we can afford. Could've shown it a bit more.'

'. . . quiet. He liked them.'

'Never used to be.'

'Growing up quiet. You know him. Still waters run deep.'

My dad's voice, louder. The screech of his chair going back. 'Still waters run deep! "Deep water's dangerous" – how's that? What's so good about deep water, eh? He'd be better for some work. I could use help anyway.'

'No.' Her voice is small and frightened and strong.

'I could use him. How long's that going to be?'

'It's almost ready now. Almost done.'

I go on through. From the corridor I can smell the horse-radish in the soup. The wooden floor tiles are loose under my bare feet.

On my dad's last birthday the TV weathermen said the moon would disappear. My father got everyone on the roof of Block C, but Piotrowski the caretaker made him pay dollars. We sat on the roof and drank Lech beer. It was evening and so cloudy, the sky looked like the inside of a bucket. The girls played the Shoe Game: lining their sandals and heels and house slippers up, and whoever's shoes reached the edge of the roof, that girl would get married next. Then the rain came down so suddenly, it was like the bucket had been turned over on us. Dad shouted that if that was an eclipse, God could stick it where the sun doesn't shine. After he shouted that, Piotrowski never spoke to us again. His skin is red under one eye, as if someone spilled hot wine on his face.

Between the Strug Blocks the little kids and old men are playing. The old men play Pan at a pink plastic table, holding the cards down with their shirtsleeves. The little kids are choosing who will jump off the Block D entrance steps. They sing the choosing song.

'Ana Dua Likka Fakka Torba Borba Ussmussmaka . . .'

When I was little I sang it often, but it's a long time since I heard it. When you are little the years go slower because they are a bigger part of your life. Time goes quicker for me now. I'm bigger; the years are smaller.

Piotr says I'm wrong. He says it's our galaxy going towards a black hole and the closer it gets, the faster we go. I think he's right too. Ideas aren't like real things. Sometimes they can be two things at once. That's what I think.

'It's you, Maria! You!'

She is bony and very small. She climbs up on to the steps' concrete edge and jumps. Her skirt flies up into her face and all the kids laugh. She comes down on her feet, slap in the dust; it doesn't look too bad. Then she falls over and balls up and begins to cry.

'Eee hee. Uuu huu. Uuu.'

I look away from them all, across the town. The sun catches in the waterways, over towards the docks. I'm facing London Piccadilly England. My mother chooses to forget and my father holds me so hard it hurts, but I can go west. When I'm big I'll do that. In the West no one will know me. In the West I can be whatever I want.

I say winiak is the colour of my mother's Baltic amber. Piotr says it's the colour of piss in summer. I say we're both right. We sit looking at the bottle with our backs against the wall of the Laboratory of Oncology. It's sleepy here with the thaw sun on us; no one comes and there are no windows for them to see us by. I pass the bottle to Piotr and he holds it up. The sun comes shining through it.

Piotr unscrews the cap and takes a swig. His eyes go all bulgy. He looks like a shot rabbit at harvest. The rabbits come out of the high rye and roll when they're hit, and the pheasants run up the air like stairs and the skylarks twirl upwards like paper ash from a fire.

'Hoooah! I need some water.'

He doesn't get up, just leans back again and closes his eyes. He doesn't pass the bottle to me either. I take it myself. He didn't drink much, but then Piotr is small. Me, I am not so small.

The screw-top scrapes against the glass. It's an old vodka bottle, there are Russian words stamped into the neck. I raise the bottle and toast Piotr and Poland and my mother. When Dad drinks he toasts Stalin. He dedicates the winiak, the coffee cups, saucepans, the blue-green curtains and the four boxes of shaving foam aerosols stacked in the hall: *To the name of Jozef Stalin! Na zdrowie, Na zdrowie!* Throwing his arms about. It's one of his jokes. He doesn't care if no one laughs. He laughs himself.

When Mother drinks she toasts no one. Drinking is another of her secrets. I take a good long swig.

'Hoooah! Christ. It's fine, isn't it?'

The sun is also fine. It feels like my guts are on fire with the season. Seagulls go over towards the canal, calling and laughing. 'Here. You want some more?'

'Her body tanned and wet down by the reservoir.'

We walk along by the canal in the hot sun, looking for pike. It's me and big Wladislaw and Piotr and Karol. Wladislaw sings.

'River was dry. Down to the river. Ay. Ayayay. That's the best song. He's the king. Isn't he, Piotr?'

'Sure.'

'You don't even know who he is. Do you have a music centre, Piotr?'

'Yes.'

'*Borja!* Farm boy. You're such a liar.'

'I do, though. My grandfather Roman does. Because Roman loves to listen to Iron Maiden.'

Our laughter goes bouncing away along the towpath wall, towards the docks and factories. Scrawled on the brickwork are gibbet pictures in red chalk and white paint. In each noose is the letter of an enemy: L for Legia Warsaw, J for the Jews. Piotr kicks up against the wall. For two steps he's running sideways. It's February. You can still feel the cold on your face.

We took the winiak from Piotr's dad, who gets it free from Mr Krajewski, who lives on the fourteenth floor of Block A and married a German before the war and now he sells rotgut to half the town.

Everybody wants to be friends with Sir Farmer Wittlin. Even now when there is nothing in the shops except glass shelves, he has food. This last Easter, Piotr had pig's knuckles and duck's liver. There is still one pig left. It's Lech, who is the fastest and has warts. Piotr tried to save some for me but his mum wouldn't let him. We had mushrooms in soured cream, and the cream was too sour.

I have many secrets now. Hanna Tuwim is one. When I learned how to come I thought of her. At night I stood at the window looking out across town, thinking of her until I came into my hand. No one taught me how to do it, I just knew. I was glad when she went away. It's too late now.

My mother is another. The way she sings in her foreign language sometimes when she works. Quietly, not to be heard, only to make sound. I know she sings in the language of Jews.

'See anything?'

'No. Just a bottle. I thought I did.' Karol slaps his knees clean and stands up and we go on.

Lots of things get frozen into the canal ice. Just here there's green bottle-glass, wooden apple crates, pages of a torn-up book, a pram with no wheels. We are looking for pike. Last thaw Karol came walking back to the Strug Blocks with a piece of ice bigger than himself. A pike was frozen into it. It was striped green and gold and the belly was white. That year there were pictures of dinosaurs in 7c's biology books. The pike was the colour of the dinosaurs. When the ice melted Piotr cut it open and inside were eggs, like green caviare, and seven fish, each one smaller than the one before. So here we are.

'Have you got more than ten records, Casimir?'

'I don't have any records.'

'Who's your favourite band? Is it Iron Maiden, like Piotr's grandad?'

'I don't like music.'

'Everybody likes music.'

'Not everyone.'

'Why not, then?'

We stop to look at the ice. Already it's melting at the edges and around the bridges. All winter the dock boats break it and then it freezes again behind them. Now it's heaped up like broken windows. Some of it's milky and some clear.

'Why don't you like music, Casimir? Is it because of those foreign songs your mum sings? Karol heard them.'

Across the canal is wasteground, then a red building with a big sign for the Association of Cattle Head De-Boners. There are girls across the next bridge, walking together in last year's long grasses. I recognize Monika from the way she walks, her arms folded across her belly. She's wearing a skirt. I wonder how she got tanned so quickly.

'Is your mother foreign, Casimir?'

I look round at Wladislaw. I wait for him to say anything more but he doesn't. He sees I'm waiting and so he gets a stone and throws it whickering across the ice. I look back at the girls.

'What do you see?' says Piotr. Light reflects off the white-washed bridge. His face is all freckles and wrinkles, screwed up against it.

'Them.'

When I was small we played with Monika all the time. Now I don't know her. The girls are separate from us. It's like the dinosaur pictures from last year's book, each different-shaped creature standing in its own group. It's not really like the dinosaurs. I made that up.

Piotr looks across at them with his screwed-up face. 'Which one would you have? If you could.'

'Monika.'

Karol comes up beside us. 'The Tomassi sisters have got a notebook with all Led Zeppelin in it. English and Polish.'

The girls are closer to us now. One of them sees us, her face lit bright and heart-shaped, turning away.

'Wait –' Piotr squats down at the canal bank, arching his head first left, then right. 'There's something under the bridge.'

We all look round where Piotr points. There is something, for sure. It curves like a tyre where the ice has melted, twisted out of the slush.

'One of us could walk to it. Piotr, I dare you.'

'The ice is too thin.'

'Karol? I dare you.'

'No.'

'Casimir, can you see it?'

'Casimir, you see the best.'

Piotr is taking off his glasses, wiping hair out of his face. I look away from him, out into the shadow of the bridge. The object is smoother than a car tyre and not as wide. Green and muscular.

'I'll do it.'

'Casimir, don't. The ice is too thin.'

Wladislaw pushes Piotr back against the towpath wall. 'It's thicker than your fucking glasses. Look at the barrel, will you?'

Near the bridge are all the things people have dropped down on the ice to break it, stones and half-bricks. Close to the bridge is a metal beer tun. It's small for a barrel, but even so. The ice is grey and flat under it.

'Look at that, will you? What's wrong with you all? I dare you.'

'You do it, Wladislaw, if you think you can.'

'Who asked you? Casimir?'

I reach down the canal bank, into the cold water. There is a gap between the side and the ice. I put my hand under the ice, feeling its thickness.

'Casimir? It could have broken and frozen again. If they dropped the barrel and it floated, the broken ice would freeze underneath it –'

'I said I'll do it.'

I stretch one foot out on to the wet ice, then lean on to it. The

[156]

ice creaks like polystyrene packing. Then the other foot. Now I'm standing on the ice, it only took a few seconds. My shoes are thin and the cold makes my feet hurt.

'Bloody hell, Casimir,' says Karol. Quietly, as if shouting could break the ice under me.

He and Wladislaw are still standing next to me, close as if I was on the ground. Wladislaw smiles and stares. It scares him, which I like to see; I scare him. I can't see Piotr now. I turn around and start to move. The ice creaks at the third step, and the seventh.

'Casimir?'

I look up. Monika is on the bridge. When I wave she starts to laugh.

'Casimir, what are you doing?'

I laugh back. I start to say I don't know when the ice goes through.

At night I count red lights from the rear window, but if it's daytime like now I ride with my face against the side-window. The light catches in its dust and it changes as you drive, rolling against the glass.

We're on Constitution Street, going slow. I see the luxury shops with floured pastries in glass cases. Old women selling plastic bags by the Old Square crossing. One man with his suitcase propped open on a dustbin. There are bottles inside – Head and Shoulders, I know the shape of them. One man in a trench coat and hat with a cigarette. You can tell he's a specu-lator too, even though you can't see what he sells.

'Small-timers.' My dad kisses his teeth with his tongue, a long drawn-out tut. The steering wheel straightens inside the ring of his hand.

'How soon?' says my mother.

'Tomorrow, late. I could do with help this time.'

'No. You don't know if Jan is on duty.'

'Not yet. I can telephone.'

'Why so quick?'

My dad is going away again. Astrakhan is where he has friends in furs. It's four days' drive but the friends are what

[157]

counts. They're made from dead lambs stitched together, but the wool is soft and the inside is also soft, like skin. This is the furs I'm talking about. The friends give Dad presents. A Russian Army watch that glows in the dark. The pistol of a cosmonaut. Only the best for the best. That's what they said. Dad told me. We were playing Pan. I almost won that time.

'Michal? Why does it have to be –'

'I don't know. Because it does.'

Outside are more old women with plastic bags. Women with grey cauliflowers and dusty bilberries and branches of yellow broom laid out on newspapers. Two Gypsy men with jars of live fish around their feet, all of them turning the light slow and orange. The old women look at nothing. The Gypsy men look at everything.

'I could use him. He's big enough now.'

'I said no.'

'Big enough. We'll see.'

'Look, Mum. Mum. Mum?'

She looks. 'Goldfish.'

'They're great, aren't they?'

'Yes, they are. Beautiful.'

My mum's hand and mine hold each other; I don't look round but I can feel them. A big ball of knuckles on the plastic seat between us. When it moves the plastic burns my fingers, but only a little. I keep my face to the glass, watching the light change.

The cold rushes up around my knees, cock, chest and head. My hands go into the water last and when they are through I pull them down, wrestling upwards. My eyes have closed themselves and I open them and look.

The ice is full of light. The water is clear green from inside. My mouth starts to open itself and I taste the ice, which is sour, like iron. I close my mouth and kick upwards. The water won't let me up. Instead it turns me round to face the bridge.

The pike is there after all. It leans away from me, a long trunk the colour of the water. Its mouth is open, a white crack in the greenness. The teeth are shining white inside the hooked

[158]

jaw, the hook of it curving up through the lit ice.

The water is getting darker. I kick again and come up under ice. My face presses against it. Now I can bring my hands up and I hit through the ice, into the air. I think, 'Still waters run deep'. *Cicha weda brzegi rwie.* There are voices screaming my name and one voice breathing. The one voice is mine. I make it go on breathing. I hold on to the ice and wait until something else happens.

My mother keeps notes in her pockets. If you're in a quiet place with her you can hear the rustle of them. I've only seen her read them once. She does it in secret. We don't talk about it.

One day in June I came home from school. I called out but no one answered. I walked in through the empty rooms, which were full of light and me sighing in the warm air, stretching the work out of my arms.

The bathroom door was open and my mother was there. She was standing by the basin with her skirt hitched up. There was blood on her hands and on her legs. She was staring at her palms. I tried to look away but she looked up at me and I couldn't.

She was as scared as me. I know it was her period now but then I didn't. After that she saw Dr Berman. He said she had Alzheimer's Disease and that she should go away. That was his diagnosis. But I know he was wrong. What my mother has is not a disease. It is that she wants to forget so much.

It's getting dark when Dad goes. I push open the window to call goodbye to him but then I wait. He walks to the car, looking both ways across the railway sidings with their blue signal lights and the allotments with their tinfoil scarecrows glittering white.

Our car is navy, not blue. Against the edge of the birch woods navy is the same colour as darkness. If pine trees grew there and not birch you wouldn't see the car at all. It's the right colour for a speculator.

He stops by it, not getting in. It's just spring; the nights are still cold. His face is clear in the dark, like the birches. It turns quickly and I look down the road and there are people coming. Two men in uniform, army or Militia.

The woods are near him, so he could run. I would. But he just stands with his face turned, watching them come up the back road towards him.

At the car they stop. I count time passing by the alarm clock's tick. They couldn't stand for so long without talking. One of the men lights a cigarette, dropping his face towards the match, and I know him. It's Tomek the Militia man, Wladislaw's father. He holds out the match to my dad and lights his cigarette too and then waves it out.

They go on talking, and then Tomek and the other Militia man take off their gloves to shake hands. My dad throws away his cigarette and shakes their hands but he doesn't take off his gloves. Then he gets into the car and the tail lights come on. I lean out of the window, holding on to the Singer's heavy iron frame.

'Dad!' It's too late. 'Dad!'

One of the Militia turns his face up to me as they walk away. My father's car goes east, towards the highway.

I get into bed and think of my father. It's an insult to shake hands with gloves on. My dad insulted the Militia and they did nothing. Outside the lampposts come on. Their light stutters across the ceiling from ten storeys down. Through the wall I hear my mother's bed creak as she lies back.

'You could have died.'

'I was all right.'

We sit on the stairs, Monika and Piotr and me. You can hear the echoes coming up from each floor. Voices and doors and dogs. The clatter of pigeons around the entrance.

'I got out by myself. I was all right.'

'I could see you through the ice.'

My arms are still cold, so that I shiver a bit. Monika is warm beside me. It's good, having her here.

'You were looking up.'

'I told you it was thin. You knew. Why did you do it?'

'I don't know.'

'Was there anything there? Was that why you did it? Was it because of Wladislaw?'

'Maybe.' I stand up. I don't tell them about the pike. It's my secret. I know it must be still there, dark in the dark water. It feels good, the seeing and knowing. 'Do you want to come inside? My mum made zúr soup. There's plenty.'

I remember how it felt. The taste of ice was sour, like metal or snow. There was the terror of coming up under it. Then there was the feeling of breaking through the ice. That was great, though. I just reached up with my hands and broke through to the air. With it came the feeling of sight. It was worth doing just for that.

The Low Road

In Casimir's dream there is the Underground and the sound of the squirrel-cage. He is down in the tunnels. The ballast stones are uneven and sharp against his bare feet.

Between the rough gravel are track sleepers, wood flush with the tunnel floor. Smooth and dangerous, smelling of damp and creosote. It is a paradox of his dream: the smoothness of the danger, the pain of what is safe. He takes small steps. He has no torch, no lasting source of light.

He is holding out his left hand so that his watch-face is ahead of him. The luminosity is already fading. He doesn't take his eyes off it as he walks. The tunnel wind beats against his bare skin. Soft and insistent, like moths.

The Underground closes around him. Its dark presses against his face. It is safe as a locked room; it is terrifying as a locked door. He is shivering, his head is shaking with it. As if he is refusing to go further, even as he walks. He tries to think where he is going but in the darkness he knows nothing. It is like having no thoughts at all. He stumbles and cries out as he falls.

The ceramic bowls of the current insulators loom up. The live track is so near his face he can smell the acid wetness of its metal. The insulators are white and featureless. Faces in the crowd of a northern country.

The track hums with power. He backs up from it with his father's watch against his chest. Then he begins to walk again. The ballast stones have cut his legs and the palms of his hands. He is glad of the feel of it. It is something to be sure of.

The noise begins as a wheedling echo in the track. It is the sound of a train coming and he puts out his right hand, feeling for the point where the wall opens out. The train doesn't frighten him. He knows this dream. There is a crossover point here, the tunnel widening around a junction. There is room for him to stand and not be killed. And the train will bring light. Everything is wrong in the dark; but what he can see, he can make right.

The wall beside him gives way to space. He steps sideways, ducking under the loops of cables and the bright coppery lines of the old line-telephone live wires. Beyond is a warren of tunnels, branching away. He turns around, pressed into the space between rails.

The train is much nearer now. Already the sound of it is going wrong. Casimir can hear something metallic, a skitter of movement against wire, the sound of something wild trapped in a narrow cage. A crash on stone and the sound of water. Echoes distorted back up the sightless black shaft.

The train roars past him. Grids of light move across his face. He looks up into the train, face screwed up against the light but grinning, teeth set. The light feels so good.

The train is deserted. The carriages press tunnel air against Casimir's face and chest as they pass, windows empty and bright. He can feel himself beginning to wake and he turns, eyes closing, as if he will walk out into wakefulness.

At the last window is a figure. It is indistinct, gone before he has turned properly to see. But he recognizes Alice. She is not singing any more, just looking out at him. Looking out of her eyes but giving out nothing, no humanity. Her eyes are so familiar to him now. The colour of blood seen through muscle.

He wakes. He is cold with the late afternoon sun on his face. The rims of his eyes still sting with sleep loss. He is sitting on a bench, its ironwork hard against his spine. In front of him is a wide stretch of concrete paving. The pavement is littered with broken bottle-glass and curlicues of plane-tree bark, split from the trunks in the September heat.

He can smell river mud. A girl with red hair and blue sunglasses roller-blades past, slaloming between pedestrians. Beyond them is the Thames. A pleasure boat hoots as it passes the Houses of Parliament, light criss-crossing in its wake.

He shifts upright and immediately he is alert, the sleep leaving him cold. He leans forward, elbows on knees, head in hands. His face is warmer than his fingers.

Across the river, Big Ben strikes four. The giant clockface shines white in the autumn afternoon. Casimir makes himself stand. He has been asleep for nearly four hours and the light hurts his eyes.

He walks across to the embankment railing, passing easily between the slow rush-hour of pedestrians. Leans against the railing, stretching out hands and arms.

This is one of his routines, the embankment bench. Often when he has finished a day shift he comes here before going home, walking down from Waterloo station, past the arched glass of the Channel Tunnel terminus. He sits for a while even in winter or spring, when the cold rain drips off the plane trees and soaks his uniform. Partly he does it because he loves the river, but mostly because it is a routine. Routines are important to him. They make things clear and certain, like light.

Now he tries to remember the last time he came here. It is a week ago already. The day he heard of Rebecca Saville's death.

He blinks, and for a moment there is the overpowering sensation of Alice kissing him. Her breath, its warmth and sound and feel. He keeps his eyes closed until the memory is gone. On his work clothes the dirt is a dark sheen at the folds of the knees and the jacket lining. He feels good, still tired but sharp and hungry. Sleeping underground; he smiles at the idea of it. Like something from a children's story or folk tale. Persephone or the Ohyn.

The railing is warm against his hands and he leans over it, looks down. Low-tide mud stretches out to the water. Casimir can see people sitting down there: an old man in a torn sports shirt and stained check jacket; a woman with a bottle in her hands, light catching its clear glass. The homeless. He looks away.

The days return to him haphazardly, in distinct images. He lets them come. Photographs spread out on a grey-lit counter. A child turning, neck stretching monstrously. The wheelchair, edging away from him. The hand in the crowd, blurred by freeze-frame, reaching out; and then the crowd itself, its faces in shadow. Casimir wants the faces lit up clear. Where he can see them.

He looks upriver to Westminster Bridge, yawning as his

mind clears. The sound of car horns carries down. A double-decker bus sits in the grid-locked traffic, stranded diagonally between lanes. Casimir watches, taking in none of it. He turns away from the river and begins to walk, back along the embankment. The thin crowd moves around him and past him.

The Tube train to Camden is old rolling stock, a rush-hour replacement from the depot yards. Its green sides flare outwards at their feet, and inside the wooden floor is worn smooth, lit by light bulbs under scalloped glass. Casimir sits in the last carriage. There is less crowd this far down the train, and in Casimir's section there is only a single other passenger, a gaunt man with a purple sports bag gripped on locked knees.

The old carriages pick up speed, rocking into the dark. Casimir thinks of the first trains on the Underground. Locomotives with breathing holes in the roads above. Sleek industrial brass and steel, letting off steam like whales.

The stations pass: Goodge Street, Warren Street. The thin man unzips his bag, takes out a dozen lottery cards and scratches them out with a ten-pence coin. As the train slows towards Camden Town, Casimir sees the man is wearing a name tag on his jumper: *Sam Deane – 'The Human Fountain'*. When he has finished, the man reaches into the bag's bulk again. Takes out another handful of cards.

Casimir gets out with the crowd. He is glad of the crush as it moves him along towards the escalators, up towards the surface. He is here on his day off, on his own time, his uniform seamed with dirt. There will be questions to answer if he is seen; where he has been, where he thinks he is going. It is simpler not to be seen.

He steps out on to Camden High Street and immediately twists back out of the path of a pavement cyclist.

'Oyoyoy!'

Around the oxblood tiling of the Underground entrance are a few stalls, bunches of henna-coloured incense and oiled hotplates of thick, pepper-red pizza. Trade spilling over from the big markets on Chalk Farm Road, the Lock and the Stables. Casimir turns north towards them, moving slowly through the shoppers and sellers.

It is not often he comes above ground at Camden. There is rarely any reason to do so. It reminds him of Adams: *I'm just going upstairs.* He was right to stay out of things, Casimir thinks. And I am wrong again. Not really careful, not like Adams. Needy. Needing to know everything. Walking out over wet spring ice.

He walks north-west. The bulk of life up here surprises him. A laughing woman with a tall bucket of green sugar cane, next to a tiered trestle of black-bruised yellow peaches. White posters spiralled around lampposts, zigzagged across building site walls. Samosa salesmen leaning between shop fronts of black leather and white goods. Voices –

'Any wear you like, ladies!'

'Shh! Hash? Hash?'

'Rass, man! You need new clothes, you start looking like a tramp. Hey! Hey, big man!'

Teenagers in bright clothes and office workers in grey, all of them walking too fast in the gutters and road. A fire engine slows, thundering at them with its horn.

The pavement ahead is blocked with a red tartan blanket, an obese skinhead brooding over his merchandise. Mechanical sniper figures snake across the blanket. When they go too far the skinhead prods them back with one steeler boot. Behind him is a fenced square of clothes stalls, electric-blue halter tops and sequinned tie-dye skirts. Casimir steps over the blanket and stops, looking across the stalls.

A small building rises out of the sea of clothes. It is simultaneously anonymously placed and curiously shaped: a conning tower of pinkish brick, ventilation slits near its small, flat roof. The brickwork is covered with giant graffiti, SUB 73 on a scrawled background of silver, purple and crimson. To Casimir it looks as if the colour of the market is creeping up the walls, a bright lichen.

He turns right at the edge of the clothes market. The smell of street foods is stronger here, air sweet and fat with the fumes of chilli and lime leaves, cumin frying in ghee, almonds

[166]

browning in hot caramel. Casimir tries to remember how long it is since he has eaten, his stomach turning over with hunger.

The flank of the building protrudes to the market's edge. A metal door is set into its side. Next to the door is an intercom, an inconspicuous plaque over the verdigrised metal: DEEP SHELTER ARCHIVES INC. NEWSPAPERS & RECEIPTS. Casimir presses the buzzer and steps close to the intercom, turning his face sideways to the smell of urine.

'Yes?'

Casimir smiles, eyes resting on the brickwork. '*Jak sie'n chuyesh*, Wanda? Are you well?'

A pause. '*Jako tako*, so-so. Who is this?' The voice is female, and Polish. The heavy accent of someone too old to ever lose it.

'Casimir. From the Underground.'

'Ah? Ah. Yes, I remember you, Kazimierz Kazimierski. Wait.'

There is a rattle of metal and Casimir looks round. A diminutive man in white jeans is pulling a shop grille down. The showroom lights are still on, gleaming through rows of lava lamps. Globules and teardrops of orange and organ-pink.

When he turns back, Wanda is standing in the open doorway. Her broadness is emphasized by thick bifocal glasses, a great head of steely white curls and an oversized jumper patterned with trees, sheep and a small cottage. She is holding a large paperback in one hand, a Danielle Steele in Polish translation.

'Hello. I close soon. Is it the ventilation?'

'No. I need – there is some information I am looking for.'

She frowns. The bifocals press up against her lined forehead. 'You are not here on Underground business?' Casimir shakes his head. 'You have authorization to see the records?'

'No.' The old woman waits, looking Casimir over. 'It is important. Please.'

After a moment Wanda stands back, holding the door open with her wide, pale hands. 'Quickly. I am in a hurry tonight. I go to the club. You want to come?'

'No. Thank you.' Casimir knows she means the Polish Hearth Club, in Kensington. A place filled by older Poles, wartime refugees, critical of the new waves of immigrants from home. It is not a place in which Casimir feels comfortable. The eyes of the old people on him. Expecting little, assuming too much.

'I will not take long.'

'No, you won't. What information is this which is so important?'

'A newspaper story.'

She stops moving and turns awkwardly towards him. They have come through into a poky office room. An Elvis Presley picture calendar half-covers a bricked-up window. Both side-walls are hidden behind filing cabinets the colour of gunmetal. At the back of the office is a small red cage-work lift.

Wanda begins to cough, staring at Casimir. It is only from her eyes that he realizes she is laughing. 'This is Newspaper Storage. We have every story here.'

'A death on the Underground. Someone was caught for it – 12 June 1987.'

'Ah? That's better. Maybe I can help you.'

The archivist backs away to the lift, hauls open the folding door. It is years since Casimir has been here, checking some common ground between the subterranean properties of London Transport and Deep Shelter Archives – crossroads of ducts and pipes, knottings of cable thick as a torso. The archivist looks unchanged. Even the jumper is familiar. Casimir sees that she still limps, her left leg longer than the right, the shoulders slightly tipped.

'Come on, please. In here.'

Casimir gets into the lift. Immediately it starts to descend, jerking back against the shaft walls. When Wanda speaks again her voice is softer, adjusting to the packed space.

'It is important to you, this death? Maybe you know who died?'

'No.'

It is a long way down. Outside the lift, the concrete shaft; outside the shaft, blue London clay. He is thinking of Alice waking in the abandoned station. The smell of him on her. He wonders how she can recognize morning, without light to touch her eyes.

'Ah. Well, it is nice to have a visitor. To tell the truth, things are not so good here now. No one comes. The libraries, they have all the newspapers inside computers, and warehouses are cheaper for storage, so why come here? This is not to be repeated, you understand.'

Casimir nods. The lift is small, so that he is pressed against the archivist's soft bulk. The smell of her jumper is as strong as that of the market above: lanolin and a bitter, trapped sweat. He watches the black shaft passing outside the diamond lattice of the door.

'This week my son and my daughter-in-law go back home to Warszawa. I will miss them but I am glad. Why do you stay in England? And just to work underground. You will go blind, like a bat – I am going blind, you see? When will you go home?'

Home. He thinks of his father, an old man in misfitting clothes, wasteground around him. He wonders if it will be necessary for the old man to die before he can go back to Poland. He thinks it will be this way. Otherwise there would have to be forgiveness. Casimir cannot imagine any means of forgiveness.

'Eh? You don't talk much. Still waters run deep, that is what the English say. The Polish is better, of course. *Cicha weda brzegi rwie.* "Quiet waters break the river's banks." You should talk more, Kazimierz Kazimierski.'

Wanda narrows her eyes and he sees it is meant as a smile, although her mouth is unsmiling.

The lift slows, two hundred feet down. Wanda pulls the door open and Casimir follows her, out into the deep shelter.

'Now we will find your story.'

They are standing at the edge of a great hall, broader than a Tube tunnel, its massive dimensions sectioned off by miles of shelves and walkways. The curved walls are painted two-tone, black and beige edged off at chest height. The floor of the deep shelter lies across the tunnel's widest point, creating a single arched chamber. Casimir remembers a second level, curving downwards like the belly of a ship.

'1987 . . . 1987 is this way. Come on, please.'

Wanda turns down an aisle between the shelves. As Casimir follows her, he sees that the shelves are packed from floor to ceiling with filing boxes, cardboard caked with dust.

'Tonight is my games night, you see. We play Pan for pierogi! So I get fat, because I am so good. But maybe you are too young for games. Maybe tonight you have a girl to be with.'

Ahead and behind, the black-and-tan walls run off into the far distance. Casimir bends his head, trying to see past Wanda to the chamber's end.

'How far does the deep shelter go?'

'From here to Lvov. No! A kilometre or two. And the same downstairs. Too much room. There is space now, where the shelves end. I never go down there.' She smiles back at him. 'It gives me the willies. The willies. You know what this means?'

'Yes.'

The archivist's teeth are the same pearly grey as the frames of her glasses. They walk on. In the overhead strip light Casimir can see that the walls are marked by slight, spiral ridges. He recognizes the pattern of a drum digger, the Underground's tunnelling machines. But I am deeper here, he thinks. Under the Underground.

'Now we are back in the 1980s. Not far to go now.'

The hall itself feels newer than the train tunnels above. There is no smell of limestone and water here, less sense of a human construction becoming natural. It is because the deep shelter is wartime, Casimir thinks; six decades old. The Underground above is twice its age.

Casimir can see the end of the shelves now. They stop dead a few hundred feet ahead. The strip lighting penetrates some distance further, before fading into darkness. The end of the chamber is out of sight.

In front of him Wanda comes to a halt, out of breath, holding on to the shelves. The boxes are wedged in tight, cutting the light down between rows.

'Here we are!' The old woman's voice is sing-song, artificially bright. She edges one box out, puffing and muttering. There is a string of letters and digits on the box lid: LONDON GDN, 06/87. Wanda dumps it on the floor in front of Casimir.

Dust billows around him and he wipes his face. The boom echoes away as he reaches down, lifts off the lid. Inside are copies of the *Guardian*, wrapped in plastic, pages compressed together.

'There! Now you must look for yourself. If you want more papers, they are all here. I am going upstairs to sit down. In twenty minutes I lock you out or lock you in. Yes?'

'Yes. Thank you, Wanda.'

Casimir is already lifting out newspapers. He doesn't look up at the archivist. Her footsteps echo away as he kneels down, hair falling forward, shadowing his eyes.

Tenth of June. Eleventh, twelfth. Casimir carefully unfolds the newspapers from the plastic wrapper. The newsprint smells fresh but the paper peels apart slowly, like onion skin. The first few pages are full of election news, then sideshow stories: *'Cecil Parkinson Gets Energy'*, *'Portrait of the Artist as a Young Dog'*.

Casimir lays the newspaper out on the aisle floor. The pages hiss as they turn. After some time he stops. As he reads, light is reflected upwards from the white paper, emphasizing the flat blades of the cheeks.

'RUSH-HOUR KILLER'
Suspect Arrested at Scene of Third Death
by Li Ailema, Crime Correspondent

Police have confirmed that a man has been arrested in connection with a third death on the London Underground. Thomas Gray, 32, a mental hospital outpatient, was apprehended yesterday morning at Camden Town Underground station. Shortly before the arrest a man was fatally injured after falling on to live rails. Sean Harris, 42, of north London, was announced dead on arrival at the Royal Free Hospital, north-west London.

The death of Harris follows a chain of similar incidents over the past six months which includes the deaths of two other London Underground passengers. A poster campaign on the Underground is said to have led to the arrest, when a member of the public identified Gray on a crowded platform immediately after Harris had fallen. The victim died after injuries sustained in the fall led to a massive heart attack.

Passengers' groups were today calling for an independent government inquiry into why Gray, diagnosed as a paranoid schizophrenic with violent tendencies, was released into the community. Thomas Gray has been shunted between hospitals, hostels and prison since his release from Marginfields Home for the Mentally Disabled, East Sussex, in 1981. Pressure on NHS beds has meant that Gray has been either discharged prematurely or refused admission to suitable facilities since that time.

No police comment has yet been issued as to whether Gray will be charged with the Underground deaths of William Tull and Lawrence Cluny, who died on 10 May and 21 March this year. However, all three victims bear a clear physical resemblance to Gray. If convicted of all three deaths, Mr Gray is likely to be kept permanently in a secure medical institution, although the final period of detention will be decided by doctors and medical staff.

Beside the writing are four photographs. The first three are mugshots of the victims' faces: white-haired, white-skinned men. Their physical differences are emphasized by different lighting and background. Casimir is aware of their similarity without being able to place exactly which features they have in common. Harris is standing outdoors, a high white sky behind him as he grins ludicrously. Snapshots, taken in lunch-breaks or days out. Never meant to be this important, as records of death. They remind him of Saville, unsmiling and badly lit.

The larger photograph shows Gray being pulled along through a crowded hall by police officers. Casimir screws up his eyes, trying to make out details in the blurred newsprint. With a shock he recognizes his station, the surface concourse at Camden Town. Gray is stooped between the policemen, a head taller than either of them, light hair falling across his face. The mouth is visible, thin-lipped and curved downwards. Without being able to see his eyes, it is hard to gauge the expression. It could be anger or satisfaction. He could be crying or smiling.

Again he remembers Adams. The room full of surreal, watered light and the supervisor's voice, angry and haunted.

He was living down in side-passages. Got away with it for months, staying down there all night, out of the way of the cameras . . . In a place the size of London, there's somebody pushing all the time.

Casimir closes his eyes tight. The archives make nothing clear, disturbing everything. Thomas Gray has been locked away for life. There is no sign that this is the man who is following Alice. This is not the man he has been looking for. '*Kurva!*' He whispers harshly, under his breath. The sound ricochets away along the tunnelled walls. Away past the last shelves where the dark begins, like deeper water. He is still thinking of Gray's killings as he folds the newspapers back into their box. The repetition of a pattern. Gray killing the men who looked like him. Alice and the dead women, their hair and skin and eyes.

As he walks back along the hall to the lift Casimir can feel the dark behind him, deep and cold. Wanda is waiting for him by the exit, buttoning a woollen coat over her jumper. Casimir walks her to her car. Kisses her goodbye on both cheeks, her hands gripping his forearms. Turns back towards the station.

It is not long until evening. To the south the sky is darkening with rain, and over the market streets runs a great skewed track of cloud the colour of neon. Casimir narrows his eyes to make out the scale. It looks gigantic, curving out towards the city's western edge.

Then he is at the oxblood entrance of the Underground. He bends his head and goes inside.

By the time Casimir arrives at Waterloo the terminus is full of the sound of rain, a fine hush of water against the glass vaulting. He walks across to the side exit, out between the shining black bulks of the taxi rank, down the steps towards Spur Road.

A figure sits against the metal balustrade, one arm held out sideways, hand resting on the head of a white dog. The stray looks round at Casimir first, eyes white and pink in the rain. He remembers it from days ago, before the news of the first death. He doesn't recognize Alice until he is standing beside her and she looks up, eyes narrowed against the hazy downpour.

'I love rain. The sound of it. I miss it underground. You do too, don't you?'

She is wearing a black wool hat, and the length of her wet hair is tucked inside the collar of a green duffel coat. Water shines against the flat of her forehead and he sits down, reaches out, wiping it or warming it with his hand.

'Yes. How did you know I live here?'

Alice reaches into the coat. She smiles as she passes him a square black wallet, as if she is giving him a present.

It is his own, cheap plastic impressed with the Underground roundel. Casimir turns it in his hands, not frowning. He pockets it without checking inside for the last of his month's wages, the London Transport identity card.

'How long have you been here?'

She shrugs. The dog turns its long head away from Casimir, grinning down at The Cut market.

'You cannot have known I would come this way.'

'If I didn't know, how come I'm sitting here?'

'When did you take it?'

'Last night, when you were asleep.'

They are sitting close, not looking away from each other. Rain runs down the sharp jut of Casimir's nose and around the cavities of his eyes. 'I didn't sleep.'

'Whenever then. You told me I could come here. Stay with you.'

'Stay. Not steal.'

'It's not stealing.'

'I don't see –'

'Which part don't you understand? I gave it back to you, it's not stealing. Did you find out who's after me?'

'No.'

'You said you could.'

'I was wrong.' He stands up. Puts out a hand. 'If you're hungry, I have food.'

She gets up by herself. They walk together, down the steps to Lower Marsh. Behind them the dog stands watching, panting into the sound of the rain.

The shop front is bright and quiet. A few stall-holders sit inside, cradling tea, sheltering their cigarettes away from wet faces. A fat man in sodden black jeans and T-shirt hunches over five polystyrene bowls of mushy peas, shovelling them into his mouth, hair plastered against his forehead. Casimir goes past the shop door to the lodgers' entrance and leads Alice up the uncarpeted staircase to his room. He closes the door behind them. Plugs in the bar heater and feeds the meter. Stands, awkward, as she looks around.

'I will get some food. There will be something left over from last night.'

'I'm not hungry yet.' She walks over to the window, looks out, then draws the net curtains shut. 'How long have you lived here?'

'Eight years.'

She is taking off her hat, the coat, not turning round. When she says nothing else he walks up behind her and she leans back against him and he puts his arms around her waist, breathing in the smell of her wet hair, hardening against the small of her back. They make love there, at the window. Quietly, Alice's cries almost as soft as the sound of the rain. Once her forehead bangs against the glass and when Casimir begins to apologize she laughs, breathless, turning her face to kiss him over her own shoulder.

Afterwards he goes downstairs for food. There are reheated chicken portions on the glass-fronted hotplate, dull and crusted with old oil. He toasts thick slices of white chip-shop bread, butters them with margarine. Warms up glutinous minestrone soup, ladles it into tall polystyrene cups.

When he gets back upstairs the door is unlocked. Alice is sitting on the bed, naked and cross-legged, drying her hair with Casimir's bathroom towel. Her cheeks and breasts are flushed with heat. He feels a sharp sensation of physical desire for her near his heart, almost painful.

'I needed a shower. I wasn't sure which was your towel.'

'You chose the right one.'

'I know. It smells of you.'

'What kind of smell is that?'

'Like fish blood. It goes with the sound of your name. I like it.'

He sits next to her on the narrow bed, carefully putting

down the food between them. Alice eats quickly, head lowered, not speaking. Casimir is too hungry to watch her. When her food is gone she leans against him, side to side, breathing out once with satisfaction.

'It doesn't feel like you've lived here for eight years. It feels as if no one lives here at all. Don't you have any things?'

He drains the last soup, then looks up at the room, trying to see it as she does. 'I like it to be like this. But yes, I have some belongings.'

He puts the cup down on the floor and goes over to the wardrobe. There is a single drawer under the main cupboard and he pulls it open. Inside are his books of street-plans and poetry. His birth certificate, passport, London Transport work permit. An old shirt of soft grey cotton, rolled up and tied with elastic bands. He brings the bundle back to Alice, strips off the bands, unrolls the cloth. Inside is a black-and-greenish lump of material with the texture of plastic. It is large as Casimir's closed, white hands.

'What is it?'

'Amber. From the Baltic. It was my mother's.'

She touches her fingers against it. One side of the amber is smooth and golden-green, the colour of a pike's scales seen through water. The rest of the piece is blackened and gnarled with a hatchwork of cracks. 'It's beautiful. What happened to it?'

'It was burnt.'

'Yeah, I can see that. How come?'

He shrugs. 'A stove. My mother was cooking duck eggs. It was when I was small, before I remember.' Out of nothing, he thinks of curtains. The smell of coal, the smell of snow. He moves his hand near his forehead, as if batting the images away.

'Was she hurt? Your mother.'

'No one was hurt.'

'Don't you miss her?'

'No.' His heart judders at the lie. 'She left us.'

'Yeah? Join the family. How old were you?'

'Twelve. I went on a journey with my father. She waved goodbye to us when we left. She told me to love my father,

[176]

because she loved him. When we came back home, she was gone. No one saw her go and she took nothing.'

'Why did she leave?'

'I don't know.' All at once the words well up in him. He swallows to force them down, but it is too late. 'To put us both behind her. She should have left a long time before. She should never have married my father.'

From outside comes the sound of an ice-cream van, its mechanical music cut off abruptly, repeated, cut off again. The tune sounds familiar, although Casimir has no name for it. Already the sound of it is distant, streets away.

'Why not?' Alice's voice is soft, careful. Casimir leans back against the wall. Beyond the window, the dark rain sky has merged into early evening.

'My father never deserved her. He is a bad man.'

'So why did she marry him?'

He pauses again. 'I think it is that she loved him.'

Alice looks away. Carefully, she begins to cover the amber with its cloth, wrapping it away. 'So where are they now? Your mum and dad.'

'My father is in Poland. We do not speak. My mother I never saw again. I used to think she died at sea, but I don't know. After she left, I couldn't live with my father. I stayed in youth hostels in Praga, downtown Warsaw. Then on the streets. Then in hostels again. I lived there for some time.' He takes the wrapped amber, holds it in his hands. 'And then it was as if I woke up. And I came here.'

'What was wrong with your father?'

'There were things he did. In the war, and after.'

'Everyone did something in the war.'

Alice moves away from him towards her clothes. Casimir had forgotten her quickness and for a moment he thinks he has said too much, that she is leaving. But she is reaching out a cigarette towards the heater. The filament dulls where the tobacco touches it, flares as Alice lights up, sits back.

For a time they don't talk. He listens to the sound of the depot yards from outside, and the hoot of a river boat. Alice is warm against him, a slight pressure on his heartbeat.

'You're very beautiful.' The words sound clumsy in his

[177]

mouth, in the English which is still alien to him.

She laughs, a ripple going through her, through him.

'No. I'm the girl on the train, Ariel Casimir. That's all. I'm the girl on the train who you never see again.' Over her shoulder, he watches her smile to herself. 'But here I am. Go on, it's your turn. Ask me something.'

He doesn't stop to think. 'What is your real name?'

'Jacqueline Chappell.'

She sucks at the cigarette. It is quiet in the unlit room. Casimir can hear the crackle and wince of tobacco and ash. She shifts against him, getting comfortable.

'The other names are pretend. I used Alice when I went underground. I've got nine National Insurance cards, nine names. All you do is tell Social Security you're a traveller and your parents are travellers. Then when you've got your National Insurance number, you can get everything. The more you have, the easier it is. But my real name is Jacqueline Chappell. Do you believe me?'

'The man at the abandoned station. He called you Blip Girl.'

She picks a strand of tobacco from her teeth and tongue, then laughs. Casimir realizes he has never heard her laughter before today. It is startling. Clear and musical, like her voice when she sings.

'When I was smaller I used to get caught doing stuff. The police called me Blip Girl because wherever I was, I messed up their crime figures. They couldn't lock me up because I was juvenile. They tried to load me off on foster carers. Now I'm older, I don't get caught any more. Not much anyway.'

'What did they arrest you for?'

She shrugs, shoulders thin against his shirt. He reaches around her, stroking her breasts. The smooth warmth of her skin against the roughness of his knuckles, palms, the backs of his hands.

'Nothing bad. Just stealing. Drugs – no needles. Once there was a man who tried to hurt me, so I hurt him back. That's all.' She folds her arms, trapping him against her. 'Foster homes were the worst. Worse than being homeless. Your hands are so big. Giant, like that statue, the marble one. It'd be good, being like you. You must scare people.'

[178]

'How long have you been homeless?'

He feels her breathing change against him. She picks up her polystyrene cup, delicately stubbing out her cigarette in its wet base. 'I can't remember. A long time now. Time goes different when you're on the streets. You get old fast, but then you know that.' She shifts, looking back at him. 'I'm not staying here tonight. I'm going back underground. Do you mind?'

He wants to ask her to stay. He wants her to tell him about the seventeen scars that run from the wings of her shoulder bones to the curve of her hips. Instead he stops himself, shakes his head. 'No.'

'It's safer. I don't like the way he keeps on. He's so – in Camden at nights he was so quiet, it was like he was everywhere. But I do feel safer, underground. Don't you?'

'Yes.'

'Will you come and see me tomorrow?'

'Yes.' She is moving away, picking up clothes, pulling them on. When she is dressed she turns to Casimir. He hasn't moved from the bed. One arm is still loose, where it held her. She comes up and leans over to kiss him, fast and supple, her mouth tasting of food and cigarettes. Then she goes quickly, without saying goodbye.

For some time he sits, thinking. His eyes adjust faster than it becomes dark. Too needy, he thinks. Adams was right after all. I need to know too much; it makes me careless of myself. He remembers the pike under canal ice, white teeth in a green mouth. No one else saw that. Such a beautiful monstrosity.

After an hour the sky is the blue of slate between the half-drawn curtains. Casimir gets up and takes off the work shirt and trousers he has worn for two days and a night, dropping them to the cold linoleum floor.

He gets dressed again mechanically, pulling on a pair of lightweight cotton trousers and a blue shirt bought cheap from the weekday market. His work jacket is hung up against the back of the door and he puts it back on and leaves quietly, pulling the door to behind him. As if someone were still sleeping in the empty room with its thin curtains and half-light.

In the Stamford Street telephone box a female skinhead is arguing about money, leaning forward over the chrome machinery and dial. Casimir waits in the rain, his back to the Bull Ring and its circling traffic. The phone-box door is wedged open with a shopping trolley. In the trolley a small boy is curled up asleep next to an empty fish tank. The woman's voice yells over the sound of cars. She slams the phone down into its cradle and backs out towards Casimir.

'Fucking cunt-fuckers! Go on then, it's your turn. Hope you have better luck with the fucks than I do.'

'Thank you.' Casimir watches the skinhead walk rapidly away towards Southwark, the trolley skewing ahead of her. Then he goes into the box, dials Operator Enquiries and waits, the door easing shut behind him.

'Good evening. Which number do you require?'

'Kentish Town Police Station. London.' He memorizes the number, feeling in his pocket for change, sorting it out on the flat of his hand. Then he hangs up and redials, holding the bust receiver together.

'Kentish Town. How can I help you?' The voice is male, with the same quality of control that Casimir remembers in Phelps's speech. 'Hello?'

It is hard to speak, the words grating in his mouth. Part of him stays detached, disgusted. But he needs the authorities now. Needs their control. 'I need to speak to Phelps.'

'Police Inspector Phelps is in a meeting. Can I help at all?'

'No. I will hold.'

'She may be some time. Can I ask – hang on, she just – just a minute, please.'

The line goes quiet. Casimir looks up at the telephone-box windows. They are crammed with prostitutes' advertising cards: FRESH GIRL, PRIVATE FUNCTIONS, HOLE IN ONE. The line clicks open and he turns away. 'Phelps here. Who is this?'

'Casimir.'

'I'm busy. What do you want?'

'You asked me about homeless people. There is something I didn't tell you.' He closes his eyes. As if the movement could stop him hearing his own voice. 'There is a girl. At nights she sleeps on the Underground. She looks like Rebecca Saville and

Marion Asher. Enough for it to matter. She has been arrested many times as a juvenile, at least once for violence.'

The line goes quiet again. From outside the telephone comes a rattling sound. Casimir opens his eyes in time to see the skinhead with the trolley go running past, back towards the Bull Ring.

'I made a mistake.'

'Yes, you did. How long have you known about this?'

He thinks back, trying to ignore the checked anger in the policewoman's voice. 'A week.'

'A week. What you're saying is, you knew about this before Asher was killed. She must be pretty, your Underground girl, if she looks like Saville and Asher. A week. I hope it was good, because it may have cost a life. I hope you can live with that.'

'Nothing was clear a week ago.'

'If it turns out this girl's the killer they should put you away. Accessory to murder and withholding evidence. What about sex with a minor, can I do you for that? Now listen. I want you to tell me her name and describe to me exactly where she sleeps.'

He leans back, the root of his skull against the glass. 'Jacqueline Chappell. I don't know if it's her real name. Sometimes she is called Alice, or Jack Union. She has lots of names. She sleeps in an underground storeroom at South Kentish Town Tube station.'

'There is no South Kentish Town. Are you trying to –'

'There is. It was closed down eighty years ago. It's on Kentish Town Road, under a shop called Cash Converters –'

'All right. I know it, yes. Red-tiled building, just like Camden station. Christ, it's minutes away.' The policewoman sounds disgusted. As if she can smell the killings, like smog pollution. 'OK. Right. I'm going to call Northern Line Management, for maps and access. As soon as they get to me, I'm going down to find Jacqueline Chappell, or whatever her name is. I want you there too, in case we need to identify her. Inside half an hour, please. Is that all quite clear?'

'Yes.'

As he puts the phone back in its cradle the mouthpiece falls off, trailing wires. The telephone's liquid crystal display goes

[181]

dead. Casimir steps out of the box, looks left and right. The wet-black stone façade of Waterloo station looms up over the Bull Ring. He puts his head down and begins to run.

The sky over South Kentish Town is grey-orange, London's last evening light reflected up against the rain clouds. Casimir is still half a mile away from the abandoned station when he hears the sirens. An ambulance speeds past him northwards from Camden, its headlights flashing. He starts after it, breaking into a run again.

In front of Al Araf Saunas the pavement is crowded with police and London Transport officials. Casimir stands in the wet street, hands open by his sides, watching the mass of movement and urgent, quiet conversation.

'Mister Kazimierski?'

He looks round into the glare of a flashlight. Beside him is a policeman, his face slack and characterless under the low brim of his hat. Casimir raises one hand to shield his eyes.

'Can you come this way, please.'

The man's quick monotone turns the question into an order. Casimir follows him through the crowd towards the back of the building. Phelps is standing in the open yard entrance, talking to a small black woman, their heads bowed together. From inside the corrugated-metal wall comes the whine and growl of an electric screwdriver. Both women look up as Casimir reaches them.

'You're late.'

'You've found her.'

Phelps shakes her head, frowning, still watching Casimir. 'No. We've been through the whole complex with keys to every room, excavation plans, floor-plans and the lighting turned on. There were three juvenile males down there and a middle-aged homeless couple. None of them looks remotely like Rebecca Saville.'

'She knows the Underground too well. She is here.'

'No. But fortunately for you, it seems she was.' Phelps looks down, sheltering her notebook under its plastic cover. 'Two of the boys saw her tonight. All three maintain they don't know her name, but they described her all right. They also say that she sold them drugs, including a syringe of blue liquid we found in their room. Pentobarbitone. It's a tranquilliser used to put down mad cows. The ambulance crew tell me it's got value as a street drug.'

She glances back up at Casimir, eyes wide and staring. Aggressive. Looks down. 'The older male fell running down a flight of stairs. He's getting medical treatment now, but I'll be talking to him soon. The woman won't say anything, not unless you count "Get off me, I'm the fucking First Lady". This is Margaret Stone, by the way. From Northern Line Management.'

'I'm sorry you've become so involved, Assistant Casimir.'

'Yes.' The manager's hand is cool and dry, even in the rain. He watches her, remembering her voice clearly on the control-room telephone. Low-pitched, very calm. *It is about Rebecca Saville. It is unfortunate.* 'What are you going to do now?'

'The station will be sealed.' She speaks up over the sound of hammering from inside the yard fence, turning away from him as she finishes. Her profile is sharp, the nose aquiline and Asian. 'I have to go. Inspector, I'll need an image of the girl for the posters. A clear photograph of Asher or Saville would help.'

Casimir steps forward. 'What if Alice is still down there?' He is nearly twice the height of the Line Manager. She doesn't look round. Phelps glances up at him and away.

'We've looked. She's not. I'm afraid all I've got here is a photocopied shot of Marion Asher. PC Hill, there's a black folder under the passenger seat in the van, can you get it, please? Fast.'

'Yes, m'm.' The policeman beside Casimir turns away, pushing through towards Castle Road.

Casimir looks round. Through the open corrugated-iron door he can see the entrance to the abandoned station. Two workers in London Transport overalls are bolting a new door into place. Its blue-grey metal surface shines with rain. The wooden door lies off to one side on the decomposing piles of carpet, split almost in two. As Casimir watches, the taller worker leans a two-handed machine against the door. It whines, high-pitched, driving a heavy bolt into the old brick.

He turns back. Phelps and the Line Manager are going through a folder, the policeman a gaunt black figure behind them. Margaret Stone stands back, holding a sheet of photocopied paper.

'Will that do? I can send on a better copy later.' Phelps is handing the folder back to the policeman.

'It's a start.' The Line Manager looks down at the photograph. Casimir comes up beside her, standing close. It is the picture of Marion Asher and the second girl. Leaning forward, laughter caught and frozen. Stone's measured voice is almost inaudible. 'It is a cruel face.'

'I'm sorry?'

The Line Manager looks up at Phelps, unsmiling. 'This will do, thank you. I must go now. Goodbye, Inspector. Assistant.' She walks away towards the alley, small and hunched against the drizzle.

Casimir turns back to Phelps. 'The girl, Alice. She knows the Underground very well. Better than us. There are places she knows which we may not even have mapped –'

'Thank you for your concern, Mister Casimir. That's why I sent twenty-five officers down to look for her. She's not there, and she's not getting back down there either.'

The policewoman looks away towards the crowd, then down at her watch. 'I'd like you to leave now, sir. One of my men will drive you back to your lodging house. If and when I need you again, I'll be in touch. Until then try to live a normal life, yes?'

The police car smells of pine freshener and urine. Casimir makes himself sit back, knees against the side-door and the partition in front. There is no door handle, no window button. He looks out at the city as it goes past, smooth and quick and bright. Rain runs sideways against the car window. As if I am travelling upwards, he thinks. Away from the Underground and Alice. He wonders what he is travelling towards.

He thinks of her laughter, breathless, rippling through her into him. The smell of her wet hair, which is sweet, like her sweat.

[184]

The car stops outside the take-away on Lower Marsh. The side door clicks open. One of the policemen in the front seats looks round at Casimir.

'All right? Take a bit of friendly advice, stay in tonight, watch the telly. You won't die of boredom. There's *Blind Date*, you'll like that. Right, off you go.'

Casimir gets out of the car and goes up the lodgers' stairs without looking back. The stairwell bulb is still out and he stands outside his door, gritting his teeth against the dark, feeling for the keyhole, the key. He unlocks the door and reaches inside, batting blindly for the light switch.

The room jumps into visibility, stark in the bare electric illumination. Casimir breathes once, twice, eyes closed. There is a noise from the hallway outside, voices of other lodgers going past and down. One measured, the second roaring drunk. Female. Briefly Casimir thinks of the dog woman and his legs ache suddenly, the body remembering its hurt.

He opens his eyes. On the mussed blankets of the bed is a plate of food, stale white toast and cold fried chicken left unfinished. Casimir walks to the window and opens it, letting in air and the smell of rain. A car goes past up Spur Road, light running along its blue lamé. On the far side of the road someone is putting up posters in the rain, white rectangles trailing away from a single dark figure. Its pale face turns upwards and away.

Casimir goes to the bed, sits down, leans back. After a few minutes he props himself up on one elbow and starts to eat methodically, forcing the oily meat and dry bread down. The newspaper lies crumpled against the foot of the bed and he picks it up and reads, concentrating on the food and his own simple hunger. The headlines, distracting and irrelevant: BLOW HOLE SUICIDE. WEB BOMB FACTORY.

'Mister Casimir?'

He stands up, walks the three steps to the door and unlocks it. Mrs Navratil is waiting in the hall. Her face looks pinched and drawn in the bad light.

'You're becoming rather popular. There was another letter for you.'

'Where is it?'

'I have it. Come up.'

Casimir follows the landlady upstairs. Blue television light fills the doorway of her flat. He steps through. The landlady is bent over beside a tasselled red lampshade. It colours her face like a light bulb seen through skin.

'It came this evening. You haven't shaved.'

'I have been busy.'

'You also smell. You must take better care of yourself. Living on restaurant premises.'

In the middle of the far wall is a massive flat-screened television. A news programme is showing with the sound turned down low, the reader staring out, unsmiling. Casimir thinks of fish in tanks, mouthing oxygen. Video cases are stacked around the television. One lies empty in front of the screen. Dully, Casimir realizes that Navratil is watching her newsreader on video.

The landlady straightens. 'Here it is.' She is holding out a brown envelope. 'Maybe it's from the police. What did they want with you?'

Casimir takes the letter. His address and first name are written in thick pencilled capitals.

'I was helping them with their enquiries.' He holds the letter sideways, to the light. Something shifts inside, tiny and papery. There are stamps above the address but no postmark. 'Who brought this?'

'A delivery man.'

'What did he look like?'

'Fat. Don't bring the police here again, Mister Casimir.'

Navratil turns away towards the television. As Casimir leaves he looks back once. The landlady is still standing, her eyes on the newsreader. Her hands clasped in front of her.

Casimir goes into his own room, locking the door behind him. He opens the letter quickly, not letting himself stop to think. Inside is a folded sheet of white paper. As Casimir unfolds it, a tiny white ball rolls out. He catches it as it begins to fall.

It is a scrawled-up nub of paper, flecked and seamed with red, no larger than a bus ticket bunched up in a pocket. It is almost too small for Casimir's fingers to unpick and he goes over to the bed and sits down, leaning forward, straightening the paper out between his large, blue-white hands. When he has it done he remains bent forward, trying to understand the one line of red text: GET AWAY WITH AN AWAY DAY!

The paper is smooth with magazine ink, torn on three sides, discoloured with age. Under the writing is the edge of a picture, a faded blue line of what could be sky, a fluff of white cloud. Casimir shakes his head. The fragment of page looks to him like an advertisement or article headline. Now nothing is legible except the six words. Like an order, or a warning: GET AWAY.

Casimir drops the paper. Beside him is the white sheet, still folded. He unfolds it on his lap. His throat clicks as he reads, the muscles opening and closing, heart lurching.

HAVE YOU SEEN THIS CHILD?

Jacqueline Messenger left her foster carer in Tower Hamlets five years ago. Investigations by her carer suggest that Jacqueline has been living homeless in the London area since 1990. Jacqueline Messenger is a tall child with fine features and blue eyes. Anyone with information on Jacqueline Messenger can contact the foster carer at:

Messenger PO Box 191, WC1 8QX.

Under the headline is a black-and-white photograph of a girl. Unsmiling, staring at the camera. To Casimir she looks ten or eleven. Her hair surrounds her face, wildly tangled. The light coming through the hair makes it bright as a corona. In contrast the face is darkened, the gaze unclear in silhouette. He sees that Alice's face has changed as it has grown. It would be hard to recognize her from this child's face. Hard to be sure of what she would grow into.

He stops reading. Walks to the window. Looks out.

Along Spur Road the posters shine, a row of white steps leading up towards the terminus. The poster hanger is gone now, but Casimir remembers him. He has seen him before. A man in black jeans and T-shirt, his face large but smooth, heavy-set and muscular. Not loosely fat. Big in the bone.

As Casimir's eyes adjust he can make out the headlines on

the distant posters. The shape of the words, like those on the page behind him.

The sense of *déjà vu* is sudden and dizzying. Casimir stands still, waiting for it to pass. When it doesn't he leans his arms on the windowsill, head down.

He tries to remember how many times he has seen the poster hanger. He is present in Casimir's memory in the same way Alice once was; as a figure seen many times, a face in the Underground crowds. He remembers him on a platform crowded with commuters, sticking papers up by the telephones, moving away with an odd fluidity. In a side-tunnel, the nails of one hand broken down past the quicks. An Underground oddity; another Rose. Flashes of other memories: hallways, stairwells, back streets. The take-away – he has seen the man inside the lodging house. A figure alone at its corner table, blending into the background, casting the faintest of shadows. As if he can be anywhere.

He steps back from the window. Outside the rain has stopped and a breeze is picking up. The net curtains belly inwards, hollow and white.

What have I done? In his thoughts the question has no rising intonation. It is hardly a question at all, more a statement of guilt.

'What have I done.'

Casimir's whisper echoes in the bare room. A rustle of sound along the unpapered walls.

His eyes flicker, staring at nothing, hands opening and closing at his sides. He leaves without closing the door, the room behind him remaining in light, the bulb swung by the wind through the open window.

Astrakhan

Along the Volga is where the fish markets are. Really they're just boats but each one is big and square as Gliwice town hall, with white domes and colonnades. Two steps behind my father, I look out of the portholes and see the kebab sellers pulling kindling off the waterfront birch trees, crows belching in the branches above them. Over the market racket I can hear singing. It comes from the mosques on the far river bank. The song shakes over the water. Like heat.

This is Astrakhan. It smells of fish, spilled petrol and broken fruit. The smell is so strong that I feel drunk sick with it for a day. We've been here for two days now, looking for the Iranian.

The fish markets: I keep my lips shut against the flies. We walk together down slick gangplanks and again down unlit steps between decks. Together we go between stalls where salt sprats are weighed in kilos and sturgeon is smoked and cut, broad as logs. Down between rooms where poachers' golden caviare is measured out in small jars. Always down and always together. But we are not together. It's five days since I learned to read my father's eyes.

The second deck has more noise, less light. There are live eels in wooden drawers. Trestles of carp, their gills still working in the hot air. More kinds of fish that I've never seen in Poland. More fish than I've ever seen, so that I'm hungry but too sick to eat with the smell of them.

We are looking for the Iranian. Because there are other things bought and sold on the riverboats, not just fish. We are here for the other things. We walk together, but my father is always two steps ahead. He is scared of me now. When he asks me what's wrong, I say it's nothing. In five days this is what I've said to him: It's nothing. Nothing else. At night when he drinks Russian spirit I can read his eyes.

July, the month of holidays. Tonight we leave for Russia, and I
learn my dad's business. All afternoon he's in the guest room,
watching the football with Slawek and Chorzelski. When he's
home this is where he sits, waiting for the next trip. He drinks
Scotch or hunters' herb vodka, arms flat out on the armchair's
rests, watching daytime TV or nothing at all. Once I was getting ready for school and I went in there and he was asleep
with a blanket on him. I never watched him sleeping before.
He looked surprised. I breathed soft.

With Slawek and Chorzelski he doesn't bring out the
Scotch, though. They drink Lech beer still warm from the corner shop shelves, crackling the empty cans. We can hear them
through the wall as we pack, my mother choosing the clothes,
me getting them, she folding them into the soft plastic suitcase
with the scuffed white corners. Warm clothes for the north,
light for the south. Dad is the loudest, barking curses as the TV
whines and shouts.

If there's any beer left, my mother will pour it on the balcony flower-pots. It kills the slugs.

I can't think of Astrakhan. When I imagine leaving I go
west, not east. Astrakhan is the wrong way. Karol says Russian
girls are beautiful at fourteen but old at eighteen. Piotr says
there will be an eclipse and not to look at it or I'll go blind. I've
seen eclipses before, they're not so great. Dad says that in
Astrakhan you can buy ten dollars for a dollar. I listen to them
and think of Terespol. Sunlight in Russia, moving across coun-
tries towards me.

'What does it feel like?'

'What does what?'

'When you leave Poland. Do you feel anything?'

She looks up from the case, easy and smiling. 'Nothing!
Except in your mind. Why, what did you think?'

I go and sit on the bed beside her, looking at my hands. 'I
had this dream. Me and Dad were walking into Russia. When I
stepped across and my foot touched the ground, it was like
pins and needles going up my leg, into my chest. Then I woke

up, and I still had the pins and needles in my leg.'

She doesn't take my hand. I know she's still smiling. From outside comes the sound of a klaxon from the steel factories, two long hoots with space between them. We sit side by side, hands in laps.

'I tried to tell him no, but he wanted you to go so much and I got so tired in the end –'

'No, I want to.'

Now I look up at her, to show I really do. At the corners of my mother's eyes are fans of lines from smiling or crying. There are three lines by the left eye, four by the right. I'd like to touch them but I can't do that.

'Can we play a game when we've finished?'

'That'd be fine. What do you want to play?'

'Cards. Pan. Is there any soup?'

'There's borsht and pasties. We can play in the kitchen.'

We shut the case and lock it and go into the kitchen. It's darker on this side of the flat but we're further from the guest room. With the window open you can hardly hear Dad at all, only the ordinary sounds from outside, voices calling voices home. We drink the soup out of teacups and eat the hot pasties off the saucers.

After I've won we clear away together. There's no soap but the water's hot today. The dishes clunk and clank in the water bowl.

'It'll be your birthday when you get back. When your grandfather was thirteen, he grew twenty centimetres in a year. Twenty! And you'll be tall as him. Have you thought about presents?'

'I don't know. You choose for me.'

'No, I'll just pick something horrible. You're big enough to make up your own mind. You can tell me and then forget. I'll keep it secret for you.' Mum talks quietly, not looking up from her hands as she scrubs. 'Do you still keep lists of secrets, Ariel?'

'No.'

I wait for her to say something else but she doesn't, not yet. I'm surprised at her for remembering. It was a long time ago, when we talked about secrets and lists. We were washing potatoes then and her arms were around me. I felt as if I had four hands.

She lifts out the last cup, white with gold patterns. Weighs it in her fingers, the water running off it. Sets it down.

'Ariel, listen to me. Whatever happens in Russia, remember that I love your father. Will you do that?'

I'm standing still, the cloth in my hands. She looks round at me, staring in the kitchen's bad light. 'Why do you love him?'

My mother turns right round and catches hold of my hands. 'Because he loves me. He has taken care of us both. There is good in you that comes from him. Will you remember that for me?'

'Yes.'

'Thank you.' She lets go of my hands, the light going out of her eyes or back into them.

When we leave that night she says nothing to me. She's packing plastic bags of food into the back of the car and I look down and she's still wearing her house slippers. They're light blue, thin on the grass-cracked concrete. I kiss her and she kisses me back and then I get into the car, pressed in with the bags of food. I look out of the rear window to wave but she's already walking to the flats, head bent forward, not turning to watch as we drive away.

We drive north-east, away from home. The evenings are long in July. Outside the car is still lighter than inside. I can see strip fields, each one just a couple of tractor-widths. Rusting combine harvesters, six in a field, still like cows. Birch forest in the distance, whiter than the horizon.

I haven't been alone with Dad since I was small. It isn't the same as it was then. We sit quiet like strangers on trains, until Gliwice is way behind us. Then he turns his head. Not really looking away from the highway, just glancing back quick. I can see his eyes when he talks.

'The roads are clear. We'll be at the border in five hours. What food did we get, then?'

The plastic bags are full of newspaper parcels. Grease-stained, folded tight. I open them carefully, thinking of my mother's hands wrapping them. The highway lights come every few seconds and I hold the parcels up to the side-window. 'Cake. Poppy-seed cake. Sandwiches. I can't see what. Cabbage pasties. And a cooked sausage. And water.'

'What kind of sausage?'

I lift the parcel to my face, smelling the garlic in the warm grease. 'Silesian.'

'Hah! Good.'

'Dad, can I sit in the front?'

'No.'

'I'm old enough. I'm twelve. The law says when I'm twelve I can sit in the front.'

'Yeah, well the law in this car says you sit in the back.'

I close my mouth with the teeth together. Look out. The highway lights have gone here, and Dad swears in the sudden darkness. There are pines close up to the roadside. They flicker past like bicycle spokes. The bitter smell of a rubbish dump blows in through the open window and is gone.

'People won't see you so much back there. OK? What they don't see they don't ask about. And the less they ask, the better for us. Still, there's quiet roads round Astrakhan, nothing to crash into for three thousand kilometres. I could teach you to drive.'

'Really?'

'Sure, why not? It's about time. Anyway, you're supposed to be learning the business.'

'Great! Great, Dad. Thanks.'

East and north-east, past the fat chimneys and long hills of Silesia, on towards Czestochowa. One time Piotr came here to see the Black Madonna with his school and three boys fainted. Now we've got no time to stop. It's hours to Terespol, where Uncle Jan waits in the border-control rooms.

I close my eyes. In the dark I can see my mother alone, walking up ten floors to our flat. The *scuff* of her house slippers on the unlit flights. The creak of the bed as she lies back down.

East of Warsaw the land gets flatter and there are fewer houses. The long ploughed fields go off into the dark, rising or falling away only a little, so the horizon is way off and out of sight anyway, there being so few house lights to mark off the distance. When we come into Terespol it's bright, though. There are floodlights like in a football stadium, high up over the train yards and border roads.

Dad parks by the railway station. There are guards everywhere on the platforms and in the waiting rooms. The trains are painted red and they let off clouds of steam. The smell of burning coal is strong on them, dirty and sweet. It makes me think of home, more than anything I could see or hear.

My father stands by the car, stretching his arms and legs. 'Aargh! That wasn't so bad, was it? Russia tomorrow. When was the last time you saw your uncle?'

'Years ago. I was little.'

'Yeah. Well, you're not so little now. Keep your mouth shut with him. I'm hungry. Get us something, will you?'

We eat two parcels of chopped-egg sandwiches and wash them down with water. Then we go into a station office and Dad asks for Jan. The office man says he's on the trains. We wait ten minutes for my uncle and then he comes out and we drive back to his house. I notice how big it is, his house. Larger than our flat. There's three of us and only one of him.

'Well. You're making good time, Michal. How are you, Casimir, are you well?'

'I'm fine.'

'Fine. Do you drink now?'

'Yes.'

'Then that's fine too.'

He takes off his green-and-gold hat, puts it on the kitchen table. There are four empty vodka bottles lined up beside the back door and Jan brings out a fresh bottle and pours three glasses. With his hat on, my uncle looked the same as years ago. Now I see his hair is gone, all except a white stubble.

'Cheers.'

'Cheers!'

We knock back the vodka. It's cold and thick from the freezer, and I feel it burn my throat and the back of my nose. I swallow fast, so I don't start coughing. My dad sighs and sits down, legs sprawled out under the table.

'Damn, that's good! And next trip'll be even better. I'll only have half the driving to do then. Twice as much to drink. Casimir's learning to drive, did he tell you?'

'No. Big man, eh? When did you start?'

'Not yet. Dad's going to teach me. In Astrakhan.'

My uncle leans forward, pouring again. Two shots, for Dad and himself. I hold hard on to my empty glass. 'Good. Now, there's benzene to shift into the car. Eight cans. Casimir can give me a hand. You'll be wanting to sleep, Michal. You're clear to go across at four.'

Dad looks at his watch. It's already past midnight. 'Casimir, you help your uncle, eh?'

'Yes.'

They both stand at the same time. I didn't know they were going to do that. They even stand up the same way, pushing themselves with their hands on the table, heads down. Brothers. I thought Dad was older, but he looks younger, with his black hair and shaved white skin. His forehead slants out more and his nose is straight; Jan's is smaller and broken to one side. My dad's cheekbones are long, like the face of a dog. They're not really that long but his face feels sharp to look at, like a dog's. If he laughed you'd even see his tongue.

He goes back into the guest room. Through the open door I watch him fall asleep in a hard chair with the TV on. Me and Jan bring the benzene up from his cellar and pack it into the boot of the Polonez. There are blankets too, in case we have to sleep in the car. I stick them under the back seats while Jan checks the water and oil. The car's insides smell of garlic and old cigarettes.

My uncle works with his head down, not talking. He moves like an old man, trudging round the car, then back into the house, not changing his work boots at the door. I follow him down the corridor into the kitchen. He's washing his hands at the sink, hot water steaming as he scrubs. When he's finished I wash my own hands while he gets the vodka out again.

'You want a nightcap?'

'Sure. Thanks.' I sit down at the chipped pink Formica table. We drink without talking for a while. There's a click every time my uncle swallows. It sounds like small bones breaking. I was eight last time I was here. My bones are bigger inside me.

'Your mother, Anna. Is she well?'

I shrug. The vodka settles inside me. Warm in my gut, light in my head. 'She's OK. She forgets things.'

'Your mother's got enough to forget.'

'Like what?'

My own voice comes out high with nerves. I sound like a child asking a question, whining at its parents. But I'm not a child any more. I'm taller than my uncle, taller than my father. The outside of my glass is white with frost. Jan sits back, hands together around his own shot. It must be cold against his palms.

'Nothing you need to know. Ask your mother if you want. She might tell you. If she can remember.'

'I'm asking you.'

He looks up at me. The skin pulls back from his eyes, up into the lines of his forehead. 'What did you say?'

'I said I'm asking you.'

My voice splits on the second word, broken between high and low. Jan looks at his glass. He could be smiling but it's hard to tell. His mouth stays the same, pulled down at the ends. From next door comes the chatter of the television. Snatches of folk music, Russian voices.

'You should respect your elders, Casimir. You know why? Because they know more than you. Knowing things is what puts the grey in their hair. You want grey in your hair, Casimir?'

'Just tell me.'

Jan snaps his head up. His face has changed. It has come alive, staring and smiling. I see he grins like my father, the lips pulled back against the teeth.

'If you like I can tell you all kinds of things. Fuck with me I'll fuck you up, sonny. You just sit there and keep quiet. Drink your big man's drink and then get some sleep. You're leaving in a couple of hours anyway. And where you're going, you'll need the rest.'

My uncle stands up. I sit watching as he clears the bottle and glasses away, rinsing them under the kitchen tap. I close my fists so the nails rest on the fat of my palms, trying to hold

[196]

the anger inside me. I feel it escape. It trickles out between my fingers, like alcohol.

'I know she's Jewish.' He doesn't answer. My head feels tight and hot. 'I know what happened to Jews in the war. Auschwitz and Sobibor. I learned it in school. It wasn't so different from the Poles. They died too.'

'Jesus Christ.' My uncle talks with his back to me, putting the glasses down hard on the draining board. Water trickles out of them down the grooved wood. First his voice is low, then loud. 'You know where she's from?'

'Kielce.'

'Kielce. Your mother and father and me, we all grew up there. Different schools, same street. Your mother's family were Jews. Jews by blood, not religion. You know what happened in Kielce?'

He turns round. The vodka bottle is still in his hands. I shake my head. The table is between us.

'You wouldn't believe how many Yids there were in Poland then. It was part of everything. Quiet Fridays, I remember that. Men who mended shoes. I never saw real Polish men mending shoes like that. I knew Jews, everybody did. I thought the same about them as everyone; they were different from us. I think they thought the same.

'I was fourteen when the Germans came. Michal was a bit older. There must've been twenty thousand Jews in our town. And when the Germans left there were two. An old man and a little one-eyed girl. They were the last. But that was normal. That's not what I'm going to tell you. Since you've asked.'

He unscrews the top and swigs from the bottle, like a drunk. Staring at me over the bottle's neck. I sit ready. If he comes for me I'll hurt him.

'So the Germans left, and there were all the empty Jewish houses. Nice sideboards, nice wallpaper. People were shocked, of course, but we had our own dead to bury. We got on with life, only with new wallpaper. And then the camps were emptied. A hundred and fifty of our Jews came through alive.'

When he talks, my uncle's voice drags. It sounds as if part of him has died. 'I was walking with Michal and our mother.

We were going to meet father at the repair shop. There was a thin woman standing in the street. You could see the light through her clothes. We came up close and she started to smile at my mother. Her hand was tight on my arm, and it started to shake before she spoke, I don't know if it was anger or fear. She said, "What? Are you still alive? We thought that Hitler had killed all of you." My mother said that. She died six months later, when the Russians were settling in. The woman could have been from our street before the war, but I didn't recognize her. She looked like no one I'd ever seen. Like nothing.'

From somewhere in the house comes the hiss of TV white noise, left on after the last programme. My uncle goes on talking in his hard, slurred voice. My head is still tight but loose, too, thoughts floating in my packed skull.

'So there were the Jews. And then there was your mother. They were always in love, Michal and her. Always together, from when they were very small. Michal believed what our mother believed – that it was better if the Jews had never come to Poland. But Jews and Anna were not the same for him. He was stupid like that, your father – is stupid, I should say. But not as stupid as your mother. She should never have married him.'

'He hid her. In the war, Dad hid her. Didn't he?'

I sound proud of him. My uncle laughs and chokes. Wipes the vodka off his mouth.

'Where? Some people did, but not our mother. No, Anna went to the camps. Buchenwald. Her whole family died there. She was still beautiful when she came back. She didn't talk any more or move much, but there she was all the same. And Michal took her away. He didn't leave a note. In the west they were giving land away, driving out the Germans, but we didn't know he'd gone there for years. He was twenty-two.'

The chair grates back as I stand up. Jan looks up at me, then away. I'm so glad he has to look up at me.

'Is that it? That's nothing. You're so old, Jan, old and –'

'No, that isn't it. Sit down, big man. I haven't finished with you yet.'

I go on standing. Jan chuckles, down in his throat. His voice goes on and on. I want to tell him to stop. It's too late now.

'You are born out of hate, boy. That's what I'm telling you. You're a child of hate. I was going to tell you about the other Jews. Because in the end, given the choice of Jews or wallpaper, people chose wallpaper. Stories started going round – the Jews were killing children, the Jews were making matzo bread with Polish blood. Crazy stories. A boy went missing – he turned up in the next village months later, but it was too late by then. It was July, the holidays, and the heat was getting up. Most of the Yids were living in one house on Planty Avenue. I came cycling down there one day and there was fighting going on. I could hear chanting, *Beat the Jews, Kill the Bloodsuckers*.

'Michal was there. He was hurting them, like the rest. There was blood on him, but not his own. He was like a dog. I couldn't get him away. *Foreigners!* he kept saying, *Bloody foreigners!* There was one man killed holding on to a tree, and I remember a woman too, with blood around her. She was pregnant. I don't know if she was dead. Forty-two of them died, though. She probably was dead, don't you think? The Jews almost all left Poland after that, the ones who were left. All except Anna.

'You see how it is now? Your father hated the Jews, and married a Jew. I think he got it from our mother. Myself, I always thought he hated Anna too. Hated loving her. And now there's you. I wonder if he hates you too.'

Everything goes quiet. We watch each other across the room. Jan has the bottle clutched against his chest. My legs are shaking badly, rattling against the table. I make myself keep on standing.

'You're lying. We would have learned it in school. If that had happened I would know.'

'No. Why would they teach it? No one wants to remember Kielce. If they can, they forget. As if it never happened. What else is forgetting for?'

'You're lying about my dad.' My eyes are hot. I can't tell if I'm crying until Jan starts to smile again.

'You know I'm not.' He leans towards me. 'Because you know him well enough. Don't you? By the time you get back from Astrakhan, you'll know all about him, believe me. Just wait.'

'My mother loves him.'

Jan backs away. He looks bored with me now. 'So try not to fall in love, eh? Your mother was smart, before the war. Not now, though. I can't stand looking at her. She's like a shadow. And now I'm going to get an hour's sleep. You want to sit here and drink, you do that. Good night, nephew.'

I sit alone at the kitchen table. The bottle is there but I don't drink. Sometimes I hear the TV and sometimes not. Once I look round, through the angle of open doors, into the guest room.

My father sits in there with his back to me. Wide shoulders and big head, very still. Beyond him is the TV, its white square and the white noise coming out of it like a sigh: *Haaaah*. I look at my father sleeping for as long as I can. Then it's four o'clock and time to go and I look away.

'Is there any more food?'

'No.'

'Water?'

'No.'

'*Cholera*. I can't stand buying from these cheating Russians. Their faces when they make money off us, I can't stand that. Not that it's real money.'

He laughs without turning. I don't understand why he laughs. I watch the back of his head as he drives. The point of the skull under the thick black hair. Russia goes by around us, its birch stands and waterlands. Silver and black, vertical and horizontal.

'Having dollars here, Casimir, it's like being in a fairy tale. In Poland we're ordinary people, but here – Hey, you could buy a woman. You want to? God knows, you're big enough. In Astrakhan, you can buy a beautiful woman for nothing. The price of that Silesian sausage. Don't let me stop you either. Don't worry about your dad, eh? Casimir?'

There's a pipeline by the roadside, sometimes close and sometimes further away. Its stilts and bridges run down vil-

lage main streets and around town halls. I don't know what
it's for, gas or oil. Yesterday I would have asked my father, but
not today. There are so many questions I want to ask him and
will not ask. I don't want to hear his answers.

'Casimir? You all right back there? What's wrong?'

'Nothing.'

'You've been quiet as the dead since we crossed the border.
What is it, are you scared of Russia?'

A flock of birds is ahead and above us, falling slowly
behind. I crane back and see they're white geese, a big V of
them over the villages and factories. The village houses are
cheap wood, white birch and wet black boards. Nothing
strong in them except the heavy, sloped roofs. Every town has
a statue of Lenin painted silver, and all the statues point north.
Like a warning: *Go back*. The pipeline goes on and on beside
us, south-east towards Astrakhan.

'Jesus, you're not feeling sick, are you? That's all I need.
Eh?'

'Nothing is wrong.'

I look past my father's head. The sun is out. It's the colour of
chalk. There are flax fields all around us now, sloping away to
flat horizons. I turn in my seat, looking out. There are no
houses, no hills, no trees, only the flax flowers. A whole landscape blue as irises. My father's head black at the centre of it all.

We come towards Astrakhan at night. It's warm in the dark,
the way Gliwice is only in summer and the first long days of
autumn. For a day there's nothing outside us except rolling
dunes of earth, like a seabed. No trees except along the steep
banks of rivers. I watch the rivers coming, miles away.

The back of the car is full of maps, old books of them with
worn-out covers. I learn all the republics and states from the
Caspian Sea to China: Turkmenistan, Afghanistan. For ten
hours I try and work out if the USSR is bigger than the surface of the moon. Sometimes when I look out there are animals in the dark. I recognize flocks of sheep and small,
muscled horses. There are also tiny deer, no bigger than
horned yellow dogs. Once I wake from sleeping and there

are three camels sitting in the dunes. When I look back to see them again they are already out of sight. I don't know if they were real now.

On the outskirts we stop to piss by the roadside. I pick up handfuls of sandy dirt. Back in the car, I see my fingers are stained pink with its colour.

My father's employer is Iranian. We drive to his office on Kalinina Street but the shop front is locked and empty, grey boxes piled against grey windows. There's no sign to say where the Iranian has gone. My father stands in the street and curses the Iranian, the Russians and their rotting country. Then we get back in the car and drive on to the Hotel Lotos over the city's rivers and tributaries and canals. There's a tourist shop in the hotel lobby and my father buys forty bottles of Löwenbräu. In our room he begins to drink, steadily and in silence, his face full of anger.

Astrakhan is a city of water. The horns of riverboats carry a long way at night. The sound drifts into the hotel room with the mosquitoes. I lie awake listening, ten feet from my father.

It isn't easy to find the Iranian. My father's Russian is good, but no one talks to us. For two and a half days we search, not speaking. When my father looks at me now his pupils are tight with guilt and fear. There is no hate, though. Jan was wrong about that. I walk a few steps behind him, so that I don't have to see his face.

Old women bend down in the streets, splashing dirty water over their boots, washing away the dirt. Everything leans or bends here. There are avenues of ash trees, knotted together above the oil trucks and private cars. Houses which sag down into the mud, the wood of them carved and patterned like icing on wedding cakes. Some are grand like Piotr's house at home, with iron balconies hanging crooked from corners and under French windows. Their metalwork is the green of river water under ice. It must be cold here in winter. You can see it in the buildings.

On the third morning we go to the Volga fish markets. Across the water are golden stands of horsetail, and beyond them, the mosques. There are men singing in the mosques, and the sound of them shakes over the water, like heat. We walk between the stalls and decks, looking for the Iranian. It's five days now since I've spoken to my father.

'Hey! Look at this, look at this. You see this? Fresh sevruga! Try. You'll love it. You want it? Try. You want half a kilo? How much you want?'

'We're looking for someone.'

'A friend? Or business? Where you from?'

'Poland. We're looking for the Iranian.'

'Then why are you wasting my time? You want fish you come to me, you want Iranians, go to Iran. *Bojemoi!* Crazy Poles.'

'I can pay.'

'Listen, I have good Russian sevruga, you see? Fresh Russian sevruga from the bellies of the most beautiful Russian lady sturgeon. What about the young man, now? Maybe he wants to try. He'll like it, I can tell from his face.'

'I can pay in dollars.'

'Is that so. How much?'

'Just tell me where he is.'

When my father speaks Russian he sounds like the Gliwice Militia men, who never smile. I stand behind him, trying to understand them both. The stall-holder spits when he talks and there are cold-sores on his bottom lip. The Russian is not clear like in school. Here it is wet, blistered, thick on the man's tongue.

He leans forward for the money. Under him shine big jars of caviare, tarry black or clouded grey or green, which are the cheap eggs of river carp. I listen hard, catching what I can.

'Thank you. Well then. Go down.'

'Down? I pay you for directions, I want to know which deck and –'

'Just go down, Pole. As far as you can go.' When the stall-holder grins, the moustache pulls back over his lips. His mouth is cracked and red, like the crust of cooked meat. 'The steps are steep down there. Watch your heads.'

At the bottom of the last stairs we come to a long room. There is no door, just a thin man at a table, writing in a fat book. He doesn't look up. His skin is dark. Until Astrakhan, I'd never seen people with dark skin. Only Gypsies. There is no light except on his table.

I wipe my hands on the backs of my trousers. Here there's always dirt on me, I can feel it in my sweat. All day the mosquitoes feed off sturgeon and at night I hear their whine in our cheap hotel room and I sit up in the warm dark, reach out and kill the mosquitoes between my hands. Their blood smells of caviare. Now I wipe my hands and stand waiting.

My father coughs, steps forward. From somewhere in the long room comes the crackle of a cigarette and its glow, away from the table's light. '*Salaam aleicum.*'

'*Wa aleicum es.* You're late. I expected you two days ago.' The man at the table speaks Polish. He has the accent of a newsreader.

'I couldn't find you. Your office –'

'It doesn't matter. Our business isn't until tomorrow. Is this your son?'

The man looks straight at me. His eyes are grey, the colour of sevruga. The cheeks are sunk inwards, as if he has no teeth. When he smiles the teeth are bright and clean and I'm surprised.

'Kazimierz Ariel Kazimierski. You're a man already. Come here. Come, come!'

He waves me over. I feel Dad move beside me, shifting around, uncomfortable or uneasy. How does the man know my middle name? It scares me. I want to look at my dad, to see in his eyes what I should do.

Instead I make myself walk forward, up to the lit table. The man is turning pages. There are rows of numbers and tiny foreign writing. I recognize the writing from home, on the tins of fish in Grandad's old room.

'Do you know what language this is?'

'Arabic.'

'Good! You're a clever young man, aren't you? Cleverer than your father, I think. And quieter. These are my accounts, Kazimierz. Imports, exports. Do you know what we sell here, boy?'

[204]

I shake my head. He doesn't look up because he knows I do not know. He goes on turning the thin pages, talking in his easy voice.

'Tomato paste. I bring tomato paste into Russia and your father helps me. Do you know most Russians have never tasted a tomato? Imagine having never cooked with that flavour and colour! My own belief is that the tomato is the basis of all Western cuisines, and many Eastern too. But it's all things Western these Soviets want. Pizza, ketchup, full English breakfasts, chilli in a bowl, hamburger relish and spaghetti bolognese. So, I bring them tomato paste. One day I will have a tomato paste empire, you see? So far I have offices in Brest and Vladivostok, Moscow and here. I like it here best, because I can take the boat home once a month and see my children and sleep with my wife. And from here I will also see the eclipse tomorrow. Do you know what an eclipse is, Kazimierz Ariel?'

'When the moon disappears. I saw one before. It was OK.'

Now he looks up at me. His grey eyes are like his voice. Mild and lazy, as if he is always about to smile. 'Was it? Well, tomorrow is another kind of eclipse. The sun will disappear. I've never seen this myself, but I think you may find it a little more interesting.' The man looks away and down, voice rising. 'Mister Kazimierski, are you ready to work tomorrow?'

'Yes.'

'There will be a shipment fifteen kilometres due south off the coast at three o'clock p.m. You and the boy will go and meet it alone. Your boat is moored at the usual place, and the payment will be there for you when you return. Leave the shipment there. I'll pick it up myself in a day or two. I don't foresee any problems, do you?'

'No.'

'Good.' The man stands up. Stooping, too tall for the ceiling. He shakes my dad's hand but not mine. 'Goodbye, old friend. I'll call you when I need you again.'

'Yes. Thank you, sir. Goodbye.'

We walk back to the stairs. There are no portholes down here on the bottom deck. The walls of the market ship seep river water. My throat is dry and I gulp, trying to make it all right. But it isn't all right, not here. I gulp again and again. My father goes up the stairs first. I follow him close as I can. Each deck we go up, I breathe easier. Up we go, into the market noise and warmth and stench. Up and out into the simple light.

All day it rains and my father waits for tomorrow. He drinks beers from the rattling refrigerator in our hotel room, while the rain comes down over the wooden houses, the canals choked with lotus flowers, the churches and mosques with their golden turrets.

I leave him alone. Even in Astrakhan, it's better to be away from him. I walk for a long time, putting distance between us. It's a hundred kilometres to the sea but I go towards it anyway, past dry docks and factories. There is nothing else to walk towards. The smells of Astrakhan are in my mouth when I swallow. It's like being ill, when you can taste the sickness in your spit. I go as far as I can, down mud streets and over bridges. Then I turn back. The rain is warm on my scalp.

When I look up again I'm at the central market. People are trading or just sheltering under the corrugated-iron roofing. I push in with the crowd. There are stacks of shrivelled rosehips and fresh dates. Bunches of dill and ferny mimosa flowers and lotus, which are pink as the steppes earth. Purple heaps of shredded beetroot and rows of pike-perch, like little green dragons. Bread with caraway, coffee with cardamom, black suspender belts with brass buckles.

I come out between two butchers' stalls. Across the road is the Hotel Lotos. I count up to our room, five six seven floors. The light is still on. My father is there, waiting for me. Beyond and above the hotel there is the sky. Clouds the colour of sevruga. Only at their western foot is a puff of red, where the sun is going down. I remember the Iranian; tomorrow there will be no sun. I try and imagine it and but it's impossible. The flame of a candle after the candle has gone out.

The rain is getting colder. I walk across the road to the hotel. The lifts are working today and I take one up. On our first night they broke down and a Moscow businessman was trapped inside for two hours, hammering on the doors, enraged. The machinery shudders as the lift opens.

My father is at the window of our room, looking out. On the TV is a Russian film. In the film it's a sunny day in black and white. A postman stops his bicycle and falls asleep under the shade of beech trees.

'Did you have a good walk, eh?'

My father stands up and then sits down again. He is trying to smile but the lines of his face work against it. There's a towel on my bed and I dry my face and head with it while he talks.

'I saw you. Across the road in the market. You looked up. He's something else, the Iranian, isn't he? All that tomato crap. He liked you, though. There's a lifetime's work for you here. You could do worse than take up where I leave off. Hey, you want to know the truth of it?'

He comes and sits beside me. 'The truth is complicated. We take things out of the country, not in. There's a chain of people around us. First there are Soviets who sell goods to the Iranian, then we take the goods out of the USSR for him. Then he sells the goods all over the world. If the Soviets could do it themselves they would, but it's against the laws. They can't sell these things to foreigners, the Yanks might notice. So they hire the Iranian, and the Iranian hires us.

'We're perfect for him, you see? He needs foreigners who can walk around here, and not look foreign. Foreigners who look like Russians. Poles, not Iranians. It works like clockwork, you'll see. Years of money. You look wet as a dog. What were you looking for, out there? There are whores in the lobby downstairs, if you want them. I'll go for a walk, eh? Kazio? What do you want me to do?'

'Nothing.'

On the TV the postman is waiting for a rope-ferry. The ferryman is a beautiful woman in shirtsleeves. They watch each other as the traffic drives off the platform, picking up dust.

'Nothing nothing nothing.' He turns back to the window. Outside the rain has eased. 'You used to play a game when you were little, do you remember that? All you ever said was "Why?" Used to drive me mad. Do you remember that radio? When you filled it with – no. I suppose you were too young. Here. I've got something for you.'

I don't look up at him until he comes over and I have to. I see he's wearing a new wristwatch. The face has slipped round but the band is heavy metal, steel and gold.

'The Iranian gave me a new watch, see? Rolex Oyster. So I remember where his new office is, he said. It's a joke. Oyster. Anyway, I want you to have this. Here, put it on, take it.'

He is holding out his old watch, the one with the Lenin face and the radium dial. The strap is worn pale from years against his skin.

'Please, Casimir.'

There is need in his voice. I've never heard that before. I look up and it's there in his face too. He's still holding out the watch and I reach out fast and take it from him, strap it on. There's only one notch-hole. Tomorrow I'll make another, measured for myself.

'There you go. How does it feel?'

It feels good. More than the watch, it feels good to talk again. I look up at him and smile. Everything Jan said must be asked, and I will ask it. But there's time. We still have days together.

'It fits well. Thanks, Dad.'

'Great. Really, I'm glad you like it.' He claps me on the shoulder. My shirt's still wet, warm with my sweat. He wipes his hand dry on his trousers. 'Right, I'm off to bed. We start early tomorrow.'

'Yes.'

'Good night. I'm glad you like it, eh?'

''Night.'

'Sleep well, Casimir. Good night.'

We walk to the boat, towards the sea. First are the high brick buildings of Lenin Street, then the asphalt roads and shop fronts, then mud back streets and slumped-down wooden houses.

In the end there's nothing but shanty town. Chicken runs and dog kennels and hacked-down stumps poke out around the shacks. The back streets get thinner, become tracks. We walk single file, my father ahead like always. Little children play in the lanes. Whenever we come close to them they run ahead and stop again, like hedgerow birds. On our right are the high concrete walls of shipyards and naval docks. The wind hums in their razor wire.

The shanty town opens out on to building sites and a stand of aspens crusted grey with bird shit and lichen. A caterpillar truck moves, way off across cleared land. The river is beside us, wide and green, and overhead the gulls reel out their fishing-line cries. The sandy mud sticks to my boots. Heavy clods of it, until my feet drag and my thighs ache. We stop often, scraping off furls of mud on driftwood and slag concrete.

'How far is it now?'

'Not far. Keep up, will you? We can't be late.'

Dad's voice is hard again, as if last night never happened. I look down at the watch. We've been walking for three hours. The strap's tight, now my blood is running hard. My wrist is bigger than my father's.

In the end we come to a stretch of empty warehouses and depot yards. The ground is black with oil and rust. In the shadow of a broken trailer my father steps too near a nest of mewling grey kittens. The skinny mother spits and runs away from us between wrecked machinery. Nothing else moves here except clouds. Around us are the shapes of derelict cranes and waterfront winches, the sky grey above their giant arms and feet.

My father stops dead ahead of me. I can hear his breath coming fast. I see the whites of his eyes as he looks behind us. 'Right here. This is the place. Christ. It feels like home.'

'There's no boat here. Do we wait –'

When I look back at my father he's already moving, clambering down to the water over the iron counterweight of a toppled crane. Beyond the crane is a lorry cargo hold, its rusted trunk leant twenty metres into the river, doors swung outwards towards the sea.

My father wades in, arms and legs working, pushing out towards the container's doors. The water soaks his blue jeans and green anorak and the cloth clings to his arms in ridges and bubbles.

'Dad! Wait for me –'

He doesn't look back. I go down to the water's edge quickly, pushing between rushes and lotus stalks. The Volga is cold as sea water, muddy where my father has already disturbed the bottom. From up ahead comes a groan of metal as he yanks at the rusty container doors, treading water outside them. I move hard, the water surging against my thighs, waist, up to the heart.

'Dad?'

My feet can't reach the river bed any more. I imagine it in my mind. It feels deep. I swim out and round to the container's high doors and through them, reaching up for the sharp metal, hauling myself into the half-light.

The container is long as a church; long as St Barbary's, by the Strug Estate. At the far end water slaps at the line of floor and wall. Above me the roof is high as two rooms, sheets and pocks of metal eaten away. There's not much light, but the container is full of sound. The small whispers of water in darkness. The slap of shallows in the distance. The echoing clop of waves against the hull of a boat; the bump and creak of its tyre-stays against the walls. I rear back as it strains towards me, the wooden curve of the hull against my outstretched hands.

'Casimir? Where the fuck are you?'

'Here. I'm here.'

My father leans over the boat's side, looking down at me, and he chuckles. The noise travels on in the wrecked chamber, a shaking hiss of sound. 'Mary and Jesus. You look like a dog now, boy. A dog in a sack in a river. Here, step on the tyres, got it? Out you come. Quickly. All right?'

He turns away before I can answer. I stand on the boat's deck, the shirt heavy on my chest. It's hard to find my balance. The boat has benches around its walls, a flat planked floor, a motor with a crooked chimney pipe. The floor is crammed with rope and nets, buckets and life jackets, cans of fuel and long white boxes. I count six while my father checks the motor. They look big in the dark, looming white. I reach out to touch one. The plastic is hard and cool against my fingers.

'Simple as a rowing boat, you see? Just a big rowboat with a motor in. No one'll stop us, but if they do, you sit down and shut up. All right?'

'Yes.'

'Right. Off we go.' He pulls the engine cord and the container fills with its smoke and bellowing noise.

We edge outside, picking up speed. I take a big breath of the wind. It streams against my wet jeans and jacket and I can feel my skin cooling, cold. I look back at my father. Behind him is Astrakhan, the towers of mosques and movement of cranes already small with distance. He sits with one hand on the rudder, legs crossed at the ankles, wet blue shirt sticking to the folds of his belly.

'How long to get there?' I raise my voice over the chatter of the motor.

My father screws up his face into the wind. 'Three hours at least. Two to the coast. Sit back, get some rest. I'll tell you if I want a nap. And stay away from the boxes.'

The corners are round, clamped down with metal. They don't shift as the boat thuds against the hard green backs of waves.

I look round again. My teeth are beginning to chatter and it's hard to talk. 'What's in the boxes?'

The wind and sun have already dried his hair. It flies back from his face, twisted black.

'Dad? What's in them?'

He doesn't hear me. The river widens around us, slow and empty. There are no buildings on the banks now, just broken green where the trees are. A straggling line of sheep, down by the water. Pylons, marching away across the flatlands.

'Dad? What's in the boxes?'

He looks back down at me, face still snarled up into the wind. He could be smiling but it's hard to tell. 'Stay away from them.'

I sit still, not looking at my father. The boxes are close, I could lean forward and open the nearest. It would take almost no movement.

The motor's rhythm goes through the whole boat, settling in my bones. The smell of diesel is like home, sweet and warm. It would be easy to sleep. Easier. The sun is out now, clouds breaking up around it. I lean back against the thrum of the engine and close my eyes.

I wake dizzy with the sun full on my face, my skin tingling with it, already burnt. I can hear my father, his hard voice. Another man, calmer, answering him. What language are they speaking? I hear words of Russian, Polish, Arabic. Other voices and languages I can't understand. A shift and clank of movement, the sound of orders. I recognize orders in any language. Behind it all, the wash and hush of the open sea.

I never knew my father spoke so much Arabic. I open my eyes. The sky is blue with high rib marks of white cloud. In one side of the sun is a chip mark. Small and black, as if the sun were made of glass. It hurts my eyes and I look away.

There's a plane next to us, floating on the sea. I've never seen a plane like this. Only in films. It has us in its shadow. On the wing are two men with dark skin, like the Iranian but with scarves on their hair. Their faces are wrinkled and a deep red-brown, as if the sun has managed to burn even them. Two more stand on the fishing boat. They lift up a white box between them. Eight hands on it, talking in their quiet, urgent tongue.

I look round at my father. He stands above me, talking up to a fifth man. The man wears a Western suit of blue linen. He looks at an open box as he talks, not at my father. Listening to them move through languages is like being a child again, hearing my parents through doors and walls.

'Forty. We agreed . . . less for less.'

'. . . nothing. I just deliver them to you. Talk to the . . .'

'Still, there is this problem. I can find better quality binary systems than this sprayed from the plane, this will leave a smaller footprint. Less deaths, is it not so?'

I pull myself up. The man looks down at me and away without moving his face. His eyes are the colour of dried blood, set into crumpled skin. He goes on talking. As if I'm invisible.

'. . . take them?'

'. . . the VR 55. Only the binary form. The money I will discuss with the Iranian.'

I look into the box. Inside is a plastic tub, transparent as old ice. Inside the tub is white powder. There are labels on the tub, written in Russian: *VR-55, binary chemical 2. CAUTION: HAZARDOUS MATERIAL.* A skull and crossbones. A storage number with many digits.

I think of the flour mill, and my mother's father. I think of the little bottles in the story of Alice: *Drink Me.* Flour and water, and the clack of glass, green and white. Little bottles. If you put them together, you make bread.

The fifth man has a gun in his belt. Oiled black metal, like the chapel grilles in churches. Now he shouts to the other men and they close the last box and take it away. The plane rocks against us and I stumble forward against my father.

'Casimir? Welcome back.'

'What are we doing?'

'Making our delivery. It's just business.'

'You said you would tell me.'

My voice is thick with sleep, as if I've been drinking. My father looks round and high above us, the other man turns away. I can't get my balance. My father turns away. 'Nadir!'

The fifth man raises his hand. The sun is above him, chipped and broken and bright. The wind flaps at the man's thin blue suit. 'Until next time, Mister Kazimierski. And to your son. God go with you. And travel fast. The eclipse has already begun.'

The plane moves away, water boiling up behind it. The wind is colder now. The plane whines faster, lurching up into the air. I start to look up again but my father grabs my face, pulls my head down. '*Kurva!* Do you want to go blind? Don't look up, understand?'

I nod. My jaw hurts where he grabbed it.

'Eh?'

'Yes. I said yes.'

I don't look at him and he swears again, walking back to the engine. The boat rocks and slops under him. He pulls the engine cord and it comes to life, hacking and coughing.

'Come here. Casimir? Get back here. If you're minding the boat, you won't look up. Hold it here. Right.'

He stands beside me as I steer. The sea changes colour around us. First it's shining, you can see down into its clear green-blue. Then the light no longer goes into it. The surface becomes dull, flat as slate, the way water looks in the early evening. I can feel my father standing next to me. Too close. The warmth of his arm in the cold air.

'What was it? The powder.'

'Why? What does it matter? It's done now. We go back and get our pay. Business is business.'

There's no noise around us, only the clatter of the engine. The seagulls have stopped crying. I didn't hear until they were gone. I start to look up but stop. After a time I see the seabirds in the distance, in the low sky, flying towards land.

I laugh. 'Flour and water.'

'What?' My father looks at me as if I am mad. Keen, careful eyes.

'What does the powder do?'

'It kills people.'

'How many?'

'How should I know? Many. Many many many. How many mice dine on a loaf of bread?'

'Why do the Russians sell it?'

'They don't need it any more. They no longer require it. So someone makes money out of it, it's only natural.'

My father bends forward, lighting a cigarette. It's cold enough that I feel the smoke, warmth blown back into my face.

'Two chemicals. You mix them together, like flour and water. And it makes a poison.'

He looks up at me. 'Clever boy.'

'A chemical weapon.'

'Only the best for the best.'

There are shadows growing on the deck now, although light still catches through the gaps of planks above the water-line. I narrow my eyes to see. Through the cracks, light falls on the deck in hundreds of little crescents. The sun is being eaten away.

'How will they die? Does their skin go numb?'

He goes quiet then. We chop across the water. He looks across at me. Fearing me. 'You touched it. When you were lit-tle. You remember that?'

'Yes.'

'You've got a good memory. It goes to your nerves, this stuff. One pinch on your skin, one drop, and everything goes numb. When your lungs go numb, you can't breathe any more. Then you die.'

'You should have told me. I will never come here again.'

I don't say it. Only in my head. A shudder of feeling goes through me. It's because of the way the light is going. So fast, as if the world is grinding to a stop. It makes my skin crawl.

'Money for nothing. I told you. We buy things now, to take back to Poland – but it's just cover. Less questions asked. You don't need to tell your mother. Christ, it's getting cold. I could do with a coat now. Still, we've not far to go.'

The light is going faster. Shadows pool out around the ropes, buckets and buoys. I look down. My shadow is growing straight out eastwards from my feet. My teeth are chattering again. I shake when I breathe, the fear gathering in my arms and chest.

'Not too far. Keep on course, that's it. Watch the coast and you'll be fine. Watch the coast and don't look up. Watch it. Casimir?'

There is something happening behind us. I can feel it in the hair on my back and hear it too, a great silence. My father's voice is small beside me. I look round.

A shadow is coming across the sea towards us, racing across the flat water. It is the shadow of the moon. It is as big as Poland. It makes no sound as it swallows us, a cold mouth without language. I look up, head right back on my shoulders. Straight up into the sun's black death mask.

'Casimir? Casimir?'

I look back down for my father, but my father has gone. Beside me stands nothing but an evil man.

Care

'I'm a dentist, I know. The range of colours in people's teeth –
fabulous. Like eyes.'

'No, they're not.'

'I'm telling you –'

'People don't have green teeth, do they?'

'Not usually, no.'

'Well then. Nothing like eyes.'

He opens his eyes. The northbound train is crowded with
evening passengers. In front of Casimir is a wickerwork of
limbs and torsos and, framed through that human mass, a couple talking. There is no other sound except the roar of the train.
They are dressed for a night out, bright and dark and colour-
ful, the woman sitting forward with her knees together.
Casimir watches her nervous energy. He feels it in himself, all
his muscles sprung tight. Waiting for action.

At Kentish Town he rises against the train's momentum and
pushes through the crowd to the curved Tube doors. Their
glass is still crystallized with rain from the city surface, miles
south. The drops shiver out into roads as the train decelerates
and grinds to a stop. Casimir steps out as the doors begin to
open, hauling them apart, the grime staining his hands black.

The station is full of people sheltering from the rain and
ticket touts for the Forum concert halls, the sweet public smell
of their wet clothes carried down shafts and wells. Casimir
takes the escalator in long strides, not breathing fast yet, beginning to run harder as he reaches the street. The pavement is
jammed with concert-goers around the all-night take-aways,
eaters leaning on the unlit fronts of fish and flower shops, and
he runs round the crowds and through them, stumbling once
in the gutter as a car blares past. Drinkers yell after him outside the Vulture's Perch and Castle Tavern.

'Oy! 'Kin' 'ell.'

'Slow down, mate! She'll wait if she loves you.'

The alley beside Al Araf Saunas is deserted. Casimir goes quietly anyway, watching for police, Line Management, any of the authorities who could stop him. The door to the yard is closed with a new padlock of layered steel. Casimir leans up close to the corrugated-iron fence. Its wet surface is stained black and yellow and steel-blue, like a wall of mackerel skin.

He closes his hands around the padlock and takes a step backwards. Held up by rotting wooden palings, the metal warps and rattles, rust cracking off it. Casimir has taken four steps when it comes away, crashing and booming towards him across the concrete. He hauls the metal to one side, mouth set with the effort. Looks up at the door of the abandoned station.

There is a figure hunched up beside the door. Indistinct from the piles of rotting carpet and linoleum around it, face turned down so that the hair drips away from the eyes. Casimir doesn't recognize the man until he goes close, up to the mottled white-metal door. The figure's neck is wrapped in pink Elastoplast, its facial features flattened out like a boxer's.

'Bill.' Casimir's voice is deadened by the downpour. He tries again. 'Bill.'

The man looks up. 'Oh, it's you.' His eyes are dull, scrunched up against the rain. Now they go wide and starey. 'Well, you've been living in interesting times, ain't you?'

Casimir squats down next to the older man, catching his breath. He sees there is a tiny dog curled up inside the man's woollen coat, black and tan with attentive black eyes. Rain shines against Casimir's face and he wipes it away with the back of his hand. 'What are you doing here?'

'Waiting for Hilary. This is our emergency rendezvous. Have you met my friend? He's called Snog. Snog the dog, see? It's a joke, you can laugh. Go on, it's good for you.'

'The police had you.'

'Nah.' Bill smiles the word out, his face lit up with something, pride or pleasure. Burnt with it. 'This old Bill's quicker than that Old Bill. The hospital had me, but not for long. Bill has just left the building. I got out through the Place of Rest, down where they take the bodies away in the Black Marias. I know the hospitals, see. I've been there before.'

He leans closer. 'Where is Alice?'

Bill puts out one fist, thumb up. Turns it down. 'She was under the platforms. Creeping around in the crawl-space. They never came out with her. I watched.'

'She is still down there?'

Their faces are inches apart. Now the man leans back from Casimir, whining, his head banging against the old brick wall. The dog looks up at their faces and away, panting into the rain.

'I don't know, I don't know. I didn't want them to find her. But it's all cocked up now she's locked up.' The homeless man begins to rock on his haunches, his voice fast, hissing. 'All locked up underground, it's ironic. It's practically pharaonic, like Rameses, that's what she is, look on my doors, ye Mighty, and despair. Down below the station's bright, but here outside it's black as night – do you remember? Billy Brown of London Town? Back in the war, that was. Back in the blackouts.'

'Quiet now. Try to stay quiet. Will you do that?'

'Yes. Right.'

Casimir leans his hands on his knees, pushes himself upright. There is no guttering on the abandoned station building, and water pours down the wall and the Underground door in slow sheets. The metal doorframe is set flush into the wall. Around it, the brick is scored with unused drill-holes. Casimir reaches out and pushes a finger into one hole, up to the first joint. The soft stone crumbles against his skin. Red, like mincemeat.

'Are you going underground?'

'Yes.'

He feels around the doorframe. There is nothing to get hold of and not all the bricks are rotten. He digs at them, feeling clay collect under his broken nails. Making purchase.

'You should get a move on. Time flies but aeroplanes crash. No, that's not right, is it? Time flies like an arrow but fruit flies like a banana? No, that isn't it either.'

He leans his head forward, resting it on the cold metal. Taking the strain with his shoulders, rolling them back. Air cracks between his teeth as he pulls. Once. Twice.

'Time flies when you're having fun. That's it. Nice to know we're having fun, isn't it?'

The door doesn't move. Casimir begins to swear between his teeth in English, in Polish. Stops himself. He holds the breath inside him, a hard belt of it in his belly. Steadily, he begins to yank at the doorframe. Hauling against it with his arms and feet, like a big animal in a small cage. As if it's him who is trapped underground, not Alice, who lied to him. Who is not Alice at all.

The door warps once, booming like a drum, and immediately there is a squeal of metal as the first bolt comes loose. Casimir works at it with quick, hard tugs. Using his weight, a hundred kilos of muscle and bone forcing itself inside. When both upper bolts are loose Casimir reaches up, pulling the entire doorframe downwards. Inside is the staircase, lit up bright and dull, neon tubes coated with dust.

On his wrist the watchstrap is tight, the veins of his arms swollen with blood. Casimir takes the watch off, folds it carefully into his jacket pocket. Looks up. The homeless man is standing ten feet away. Quiet, well back, the dog still cradled in his arms.

'Well. No hiding from you, is there? What big hands you've got, Granny. Long arm of the lover, that's what you are.'

'Are you coming down?'

'No. No, we'll stay up here, thanks. Got to wait for my other half, my Hilary. Dear Hilary, without her I'm rather ex-Hila-rated. Nice to get out of the rain, though, ta. I'll see you when I see you, eh?'

'Goodbye.'

Casimir steps over the flat ramp of the door and goes inside. He takes the stairs at a run. Making long jumps down them, eight or nine steps at a time. He remembers the feeling from childhood; the delight of motion through trees, the sensation of flight.

At the bottom of the spiral stairs he waits, listening to the sound of himself echo away. In the core of the staircase the substation door has been shut. Casimir tries it but the heavy metal is locked and his arms ache to the bone. Two arches lead off into light through the curved walls. Casimir looks down for his own footprints, but the dust has been trampled away. He turns left, into the side-passage with its bricked-up lift doors and wartime graffiti.

The lights are brighter now and Casimir can see pale line-marks on the walls, as if furniture once stood against them. At the passage's dead end he can make out a pile of wooden planks and three sets of bunk-beds, their skeletal frames leant awry.

He stops still. From somewhere in the abandoned station comes the buzz of loose electricity. He can smell it in the air, frazzled and sour. He wonders if the generators are damp with groundwater or simply overloaded, unused to so much activity. There are other sounds too: the cacophony of a car alarm filtered down from the surface, the hush of tunnel air from further underground. Nothing human.

'Alice?' His voice sounds small in the ruined station.

The hush of tunnel air intensifies, gains sound. Its murmur builds to a roar as a train goes through the derelict platforms below. Casimir takes out his wristwatch. It's still before ten, hours until the Underground closes down.

There are four storeroom doors further down the passage, their old wood glossed with strip light. A metal bar has been set across each door, nails drilled into the passage's cracked tiles.

'Alice?'

He comes to the stairs with their luminous wall-stripes. Walks down through the radium light, past the last locked door and the light bulb still swinging on its flex, out into the railway. Silver parallels curve off into the dark, clean and perfect and beautiful.

She is at the far end of the southbound platform, sitting on a pile of Underground signs between high stacks of ironwork litter bins. Casimir is less than a dozen feet away when he sees her. She is smoking a cigarette, leaning back against the platform wall. Her face is still in profile, not turning to look at him.

He sits down beside her, not speaking. The smooth enam-elled metal is cold against him. Rat's-tails of unwashed hair fall straight past the curve of Alice's cheekbones. He can't see her eyes or ears, only the downturn of her mouth. From where he sits, it is hard to tell if she breathes.

'Are you hurt?' She doesn't answer, his lone voice whispering away. He tries again. 'I have been looking for you. What are you doing?'

'Waiting to get out.' She takes a drag of the cigarette. The tobacco pops and crackles. Like electricity, he thinks. 'What do you want?'

'I found him. It is a man you knew, a foster carer –'

'I know who he is.'

She looks round at him, forehead pinched between narrow eyes. Casimir remembers the Line Manager. It is a cruel face. He goes on talking.

'The lines shut down in two hours – we could walk to Camden. Or you can leave now, with me. I have removed the entrance door.'

'*I have removed the entrance door.* Christ, you even talk like Arnold Schwarzenegger. You told the police I was here.'

'Yes.'

'You cunt.'

He sees the way her throat and jaw and face move, bringing up the word. Her voice breaks on its harshness and she turns away.

'You knew it was him. The foster carer. You never told me.'

'So? You know now. *Carer!*' She spits the word out, disgusted by it.

'What is his name?'

'What does it matter? All that matters is he doesn't find me. I'll never let him find me.'

He is looking at her hands. The nails have white crescents of calcium deprivation. They are bordered with black dirt under the broken edges. Casimir imagines her at the entrance door, panicked. Scrabbling at the metal, trying not to be heard.

'You thought it was me who killed them. Didn't you? I thought you believed me. You should have. We were lovers.'

'I'm sorry.'

She leans back. Takes a long drag of the cigarette, breathes it out. Casimir sees that her face is wet. He holds himself back. Wanting to touch her, not yet touching.

'You're stupid, Ariel Casimir. You'll never find someone like me again. And that policewoman too, what a mad cow. You know what'd be funny?' She smiles at him but the expression is weak, already fading. 'If they locked me up, he'd never get to me. All the years he's been after me, and then they'd lock me away. Don't you think that's funny?'

'We can tell the police –'

'No!' Her voice rises over his, shrill and strong. Bruised with anger. 'He doesn't even know what I look like, not really. I haven't seen him for years. He used to tell me he wasn't a real dad. He told me lots of times. So it didn't matter what he did to me, that's what he said; because he wasn't real. Still hurt though.'

The cigarette is burnt down to the stub. Alice puts her arm out straight and flicks it. Casimir hears her nails click. The butt sparks off the far wall, trailing down to the catch pit.

'Care! He was careful though. He took care that no one knew. When I was little I was scared of butterflies, I hated summer. Because I thought they'd hurt me. Like butterfly knives. He liked knives. It was all right when it hurt, though. Because what we did was wrong. It was worse when it didn't hurt any more. When it stopped hurting was when I left.'

'There are other places to go. Away from London. I can take you to Poland.'

'And then there were the posters. They were everywhere, it was like –' Her voice is weaker now, and querulous. 'He's crazy. I don't know how he does it. It feels like he's everywhere.'

'He was in Lower Marsh. In the restaurant.'

She looks round at him quickly, as if she had forgotten he was there. It reminds him of Adams, but the supervisor's private voice was quiet, thoughtful. Alice's is different. Cold and clean-cut, like raw meat.

'He sent me a warning. To stay away from you.'

'No. He sent you something to scare you, and then he waited for you to find me. He's clever like that. He'll be here soon.'

She stands and reaches a hand back down and he takes it. There is almost no flesh on the hard bones of her fingers. It is the hand of an old woman and for a moment he feels the urge to pull away.

'It's not your fault. We should go now. Are you coming with me?'

'Yes.' He grins with the effort of standing, the muscles of his thighs and shoulders aching around the joints and bones.

They go together up the green-lit stairs, along the tiled passages, between locked doors. The light bulbs gutter as power spits and hums above them. Alice talks fast, breathless with movement. Close to him, so that their fingers connect and catch, and then they are walking like lovers, hand in hand through the abandoned station.

'How old are you, Casimir? It doesn't matter, though. My grandad was fourteen years older than my nan. She had cataracts, all white. You've got nice eyes. You kept looking at me on that train, and then I saw you in Camden. And he was there already, my carer. I knew you'd help, though. I could see it in your eyes. We can go somewhere, can't we? Poland. What's it like? Casimir? What's Poland like?'

He walks slower, head bent forward as he comes to a standstill.

'What?'

'There is someone here.'

She stops. From ahead and above comes a *scuff* of friction, echoing down the stairwell. A soft clicking of movement, like dominoes falling. The rhythm stops, then begins again, faster and deadened as it approaches. As if the runner is barefoot, racing down the spiral stairs towards them.

In one movement Alice crouches and turns, fast as a sprinter off the blocks. From the stairwell come two claps of sound, almost together; the sound of feet hitting the shaft floor.

Casimir stands quite still, facing the entrance arch. His eyes hurt in the flickering light and he blinks once, twice, clearing them.

No one comes out of the archway. From where he stands Casimir can see a section of stairwell core. Beyond that the second lit archway, leading down. A current of air susurrates through both archways as another train comes closer, along the Tube tunnels.

There are two ways down, he thinks. Panic begins to rise inside him and he forces it back, turning, running on the turn. One of the strip lights has gone dead and he sprints through its band of darkness, down the staircase, out on to the south-bound platform.

'Alice!'

He can see her, way ahead of him and still running, down towards the southern tunnel mouth. The noise of the train is building up now and Casimir's voice is drowned out as he shouts again.

He looks round. A hundred feet back up the platform is the flickering light of a second cross-passage, orange Portastor units piled high around its mock-Tuscan archway. Casimir stares at it as the tunnel air begins to roar around him. But there is no one there – he can see no one, no movement of shadows. Lit up red and grey, a fold of newspaper is blown past him towards Alice. She is at the platform's end wall, kneeling by the tunnel mouth. He runs to her. The newspaper catches at his feet, tearing apart.

'Told you. I told you. He made you come to me.'

'I didn't see him.'

He kneels beside her and she reaches up, kissing him. Hands around his head, feverishly stroking the back of his skull. The train batters by next to them, a flickering arcade of light and faces.

Her mouth tastes of cigarettes, hot and rancid. She breaks the kiss and whispers up at him, mouth to mouth. 'How long until the next train?'

'Not long. Maybe five minutes.'

'I don't care, if he's here. I'm going through to Camden. Will you come with me?'

'Yes.'

'We won't get hurt, will we?'

'No. Stay away from the tracks.'

'Help me down.'

'Wait. Please.'

But she doesn't wait. On the platform's end-wall is an alu-minium socket cover and Casimir flips it up and clicks the switch underneath. There is an echo of sound like hands clapped once and lights come on along the curved tunnel wall, strung out towards Camden Town. He can see Alice moving away through the bands of illumination, leaning against the ribbed metal wall.

Casimir climbs down, finding his footing between ballast stones. He enters the tunnel a dozen feet behind Alice. Instinctively, his shoulders hunch forward. The light here feels more temporary than at South Kentish Town, the dark closer and more permanent. For the first time tonight, he is glad to be with Alice. There is no sound except the clatter of their feet on tunnel ballast, their breathing carried off in the tunnel's wind.

'The nearest track is a signal line. The next is the negative current.' His voice echoes oddly, struck off the Tube's metal walls. 'Stay away from both. Even the signal rail has some power. If you fall, keep away from the furthest track. That is the most dangerous. Alice? The furthest track.'

'I heard you the first time. Is he behind us?'

'I don't know.'

'So listen. You're closer. Do you hear anything?'

He slows, head cocked. He can hear nothing but the slight hollowing of air currents as they fill out into the abandoned station, two hundred feet behind them.

'No. There is –'

He stops speaking. From around the tunnel's northern curve comes the clatter of stones on the wet concrete. Only once; then there is quiet again. His mind races, trying to picture causes. But there is nothing animate in the tunnel. Nothing to move or fall, except them.

'I hear him.'

'Oh no.' Alice's voice sounds miserable. Like a child, knowing what is happening, not wanting it, and without the power to change it. Casimir takes hold of the wall's metal ridges and begins to haul himself along. Tunnel stones clack around him as he closes the gap with Alice.

A step away from them the signal rail shines, curving south-west.

'Say something, Ariel. Tell me something nice.'

[225]

He tries to think of what to say. The effort of speech and movement takes his breath away. In his head he counts the line-lights, measuring off distance. Twenty-nine, thirty. 'I had a dog. When I was a child. It was called Bison.' Thirty-two, the bulb flickering in its bracket. 'Because in Poland there are great forests full of bison, they are big as Russian tanks and the steam comes off them like the smoke from Russian trains –'

Her laughter comes from deep in her throat and he is glad of it. 'You fucking liar. I bet you never even had a dog. Did you?'

'No.' He is close enough to touch her now. Her hair is pulled over one shoulder and he can see her bare neck under the grimy collar of her jacket. The skin and cloth are sheened with sweat. She doesn't look round.

'I didn't have a dog either. I always wanted one. Something big with real teeth. My carer said I wouldn't look after it but I would have. Then it would have looked after me –'

Alice stops talking. Casimir walks into her as her pace slows, his hands going out against her warm back. 'He's getting closer.'

'No, not him. Don't you hear it?'

He feels it first. Through his feet, a vibration in the tunnel floor. There is a noise behind them, still distant. Pressure building underground.

'It's a train. Isn't it?'

'Yes.' He counts the line-lights. Thirty-nine, forty. 'There is a junction ahead of us. Go as fast as you can.'

'How far is it?'

'A hundred feet. Go faster.'

'Is there room for us? If the train comes first.'

'No.' The train is louder now. It sounds as if earth is moving southwards. Piling towards them through the half-dark.

There is another clatter of stones behind them and a noise that might be human, an echoed *hah* of effort. Alice starts to run. Almost immediately her feet slip on the ballast stones and she stumbles between the nearest two tracks, finds her balance and keeps going.

Casimir picks up speed. The sound of the train is intimately familiar to him, air avalanching before its flat head. Part of him knows how close it is and his mind blanks out, not allowing him to estimate the distance behind them, the distance ahead. The tunnel dream comes to him, very clear. The alcove always beside him. At the last window of the train, Alice's face.

'Where is it?' She is screaming now and as she does so another noise starts up behind them, a braying roar. It is hard to make out as a human sound. Alice cries out again. There is a rhythm to the other voice, violent and reflexive, like sobbing or hysterical laughter. The force of it and the force of the train come barrelling towards them along the metal tunnel walls.

Shadows flicker around Casimir, thrown ahead by the last line-light. Then the junction alcove is beside him. He almost runs past it, so that he has to reach out for Alice, hauling her back under the tangle of cables, holding her into the dark space. Pressing his face into her hair.

The noise reaches them, a deafening rumble. It sounds volcanic, a great force trapped underground. It sweeps on and under them, the ground shuddering like a motorway. A light rain of dust falls on their bent forms from the mare's nest of cables. The roar of air begins to fade southwards, towards Camden Town.

Casimir puts his head back against the alcove wall. Sweat stings his eyes and he blinks it away, breathing hard. After a moment Alice begins to move. Pulling away. Her laughter is high and keen, on the edge of hysteria.

'What was that, what was it, was it a ghost train? There was nothing there, was there? I didn't see it.'

'No. I think it was a postal train.'

She closes her eyes, shivering. 'What's a postal train?'

'There are mail Tubes. Unmanned trains. In some places the tunnels go near ours. I've never been so close to one before.' His hands are shaking and he closes them around her biceps.

Alice opens her eyes. The control is back in them, the pupils dilating, adjusting to the dark space. 'It went underneath us, didn't it?'

He nods. She leans her face against his, forehead to forehead. Whispers to him. 'He would be dead, if it'd been a real train. My carer. And now he's not.' He can feel her breath and the lashes of her eyes as she blinks, almost smiling. Her breath and his steadying together. 'What a shame.'

She kisses him gently. Pulls away, pressing her hand against his lips as she leans out of the alcove, rises to her feet, already starting to run.

Casimir hauls himself up and out. He can see the paleness of Alice's hair, flickering south between line-lights. He opens his mouth to call after her and as he does so, the roaring begins behind him. Gut-deep and angry, rising into a ragged wail. Casimir feels a switch kicked over in his head. The darkness around him, the desperate sound of fear behind him.

He starts to run. On the tenth step his ankle twists, the calf dragging against the signal rail's cold metal. He hears and feels the electricity snapping his leg rigid. Alice is calling from up ahead and he stumbles against the wall and on.

'I can see the end! I see it! Don't look back. Casimir! I can see –'

Still running, he looks back. The carer is less than a hundred yards away. In themselves his movements are not frightening but almost comical, like something in an old film. Sped-up. His T-shirt flaps loose from his jeans. Casimir can see the fish-white flesh of his belly, big but muscular, fat only in the way wrestlers are fat. But so white, like something not used to the light.

And now there is less than fifty yards between them. He moves like Alice, thinks Casimir; the quickness and silence are deceptive. He is surprised at the human face, as if part of him expected something animal. The man stares past Casimir, eyes fixed ahead in their wide-boned cheeks, the roar echoing away around them. There is something in his bunched left hand, the long nails curled around it. Shiny, a vestigial metal finger.

'Casimir!'

He runs harder. Methodical, making himself move. He hears the carer's breathing and laughter bubbles up inside him. The hysteria is not unpleasant but exciting, like the thrill of a childhood game. A hunt in the backwoods, Piotr's laughter echoing away through the stilted forest light. Now he can feel the muscles in his back spasming, expecting pain.

There is a hole in the darkness ahead. He has looked up to see it several times before he takes it in as the tunnel's end.

Beyond it are platform lights. The bright, dark clothes of an evening crowd. The distant glitter of a timetable light-board.

He comes out into bright light. Its clear surface falls across him and he gulps at it, not looking back at the tunnel's mouth. Alice is beside him, kneeling in the thin crowd, and she reaches down and helps him up. There is panicked laughter and whispering around them. The small, clear voices of children.

The human noise seems peripheral, as if part of him is still running. Casimir presses his face against Alice, breathing in the smell of her neck. Against his face, the hardness of her collarbone under the skin.

'Daddy, are they Underground people?'

He opens his eyes. There are two small girls watching him. The same dark irises, dark plaited hair. Their father pulls them back into the gathered platform crowd.

'What's the Underground lady saying, Daddy?'

'The man's got all blood on his feet.'

Casimir feels the wetness on his calves, colder and more painful where the jeans touch the flesh. The wounds there have reopened and he remembers the dog woman, days ago. *Don't hurt my lurching girls.* Alice is talking to him, close and urgent.

'Casimir, come on. Please don't stop now.'

He shakes his head to clear it. Looks round at the tunnel mouth. There is no sign of anyone following. Nothing except the line-lights, bright beads strung out into the dark curve.

'He could come out another way. Could he do that? He could be anywhere. Casimir?'

Over the heads of the crowd he can see a cross-tunnel bridge. It cuts straight and high across the platform's curvature. There are people there, not looking down, hurrying on to other platforms and destinations. Beyond the bridge is a sign in green, EMERGENCY EXIT; beyond that, the control room's passage entrance.

'The control room. We will watch for him.'

Casimir starts towards the passage, Alice just ahead of him, almost running. The crowd moves away from them both. Trying not to touch.

The control-room door is unlocked and Casimir goes straight in, heading for the camera screens. Weaver is by the equipment racks, changing into orange tunnel overalls. A skinny figure in white Y-fronts, his back blotched with wine-stain birthmarks. He looks round, gawping at Alice.

'Who are you? Cass, is she public? You can't have her in here if she's public –'

'Weaver, listen to me.' Casimir leans over the counter, monitor light dulling his face. The four platforms curve away on their separate screens. They are almost empty, a few weekday late-nighters clustered by exits and entrances. 'You must call the police. Tell them – just tell them to come. Weaver?'

The worker is staring at Alice. His face is blotched red and white as he blushes. 'You look just like them. The woman who fell and the other one. What's your name?'

'Alice.'

She has stopped moving. Watching him. Casimir keeps his eyes on the screens.

'Hurry now. Call the police at Kentish Town. The number –'

'Yeah, all right. I know the number.' The trainee's voice is puzzled but light, accepting. There are cellular telephones slung from the equipment rack and he reaches one down, fumbling with the buttons. Alice comes up beside Casimir. She cranes back to see the screens.

'He could go away again. He could wait for us.'

He remembers the carer's face and, more than that, his screaming. A basic, animal sound. On the screens, three of the tunnel mouths are dark. The fourth is beaded with line-lights. A few people still wait there, peering into the half-dark.

'Sir? I can't get through to them, it's busy.'

'Ring 999. Explain to them.'

Casimir's voice is soft with concentration as his eyes go from screen to screen. In his mind he imagines the carer crawling up on to the platforms.

But there is nothing to see. A train comes in, heading south through the City. Pulls away from an emptied platform. Casimir feels his breathing becoming even and slow. The image is so familiar and mundane.

'Cass? What am I explaining again?'

He turns towards Weaver. The trainee flinches away as he grabs the telephone. There is blood on his hands, where they have touched his trousers. His fingers leave tacky print marks on the cell's green-lit buttons as he starts to dial.

Behind him Alice starts to talk. Her voice is quiet, conversational.

'He's still here. Here he is. Come and see.'

Casimir pushes the cellular phone back at Weaver as the line connects. Runs to the counter, eyes jittering between monitors. Alice's voice is soft, as if the carer might hear her through the screens.

'He came out of a different tunnel. He could be anywhere now.'

Casimir doesn't answer. His eyes are settling on one of the cross-tunnel screens. A man runs under the camera's steep angle and goes up the emergency stairwell, out of sight. The camera blurs his movement and the heavy, rounded shoulders, a grey trail fading behind the figure as it disappears up the spiral.

'There.' Her voice is a sigh. As if seeing the carer relieves her of something.

'I saw him.'

'The stairs only go up, don't they? We could catch him.'

'Maybe. I don't think there is another way –' Casimir stops talking, features relaxing.

He goes over to the equipment racks. His work jacket hangs torn down one side and he takes it off and puts on an orange visibility vest. There is a pair of his work boots at the rack's foot. He shucks off his shoes and pulls on the boots, glad of their thick rubber soles. There is a bunch of emergency keys and he takes them too, sliding the cold metal into his pocket.

He turns round, taking in the room. Weaver standing, his thin chest still bare. Alice sitting on the counter, her knees together and her shoulders hunched up; watching him and saying nothing. Casimir wants her to say something. To tell him to take care. Anything will do.

'Weaver. There is someone I have to find.' He reaches out and takes the telephone. 'I know where he is. Stay here with Alice. Don't leave her.'

The trainee stares sideways at Alice, as if she might jump at him, mad as the dog woman. 'What about the police? I can call them again.'

'I don't need them. I can do it myself.' Casimir clips the telephone to his belt. It bangs against his thigh as he walks to the door. A familiar weight, reassuring. 'Watch the screens while I'm gone. Call me if you see him.'

'Casimir.'

He looks back. Alice hasn't moved. There is nothing in her face he understands. 'Take off the vest. You don't want to be seen.'

He stares back at her, not breaking the gaze. Reaches back over his head, pulling off the bright orange material. When she says nothing else he opens the door and goes out without looking back.

It's not long until closing time. He can hear it in the cross-tunnel, the sound of the station hollowing out, the few last footsteps becoming isolated. Casimir turns past locked doors and the dirt-thick grilles of ventilation shafts. The air is cloyed with the smell of cooling kitchens above, Camden restaurants winding down for the night.

There are so many doors, he thinks. He passes them as he reaches the emergency staircase. The walled-up lift portals, the substation entrance. Storerooms and the metal shutters of old cross-passages. So many places to hide. He goes slowly, listening to the station, moving up the metal spiral of cross-hatched steps.

Ten feet up there is another doorway in the shaft wall. Its metal surface has been painted over, not once but many times, the yellowed surface itself scrawled with graffiti four or five layers thick. The mortise lock is covered with paint, up to the keyhole's circular rim.

Casimir tries to imagine how many times he has passed this way, the daily pattern of work making him part of the crowd. It is hard for him to see the deep-shelter door in detail. Familiarity has faded it. He screws up his eyes. Leans close. Looks up.

The painted surface is no longer seamless. Running between the door and its jamb is a fine line, the paint not chipped or cracked but evenly cut through. To Casimir the detail seems odd in its care and violence. He imagines the carer, out of sight, bent forward. His knife opening out like butterfly wings.

He takes the keyring out of his pocket and sorts out the familiar flanged shapes: platform tannoy, crawl-space, surface concourse. He has never been into the deep shelter this way, and he wastes time on three keys before trying a grooved stub of bluish steel. Casimir works it into the mortise lock. Turns it twice, opens the door and steps through.

The smell and the dark hit him together and he raises his hands against them. The deep-shelter air is sour here, as if the trapped dust has fermented over decades. There is no wind on Casimir's face. The bottled-up air hangs around him, pungent as battery acid. He reaches out his hands, feeling along the walls until he finds a panel of light switches.

He flicks them on. At the end of a short corridor is another staircase, spiralling down. Keeled over by the stairwell is a block of machinery, LAMSON PNEUMATIC COMMUNICATION cast into its side.

He walks to the stairwell. The shaft is narrow, and Casimir can see down less than ten feet. But there is a sense of space below. The sound of an Underground train comes through the stone and is carried on into the intervening air. Casimir starts towards the staircase, clumsy with anxiety. One boot clangs against the side of the communication machine.

There is a skittering from below. A rhythm made quiet. The sound of something alive. Casimir follows it down and out, into the deep shelter.

He is standing at the far side the upper hall, thirty feet across from Wanda's red cage-work lift. Casimir's footsteps whisper ahead of him as he starts to walk, northwards, between the shelves and aisles. The neon strip lighting is dead, but Casimir's switch has turned on a series of emergency lights. He recognizes their grille-work brackets, like those in the train tunnels above.

There are other sounds now, softer than those Casimir makes walking. The drip-drop of water falling, far ahead and

[233]

out of sight. A whirr of ventilation fans, somewhere off in the lengths and turns of the Underground.

Casimir stops by one of the shelves. The wooden frames are familiar now; they are bunk-beds, plain and functional, like those in South Kentish Town. There is space here for thousands of people, he thinks. He goes on under the bars of emergency light.

After some minutes he comes to the end of the archives. Beyond is the empty hall. The line-lights trail off into the distance, clear as a runway. By their illumination Casimir can see stalactites, very white and thin, longer than those in the abandoned station. Storage units, big as truck trailers, their labelled doors locked and dark.

He takes a step away from the archives. There is a difference in the quality of the air here. A greater humidity, a wet coldness and the smell of lime. The environment changing, as if Casimir is swimming out over some oceanic shelf.

The lights help him. It is easier to keep going with the light strung out above him. For a long time he cannot see the chamber's end, and then it looms up abruptly. Casimir reaches a hand out to the flat black concrete. Spurs and surfaces of metal stick out and upwards in three places, as if a massive piece of machinery has been walled up inside. A staircase leads down to the left, light filtering up from the floor below.

It is like being under water, Casimir thinks. Underground and under water are not so different. There is the need to see everything that is hidden, and the desire to get back up to the light. The desire to get out is stronger now. Casimir takes a deep breath, shuddering, glad of the air. Then he goes down the narrow stairs.

The deep shelter's base is more cramped than the hall above, the ground levelled out several feet above the tunnelling machine's original curve. Many of the lights have burnt out, patches of brightness and dark scattered into the distance.

Casimir turns slowly, eyes wide, taking in everything. Under the last spiral of steps is a cavity, narrowed down at its curved end like the volute of a shell. He sinks down to his knees, peering inside.

There is a tiny scuttling in the cavity, insects or tunnel mice, nothing larger. Casimir straightens and begins to walk again. The dust is thicker, matting the concrete under his feet as he moves between shelves.

It is hard to keep track of time. He gropes around for the watch at his wrist, brings it up to his face. But the luminosity is fading. He has been close to the dark for too long. Casimir takes another shuddering breath and goes forward again, eyes wide open.

Without warning he comes to the south end of the shelves. Beyond there is nothing but darkness, the line-lights dead or never installed. Casimir's arm catches a filing box and it falls to the chamber floor. The impact booms dully in the long hall. He kneels down, gathering up spilled papers, marring the hall's thick dust with his movement.

The papers are printed with faded blue shop-till ink. Casimir holds one strip up to the light, then another: '*Asha's World of Booze, 291 Parkway. 17/05/74. Cheque #248285. AC#90887121. Holder: T. T. Cheam. Sun (The) Tuesday, 20 x Skol Lager, 1 Liquorice Allsorts. £6.30.*' '*Ashbery Health Clinic, 2b Pleasant Row. 17/05/74. Cheque #188803. AC#01076458. Holder: D. Falconer. Spinal Massage Treatment. £85.00.*' '*Ashen Entrail Patent Leather Goods –*'

Casimir looks away. Light spills forward from the last line-lights above him, into the dark. There are more storage units ahead of him. Between them, the accumulations of dust are scuffed by movement. Hundreds of feet into the dark is a right angle of light.

He straightens. He can feel the last line-light above him, the slightest warmth of its illumination. Casimir looks up at it, closes his eyes and breathes in. As if he could inhale the light, hold it inside himself. Then he opens his eyes and steps out into the dark.

The shivering begins almost immediately, starting in his legs and creeping up to his arms and chest. After fifty steps Casimir realizes he is still holding his breath. He begins to exhale and then stops himself. He goes on walking. If he looks down he sees nothing, but from the edges of his eyes Casimir can see the dust around him, disturbed ahead of him, a darker path curving towards the right angle of light.

It is clearer now. Casimir can make out the line of a door. He is walking towards the last of the storage units, up against the southern end-wall, as far into the deep shelter as he could go.

It is a dozen steps to the door. Quite distinctly Casimir can feel his heart, its spasmodic movement against his ribs, and the pulse of blood up near his brain. He comes to the door with his hands stretched out, touching the light. Feeling along it as the breath goes out of him.

He stands outside the door while his breathing steadies, one hand by the hinges and one by the handle. There is no sound from inside. Between Casimir's hands is a stencilled sign:

Portastor #62. Licence #62. Renew 01.01.01

CARE

He reaches out and opens the door. Steps forward, out of the dark.

There is no one inside. The cabin's walls are bright sheet metal. Light strikes off them from two long-life bulbs. Against the far wall is a red-striped mattress, a metal tool box and two stacks of posters which reach up to the ceiling, white paper pillars. A narrow path is cleared to the bed. The rest of the floor is covered with objects, laid out in neat rows. Reflections glare off tall glass jars, tiny droppers, assemblies of green bottles.

There is a whisper of sound outside. A scutter of feet, moving away. Casimir doesn't turn round. For the moment what is here matters, not the man outside. His foot catches against a stoppered jar and he kneels fast, stilling it before it falls.

The jar is full of a dense, oily dust. It is impacted down into layers of lead-grey and brown, like exotic sands in souvenir glass. The folded texture and colours look almost fungal, Casimir thinks.

There is a label on the far side of the jar. Casimir turns it to see. BEDDING SKIN is printed in old typewriter letters, the Ds bluish and faint.

He puts the jar down, looks up. The room is full of a sweet odour, comforting and intensely familiar. A stack of translucent Tupperware boxes is stacked next to Casimir and he picks up the top one, shakes it. The box is almost weightless, full of a soft flopping sound.

He opens the box. It is packed with Kleenex tissues, pink and white and green, compressed in tightly so that they topple out towards him.

Casimir picks the tissues up. They are all used, the stains clear and dry. In the second box he can see more tissues. Darker stains. A label and date. ACCIDENT BLOOD.

It is hot in the small chamber. The light seems to beat back off the metallic walls in waves. Casimir's breath is becoming harsh and quick.

He looks round him, dazed by the light. Along the left wall is a row of bottles, their necks wound shut with masking tape. It is hard to tell what they hold through the green glass. Beyond them is the mattress, the tool box. A wooden container, polished as a music box.

Casimir steps through to the bed. Reaches down for the box. It is heavy, full of the dense chuff of written papers. Casimir clamps the lid in one hand and the base in the other. Pulls against the tiny lock. There is another label on the base of the box, HEAD, in faded blue.

The lid creaks. Casimir's face is snarled up with effort, eyes fastening on nothing. The objects, the mattress.

He stops. Laid across the mattress are pieces of cloth and clothing. A grey sweatshirt, arms folded. A plain white towel.

The chamber is baked in long-life light. Casimir can feel the sweat on him, trickling down his sides. The towel is folded in four, carefully kept. Casimir puts the box back down, takes the towel. Turns it in both hands. Presses it against his face.

It smells of himself. The odour is acrid, not unpleasant. He remembers Alice's voice: *Like fish blood.* To himself his own sweat smells more mineral; if metal could be smoked it would smell like him. It is familiar as the sounds of the Underground. He thinks of Lower Marsh. The narrow corridors and cheap rented rooms.

He breathes again, closing his eyes. Beyond his own smell is another. Bitter and sweet and lovely, like honey. Alice.

There is an electric buzz of sound, violent in the harsh, bright room. Casimir drops the towel, twisting round, hands finally going to the cellular phone at his belt. He raises it to his face and clicks the line open.

[237]

'Yes?'

'Where are you?'

I am in storage, he thinks. In storage with Alice. Laughter rises up in his throat like vomit. He forces it back, throat clicking tight.

'I don't know, I – is that you, Ian Weaver?'

'Sievwright. Where are you? He's here, the guy you – he's right here now!'

He closes his eyes. Holds them shut. 'Sievwright, where is he going? Which screen do you see him on?'

The line crackles with interference, the worker's voice fading in: '. . . the one with the tunnel lights on. Going back where he came from –'

Casimir clicks the cell off. Looks up. In the Underground he knows everything, his mind racing ahead up the shafts and passages. It is two flights to the deep-shelter entrance. Five hundred feet to the tunnel mouth. He knows the way. It isn't far now.

He runs across the room. Bottles and jars scatter around him, crashing together. Outside is the dark but the light is ahead of him now and he runs hard, back towards the deep-shelter stairs. Making it easy for himself, struggling back up towards the light.

At the outer door the telephone catches the wall. Casimir lets it clatter down the emergency stairs as he jumps down to the cross-passage, pushing hard with the muscles of his chest and arms and legs. Leaning into the run as he comes out on to the empty platform.

For an instant the station fades back around him. He can smell the forest, which is also the smell of home. The sap of pines like mint and blood. Voices behind and the squirrel ahead of him, not running. Waiting for him, under the trees. Then he is at the tunnel mouth and he can see the carer ahead of him, or if not the carer then someone, the figure disappearing round the tunnel's curve, the bright beads of line-lights strung out into the warm darkness.

He stops at the platform's edge. Sits down on the white line, reaching out with his feet towards the shining metal tracks. Glances back along the platform. The timetable light-board is a hundred feet away. The arrival time of the next train glitters as the minutes change. Casimir narrows his eyes but they are tired, strained by bad light. He can see only one digit by the train's destination. An eight, or a six, or a three.

'Oy! You can't all be just going in there. That's breaking the law.'

He looks up. Sitting on the last platform bench is an old black man, curls of white hair sticking out under a brown pork-pie hat. Leaning forward, a wooden walking stick across his knees.

'I'm sorry. I have to go.'

'Breaking the law. Tch.' The man goes on frowning, shaking his head. Angry or uncomprehending. Casimir turns away, pushes himself off the platform, and starts forward into the tunnel.

The air here is colder now, the city above cooling towards midnight. From up ahead Casimir can hear the carer. He is no longer moving quietly or even with speed. The chuff of his steps against the gravel is slow and measured, like a spade cutting into stony ground.

Around the first bend the tunnel straightens out. Now Casimir can see the other man. A hundred yards distant, the dark round of his shoulders is sketched into the gloom. He leans a hand on the tunnel wall as he walks and his breathing echoes back down the tunnel. It is monstrous, the breath rattling. Casimir calls out, still moving.

'I see you. I know who you are.'

The other man slows to a halt. He is at the periphery of a line-light's illumination, stark and clear. The face is broad and moon-like. Without expression. He looks through Casimir, as if he sees no one there. After a moment he turns and begins to run again. Not fast but regular, finding his rhythm.

He is limping, Casimir thinks. The carer is hurt. If he is hurt, I can catch him.

He picks up pace, boots crunching against the ballast. Once he thinks he hears another train, a sighing of air, but when he tries to listen it is only the other man. Breathing hard, not so far ahead.

The carer looks back as he runs now, craning round every

few steps. The skin of his face and hands is unnaturally white. Whiter than skin, as if he has been washed in formalin.

'I know what you are. What you want, I mean. Wait, I –'

Talking is no good, he thinks. It takes his breath away. A stitch is forming in his gut, a slow twisting pain. He thinks of Poland again; the birch trees, whiter than the snow. The carer's skin is white as the birch. There is still fifty yards between them when he feels the movement of air against his face. Casimir keeps moving, remembering the postal train.

But there was no wind when the mail Tube passed them. Now he can feel the air pressure; its current, dangerous as electricity. A slight coolness against the line of his nose, as there was eight days ago. Adams beside him on the platform, telling him about the woman who fell.

'Wait – there's a train coming. A train –'

It is closer now, the air building up, acquiring sound. Casimir stoops down. Already there is sound in the tracks. Faint, the whicker of ice warping or water boiling.

'Can you hear me? Listen!'

He is shouting now. Ahead of him, the carer stops. Turns round.

This time he is standing between lights, in a bar of darkness. Casimir cannot see his expression, only the white of his skin. His face, his hands.

There is metal in the carer's right hand. And now there is sound coming from him too, not speech but a chatter of metal, like ticker tape. It takes a moment for Casimir to connect it with the movement of metal. In the carer's hand, the knife opens and closes. Irregular but purposeful, like the spasm of a butterfly in sunlight.

'Come back! We have to go back –'

The sound of the butterfly knife is already being drowned out by the roar of the train. It is faster than the postal train, thinks Casimir. Already it is much too late to turn back.

The sound of the knife stops abruptly. Now there is only the rumble of air. It buffets against Casimir's face and he narrows his eyes. Very still now, watching the other man. Seeing him. In the dark, the carer is smiling. An open-mouthed smile, the jaw thrust out, the bottom teeth a hard crescent.

Like the pike, Casimir thinks. Beside the carer, cables run on along the tunnel walls. In the glare of the next line-light the cables curve up in an arch of grime-black, green and orange plastics. Under the archway is the junction's black hole.

The alcove is less than ten feet behind the carer. The noise in the tracks is more violent now, the train's weight carried down the electrified metal. Casimir shouts into the wind as it builds and thunders.

'You let me follow you.'

The carer smiles again; teeth out, grimacing. He walks backwards two steps, hand brushing along the wall. Now he is standing in the light, the junction alcove beside him. In his fist the knife points towards Casimir. Edge and point on, it is almost invisible.

The wind roars past them both, tugging at their soiled clothes. Casimir can see the other man's face now. He doesn't remember seeing him this still before. He is surprised by the lines of old expression in the man's face. The carer looks like he is flinching away from something, some pain or violence. The feeling is set hard into his features. It is the face of someone used to losing and loss; the expression of a victim.

From their sockets the eyes stare out at Casimir. Hard and narrow as the face is soft and wide. As if it is his own eyes the man flinches away from. They are Alice's eyes. Blue as blood seen through muscle.

Two hundred feet northwards, the Underground train comes round the tunnel's curve. To Casimir its flat head seems to move with great slowness. There is time to see the driver in the bright cabin, leaning down over the gears. A face in the first carriage, leant back against the dirty window. Blue sparks and fuse-light spat between rails and wheels. Light thrown out across the tunnel's roof, racing across its iron ribs with the quickness of sunlight across fields.

Then the Tube is into the straight, picking up speed. Ahead of it, the carer stands unmoving, a giant black silhouette with the headlights behind it. The Tube's horn blares out, deafening loud, the sound rifled against Casimir's eardrums. He bends away from it, eyes squeezed shut. Reaching out for the tunnel wall with one hand, then with both hands.

The wall cables are under his palms, caked with grime. Above them are the old line-telephone wires. In his mind's eye he sees their parallel lines. The bright, live copper.

He scrabbles upwards. For a second he is hanging off the negative wire, feeling it bend as he hauls upwards. Then he has both wires, their electricity buzzing against his palms. He cries out against the train's roar and brings his hands together above his head. Like a prayer, or a fist.

For a moment there is light everywhere, the entire section of line short-circuiting around Casimir. The train screams down on him. Even in his hands there is light, and a rhythm of pain. Then all the lights go out.

Out of Depth

He drives fast, but the sunlight is faster. It goes ahead of us, over the fields and woods. When the birch trees are in darkness the trunks are pale as lightning marks, struck upwards through the black hemispheres of their branches. But when the sun moves on to them the forest is green on top and yellowish underneath, the colour of hair or dry grasses.

The signposts are blue and white, like paintings of July sky. It is ten kilometres to Gliwice. I will be home soon. I will not be home again. How can my mother love my father? How is it that I came to be born?

My father drives without speaking. Around us is the wind, it comes in through the front windows, out through the back. Two front, two back, like blood through a heart. Soon I will see my mother.

The sun moves on to us again and I sit back. When it passes us my muscles harden. It makes me think of Astrakhan, every time. The shadow of the moon, big as a country, coming across the water towards us. The surface of the moon, the surface of Russia. I was calculating them together, but I never finished. I remember my father's expression when he turned to face the moon's shadow. He looked terrified. It was like looking into a mirror. This is the last time I will feel for my father.

He changes down gears at the corner of Aleksandra Fredy Street. Changes to fourth again, picking up speed. I look across at him: his face is curious, as if he is waiting to be hit. I don't understand it. I look away. Out of the side-window I can see the Strug Estate. The blocks stick up, arranged in pairs, like the points of electric plugs.

'Fire.'

His voice surprises me. I look round at him and then follow his eyes, back to the estate. From one of the blocks smoke is rising. A or B Block; not ours, which is further away. It is not like coal smoke, which is brown; this is black and thin. It is a small fire, but the smoke still goes up and up. I am surprised at how far the smoke goes. Miles up it drifts away, east towards Oswiecim.

'Maybe it's your mother. She's been burning duck eggs again.'

I say nothing. Now we turn off Energy Street. The smoke is coming from A Block, and I roll down the window and look out. The afternoon sun catches off the flat windows. Only high up there is one burnt-out window. The glass is all gutted out, the windows dulled two flats above it.

'At least it's not us. At least we're all right, eh?'

We are all right. Not good, not bad. I try to picture my mother's face and it has gone. I put my head right back to see the fire. I count up the floors. Five, six, seven. The sunlight races over and past us.

Still

He opens his eyes.

Nothing happens. It is as if his face is paralysed without his mind knowing. As if he is blind. The tunnel dark lies against his face. Somewhere there is the sound of shaking metal and shouting. But he no longer understands this. In the dark he understands nothing at all.

It is something he has been waiting for all his life. And now the darkness is here again, and he is not ready. He is eclipsed. It is as if the life has gone out of him with the light. His legs buckle and he falls although there is nowhere to fall, only a movement through darkness into darkness. Something hits his head and it fills with stars. Their brightness hurts and he is glad of it.

He feels his head with his hands. There is blood, but not so much. The track metal is there, cold and hard, all the power gone out of it. The hammering comes again and the shouting. It could be near and faint, or far and loud. He doesn't know. You know nothing, he thinks.

'Casimir.'

His name comes hissing through the dark. Casimir. It sounds like blood. In the dark, someone is saying his name over and over.

'Casimir Ariel Casimir Ariel –'

A rattle of sound. He closes his eyes again, trying to understand it. It sounds human. He thinks of laughter.

He knows who the voice must belong to, although he has never heard it. For the time being he has no name for it. He reaches down, feet and hands spread, holding on to the track for balance. Sways upwards. Now he is standing in the dark. The balance leaves him and he goes on standing, unable to move. The voice sighs and cries, near or far.

'Ariel Casimir.'

'Here. I am here.'

The words come to him like light. With them, he finds the strength to walk forward. Two, three steps. He closes his eyes again. It is easier with his eyes closed.

On the tenth step he walks into the great flat head of the train. He reels back, arms going out as he falls again. He doesn't cry out. On the tunnel floor he rolls over on to all fours, head down between his shoulders. Teeth together, finding his breath.

'Ariel Casimir.'

There is light in his hands. On the left hand. He raises it towards his face. It is the wristwatch, the only thing of his father's he has kept. The glass is broken and the face is bent inwards, like a bottle top. But the luminosity is still there, shedding its faint limelight.

His eyes adjust. In the pitch-black tunnel, the glow of the watch-face is enough to pick out the whole of Casimir's hand. He presses it against his face, breathing in long sighs, feeling the pulse slow in his wrist, forehead, heart.

'Help me.'

He holds the watch out ahead of him. There is a figure, slumped face-up across the tracks. Casimir moves over, squatting above it.

The carer's face is discoloured, the whole surface bruised dark. The crash has thrown him forward, twisting him in the air as the bones began to break. Ribs have been pushed through his shirt from the strength of the train's impact, Casimir can't see how many. The man's arms are flung out, palms upwards.

'Let me see her.'

'Lie still.'

'I'm sorry. I love her. I'm sorry for all of it.'

The man has been made monstrous with damage. His eyes are crusted with blood and tears but open, staring up into the green light. It reminds Casimir of his father, and he tries to picture him. A weak man, twisted by amorality and a brutal, simple nationalism. There was a photograph, he remembers. He had torn it up, letting it fall from the window, not wanting even to look at it.

[246]

He remembers Anna's voice: *There is good in you that comes from him.* He wonders if it is true, and if the opposite is true: he wonders if he can be the monster his father was. Casimir thinks how easy it would be to kill the carer, here underground, where no one can see. To finish it cleanly, for Alice and himself. To make an ending of things and never have to look over his shoulder, back into the dark. He could do it with the strength of one hand.

'Please.'

'Shut up.'

Gently, he touches the man's body. Feeling for damage, drawing back. The hammering and shouting come again, somewhere behind him. He ignores it. Holds the carer's eyes with his own, steadying them.

'I'm sorry. Can I say sorry to you?'

'No. Not to me.'

'Take me to her.'

'Quiet now.'

He reaches under the man's waist and head. Lifts him in one movement, head and spine held as still as he can manage. He waits for a few seconds, making sure of his footing. Then he starts to walk. Away from the train, southwards towards the station. He measures the steps out, cradling the carer.

'I'm dying.' The man sighs. Turns his head forwards. 'It hurts. You wouldn't believe how much.'

His feet crunch against the ballast stones. He moves with care. A parent or an undertaker. He remembers how strong his father was, and wonders whether Michal would have used his strength for this. Casimir thinks that perhaps he would.

He thinks of how old his father is. It occurs to him that there is still time to go back to him, in Poland. He wonders if the old man will ask him for forgiveness, and if he is the one to give it.

It takes a long time to round the tunnel's curve. Now Casimir can see the light of the tunnel mouth. A tiny white oval, it becomes imperceptibly larger with each step. He keeps his eyes on it. He tries to remember where he is coming out. London or Poland. The deep forest or Astrakhan.

'Can I see her?'

'Yes.'

The tracks shine beside him, catching the distant light. Against the carer's body, the palms of his hands ache and burn. The dark is still around him and behind him, but ahead of him there is light.

'Are you taking me to her?'

'Yes. Lie still.'

Now he can see Alice in the tunnel mouth. The light is behind her. He walks towards it, not looking back.

With thanks

For their help: the Figurski family in Warsaw, the London Wiener Library, the London Polish and Nigerian Embassies, the London Polish and Jewish Museums, the London *Jewish Chronicle*, the Astrakhan Kremlin staff, Jerry Murray at Goodge Street deep shelter, and London Transport staff at Belsize Park, Green Park, Down Street, British Museum, Camden Town and South Kentish Town. For rhythm: Charles Perry, 'Portrait of a Young Man Drowning'. For financial assistance: the Harper-Wood Studentship for Literature, administered by St John's College, Cambridge University.

FATEFUL VOYAGE

*A voyage to New York changes the path
of one woman's life...*

November 1907. Hester Shaw is hidden
away in a small London flat paid for by
Alexander, her wealthy married lover. When
he persuades her to accompany his aunt on
a trip to New York she meets young Charlie
Barnes, who falls in love with her. This is her
chance to put her shadowy past behind her
and start afresh, but the decision to leave
Alexander, a powerful senior policeman, will
prove disastrous...

Pamela Oldfield titles available from Severn House Large Print

Loving and Losing
Full Circle
Jack's Shadow
Summer Lightning
Henry's Woman
Turning Leaves
Intricate Liaisons

FATEFUL VOYAGE

Pamela Oldfield

Severn House Large Print
London & New York

This first large print edition published 2009
in Great Britain and the USA by
SEVERN HOUSE PUBLISHERS LTD of
9-15 High Street, Sutton, Surrey, SM1 1DF.
First world regular print edition published 2007 by
Severn House Publishers Ltd., London and New York.

British Library Cataloguing in Publication Data

Oldfield, Pamela.
  Fateful voyage.
  1. Mauretania (Ship)--Fiction. 2. Transatlantic voyages--
  Fiction. 3. Great Britain--History--Edward VII,
  1901-1910--Fiction. 4. Love stories. 5. Large type books.
  I. Title
  823.9'14-dc22

  ISBN-13: 978-0-7278-7812-0

Printed and bound in Great Britain by
MPG Books Ltd, Bodmin, Cornwall.

One

The church clock struck midnight. The sound echoed through the silent London streets, where only the barking of a dog or the wail of a cat disturbed the dark alleyways, and the clatter of a hansom cab was less likely. Still awake, Hester closed her eyes, determined that somehow she would make sleep come. It was the third night in a row that she had remained awake until the early hours of the morning. Around her she heard the familiar sounds of the little attic room. The flutter of the curtains as the wind reached them on its way past, the regular tick-tock of the small brass carriage clock that had been Alexander's first gift to her, and the occasional sound of the wooden rafters that always contracted as soon as the fire turned to ash and the temperature of the room dropped.

Beside her in the bed, Alexander stirred.

'I can't sleep,' he grumbled. 'Thinking about that damned man, Drummond! He

5

undermines me at every turn and I won't put up with it any longer.' He turned on to his back, wide awake and simmering with anger.

Hester said nothing. The past six years had taught her when to keep quiet.

'He thinks he's getting away with it,' Alexander muttered, 'but I've got his measure, and I'm going to break him! He'll be very sorry he crossed me.'

Frank Drummond, Hester knew, was a colleague with connections to people in the Home Office. She also knew that Alexander hated him for some reason she had never understood.

'He won't know right from left once I've finished with him,' he threatened. 'No man treats me like that and lives to tell the tale!'

She laughed dutifully. 'Poor chap.'

She wasn't sure what the man had done to anger Alexander, but she knew better than to ask. He kept his professional life remote from his personal life, and she had no wish to share such problems.

'He's gone too far this time, damn him, and I'm going to nail him.' He sat up, sighing heavily to let her know he was less than happy. 'It's stuffy in here, Hester. Is the window ever opened?'

He was fanatical about fresh air.

'It won't open properly, it—'

'Don't remind me. It sticks. My fault, I suppose.'

Hester remained silent. It *was* his fault. She had offered to arrange for a carpenter to adjust it, but he had refused, saying that *he* would see to it.

He broke the silence abruptly. 'How would you like a trip to New York?'

'Together?' Foolishly, for a moment or two, she allowed herself to hope.

'Don't be ridiculous! To accompany my aunt. What time is it?' He reached for his pocket watch and squinted at it in the moonlight which filled the room. 'A trip on the *Mauretania*,' he elaborated. 'Her maiden voyage, no less.'

Knowing that without his spectacles, Alexander could not see properly, she said, 'It has just struck twelve.'

The *Mauretania*, she thought, her eyes widening. His aunt must be very wealthy. She was a brand new transatlantic steamship which doubled as a liner, sister to the *Lusitania* which had sailed for the first time a couple of months earlier. The maiden voyage sounded wonderful, but it also meant being apart from Alexander which made her hesitate.

He slid from the bed, walked into the lavatory and returned a couple of minutes later. Standing by the bed, he rubbed his eyes and then ran fingers through his hair, a mannerism he had when he felt guilty. He was eating too well, she thought a little critically, and

7

becoming a little grey on the temples. Soon he would look like any other middle-aged man – not that it would bother him. Alexander had too much confidence to worry about how he might appear to others.

He swung his arms: forward, up and down, sideways, then up and down again. The 'loosening up' exercises he had learned as a boy at his very expensive private school.

'I told my aunt you would accompany her.'

'Not...' Her face fell.

'Yes. Edith. She's still nervous of the sea and refuses to travel alone. You've never been to New York so I said you'd go with her.' He sat down on the edge of the bed. 'She has to see a specialist there. Her friend has recommended him. Dr Guy Stafford.'

'What's wrong with her this time?'

'Goodness only knows. I don't.'

'What happened about the kidney trouble?'

'Nothing as usual. It went away as soon as she lost interest and turned her attention to a heart problem.'

'She suspects heart trouble now?' Hester shook her head. Travelling with a cranky old woman held no appeal. 'Why doesn't she advertise for a travelling companion? She can afford to pay well. Some women would jump at the chance.'

Hester considered what she knew about Alexander's elderly aunt. Edith Carradine was a widow – a silly, bad-tempered woman with more money than sense, according to the nephew she adored. She apparently thrived on imaginary illnesses and enjoyed the attention that came with medical consultations.

Alexander laughed shortly. 'She did advertise. No one would take the money.'

'I'm not surprised. From what you tell me, I can imagine her interview technique!'

Alexander touched his toes ten times, then straightened, puffing slightly. 'I told her it was settled. You have to go.'

Annoyed at being manoeuvred, Hester began to resist. 'Why can't one of her daughters go with her? That makes more sense.'

Alexander snorted. 'Because they both produced convincing excuses the moment the idea was mooted. One is apparently nursing a sick friend, the other is preparing for an exhibition of her watercolours. It has to be you, I'm afraid. It's not too much to ask, is it? A favour to me. I'm very good to you.' He leaned forward. 'I make you happy. I buy you beautiful clothes, I...'

'I make *you* happy in return.'

'I don't deny it.' He kissed her hand, her arm, her neck. 'Say you'll go. Please, Hester.'

She was wavering. A trip on a liner to New York and back would be an adventure, but Edith Carradine was a definite fly in the ointment. The other reason for Hester's

9

hesitation was a permanent worry that one day Alexander would find another woman. It may be that leaving him for several weeks would be too great a strain for him. He might find someone, intending only a brief fling, but then ... She frowned. He was still an attractive man, despite his age, and he was influential and comparatively wealthy. Few women could resist his charm if he put his mind to it.

'How long would we be gone?' she asked.

'As long as it takes. She might be over there for several weeks. Five or six, perhaps. It would do you good, Hester. You lead a very uneventful life. I'm a selfish brute, keeping you all to myself. Aunt Edith will probably sleep a lot. Early to bed, afternoon nap and all that. You can enjoy life at sea.'

'Five or six weeks? Then I definitely won't go.' Hester propped herself up on one elbow. 'Are you trying to get rid of me? Is that it?' She tried to sound light-hearted, but she was actually very nervous now. Was she being naïve? Was he trying to tell her something? Was he tiring of her after all this time? She suddenly saw a frightful image – herself returning from the trip to find the flat was no longer her home. Would he do that? She didn't think so, but the hateful vision made her draw a sharp breath.

He stood up, crossed to a chair, and began to dress himself. 'I don't want to argue,' he said. 'I've said you'll go. That's the end of it.'

Defeated, Hester gave in to the inevitable. To annoy him, she asked, 'Who did you tell your aunt I was? Your mistress?'

He gave her a withering look, sat down, and began to pull on his socks and shoes. He combed his hair without looking in the mirror and shrugged on his jacket.

'The question was a serious one, Alex,' she insisted. 'Who will you say I am?'

'I told the odd lie!' He grinned and suddenly looked much younger. 'I said you were once the dressmaker to the wife of a friend of a friend...'

'I can't sew for toffee!'

'And that I know you to be utterly reliable and of a dutiful disposition.'

'Dutiful!' Pushing the negative thoughts aside, she laughed. 'Oh, Alexander! You didn't!' She hoped she was not dutiful. It sounded horribly submissive.

'It was what she wanted to hear, Hester. Don't fuss. By the time she finds out that you are *not* dutiful it will be too late. You'll be travelling on the finest ship ever built in this country. If she goes fast enough, she might take the Blue Riband from the *Lusitania*! It will be a wonderful experience. An elegant cabin, good food, games to play, a library...'

'Games?' She raised her eyebrows.

'Shove halfpenny, Ludo, deck quoits.' He grinned.

11

Since it was inevitable, Hester allowed herself to hope she just *might* enjoy it.

'When is this trip, Alex?'

'In ten days' time. You can go for walks on the deck.'

'Walks on deck? It's November!'

'Wrap up warmly. It will do you good. Blow away the cobwebs.' Ignoring her protests, he rushed on. 'I'll give you some money and you can buy a few new clothes in New York. You'd like that, wouldn't you?' He kissed her. 'Now, I must go. Marcia...'

'Will be wondering where you are ... I know.' Hester drew up her knees and hugged them defensively. This was the worst moment, the one she always dreaded, when he left her with so little apparent regret. As though he had just completed a business transaction and was eager to leave the office and return to his other life. Perhaps, for him, that was exactly how it felt. The idea tormented her and she had to bite back a cry for reassurance. She had told herself many times never to reproach him. She had entered into their arrangement with her eyes wide open. It was swings and roundabouts. Often being with Alexander was a joy, sometimes a habit, but at other times it brought pain.

She said brightly, 'It's a good thing you don't have far to walk.'

He waited as she remained sitting on her bed. 'Well, don't just sit there. You have to lock the door behind me.'

'I will,' she said.

'I like to hear the chain go on. I've told you that London's a dangerous place. I ought to know – the streets are full of villains.'

He worries about me, she thought, slightly cheered, and slid from beneath the sheet, followed him out of the bedroom and along the narrow passage. He opened the door, turned back to give her a perfunctory kiss – and then was away, clattering down the stairs.

'That's right,' she muttered. 'Wake all the other occupants.'

Remind them that it's midnight, she thought unhappily, and you are hurrying back to your wife. Let them know, if they don't already, that I am merely a kept woman, to be abandoned every night on the stroke of midnight like Cinderella's slipper.

The street door opened and closed, and she hurried to the front window as she always did, and, with fear clutching at her heart, watched Alexander stride out along the street in the direction of his wife and their home.

'Don't betray me while I am in New York,' she whispered. 'Please don't betray me.'

As soon as he was out of sight, she went back to the empty bed and lay staring up at the moonlit ceiling. She was thirty-one, her youth was gone – and she needed him.

Marcia pretended to be asleep when her husband returned, but when he finally slid into bed beside her, she mumbled sleepily and opened her eyes.

'How did the meeting with Grey go?' she asked.

'So-so. He's an idiot, that man.'

'But did you get your point across? You were there for long enough.'

'Which point?' He yawned.

She breathed in through her nose and recognized the woman's perfume. No doubt she would again find red gold hairs on the collar of her husband's jacket and maybe a smudge of rouge on his shirt. Was he really so careless of discovery or did he think her totally unobservant? Did he think she was ignorant of the small flat he had bought in Chalker Street in which to squirrel her away?

Whoever the woman was, Marcia did not care. She was welcome to him. He would never leave her because she had brought a great deal of family money to the marriage and had made life easier for him while he climbed the career ladder to a senior position within the police force.

Alexander Waring had been a young police sergeant when they first met, mixing with the worst ruffians in the criminal under-world. He had claimed, laughingly, that he was on first name terms with all the best villains. He had thrived on the challenges, relishing the hostilities, the plotting and counter-plotting, frequently risking his life. He had succeeded where lesser men had failed, bringing a record number of miscreants to justice. It had been a long, hard struggle, and she was pleased and proud that, with her money and her social contacts, she had eased the way upward for him. He was now a detective chief inspector at Scotland Yard and she felt he deserved it.

But he didn't know everything. Marcia knew something he did not – though only forty-nine, she was seriously ill and would soon die. She was therefore grateful to the other woman who satisfied her husband and left his wife free to end her days in comparative peace. The drug the doctor gave her allowed her to pass many hours in a dreamy half-conscious state that was more than bearable. It was positively euphoric. Only towards the end of the evening did she allow herself to emerge into full reality, and accept the pain that went with it. She did it willingly to spare him unhappiness. When she died he would be free to remarry. By then she would be in another, hopefully better, place.

'Which point?' Marcia echoed. 'Why, the point about the increase in manpower. That was why the meeting was held. You knew it would be a late one – and then you were popping into the club.'

15

He had lied. She knew it. Not that the lies troubled her, but it riled her that he thought her so easily tricked. One day she might surprise him.

'Oh, that!' He recovered quickly. 'Yes. The manpower issue. He's going to consider it – or so he says. He made a half-promise, but he's a slippery customer. How have you been today? Any better?'

Instead of answering, she asked, 'Was Fanshawe there?'

'Fanshawe? At the club, do you mean? Of course he was. The old blighter's always there. It's his second home!'

'Last night you said he was ill and you'd had to take him home in a...'

'Taxi. Oh, yes. That.'

She smiled in the darkness. Poor Alexander. He was a hopeless liar – at home, anyway. He could never remember from one day to the next, but perhaps that was better than being a good liar. She was not complaining.

'Yes, of course,' he went on hastily. 'He wasn't ill as it happened. Just drunk. Paralytic, in fact. Stupid old fool!'

'I thought you said he'd collapsed and you kindly offered to...'

'I was being charitable, Marcia. One does not care to malign one's friends. He's practically an alcoholic.'

'Still, it was kind of you to look after him and see him safely back to his flat. It made

16

you terribly late home.' She crossed her fingers and hoped she hadn't gone too far.

'I found a woman for Aunt Edith,' he said, changing the subject abruptly. 'She's travelled before and is eager for the trip.'

'Wonderful. What does she charge?'

'We didn't discuss that. I shall leave the financial arrangement to the two of them when they meet.'

'What's her name? How did you find her?' Now Marcia was genuinely interested. Years ago, as a young wife, she had been persuaded to travel with Edith and it was an experience she'd rather forget.

'Someone at the club mentioned her. Hester Shaw. She used to be a dressmaker and loves travel but cannot afford it.'

'Hester? I like that name.' Marcia yawned. 'Have you given any more thought to the carpet in your study? It's positively threadbare in places and Mrs Rice is always grumbling about it. It holds the dust apparently.'

'No, I haven't, and she should mind her own business and get on with her job. I've actually had more important things to think about than a worn carpet. That may surprise you.' His tone was caustic, a sure sign his wife had irritated him.

Marcia turned over on to her left side. 'Goodnight, dear,' she said, in a sickly sweet tone that she kept for such moments.

'Goodnight, Marcia.'

Her pain was murmuring already, agitating like a pet dog waiting for a treat, but knowing it would soon be over made it bearable. As soon as her husband was asleep she would go downstairs and take some medicine.

'Don't wake me if I oversleep in the morning,' she said. 'I've had a busy day and I'm tired.'

'Mmm...'

He was already half asleep. When his breathing changed she would recognize the sound. Marcia thought of the coming pleasure and smiled.

At three thirty that same night, Charlie Barnes was making his way through the silent back streets of Liverpool. He had just come from a late-night poker game in which he had lost the last of his wages, and his usually sunny expression had given way to one of disappointment and growing anxiety. At the corner, he turned into Marlin Row and headed for number five. Outside the door he paused to run his fingers through his curly brown hair which was more dishevelled than usual. He rubbed his grey eyes, which were smarting from the smoky atmosphere of the room at the Jolly Sailor, tugged down his jacket and fixed a carefree smile on his face. Instead of knocking at the front door, he tapped five times on the front window and, when nothing happened, he repeated these taps with a little more force.

Under his breath he said, 'Wake up, Annie!' and stared round at the neighbouring houses to see if anyone was watching from behind twitching curtains. After a few moments, while he tapped his foot impatiently, the door opened, a hand reached out and a young woman pulled him into the narrow hall.

'Charlie,' she whispered, as he pushed the front door closed with a practised movement of his right foot. 'I thought you was never coming. You know what time it is?' She was tugging at his jacket, trying to take it off.

'Course I know.' He pressed her against the wall and kissed her hard on the mouth. Annie was a pretty little thing – with blue eyes and fair hair which curled carelessly around her face – and she adored him. He'd been seeing her for more than a year and Charlie knew she'd do anything for him. She had no husband, jealous or otherwise, although poor Stan Holler had been after her since their school days and made no secret of his feelings for her. (Not that he stood a chance while Charlie Barnes was around!) So she had no kids to distract her *and* a place of her own. He was lucky and he knew it.

'Wait,' she said, wriggling free. 'We can't do it here. Someone might see.'

He followed her into the room which she rented from Mrs Fisher, who owned two other houses in the street and was considered a wealthy skinflint by her tenants. The room served as a bedroom-cum-living room and was sparsely furnished with a second-hand bed, table and two chairs. Within minutes they were both naked on the bed, eager for each other after the days they had been apart.

Afterwards, Charlie felt cheerful again and a little better about the money he had just lost. He had his arm around her and in the light from the street he saw that Annie was smiling too.

'I told you I'd be back,' he said. 'I promised and here I am.'

'Like a bad penny.' She snuggled closer.

'Not so much of the "bad", Miss Green.' He kissed her shoulder.

Charlie knew that whenever he was away on a trip, she worried that he would meet another woman and she would never see him again. Not that she had ever put her anxiety into words, but he knew. Charlie understood women. He loved them and would never deliberately hurt one of them. But he was good-looking and they buzzed around him 'like bees round a honeypot'. That was how his mother had described it when he was eighteen. Now he was twenty-five, and in love with life, he knew what she'd said was true and enjoyed himself.

Most of the time, that is. It was hard to enjoy himself when he was skint after a poker game that had robbed him of his last sixpence and left him with an IOU for a pound.

He sighed then quickly turned it into a cough.

She said, 'So where was you?'

She spoke lightly, but he sensed her unease.

'Here and there,' he said, hugging her. 'How many times do I have to tell you that I'm footloose and fancy free. Always have been and always will be. Not the marrying kind.'

'But ... you weren't ... in trouble again?'

'In trouble? When do I get in trouble?'

'You were in that fight once. Just after Christmas.'

He rolled his eyes. 'That was nothing. A bit of a falling-out, that's all that was. Me and Stan Holler. He was always on to me because of you. They never even fetched a copper!'

'But they threw you both out into the snow.' She giggled.

'It cooled us off. No harm done. We shook hands afterwards. You know we did.' He dismissed the incident with a shake of his head. 'A bit of a dust-up, that's all. A misunderstanding, you might say.'

'You might have got hurt.'

'Course not! You shouldn't worry, Annie. You'll get wrinkles.' He kissed her again. If he ever decided to settle down – and it was a mighty big 'if' – it might be Annie, but marriage held no appeal for him and he made no bones about it. Annie knew the score.

'I'm off again on the sixteenth of this month,' he announced. 'On the *Mauretania*, no less! Maiden voyage. I'll earn more and there'll be lots of rich people so lots of tips! I'll be rich when I get back. We'll go somewhere nice. Blackpool maybe. See the lights.' He hugged her. 'Might even stay the night!'

'Stay the night in Blackpool. Oh, Charlie! D'you mean it? In a hotel? Oh, we couldn't, could we?'

He could hear the excitement in her voice.

'Why not? You're a good girl. You deserve a treat.' Somehow he had to steer the conversation the right way. He hated borrowing money, but if he went to New York without settling the debt, they'd be waiting for him when he got back and he'd probably face a beating. 'The thing is, Annie, I'm a bit short at the moment and I want to book the hotel before I go away. I don't suppose you could help me out, could you? If not I'll chance it and try to book when I get back.'

'Oh, Charlie,' she wailed. 'You haven't been gambling again, have you? You still owe me two shillings from the last time you lost.'

The reproach in her voice was obvious and Charlie counted to ten.

'Then I'll buy you something nice in New York,' he offered. 'You'd like that, wouldn't you? A present all the way from America. That would be something to show your friends, eh?' He idled his fingers through her blonde curls. 'I quite forgot I owed you that two bob so you'll forgive old Charlie, won't you? And as for the gambling, well, it's not real gambling. Just the odd poker game. I'm trying to save up.'

'But so am I and...'

He sat up. 'No, Annie! Not another word. You're right. I shouldn't have asked you. I only needed a couple of shillings, but one of my mates'll help me out.'

She was silenced and he knew that now she felt guilty. She thought she'd been mean, a poor friend and less generous than his mates.

Charlie pressed home his advantage. 'That is enough about money. What shall we talk about now? I know, you haven't told me about that new job you went for – the one at the florist where they would train you to arrange flowers. Did you get it?'

'No.' She held his hand to her mouth and kissed it. 'They said I was not mature enough. I'm still at the laundry and Ginnie's still hanging on in the ironing room. If she'd go I'm definitely next in line for her job. The ironing would be better than nothing, but not as nice as the florist. Charlie, about the money. If you—'

He put a hand over her mouth. 'What did I say? No more about money. I shall manage, don't you worry. Not mature enough to work in a florist shop? But that's nonsense, that is. Suppose I have a word with them. Sweet talk them. How would that do, d'you suppose? Anything I can do to help you. You know me.'

'It's kind of you, Charlie, but it's too late. There's a new girl working there since Monday. But there's another job going at the greengrocer's and I might—'

'Which greengrocer is it? Suppose I come with you. A bit of moral support.'

'They won't listen to you. It's me they—'

'I could say we're engaged. They're not to know.'

'It's not just that, Charlie. They made me do some sums in my head and I got them wrong.'

He ran a hand gently down her body then up again until it cupped her breast. 'You do still love me, Annie, don't you?'

'You know I do!'

'Then there's something you can do for me. It's a lot to ask, but...'

'Anything I can.'

'Then make me a cup of tea! I'm parched.'

Her pretty laugh rang out as she cuffed

him playfully. 'You are a one, Charlie! You'd get away with murder, you would.' She scrambled from the bed, pulled on her flannel nightdress and crossed the room to the corner she called her kitchen. A single gas ring stood on a wide shelf and a saucepan hung on the wall. There was a single tap and she half filled the saucepan and lit the gas ring. While she found two cups, tea, sugar and milk, Charlie waited, sitting up in bed with the blankets pulled up to his neck. The room boasted a small black iron fireplace, but the fire had long since gone out and the room was chilly. He had hurried through a damp fog to reach Annie Green and was thankful he need not go out again until six. He could then sneak away before Mrs Fisher was up and about next door.

Annie returned to bed with the tea and Charlie sipped his gratefully. He told her about the RMS *Mauretania* and about the preparations that were being made for her maiden trip.

'You should come to watch us leave the harbour,' he suggested. 'There'll be a band playing and the ship will be decorated with bunting – and you can watch all the toffs going on board.'

'I might do that, Charlie. Then I can wave to you.'

When they had drunk the tea Charlie slid down under the blankets and closed his eyes sleepily. Annie rinsed the cups and then crossed to the small wardrobe where she kept her few clothes. While Charlie dozed, she opened the drawer at the bottom and took out a small tin where she kept her savings. Annie extracted a shilling and two sixpences and counted what was left. After returning the tin to its hiding place, she tiptoed round to Charlie's side of the bed and placed the money on the small table which contained a candleholder and a dish of withered rose petals.

Charlie grunted and opened his eyes. 'Oh, you sweetheart,' he murmured. 'That'll see me through until I start back at work. Give us a kiss!'

The kiss led to another and then somehow he was not sleepy after all, but soon after, once the passion passed, flushed and satisfied, he forgot about the fog and the unsuccessful poker game and finally slept.

A few hours earlier, while Charlie Barnes had still been hoping to win at poker, an elderly lady had sat at her writing desk in an elegant apartment overlooking the small green area optimistically known by the inhabitants of Tessingham Terrace as 'the park'. Her thin grey hair was plaited and hung down to her waist. Her crumpled face shone with an application of expensive skin cream and the bony hand that held the pen showed signs of a professional manicure. Her faded grey eyes stared at the page through small, round-lensed spectacles while her small mouth moved approvingly with each word that she wrote.

Edith Carradine, at eighty, no longer remembered her birthdays out of choice, and she also no longer remembered anyone else's birthdays. Her days, she told herself, were too full. She had to watch her wealth, monitor her servants, and ensure that she stayed healthy. All three aims were fraught with difficulties because she could not trust other people to do their work properly or get them to understand the quality of service she had been brought up to expect. Her father's family were descendants of land-owners in Surrey where several large farms remained and were worked by tenant farmers. Her mother's money had come from overseas investments, mainly India – money that had been wisely invested in the City. She had married well, too, and her husband had left her a large sum of money when he died twenty years ago.

She had, she believed, two ungrateful daughters, who were more than willing to spend her money, but refused to allow her a say in how it was spent. They even rejected her advice whenever they could. After the death of her husband they had finally rebel-led against her autocratic ways and the resultant relationships were fragile. Entries in her daily diary over the past years provided evidence of the many and varied quarrels and estrangements between mother and daughters.

She glanced back at the many and varied complaints she had confided about them. Dorcas had refused to take her advice on footwear, as usual, and had bought laced shoes instead of buttoned boots – and had had the audacity to suggest that at the age of forty-five she was old enough to choose her own shoes. Cheeky young madam! Evelyn had employed a housemaid from an agency instead of training a young girl straight from home. Lazy, that was Evelyn's problem ... And only recently Dorcas had lied to her in order to avoid including her at a dinner party. Selfish creature. Her mouth tightened at the unhappy reminders.

This particular night, however, Edith Carradine had nothing unpleasant to record about either Evelyn or Dorcas. Her mind was on the approaching trip to New York on the RMS *Mauretania* and the woman her nephew had found to accompany her.

Wednesday, November 6th, 1907 – Young Alexander has come to my rescue, bless the boy. He has found a suitable companion for me who comes highly recommended by a friend of his. Her name is Hester (or possibly Esther) and he says she was once a dressmaker but presumably has now fallen on hard times. 'Not a "fallen woman," I hope!' I said, being unusually flippant. I expected him to laugh, but he gave me a very odd look and changed the subject. Perhaps he found it somewhat out of character, which I daresay it was. Alexander describes her as 'biddable' (or was it dutiful?) so we should get along. I shall take no nonsense from her and at the first sign of unsuitability shall not hesitate to send her packing. I can always hire another companion for the return crossing when we reach New York. I shall take two of my dresses that need alteration since the Harley Street man (I forget his name) advises me to wear a less restrictive corset as he suspects that the present one is putting undue pressure on my digestive organs. A little sewing will keep Miss Shaw out of mischief. There will be no 'shipboard romance' for any companion of mine. I shall firmly discourage 'followers' and will keep a strict eye on Miss Shaw from day one.

Blotting her writing carefully, Edith reread her words with satisfaction, but as she replaced the pen she frowned at the backs of her hands which were liberally sprinkled with dark freckles. It seemed that no amount of lemon juice would fade them and that irritated her. She had plenty of time and money to spend on herself and enjoyed buying expensive clothes and cosmetics. She had once been a great beauty, and although she was now a mere shadow of her former self, she still had the satisfaction of having outlived many of her friends. Age was her enemy, but, she told herself, she was prepared to go down fighting.

Two

Annie Green would not have recognized her lover in the smart uniform of ship's steward. Charlie hurried through the public rooms of the *Mauretania* on a tour of inspection with his friend Chalky White. He had waved 'goodbye' to Annie on the quayside two hours earlier and had parted from her with real regret, but had forgotten her immediately. Now some of the crew found themselves with time on their hands because the boat train from London had been delayed and it would be another hour at least before the eager passengers reached Liverpool and could start boarding.

'A drawing room for the women. What next?' Chalky rolled his eyes. 'They're pampered, they are.' He stared round the large room in undisguised awe. 'Look at that! Oak panelling. What did that cost?'

'It's maple, not oak,' Charlie told him loftily. 'Wait until you see the men's smoking room. Their panelling's walnut.' He had overheard many useful facts earlier by loitering near to three of the ship's officers who were escorting important passengers around the new ship.

Although the ship was an express liner, her title was Royal Mail Ship since she had been designed primarily for the speedy carrying of mail to and fro across the Atlantic, but certain concessions in the way of comfort had been made to the travelling public and the interior decoration was elegant enough to impress them.

Chalky frowned. 'They say it's not a patch on the *Amerika*.'

Charlie rushed to the ship's defence. 'But the *Amerika* is slower, don't forget. We did twenty-six knots during the trials. Wish I could have showed Annie round. She'd have been knocked sideways. Be like a palace to her, this would.'

'It's like a palace to *me*!' Chalky grinned suddenly. 'When you going to marry this Annie, then, if she's so wonderful?'

'Don't rush me. We haven't mentioned wedding bells and I don't intend to. You know me, Chalky. Do I look like someone's husband? I don't want to end up like you with two kids and another on the way. You know what one of my lady friends told me? She said I wasn't husband material! Elena her name was. A real darling. Father was an Italian and owned his own restaurant. You can get to like spaghetti if you try hard enough and it's free!' He laughed. 'Not "husband material". I took it as a compliment and her mother took against me. But it's the truth. I want my money for myself.'

'To pay off all your gambling debts!'

'Who says I've got any?'

'You always have gambling debts. You can't play poker because you've got an honest face.'

'That's all you know.' Charlie tapped his chest. 'I'll be rich one day. You never will. Come on, let's take a dekko at the Grand Salon.'

They were not disappointed. In fact nothing disappointed them, although they were careful not to appear too impressed and passed semi-critical comments from time to time in order to appear blasé.

Half an hour later, the passengers began to embark and Charlie was back at his station in the bar reserved for first-class passengers. People swirled around him, mostly lost and asking for directions, but some were already settling into the comfortable chairs with a drink, determined not to miss a moment of the good life they had been led to expect from the publicity literature for the 'floating palace'.

Charlie slipped between them with practised ease, a tray of drinks balanced on one hand, a cheerful smile on his face. First day aboard the new ship, but he knew it didn't show. Like his colleagues, he managed to look entirely at home as he ministered to the passengers' every need and anticipated the tips he would receive when the crossing came to an end.

An elderly woman laid an imperious hand on his arm and stopped him in his tracks.

'How can I help you, madam?' he asked smoothly, his handsome face creased into a smile, his eyes on the powdered face and elaborately coiffed hair.

'You can show me the way to my cabin, young man,' she answered. 'All this muddle and confusion – it's a disgrace. First the train from London is late and now we are supposed to make our way through this frightful crush of bodies. It's quite unnecessary.'

'I wish I could help you, madam, but the bar staff are not allowed to leave the area. However, I...'

The woman turned to her much younger companion. 'What did I tell you, Miss Shaw? No respect for age or class these days. Standards are falling everywhere you look. We are paying for first-class service, but look what we get!'

'I'm afraid, madam, that on a maiden voyage the crew are not always familiar with the layout of...'

'Don't make excuses, young man. The fact that this *is* the maiden voyage is all the more reason why the trip should be superbly comfortable for the passengers. I shall write to

Cunard as soon as the voyage is over and shall tell them exactly what I think of their efforts!' Her eyes narrowed. 'Where do you come from? You're not a Londoner. I can tell from your accent.'

'No, madam. Liverpool born and bred!' He smiled, but she refused to be charmed.

'A pity.'

Charlie gave a polite shrug and took a second look at the woman who he now knew as Miss Shaw. So she wasn't married. He guessed she was a little older than him, not beautiful but definitely attractive in a restrained way and with a just perceptible air of sadness about her that Charlie immediately found intriguing. He was also a great admirer of bright auburn hair, especially when it was allied to green eyes. He wondered if she had a fiancé. He thought it more than likely. He could imagine her asleep in a silky nightdress, her hair tousled on the pillow.

She turned to face the old woman. 'Don't worry, Mrs Carradine. We'll find one of the officers. Or would you like to wait here with a glass of lemonade while I go in search of our cabin?'

'Lemonade? In this weather? Certainly not.' She tossed her head. 'However, I'd not refuse a pot of tea and a biscuit while I'm waiting.'

Charlie tore his gaze away from the

35

younger woman. 'You might try the Verandah Café, madam. It's a brand new concept and we think...'

'Certainly not.' She turned to her companion. 'I shall stay here and you may fetch me—' She broke off. 'Oh! I see no vacant tables.'

'I'll find you one, madam,' Charlie told her. He leaned towards her confidingly. 'I know the very place – tucked away in the corner where you won't be jostled.' He smiled at her and then at the red-headed woman. Was it his fancy or did the latter brighten slightly under his attention? Women responded to him, he knew. He had once boasted that given time he could have any woman he wanted. It wasn't quite true, but he did have a great deal of success with what he called 'the ladies'. He put it down to being slim, handsome and a smooth talker – and to loving them and letting them know it. This young woman, however, was a different kettle of fish altogether. He had never chanced his arm with a first-class passenger but he was tempted. How would she react, he wondered. She might be flattered or she might be offended or consider him impudent. The more he thought about it, the more he fancied the challenge.

The old lady agreed to the pot of tea with a show of reluctance and the younger one went on her way in search of their cabins.

Charlie led his elderly charge to an empty table and, with a slight pressure on her arm, helped her to settle in the seat. Moments later he returned with a pot of tea and a plate of biscuits.

'What is your name, young man?'

'Charles Barnes, madam.'

She gave him a condescending nod. 'Thank you, Mr Barnes.'

'Shall I fetch a drink for your daughter?' It was meant to be not-so-subtle flattery but it failed.

'My *daughter*? Don't be ridiculous. I hardly know the woman. Miss Shaw is my travelling companion. Nothing more.'

She gave him a dismissive wave of her hand and Charlie escaped. Silly old bat, he thought and gave a few moments' thought to the unfortunate Miss Shaw, until a trio of smart young women appeared and asked for his help, and the old lady and her unfortunate companion were at once forgotten.

Fifteen minutes later Hester was ushered into her cabin by Mrs Pontings, a kindly stewardess who confided proudly that she was the sister of one of the ship's officers.

'And if you need me, just press the bell and I'll come along right away,' she promised.

'When do you go off duty?'

'We're always available, madam, so if you're taken ill in the night don't hesitate to ring. That's what I'm here for.' She smiled. 'Enjoy your trip.'

She closed the door and Hester was left alone to get her breath back and marvel at her surroundings. The carpet was a pale green, as it was throughout the rest of the passenger areas. The hand basin was fitted into a marble surround. The bed linen was of a high quality and matched the curtains which framed the porthole.

Edith Carradine had booked them into adjoining rooms, solely for her own convenience, as she had explained coming down on the train from London.

'If you are in cheaper accommodation elsewhere, Miss Shaw, I should not be able to summon you so easily. There would be no point in paying for a companion who is not on hand if I am seasick or otherwise inconvenienced. I hope you appreciate my generosity.'

'I do indeed. Thank you.'

The truth was that being next door to her employer might prove more limiting, thought Hester, who had secretly hoped for some opportunities to explore the ship's facilities on her own. Still, there seemed little she could do about it, and she was certainly grateful for the luxury the cabin afforded her. It was a far cry from the small flat which Alexander had bought for her. Not that she wasn't grateful – she certainly was. He had met her at a desperate time in her life which she wished to forget.

Mrs Carradine might be an irascible old woman, Hester thought, but she knew how to do things in style.

Hester had also learned, on the train, of the garments Mrs Carradine was expecting her to alter. She would do the best she could with them, but if her employer found fault with her work, she planned to claim that her eyesight was failing. A lie but what else could she do? She could hardly betray Alexander who had lied on her behalf – albeit for his own benefit. Presumably he had thought Hester would enjoy the trip despite her responsibilities to her employer. Or had he? Had he perhaps been eager to get rid of her so that he could pursue someone else? The worry never left her. He had promised Hester that when his wife died he would marry her. Marcia was much older than him, but Hester realized she might live for another ten or twenty years. Her own situation was far from ideal, but the life into which she had been drifting when she and Alexander met would have been far worse.

Hester now went into the adjoining cabin to see if it varied in any way from her own. It looked similar but with the addition of a telephone on a stand in one corner. She shook her head in amazement and wondered who Mrs Carradine would want to contact.

Her uncooperative daughters? More likely her nephew Alexander, to complain about the unsatisfactory companion he had found for her!

There was a knock on the door and when she opened it a porter stepped briskly into the cabin, wheeling a large trunk.

'Your luggage, Mrs Carradine,' he said with a smile. 'Will you need help with your unpacking?'

'I'm Mrs Carradine's companion and no thank you. I think the unpacking will probably fall to me.'

'Right, madam.' Deftly he manoeuvred the trunk into position beside the chest of drawers and then loitered hopefully. He did not outstretch his hand, but Hester realized that he was expecting a tip. 'I'm so sorry, I have no money with me. It's in my cabin next door. If you'd wait a moment.'

He stepped outside and waited in the narrow passage as she found a sixpence and handed it to him. Hiding his obvious disappointment, he smiled and hurried away with his trolley.

Ten minutes later Hester had collected her employer from the bar and installed her in the cabin.

Mrs Carradine stared round with narrowed eyes. 'Where's the bathroom?' she demanded. 'Every first-class cabin on the *Mauretania* has a bathroom. There must be some mistake. Ring for the steward at once.'

Hester had also read the brochure. 'I think it said that *some* of them have bathrooms.'

'When I want your opinion, Miss Shaw, I'll ask for it. Please ring for the steward.' Her glance fell on the trunk. 'Who brought that?'

'A porter. I gave him sixpence.'

'More fool you!' Abruptly she sat down on the edge of the bed as though wearied by the day's events and Hester felt a sudden compassion. She was, after all, very elderly, but her habit of fighting everyone who tried to help her was inevitably going to drain her energy.

Mrs Pontings arrived, smiling, but Edith Carradine soon changed that by interrupting her introduction with a demand to know where the bathroom was that she had expected.

'The number of cabins with bathrooms is limited,' Mrs Pontings explained soothingly. 'But you'll find that...'

'Limited?'

'I expect they had all been snapped up by the time your booking was received. They do cost a good deal more and many passengers find...'

'I am not one of your "many passengers", Mrs Bunting. I am—'

'It's Pontings, madam.' Ignoring Edith Carradine's icy tone, the stewardess continued. 'My name is Pontings. Not Bunting.'

Edith Carradine looked at Hester. 'Get rid of this woman,' she snapped. 'I'll take the matter up with someone more senior.'

Hester looked at the stewardess apologetically. 'I'm sorry,' she stammered. A look of understanding passed between them before the stewardess withdrew.

When the door had closed behind her, Hester hesitated, then said, 'She's a very nice woman.'

'How would you know? She has no manners. She interrupted me.' Edith stared balefully round the cabin, but found nothing else to annoy her. 'Unpack my trunk, please, and then go next door and unpack your own luggage. I shan't eat this evening – it is already too late thanks to that stupid train driver. I will go to bed at ten o'clock. If I need you I shall knock on the wall. Let's hope for good weather. Are you a good sailor?'

'I don't know yet.'

Edith Carradine snorted. 'Well, don't expect me to look after you. You're the companion! If you want dinner tonight you will have to go down on your own. I shall rise at eight and will expect you to accompany me to breakfast in the dining room at a quarter past nine on the dot. Life, I have discovered, needs careful supervision, and time has to be properly disciplined. You will, I'm sure, find that out for yourself as you get older.'

The cabin was silent for the fifteen minutes it took Hester to unpack the trunk and stow away the various items of clothing. The long skirts and dresses went into the small wardrobe with the five pairs of shoes while the underwear and small garments fitted into the drawers.

Since the old lady made no comment, Hester decided her work must have met with approval, but when she turned to leave she was given a nod but no thanks. She closed the cabin door and hurried into her own room where she let out a sigh of relief. Exhausted, she sat down on the bed and covered her face with her hands. How on earth was she going to survive the rest of the crossing?

That evening it rained hard as RMS *Mauretania* pulled away from her berth at the Princes Landing Stage and only the boldest or more foolhardy passengers braved the outside decks to watch the departure from Liverpool. Hester was not among them. She had decided to explore the ship more thoroughly and then go for dinner at eight o'clock. She moved quietly along the passage between the rows of cabins, making little sound on the tiles underfoot. They had been specially designed to reduce noise and would ensure a minimum of disturbance from late-night revellers for those already in their beds.

Hester began to enjoy herself as she blended in with passengers and crew, the latter busy about their duties, the former in the process of settling in. Hester found the library, it was almost empty, and then peeped into the men's smoking room before arriving at the bar where her employer had waited for her pot of tea.

At once a young purser appeared at her side, his tray at the ready, his smile broad. His dark hair was parted in the centre and smoothed down with what smelt like patchouli oil and his dark eyes surveyed her with obvious approval. But he was not Mr Barnes, she noted, and was ridiculously disappointed.

'Can I get you anything to drink, Miss Shaw?' he asked.

She blinked in surprise. 'You know my name?'

'Charlie Barnes mentioned you to me. He said to look after you if he was not around.'

'Goodness!' She laughed. 'That *is* good service.' She felt herself colour with pleasure at the idea that the young steward had spoken about her to a colleague. 'I'll have a glass of orange juice.'

'May I recommend a cocktail, Miss Shaw?' He indicated a menu standing on the table. 'A Tequila Sunrise might suit you. It's very pretty. Most ladies like it. Or there's the Manhattan. That's—'

'I think I'd better not,' she said reluctantly. 'I don't drink a lot of alcohol and it might make me dizzy.' Her employer would throw a fit if she thought her travelling companion had taken to drink!

At that moment, to her secret delight, Charles Barnes materialized beside them. He raised his eyes and turned to Hester. 'This is Chalky White, Miss Shaw. Don't believe a word he says.'

Both men laughed at this.

'I'm only trying to advise her on a suitable cocktail.'

Charles Barnes tutted. 'If Miss Shaw wants any advice she will come to me. You go and serve the old gentleman over there. He looks thirsty.' With a nod of his head, he indicated a burly be-whiskered man who at once caught Chalky's eye and beckoned.

Chalky rolled his eyes. 'Must I?'

'Remember your wife and kids.'

'Oh, I do!'

Fixing a friendly smile to his face he moved away in the direction of his next customer.

Hester said, 'That was unkind, Mr Barnes.'

'I hope you'll forgive me.'

'I'm sure I will. He doesn't look old enough to have a family.' Goodness, she thought. Am I flirting with this man? How ridiculous.

'He made an early start. Married at twenty, regretted it at twenty-one. Not like me. No wife. No kids.'

45

'And no lady friend?' The words slipped out unbidden. Hester was appalled. Stop this, she warned herself. You're making a fool of yourself. You have absolutely no interest in this man or his friends.

'No special lady, if that's what you mean. So, now, if there's anything I can get for you...'

Hester took a deep breath and let it out while she made an effort to take her own advice. *This stops right now.*

'I was going to order a glass of orange juice.' She softened the words with a smile. 'I hope you're not also going to try and sell me a cocktail instead.'

'Maybe tomorrow,' he said, winking. 'No pretty young lady should travel on the *Mauretania*'s maiden voyage without trying one of our cocktails.' He moved smoothly away, unaffected by the ship's movement.

Hester felt the faint vibration from the engine room and was aware of a distinct lightening of spirit. Blow Mrs Carradine! she thought. She can be as awkward as she likes. I shall still have some free time and I intend to enjoy myself. She felt like a young girl let out of school and then felt guilty. Being with Alexander was a permanent constraint, but that was not his fault. He could only be with her when work and his home life permitted and she understood that he had meetings to attend which occasionally lasted well into the night. They could never venture outside the flat together in case they were recognized, and even when she was alone, she did not feel free. She was constantly afraid of meeting someone she knew – an old friend, perhaps – who might ask her difficult questions about her present situation or ask for her address so that they could 'pop in' and see her. Casual friendships Alexander had forbidden because he hated the idea of finding someone there when he called in unannounced.

As she sipped her orange juice and watched Charles Barnes mingling with the other customers, she realized with a start that here on the *Mauretania*, if she discounted Edith Carradine, she was unknown and could move anywhere she liked without fear of being recognized or embarrassed. She could sit in the library, stroll on deck or scan the shelves of the on-board newsagent in search of a suitable magazine. She could then sit and read it in a sheltered corner of the deck, with a rug over her knees to keep her warm.

There was no one to point the finger. Yes! she thought, growing bold. Tomorrow I will choose my first cocktail.

With a faint smile on her lips, Hester plucked the list of cocktails from the table and gave it her whole attention.

The night passed smoothly as the ship's bow

cut through the cold grey water on her way to Queenstown in Ireland. Twelve and a half hours later she docked, to the delight of her crew and those passengers who appreciated the speed she had maintained. At this rate, they told each other, the *Mauretania* might well equal the *Lusitania*'s speed record and that would be a matter for huge rejoicing as a friendly rivalry already existed between the two sister ships.

For a while Hester and her employer stood at the ship's rail with other passengers and watched the huge sacks of received mail being hauled upwards by winches. Once in New York it would be sorted and sent on its way, while mail destined for Great Britain would be taken on board.

A smart middle-aged man standing next to Edith Carradine turned to them, introduced himself as Dwight Leonard and asked how they had slept. 'It was a good run down,' he said, with a noticeable twang which immediately labelled him as an American, even if his name had not immediately done so. 'Cunard can be proud of her new ship. Yes, ma'am! This company doesn't cut corners. No expense spared on this vessel. Mind you, we still have to see how she copes with the Atlantic. The sea can sure be rough at this time of year, but the *Mauretania* will take it on the chin.' His laugh was a loud, proud bellow which made the two women smile.

His face changed. 'But that can slow us down. That's the only problem. Nothing else to worry about on a vessel like this. You can rest easy. Yes, sirree! I slept like a baby last night. How about you two ladies?'

Before Hester could reply, Edith said frostily, 'We went to bed early and slept well enough, thank you.' Hester realized that she was not enjoying the man's well-intentioned conversation.

Undeterred he continued. 'Not that we need to break any records. The *Lusitania* has already snatched the Blue Riband from the Germans.' He laughed and Hester joined him, but Edith stared grimly ahead, saying nothing.

Below them the relentless activity proceeded at what appeared to be a snail's pace. Passengers were boarding – men carrying hand luggage, women with young children, elderly people helping each other up the gangway and disabled people in wheelchairs being pushed up by sturdy crew members.

The man said, 'Did you folks know we took on bullion back in Liverpool?'

Edith finally showed an interest. 'Do you mean *gold* bullion?'

'Indeed I do, ma'am. Twelve tons of it, so they say. Twelve tons of pure gold! Now, doesn't that give pause for thought?'

Hester said, 'A very expensive ballast!' This brought another bellow from Leonard, but

Edith had once more relapsed into silence.

'Take a lot of slaving in a creek in California to pan that kind of gold! My granddaddy did a spell there back in '49 and thought himself lucky to end the day with half an ounce of the darned stuff. All he got at the end was a bad back and empty pockets, but he had to try. They all did. Some won out, the rest didn't.'

'It must have been exciting,' said Hester.

'You bet. Hard labour, too, but it was an adventure.' Making a final effort with Edith Carradine, he gave her a smile and said, 'It's a pity you turned in so early last night, ma'am. There was one helluva fireworks display as we passed the New Brighton pier – to wish the ship Godspeed.'

Hester expressed disappointment that she had missed it.

'Very over-rated, in my opinion,' Edith said. 'All that noise. I'm afraid I value my rest. In my state of health a regular and early bedtime is essential.'

Hester recalled what Alexander had told her and wondered what these ailments amounted to. Was her health really at risk or was it all in her mind? Maybe she should enquire. If Mrs Carradine were ever taken ill on board, her travelling companion should be able to offer some insights into the problem. If the old lady regularly took tablets, Hester ought to have some idea what they were and when she should take them and what the dosage should be. She thought about the ship's doctor and wondered how well qualified he was. For the first time she realized that being a travelling companion had its responsibilities and decided to approach her employer on the subject of her health at the first suitable opportunity.

Almost as though she had read Hester's mind, the old lady turned abruptly from the rail. 'We must go inside, Miss Shaw. I've seen quite enough. This cold damp weather is bad for the lungs and mine are weak enough already. We will go for breakfast and discover what sort of kitchen the *Mauretania* has produced. You can always tell by the toast. A decent kitchen will offer diners toast that is well-browned but not burnt.' With a brief nod to their American companion, she walked briskly from the rail towards the companionway.

After a moment, Hester said, 'It was nice talking to you, Mr Leonard.'

He doffed his hat. 'Your aunt, perhaps?' he asked, raising his eyebrows.

'Hardly,' Hester said. 'I'm her travelling companion. In other words, Mrs Carradine is my employer.'

As she hurried away from him in pursuit of the old lady, she thought, I'm actually being dutiful now! How terrible! But Mrs Carradine was paying for the trip, she reminded herself, and was entitled to her money's worth.

Fortunately breakfast – served in the dining room, an elaborate area built on three levels – satisfied Edith's high ideals in most respects. The porridge was free of lumps, the milk was fresh, the stewed apples were just sharp enough and the toast was the right shade of brown. Her only grumble resulted from the fact that they had to share a table with four other people. These were a mother and her twelve-year-old daughter and an elderly couple. As these four had turned up earlier for their breakfast, Hester and Edith only shared the table for twenty minutes and, to Hester's relief, her employer managed to restrain herself from making any critical remarks. However, as soon as they had left the dining room, Edith gave an exaggerated sigh of relief.

'What frightful people! I shall speak to the management. I had no idea when I chose the *Mauretania* that we should be forced to share a table with strangers.'

'I thought they were very pleasant. The girl was very well behaved...'

'She was sullen.'

'I thought her shy.'

'Believe me, Miss Shaw, I have two daughters of my own. The girl was sullen. Boys of that age are also sullen – with the exception of my nephew, who was perfectly capable of conversing with adults from a young age.' She spread marmalade on her toast and cut it carefully. 'And the mother's accent! Goodness knows where they hail from.'

Refusing to be drawn into the attack, Hester said, 'It sounded like a West Country accent to me. Maybe Devon or Cornwall. The other two were cheerful souls.'

Edith gave her a withering look. 'Mr and Mrs Gutteridge? They never stopped talking, if that's what you mean by cheerful. Practically told us their life stories. So they run a successful grocery chain. It's of no interest to me. I'm not used to being bombarded with information over breakfast. It's bad for the digestive process. If we can't have a table to ourselves I shall write to Cunard and complain.'

Hester's mind was working fast. 'I'm sure you could have your breakfast in your cabin if you wished for privacy. The stewardess could probably see to it for you.'

This would release her from her employer's company for the best part of an hour each morning. Edith's company was already proving wearing, Hester reflected.

Concentrating on her boiled egg, she tried not to show her enthusiasm for the idea. She said innocently, 'I think you're right, Mrs Carradine. Doubtless many other like-minded people are making similar arrangements.'

Mollified by her companion's encouragement, and beginning to think it her own idea, Edith finally left the table and went in search of Mrs Pontings, leaving her travelling companion to enjoy a second slice of toast in peace. She was about to leave the dining room when one of the waiters came to her table.

'Miss Shaw?' he asked.

She nodded.

'I've been asked to give you this.' He handed her a small envelope and hurried away.

Startled, Hester opened the envelope with fingers that shook slightly. Who would send her a note? Unless it was from Mr Barnes ... It was!

> *If you fancy a drink later and need an escort, I'll be at the Verandah Café at eleven tonight. Charlie Barnes.*

'Oh, no,' she whispered as her insides tightened with a mixture of excitement and fear. 'No!' she insisted, as her pulse quickened. An assignation with one of the ship's stewards? It was quite out of the question. Edith Carradine had made it clear that she was not to become involved. No shipboard romance. That was how she had put it. And there was Alexander to consider. Not that he had extracted any such promises, but there was such a thing as loyalty. 'Quite impossible,' she muttered and crumpled up the note impatiently.

But a drink sounded harmless enough. Probably all the crew members were trying to find a woman to flirt with to brighten up the crossing. Was that all it was? Maybe all the single women were hoping for a mild flirtation to while away the time as they crossed the Atlantic. Perhaps it was normal. Perhaps she was being paranoid.

Only one quick drink. She told herself she was making a big deal out of nothing.

Adrenaline was coursing through her at the idea of a late-night meeting with Charlie Barnes, but, perversely, she wished he had not written to her in this way. She was probably ten years older than him so why hadn't he picked on someone else? Someone younger and unattached. The ship was full of pretty young women, all eager for romance. It was written on their bright faces and the provocative way they tossed their hair and glanced beguilingly from beneath their little hats. By comparison, Hester felt quite dowdy. So what was Mr Barnes playing at?

She smoothed the rumpled note and read it again, trying to imagine what had been in his mind while he was writing it. Was it some kind of joke? Maybe his friend had dared him to do it. Or they might have made a bet on whether or not she was the kind of woman who would be flattered into accepting an invitation from a stranger.

Throwing down her table napkin in frustration, Hester stood up and hurried from the dining room, looking neither left nor right for fear that someone might be watching for her reaction. Unable to face Edith while her mind was in turmoil, she went out on deck and stood with some other passengers at the rail, staring blankly at the busy scene. Soon after eleven she knew they would weigh anchor and leave Ireland and head out into the Atlantic for a four or five day crossing.

What would happen, she wondered, if she failed to turn up at the Verandah Café? He might take offence and ignore her in future, making sure that she would see him being charming to another woman. But suppose she *did* go there and he stayed away. Was it just a test of some kind? Coming straight from the dining room, Hester was wearing no coat or jacket and the wind was cold. She wrapped her arms round herself, shivering inside as well as outside. If she was honest, she *wanted* to meet Mr Barnes, but common sense warned her against it.

But I like him, she thought. He was like no one she had ever met before. Breezy and seemingly uncomplicated, he was everything that Hester was not – but would like to be. And so unlike Alexander who took her for granted and rarely paid her a compliment –

except the one of sheltering her from the hardships of life. She owed so much to Alexander, she thought with a resigned sigh. Had she, after all, made a mistake in allowing him to snatch her from the slippery path on which she was about to embark when they met?

The moment was engraved on her memory. Expelled from the house that had been her home and employment for three years, she walked away with tears in her eyes, the bitter accusations still ringing in her ears. Her last glimpse of the family had been little Davina's frightened face, pressed against the window of the front room. Amelia Cartwright had refused to believe that Hester had not encouraged her husband, and Clive himself had denied that he intended any impropriety. Only Clive and Hester knew how badly he had behaved towards her, invading her room, night after night, until in desperation Hester had asked his wife for a key. That had been a mistake because it had aroused Amelia's suspicions.

'I want you out of this house,' she had cried, her face white with anger and contempt. 'To think I trusted you. To think I allowed you to be with my daughter. I thought you were a respectable woman, but Clive tells me how you flaunted yourself. Oh, you disgust me. You can pack your bags and go ... and don't you dare ask me for a reference! You call yourself a nanny, but you are no more than a...' She choked on the words and turned away, tears rolling down her face.

What exactly had Clive told her? Hester would never know because he had kept well away until she had left the house. Disgraced and with no reference, Hester had found herself homeless and without the means to support herself. She worked for a month as an assistant in a sweet shop, but the wages had been insufficient to pay for her miserable lodgings and she had been forced to pawn some of her clothes to make up the difference.

One dark winter evening, Hester had been spotted by Alexander as she made her way along a street frequented by fallen women. She had never admitted to herself her reason for being there, but she had thought she might be accosted by a passing gentleman. Stumbling on the cobbles, however, she was thrown headlong and her inelegant fall was seen by a gentleman passing the spot in a hansom cab. Alexander had stopped, helped her to her feet and had given her a sixpence to buy herself 'a hot pie'. As she stood at the stall enjoying the luxury, he had returned. Apparently impressed by what little dignity she retained, Alexander had been attracted to her and the chance meeting led to a second meeting and then to a relationship.

When he suggested renting a small flat where they could meet regularly, she had gratefully accepted his offer.

Now she was facing another offer and she didn't know what to do.

Three

The furious grey seas surprised many of the passengers as the ship left Ireland and headed into the Atlantic. The *Mauretania* began to react, pitching into the huge waves with a shock that sent tremors through the hull, or rolling from side to side, so that the passengers, both young and old, staggered drunkenly as they moved around the vast liner. At first people treated it as a joke and the children found it hilarious. As the hours wore on, however, the adults found it challenging, the older people grew wary of an accident and the children lost interest. Only the crew members moved easily round the ship, enjoying their superiority while handing out soothing comments.

'Don't worry, sir. You'll soon adjust,' or 'It's a matter of time, madam. By tomorrow you'll have your sea legs.' Neither was true. Most of the passengers would become queasy and lose their appetites while an unfortunate few would be seriously seasick and confined to their cabins.

To Hester's surprise, by lunchtime she was

still feeling reasonably well and went into the dining room with Edith who, although slightly off-colour, refused to be cheated of a delicious meal which was included in the overall price of the trip. As they settled themselves at the unoccupied table, the old lady smiled triumphantly.

'Hah! Not up to it! I might have known.' She regarded the empty seats with satisfaction.

'Good afternoon, ladies.' The waiter smiled. 'How can we tempt you today?'

Edith picked up the menu and studied it without much interest.

Hester asked, 'It all looks wonderful. Can you recommend anything?'

He leaned over confidentially. 'The lentil soup is very good for lining the stomach, miss. Afterwards perhaps the lemon sole – that's very light – and, if you're still hungry, an ice cream is easily digested.'

'That's what I shall have then. Thank you.'

Edith was frowning. 'I'll have just the soup with some thin bread and butter. Brown bread, of course.'

He wrote busily. 'No main course?'

'I said "just the soup"!'

As soon as he had brought the soup, Edith toyed with it, apparently unwilling to eat it. She nibbled a triangle of brown bread and looked rather unhappy.

Feeling sorry for her, and to take her

employer's mind off the ship's movement, Hester brought up the subject of the three dresses she was supposed to be altering.

'I had no idea you expected me to do some sewing,' she told her. 'I had to give up that line of work when my eyesight began to deteriorate. The problem—'

'Don't bother me with that now!' Edith took a spoonful of soup and swallowed it nervously.

'I just wanted you to understand. I'll do the best I—'

'What did I say?' Edith glared at her. 'I've other things on my mind.' She laid down her spoon and stood up. 'I don't feel too steady. You can help me back to my cabin.'

On the way out they were intercepted by the waiter and Hester informed him that she would be back shortly to finish her meal.

'I shall sit in my chair,' Edith informed her when they were back in her cabin. 'Put a glass of water beside me on the table and leave me to my own devices. I hate fuss. As long as I know you are next door, I shall be quite all right.'

Hester promised to return as soon as she had eaten and hurried back to the dining room. The twelve-year-old girl had now taken her place at the table and without her mother's presence, proved surprisingly talkative.

'Everyone calls me Elly or Nora which is

nearly as bad,' she told Hester between mouthfuls. 'And I hate them both so please call me Eleanora – unless you want to call me Monique, which is a name I really like, only don't let my parents hear you or they'll blame me because it's French and they think it's silly because I'm not French. Could you pass the salt, please?'

Puzzled, Hester did so. The girl poured some on to the table, took up a pinch and tossed it over her shoulder.

'Isn't your mother hungry?'

'No. She's been sick and the stewardess brought her a tablet to take and I know she won't take it because she says tablets aren't natural and we should let our bodies deal with it naturally because it's not an illness, it is only because of the ship's motion. If I get sick, I shall take a tablet. They're made of dimenhydrinate in case you need one. And I can spell that, in case you're wondering.' She took a gulp of air and studied the menu.

'Thank you, er ... Monique. I'll remember that.'

'I shall have the duck pate' – the girl glanced up at the waiter – 'and the roast beef and then the meringues – are they those white crunchy things?'

'Meringue, miss, is a crunchy mix of egg white and—'

'Egg white? Really? Ugh! I'll have apple pie instead.'

Hester's lemon sole arrived and she thanked the waiter. The girl's food arrived and the meal passed amicably. Hester was beginning to relax. Monique alias Eleanor amused her even though her presence reminded her of the fact that she would probably never have children of her own. Alexander, childless, had once talked about the family he had wanted, but lately, as Hester grew older and Marcia lingered on, the subject had been avoided. A shame, because she thought Alexander Waring would make a good father.

After lunch, she let herself in to check on Edith and found her asleep on the bed. Obviously she had agreed to take a tablet. Knowing that she might be needed any time, Hester bought herself a magazine and settled in her own cabin to read it. Try as she would, however, she could not concentrate, but allowed her thoughts to stray to the crumpled note in her purse. She had decided not to accept the invitation, but was regretting her decision more and more as time passed. Around five o'clock, Mrs Pontings knocked on the door to check on Mrs Carradine.

'I gave her a seasickness pill and I expect she's sleeping, but when she wakes she should drink a glass of water as her mouth might feel a bit dry.'

'I understand she's travelled before so she should know what to expect, but thank you for the advice.'

'They do rather knock you out, those tablets, but anything is better than feeling queasy all the time. She might need another to get her through the night, we'll see.'

'Are we expecting a rough night then?'

Mrs Pontings rolled her eyes. 'Oh, yes, dear! Very rough, I'm afraid. The Atlantic is hardly ever calm and rarely so in winter. But we're in good hands. We've got a good captain and that's the main thing.'

As soon as she had gone, Hester took the note from her purse and reread it. Suddenly she pressed it to her lips. More than anything she wanted to be at the Verandah Café to meet Charles Barnes. Just thinking about it made her feel younger than her years. A charming, fine-looking man was eager for her company, and that made her feel alive for the first time in years. She had made up her mind not to go, but she couldn't resist imagining how the meeting might go if she had decided to accept. She wondered what she would have worn. And who else would be there? Other crew members? Young married couples, perhaps. Or honeymooners. Older men travelling to New York on business, dallying in the bar late at night, hoping to 'pick up' an unaccompanied woman. Single women hoping to be picked up. She had heard that high-class courtesans used to travel on the liners in search of rich patrons.

It all sounded wonderfully romantic and risqué and exciting ... and she would not be there. She sighed as she imagined herself standing close to her escort, or sitting at a table, heads close as they chatted intimately.

'Oh, Alexander!' she groaned. He was her conscience and in a way she was grateful. Without him she knew she would be hurrying to the Verandah Café bar as soon as the big hand of her small travel clock showed eleven o'clock. Instead, she would probably be fast asleep by then for she had made up her mind to go to bed at ten. Charles Barnes would no doubt be annoyed to be 'jilted' in front of his friends, but he would quickly find another woman to take her place.

As though a voice had called her, Hester awoke later that night, sat up and peered at the clock. Twenty past eleven! Without a second's hesitation she scrambled desperately from the bed, splashed cold water on to her face and washed her hands. She ran a comb through her hair, pulled on her best skirt and prettiest blouse, slipped her feet into some shoes, snatched up her purse and let herself out of the cabin. Her heart was pounding. She would be too late. He would not wait. He would never speak to her again and it was her own fault.

'You coward!' she said out loud.

Turning a corner she almost collided with

a stout gentleman who recoiled with a muttered, ''Pon my soul!'

The passageways were eerily quiet as she made her way with difficulty, lurching from side to side with the roll of the ship.

Wait for me, she thought. I'm coming!

What a fool she had been, too timid by far. Where was the wrong in meeting a friend for a late-night drink? What harm could she come to? Charles Barnes was a member of the crew. He was hardly going to molest her and disappear into the darkness, never to be found again. He had a job to do. He was not going to risk his career in any way by bad behaviour for fear she report him to his superiors.

She stopped suddenly and looked around her. Where was she? Surely she should be there by now – or had she taken a wrong turn?

'Please,' she asked nobody in particular. What on earth was the time? His friends would tease him, but she was on her way. A stewardess appeared carrying a pile of towels and Hester asked for directions.

'You're on the wrong level,' said the stewardess. 'Go left and then right, then up one level in the elevator. Turn right and you're there.' As Hester thanked her and turned to retrace her steps, she added, 'Don't worry. He'll wait. They always do!'

Hester was in the elevator when it struck

her. Suppose she rushed in and ... and he had grown tired of waiting and ... and she found him with someone else. He wouldn't find it difficult. Leaning back against the panelled wall of the elevator, she took several deep breaths.

Don't even think it, she told herself. Calm down or else you will look desperate and people will pity you. Think of an excuse for your late arrival. Or pretend you did not notice the time ... Say you were finishing a letter ... or delayed by your companion.

Five minutes later she saw the words Verandah Café and almost cried with relief. Slowing down, she managed to fix what she hoped was a casual smile on her face and stepped inside. Despite the ship's move-ment, the room was packed with happy people, some sitting round the small tables, others standing along the bar. Some were even leaning on it for support! Whenever the ship rolled further than usual there was a concerted shriek followed by laughter. Hes-ter envied them. So young and so carefree. They seemed like people from another planet. The lights were low and a small group of musicians played popular ballads. Searching among the crowd, she caught sight of Chalky White, who was with a group of young men and women. One look told her that they had already had a little too much to drink. There was no sign of Charles Barnes and her hopes began to fade.

'Over here!' It was Chalky who had spotted her. At least he seemed friendly enough, she thought, as she threaded her way between the tables and swaying crowds with murmured apologies. He had his arm through that of a young blue-eyed woman with a tumble of fair curls whom he introduced as Nurse Dulcie Anson. She was looking up at him adoringly, but when Hester reached him, he put an arm round her as well and gave her a brief hug. Despite her recently made plans, she found herself stammering excuses for her lateness. He shook his head.

'He thought you weren't coming, that's all. He was a bit cut up.'

'Cut up?'

'Yes. He's taken a real shine to you. Poor old Charlie! He's not used to being "stood up". Dented his pride, if you see what I mean.'

'Stood up? Oh, no! I didn't mean to ... I was delayed by Mrs Carradine...' She could not quite manage to finish the lie. Had he actually been upset by her absence?

Freddy, the barman, leaned across. 'You Miss Shaw by any chance?'

Hester nodded.

Chalky said, 'Better late than never! A cracker, isn't she, our Miss Shaw?'

The young women regarded her critically as if assessing the truth of this. Hester felt her cheeks burn. Envying the peachy complexions and bright eyes around her, Hester realized she must be at least ten years older than most of them, if not more. Mortified, she hoped she wasn't old enough to be anyone's mother!

'I'm Freddy to my friends,' the barman told her with a broad wink. 'Charlie said, if you *did* turn up, to give you a cocktail of your choice – from him!' He grinned. 'What's it to be?'

Egged on by Chalky and his friends, Hester settled on a Manhattan. She sipped it dutifully but couldn't enjoy it. Nor could she join in the light-hearted banter of the crowd. They seemed so carefree that she felt old by comparison. Old and dull. When the music became romantic, one or two couples began to dance, and she made her excuses and left.

Finally finding her cabin again she let herself in and sank down on to the bed. Never again, she vowed silently. You are not one of them. You can't expect to be accepted. You will never fit in. She pulled off her clothes and tossed them on to the chair, neglecting to fold them, regardless of how they would look in the morning. They would be talking about her, she thought, and laughing at her behind her back. Or worse, they would already have forgotten her existence. What would Chalky say about her when he next saw Charlie? That she looked like a fish out of water.

Stick to what you do best, she urged herself as she lay in bed and stared at the ceiling. You're a travelling companion ... and a kept woman. The mistress of a middle-aged man with a wife who is going to live for ever. She got out of bed again and cleaned her teeth and climbed back into bed. *Forget tonight. Forget Mr Barnes. Count your blessings.* She laughed aloud. How many times had her mother told her that ... But she did count them. She had her health. She had Alexander. She had enough to eat and a roof over her head. She was crossing in style on the *Mauretania* and soon she would be in New York where anything might happen. She closed her eyes and waited for sleep to claim her.

The crew's quarters were a far cry from those of the first-class passengers or even the cheapest accommodation favoured by the emigrants, but the food in the dining room was reasonable and plentiful, and the hundreds of hungry young men and women who made up the staff ate well most of the time. The seasoned crew were never seasick, but the newcomers took time to become accustomed to the rolling of the ship. At breakfast the next day, as most of the *Mauretania*'s crew were seasoned by virtue of duty on previous vessels, the behaviour of the seas did nothing to dampen their spirits, and the conversation was lively.

It was a vast room, the lights already lit because of the dark November sky outside, but steam rising from the tea urns gave the place a cosy, contained feeling and enticing cooking smells added to its cheerful atmosphere. On this particular Monday morning, the weather was growing worse as strong winds and gigantic seas battered the *Mauretania*, but few people took any notice of the forecast. It was time for breakfast, a time to 'stoke up' for the gruelling day ahead. Chalky White, short on sleep, but still cheerful, tucked into his egg and bacon, mopped up the juices and then wiped the plate with a thick slice of buttered bread. He grinned when his friend sat down next to him with his own breakfast.

'Cheer up, Charlie! It might never happen.'

'Stow it!' Charlie reached for salt and pepper. His usual sunny expression was missing and he glanced at his friend irritably. 'Don't say it,' he warned.

All around them, the benches were filling up. There was a choice of menu and some were eating kippers. The noise was tremendous as voices rose above the clatter of knives and forks.

'Don't say what?'

'That you warned me. That you were right.'

The man opposite asked, 'What's up with heem?' He was Italian.

'Mind your own business, Stefano.' Charlie glared at him across the table.

Chalky reached for a fourth slice of bread and butter and took a large bite out of it. 'What's it worth...' he began, 'for some good news? Ten bob?'

'Ten bob? You're mad!' Charlie began to eat.

'All right then, five bob? Two?'

'Sod off, you silly devil!'

'Good news ... about Miss Shaw.' He grinned.

Charlie gulped down a half chewed mouthful and almost choked. 'What about her?' He looked round as though expecting to see Miss Shaw hovering somewhere.

Chalky beamed. 'She turned up looking for you but you...'

'She turned up?' His eyes brightened at once. 'You're not having me on? Miss Shaw turned up?'

'Yep. All dollied up, smelling of roses – or violets or whatever women smell of these days. Not a patch on my little nurse, mind you, but she looked very pretty.' He launched into the details.

Charlie's appetite suddenly returned and he began to enjoy his breakfast. 'I knew she'd turn up!'

'That's not what you said last night when

you left in a sulk.'

'Me sulk? I was tired, that's all!'

'Tired my eye. You were as sick as a parrot. I swear there were tears in your eyes.'

'You need your eyes tested, chum.' A broad smile lit up Charlie's face. 'What? You thought I didn't think she was coming? Course I did. I left her that drink with Freddy, didn't I? I knew she was interested.'

'You were fed up to the teeth because she didn't show. Admit it.'

'Please yourself. So why was she so late? Did she say? Did she look sorry that I wasn't there? Did she give you a message for me?' He gulped down steaming tea and gasped. 'Christ! That's hot!'

'Comes from a hot place and ... No, she didn't leave you a message. But she chose a Manhattan. Forced it down like it was poison, but tried to make out she liked it. The truth is she was like a fish out of water. We were all nice to her, but she was nervous. On edge. She's a funny one.'

Charlie beamed. 'Nothing funny about Miss Shaw, Chalky. She's just a cut above the rest. You wouldn't appreciate a woman like that.' He was rapidly recovering his confidence. Miss Shaw had accepted his invitation. Miss Shaw was interested in him. 'She has class, Chalky. Class.'

'I thought you said she was a travelling companion. A *paid* companion. What's classy

74

about that?'

Charlie paused to consider. 'Probably down on her luck. Rich Daddy went broke and shot himself and she's forced to work for a living. You know how it is.'

Stefano showed some interest. 'Who ees shot heemself?'

'Who's talking to you?' Charlie blew on his tea and sipped it cautiously.

Chalky stood up. 'I'm off. Word from above is that the weather's getting worse. It's going to be a tough day for the pampered darlings! All being "icky" and little piles of sawdust everywhere. They pay all that money just to be thrown around and lose their appetites.'

Stefano laughed. 'Tell us something we didn't know!'

Charlie simply smiled. His day was going to be brilliant, he thought. The world was a wonderful place. Miss Shaw was interested.

When Hester went into the next cabin around nine thirty, she found Mrs Carradine nibbling a small chicken sandwich. She was sitting up in bed wearing an expensive crocheted bed-jacket and seemed reasonably restored.

'Mrs Bunting brought it,' she told Hester, indicating the sandwich. 'She says it's the very best thing when one is recovering from any sickness. Because it's bland, you see, and light, and easily digested. Sit down and tell me that we are going to have better weather today.'

Hester obeyed. 'I can't agree about the weather,' she said. 'I haven't been along to reception and haven't heard the forecast. But you look much better. Perhaps you've got your sea legs.'

'Mrs Bunting – oh, no, it's Pontings – says if the weather doesn't improve I shouldn't venture far for fear of a fall. Her brother says it's not uncommon for elderly people to break an arm or a leg because we have such brittle bones. So I shan't be going far. I take it you've had your breakfast.'

'I did, but I shared the table with the girl. No one else appeared. Now, how can I be of help this morning?' She crossed her fingers and hoped her employer had forgotten the dress alterations.

Mrs Carradine seemed to be in a better mood. 'I fancy a little conversation – or would you care to read to me from the Bible. I used to read from the Good Book for my husband when he was ill. In his latter years he suffered with his eyes and reading small print tired him.'

Hester chose conversation. 'I visited the Verandah Café,' she confessed, leaving out the lateness of the hour. 'I thought you might enjoy it, but in fact it was a disappointment. It was entirely inhabited by bright young things and rather noisy.'

'Did you stay long?'

'No. I had a glass of orange juice and then left. I don't think you'd enjoy it.'

'Was there music?'

'Yes, a few people danced.'

'Danced? What time was this?'

'Early evening.' Hester was now wishing she had never mentioned the Verandah Café. She waited for the next question which would no doubt inspire another lie, but her employer had grown tired of the subject.

'Tell me something about yourself,' she suggested. 'My nephew was terribly vague. How did you two meet?'

The shock sent a shiver up Hester's spine. She must be very careful. Edith Carradine might be elderly, but she was certainly not slow-witted, and Hester could imagine her pouncing on any slip. She wondered desperately what Alexander had told her.

'Cat got your tongue?'

'No ... that is ... I don't quite know where to start.'

'Start with your parents, then.' Edith settled back comfortably. 'What did your father do? What sort of education have you had?'

This was safer, Hester thought. She could tell the truth.

'My father was in shipping – exports and imports. The company owned four ships. He was away quite often, travelling as part of his job – in Greece mostly.'

'Ah! Then presumably there was money for your education.'

'Yes. I was sent to boarding school in Sussex when I was nine.' She didn't explain how unhappy she had been.

Edith frowned. 'Then why did you become a dressmaker? I would have expected you to make a good marriage.' Seeing that Hester hesitated, she pressed her. 'Did something go wrong? Was that it?'

'Yes.' At least she could tell this part of her background. 'It was embezzlement. One of the directors went to prison for his part in the scandal. My father was not involved and was cleared of any part in the deception, but he never recovered from the blow. My mother says it was the shock that killed him. A heart attack when he was forty-five.'

She could still hear the tick of the clock as she waited outside her parents' bedroom where his body lay in the open coffin. She had to lean into it to kiss the cold hand and whisper a 'goodbye'. She could smell the burning candle wax from the four black candles in their tall brass candlesticks, one of which stood at each corner of the elaborate coffin. She was thirteen years old.

'My dear, how positively frightful!'

Edith's voice jerked Hester back to the present.

'My mother married again – a farmer in Hertfordshire. Life was very different after that.' The only good to come out of the second marriage, she reflected, was that she had been taken away from the hated boarding school.

She recalled her mother's face as she'd left her nine-year-old daughter in the care of one of the prefects on her first day at boarding school.

'If you aren't happy, Hester darling, you must write and tell us and we'll take you away.'

Hester had written countless letters, but later her mother insisted that the school had never forwarded them. Hester had felt utterly betrayed.

'Well! That is interesting.' Edith was regarding her with astonishment. 'How are the mighty fallen!' she said tactlessly. 'Was the second marriage fruitful?'

'No. I'm an only child.'

'So, who taught you to sew?'

'I suppose I picked it up as I went along.'

Edith was startled. 'You picked it up? My dear, dressmaking is an *art*. Not something you "pick up"! My last dressmaker was wonderfully talented. Show her a picture and she could copy the garment perfectly. She would take my measurements, draw out a paper pattern, cut the material and make it up! She had been properly trained.'

Hester hurried to correct the slip. 'I daresay I am more a seamstress, but ... but I have cut out and made dresses. My mother didn't want me to be away from home because she was very lonely and anxious after Papa died, before she got married again. She helped me at first, but then I gradually taught myself.' More lies. When she returned to Alexander, she decided, she might well throttle him! 'I wouldn't compare myself to your last dress-maker.'

'I should hope not,' Edith huffed. 'And that's how you met my nephew, Alexander?'

Hester took a chance. 'We've never actually met – at least, he may have been among the company, but I don't recall ever being intro-duced. I think he probably heard of me through a friend's wife.' Don't ask me her name, she begged silently. 'I did some sew-ing for her. I cut up a ball gown to make dresses for her twin girls.'

If the old lady queried this, she would pretend that Alexander had been confused. Holding her breath, she wondered how she could change the direction in which this conversation was going. Perhaps she should suggest a walk – but the ship was rolling heavily so that was hardly an enticing pros-pect. In desperation she said, 'Shall I read to you now? I always feel the psalms are very soothing.'

But Edith was not listening. Her mind had taken her in a different direction. 'So you haven't met my nephew – my sister Imogen's

boy. You'd like him, I think. He's a gentleman.' She sighed. 'He married a poor little
thing. Marcia Harcourt she was then. Not
poor financially, but poor in spirit and
entirely lacking in energy of any kind. She
seems to dream her way through life,
imagining that she is ill. Her mind seems to
drift at times, as though her thoughts are
elsewhere. I think she'd *like* to be ill, if the
truth were known. She loves to lie about on
the chaise longue and have people wait on
her hand and foot.' She shook her head.
'Poor Alexander. She must be a great trial to
him, but he never complains. That's what I
mean by a gentleman ... If you think you
have something wrong, demand to see a
specialist, I told her. That's what I do. That's
what I'm doing now, isn't it?'

'Indeed you are. We must pray he can help
you.'

'Well, naturally he can help me. I'm told
Mr Stafford is an excellent heart man and
his techniques and treatments are far ad-
vanced compared with those in England. So,
that's where I'm going. Alexander suggests
his wife should seek a second opinion,
abroad if necessary, no expense spared. But
she refuses.'

'But if she really is ill ... she might die. That
would be—'

'Die? Of course she won't die. She's not
even ill. She's a malingerer! Poor Alexander.'

This was not at all what Hester had wanted to hear. Alexander was promising to marry her when Marcia died, but from what she was now hearing, she could expect a long wait. All her doubts resurfaced. Would he then prefer someone much younger who could give him a family? If she were to have a child with Alexander, their marriage would have to be sooner rather than later. Dare she raise the question with him on her return? She desperately needed to know but dreaded his answer. Suppose he said honestly that he had no immediate expectations of being a widower. What would she do? Leave him? Would he be prepared for her to go? Did he *want* it to happen that way so that he would not have to end the relationship himself?

With an effort Hester abandoned that line of thinking. Daringly, she asked, 'What is he like, your nephew? Apart from being a gentleman.' It would be interesting, she thought, to hear his aunt's opinion.

'Alexander is quite charming, very good-looking, due quite shortly for another pro-motion – and is very devoted to his foolish wife. A lesser man would have given up on her, but he is patience personified.' She smiled suddenly. 'As a boy he always loved his Aunt Edith. I used to take him to feed the ducks in Regent's Park and to run around with his hoop. I have a photograph of him somewhere in his little sailor suit. He was sweet natured, never a bully. He always abhorred cruelty and injustice.' She paused in thought. 'He once came home from school with a bruised eye and his parents were shocked to discover he'd been fighting the school bully! Defending a weaker boy. That about sums him up.'

'He sounds a nephew to be proud of.'

So Alexander was due another promotion, thought Hester. He had kept that to himself ... and he was devoted to Marcia! She was beginning to doubt that she knew him at all.

'Indeed he is. He's the only one I approve of. My younger sister Imogen has another son, Bartholomew, but he is a bit of a wastrel, and they have sent him abroad to friends in South Africa to work. Always a sickly child, they were always too soft with poor Barty!' She shrugged. 'Not like Alexander. As he grew up he made up his mind to enter the police force, much against his parents' wishes. I encouraged him though. He wanted to do some good in the world. He's very high-minded and he's worked his way up by sheer hard work and a determination to succeed. Promotion is hard to come by in the police force. Too many men chasing too few opportunities.'

Hester was regretting that she had pried into Alexander's life. Depressed, she decided she had heard more than enough. 'Shall I read to you now?'

When Edith agreed and reached for her Bible, Hester didn't know whether to be pleased or sorry but at least she need not tell any more lies.

Four

It was after two in the afternoon when Charlie found Miss Shaw. She was in the reading room, surrounded by elderly ladies and ruddy-faced men with thinning white hair. The women were reading, but most of the men were enjoying the sight of Miss Shaw – and who wouldn't be. Charlie's heart thumped as he crossed the room towards her. She was wearing a soft tweed suit in grey, and a white collar showed at the neckline. Slim and elegant, he thought.

He bent over and whispered, 'May I speak with you outside, Miss Shaw?'

Startled, she nodded and he fancied he saw a faint blush illuminate her face. She marked the page and left the book on the small sofa where she had been sitting. As soon as they were outside Charlie closed the door behind them and, checking that no one else was around, pulled her close and kissed her before she had time to know what he intended.

For a moment, she stared at him, shocked and embarrassed.

He said, 'If I've offended you, I expect

you'll slap my face! And I'll deserve it.' He had expected her to return the kiss with fervour – he had hoped the young woman would be thrilled and excited – but the expression on her face set alarm bells ringing. 'I apologize, Miss Shaw,' he told her desperately. 'Will you forgive me?'

It occurred to him that he had misinterpreted the situation, but if she didn't want to be kissed, why on earth had she turned up at the Verandah Café? And suppose she was really offended and reported him to one of the ship's officers. Fear was almost unknown to Charlie, but he felt a prickle along his spine. 'I thought, Miss Shaw ... that is, I think I've made a mistake,' he stammered as his stomach churned.

Watching closely, he saw the shock fade to be replaced by confusion.

'No, Mr Barnes. It's I who should apologize.' Her voice shook slightly. 'I didn't mean to meet you last night – it didn't seem prudent – but then...' She shrugged. 'Somehow I changed my mind at the last minute and I knew that I wanted to see you after all. I rushed along and got lost and then, when I found the café, you weren't there and the barman said you'd paid for a drink so I couldn't not drink it without offending you, and ... Oh, Charlie! I shouldn't have ... have led you on.'

'But I wanted you to!' Hope flared suddenly. She had called him Charlie! He knew it was a mistake on her part – a slip of the tongue – but it thrilled him, anyway. 'I mean, I shouldn't have sent the note,' he told her. 'I should have asked you properly.'

But the reason he had not done so was in case she refused to his face. He wasn't used to rejection. He went on earnestly. 'I just can't stop thinking about you and wishing...'

Her eyes were large and intense and he struggled not to kiss her again.

'Mr Barnes, I – I don't think I'm at all suitable. For you, I mean – or anyone else for that matter. My situation is ... complicated but there are plenty of other young women. I don't think it should be me because ... I have attachments – of a kind. There is someone at home.'

'You're not married. You aren't wearing a wedding ring! Are you secretly engaged? Is that it?' Suddenly he realized just how much he wanted the answer to be negative.

'Not exactly, but ... You really mustn't ask all these questions, Mr Barnes. You're embarrassing me.'

'Please call me Charlie.'

'Oh, no, I couldn't!'

The more she protested, the more he longed to throw his arms around her, but he fought off the urge and tried to remain reasonable. Women never held him at arm's length for long but this one ... He was becoming worried, but before he could rustle up a more convincing reason why she should forget whoever was in England, the library door opened inwards and she almost fell into the arms of a plump bearded gentleman.

He cried, 'Whoa there, madam! You'll be sending up my blood pressure.' Laughing, he waved away her apologies and winked at Charlie before lurching his way along the passageway. Charlie had Miss Shaw to himself once more. But now they were both laughing at the incident and the earlier coolness seemed to have vanished. She looked beautiful when she smiled, he thought, his heart contracting a little.

'Could we start again?' he asked.

'Why not?' Her smile broadened. 'Good afternoon, Mr Barnes. What is the weather forecast for the rest of the day?'

'Not promising, Miss Shaw. The gale's getting worse. Some waves are breaking right over the ship and a few windows have been broken on the upper decks.'

'Really?' Her smile faded. 'Are we in any danger, Mr Barnes?'

He put a hand over his heart. 'If we are, then I will be at your service. If the ship sinks I shall rescue you.'

'Can you swim then, Mr Barnes?'

'Swim? Certainly not, miss! But I'm a very quick learner.' He closed his eyes in case his intensity frightened her away. With his eyes still closed, he said, 'I have a confession to make.' Opening them, he said, 'I'm not sorry I kissed you. I've been imagining it ever since I first saw you, but I *am* sorry you didn't kiss me back. Will you ever, do you think?'

He could almost hear the struggle going on within her mind. At last she said softly, 'I should hate to think I might not.'

The seas continued to become increasingly rough, with waves up to sixty feet high, and, like most of the elderly passengers, Edith Carradine refused to leave her cabin for fear of a fall.

'I could break a leg, the way this ship is behaving,' she told Hester. 'Mrs Pontings says there has already been one accident. An elderly man lost his balance and has hurt his elbow. They say the ship's photographer has given up in despair because his clients can't stand still long enough for him to take the photograph.' She paused for breath and went on. 'Mrs Pontings' brother told her the galley is in a mess – everything that isn't nailed down has fallen over. And even a few crew members are sick.'

Despite these proofs of the roughness of the sea, Hester was sent on various errands. The third of these was to fetch the doctor because Edith complained of her heart, saying she was feeling dizzy and that her pulse was erratic. Hester was on her way up the main stairs when the ship's bow dropped into a steeper than usual trough and a man, coming down the stairs, lost his footing. With a cry of alarm he tumbled down on top of her. She was crushed against the woodwork and struck her head...

Twenty minutes later the doctor looked at the prone figure in the bed and tutted irritably.

'Why don't people behave in a sensible manner?' he asked. 'Isn't it obvious that it's not a good idea to go wandering around the ship in weather like this?'

The young nurse nodded earnestly, her blue eyes wide, her fair curls confined by her nurse's headdress. This was her first step into the real world since completing her medical training, but what she lacked in experience, she made up in enthusiasm. 'Will she come round, do you think? I mean, she isn't...?' The word 'coma' buzzed in her brain as did the phrase 'vegetative state'.

The doctor rolled his eyes. 'No, she isn't. Nothing dramatic, so don't get excited. A bit of concussion and a nasty bruise. That's all. She might be a bit delirious or disoriented, but she'll be up and about before long. If she says anything intelligible, make a note of it.' He took out his watch and frowned at it. 'I'll notify the captain, and then I'll be in my office writing up my log. When I get back you can find her cabin and see if she has anyone travelling with her who'll be wondering where she is.'

Left alone with her patient, Dulcie Anson busied herself smoothing the sheets around her patient and gently plumping the pillow.

'Nothing to worry about,' she said to her sleeping patient. 'You're in good hands.' There was something familiar about the woman, she must have seen her somewhere.

It was a pity in a way, that it wasn't worse, she reflected. They might have hit the newspaper headlines in New York. DISASTER ON NEW LINER'S MAIDEN VOYAGE. There might have been a mention of the devoted doctor and nurse pulling the patient through. Not that the ship would want headlines like that. They would obviously have to avoid anything which suggested that RMS *Mauretania* was not a stable ship. No bad publicity for Cunard. She understood that.

She tried to concentrate on the job in hand. The patient might wake up and vomit. She hurried to fetch a suitable bowl. Then she found a notebook and pencil and sat down next to her patient. Staring at the pale face, closed eyes and slack unresponsive mouth, she wondered if perhaps she was someone famous, although she hadn't been wearing expensive clothes when she was carried in, barely conscious. Now she wore a hospital gown. She frowned. Where had she seen her? It came to her suddenly.

Of course! This was Charlie Barnes's lady friend – the one who stood him up!

Half an hour later, Dulcie was tapping on the door of the cabin occupied by a Mrs Carradine.

The door opened and a cross-looking woman glared at her. 'I didn't ask for a nurse,' she said sharply. 'I asked for the doctor, but that was nearly an hour ago.'

'Mrs Carradine?'

'Yes, but they are not fobbing me off with a nurse. I have a heart problem and am on my way to New York to see a specialist.'

'It's about your travelling companion, Miss Shaw. I'm afraid...'

The door opened wider. 'You'd better come in, I suppose. What has she done?'

Dulcie stepped into the cabin, hiding her astonishment at the luxurious fittings and furnishings which compared so favourably with her own cramped quarters. 'I'm afraid she was knocked down by a fellow passenger who fell against her, but—'

'Drunk, was he?'

'Oh, no! He simply lost his balance. Fortunately he escaped serious injury, but poor Miss Shaw was sent flying and hurt her head. She's in the ship's hospital under observation.'

'In the hospital?' The old lady sat down

heavily. 'She is supposed to be taking care of me, not being knocked down! I sent her to ask the doctor to come here.' She put a hand to her heart.

The nursing training came to the fore and Dulcie spoke soothingly. 'The doctor assures me it is only a mild concussion and she may be released from the hospital later today or first thing tomorrow morning.'

'So is the doctor coming to me or isn't he? I sent my companion to summon him almost an hour ago. I could be dead by now!'

'I'm afraid he didn't receive the message because of your companion's injury. She was in no state to deliver messages to anyone. We had a job trying to find out her name. I'll let Doctor Dunn know your anxiety.'

'Ask Miss Shaw to explain it to him.'

Dulcie counted silently to ten. What an impossible old lady. Miss Shaw was probably better off in the peace and quiet of the hospital room. She tried again. 'Miss Shaw hasn't been able to say anything very coherent yet. She's still unconscious – although she has called once or twice for her husband.'

The old lady snapped, 'Aren't you listening? She is a Miss Shaw. *Miss* Shaw. She isn't married and doesn't have a husband.'

'So who is Alexander?' Taken aback, Nurse Anson frowned. 'She keeps muttering his name. I thought she said, "I'm sorry, Alexander." I thought quite naturally ... Oh, dear, how silly of me. Perhaps it's her brother or her fiancé.'

'She doesn't have a brother or a fiancé.' She was staring at the nurse. 'Or if she has, it's the first I've heard of it. Are you sure it was Alexander? Maybe it was Alec.'

'I don't think so because once she called him Alexander.'

'Not Mr Waring?'

'Waring? No.'

'What else did she say? Think, girl!'

Dulcie objected to being referred to as a girl, but knew better than to say so. She tried to concentrate. What else had she written in her notebook? 'She said something about Chalker Street. "Being safely back at Chalker Street." Something like that.' She looked hopefully at the old lady.

'Did she now! Chalker Street ... Chalker Street, London?'

'I don't know, ma'am. I don't know London. I come from Sutton in Surrey.'

'Hmm? This is very odd. I'm beginning to wonder—' She covered her mouth with her hand as though to prevent her thoughts escaping into speech.

For a moment neither spoke. Dulcie was brightening. Perhaps, after all, there was a mystery here. Was the patient using a false name? Travelling incognito, the way they did in novels? Was she running from her husband to her lover in New York? An heiress, maybe? NURSE UNRAVELS PLOT ON BOARD LINER!

This interesting line of thought was interrupted at this point by a new sensation which gradually distracted them from their conversation. For a moment or two they regarded each other in surprise, waiting to have their suspicions confirmed. Instinctively they both turned towards the porthole through which the clouds now seemed to be moving in a different direction. The sound of the ship's engine had also changed. Mrs Carradine was first to break the silence.

'Am I imagining things or are we changing course?'

'We're slowing down!'

They looked at each other in alarm. Altering course mid-ocean sounded most unlikely.

On deck, dozens of the crew had been called out to fight a very real danger. The violent movements of the ship had caused a spare anchor to break free from the moorings on its cradle and this enormous piece of ironwork was sliding around the deck creating a serious threat to the superstructure as well as to the men who were desperately trying to secure it. It weighed nearly ten tons and its erratic shifts of position were difficult to anticipate and deal with. Adding to their problems were the giant waves which crashed over the deck and threatened to sweep the unwary overboard. To lessen the impact of the waves, the captain had decided to change the ship's course so that she would not strike the mountainous seas head-on and would thus provide a somewhat safer environment for the men whose hazardous work it was to return the anchor to its cradle and lash it down.

Meanwhile, Hester lay in bed unaware of the crisis on deck. She had dimly recognized the nurse's uniform and knew she must be ill or injured, but had no recollection of the accident on the stairway. At some stage, she had had flashes of memory and fancied that she had fallen and hit her head, but how, why or where escaped her. When she moved her head an ache began behind her eyes so she kept them closed most of the time and kept her head still. She had glimpsed the small room with its white cupboards and tables, each stocked with stainless-steel dishes and utensils – and she also recognized the antiseptic smell. Slowly her memory was returning. She finally remembered that she was on board the *Mauretania* ... and then she recalled Mrs Carradine.

'Oh!' she groaned as more memories emerged from the corners of her confused mind. She put a hand to her head and felt a large lump on the right side above her ear. At that moment the door opened. She opened her eyes, as a man in a white coat appeared and introduced himself as Doctor Dunn. He was portly and his manner was brisk. He explained briefly what had happened to her, in a voice that suggested she had somehow brought it all down on her own head by careless, ill-advised wanderings. Finally he enquired how she felt.

'My head aches and I feel rather dizzy, but I'm probably well enough to go back to my cabin. My employer will be worrying about me.'

'She knows the situation. We found your room number on the key in your purse – I hope you'll forgive the intrusion – and then went through the passenger list. Nurse Dulcie Anson is with your employer as we speak. Mrs Carradine will expect you later this evening if you feel well enough. If not we will keep you under observation overnight. We shall see.' He held up a hand when she began to protest. 'We can't take any chances, Miss Shaw. We have the matter of insurance to consider. We can't have you wandering around the ship half-dazed, can we?' He gave her a humourless smile, made his excuses and hurried out.

With a resigned sigh, Hester settled herself for a long wait. She didn't mind being kept from Mrs Carradine for an hour or two. It would give her time to think about the pressing matter of Charlie Barnes. Did she dare see him again? She was almost certain she would manage it somehow.

By evening, despite the continued bad weather, a small number of hardy souls had managed to reach the bar where Chalky and Charlie were on duty. One of the women, pressing a handkerchief to her mouth, looked apprehensive, as though at any moment she would stagger back to her cabin. The men looked uncomfortable to a lesser degree and appeared determined not to be done out of their evening tipple. The atmosphere was subdued and the barman, with little to do, was wiping the bar counter to remove the spills due to the ship's erratic motion.

Since everyone had been served, the two stewards were able to stand together while keeping their eyes on the clients, ready to rush forward when anyone raised a languid hand or made eye contact.

Charlie said, 'Is Lizzie sure it was her? Miss Shaw doesn't look the type to go falling down stairs.'

'I told you!' Chalky rolled his eyes in mock frustration. 'Dulcie had to go and talk to the old lady and tell her what had happened. Anyway, she didn't fall down the stairs, this man fell down on top of her and knocked her over.'

'I'll send her some flowers then!'

'A florin says you won't!'

'And a get-well card!'

'What will the old dragon think?'

'Ah! Good point ... I'll say they're from the crew, but I'll wink at her – Miss Shaw that is, not the dragon.'

Chalky looked at him. 'You're not going soft on this one, are you? She sounds a bit out of your league, if you ask me.'

The smile faded. 'I'm not asking you and what if I am soft on her? So what? I'm not married or anything.'

'What about Annie Whatnot back home? I thought you said if you ever tied the knot it would be to her.' He caught someone's eye and hurried away to collect the order, then over to the bar to load his tray with a sherry and a double whisky with ice, then back to the man and woman who had ordered the drinks.

And then he came back to his friend.

'Annie ... yes,' Charlie said. 'I did think she might be the one, but I never said that to her, and I didn't say I would marry her. You can ask her. She'll tell you. But now I've met Miss Shaw, I realize Annie wasn't the one. I'll have to tell her.'

'A letter? After, what is it, three years? Poor Annie!'

'Two years not three. No, I couldn't do that to her. I'll tell her myself, face to face. I'll tell her the moment I get ashore.'

Chalky grinned. 'You don't know yet

whether Miss Shaw will have you! She might turn you down. You don't know much about her. Then you won't have either of them.'

To his surprise this argument stopped Charlie in his tracks. He said, 'Turn me down? Oh God! She wouldn't, would she?' He regarded his friend with dismay. 'I'm not fooling, Chalky. It has to be Miss Shaw. I just know it. If she turns me down I'll ... I don't know what I'd do! I just feel for her – in my heart! And don't laugh. I mean it. Didn't you know it when you met your wife?'

'No. Nothing of the sort.' He raised his eyebrows. 'She told me she was expecting a baby, mine, and said her ma would throw her out into the street and her pa would come after me and beat me up. So I asked her to marry me and she said, "Yes." And we get along fine.' He shrugged. 'Women are all the same.'

'Not what you'd call romantic!' Charlie shook his head.

'It doesn't have to be romantic.' Chalky tapped his forehead meaningfully. 'You're taking it too seriously. Believe me, marriage is not romantic. My wife's a good sort. Could have done a lot worse.'

'Well, it's not like that for me. I've fooled around a lot, I admit, but this is different.'

I want to protect her, he thought. Chalky would never understand. I want to be everything in the world to her – but I can't tell him that. He swallowed hard, taken aback by the strength of his feelings for Miss Shaw. He must stop calling her that. He must find out her Christian name ... and he would send her some flowers. Better still, he would take them to her. He was suddenly overwhelmed by a need to see her, hear her voice and see her smile. He would find the little nurse and ask for Miss Shaw's room number. They would be in New York in a few days' time and he might never see her again. A cold shiver ran through him.

'I'm going to marry her,' he said doggedly. 'Whatever it takes.'

'She might be a widow with five children!' Chalky was determined to torment him.

'Miss Shaw,' Charlie reminded him. 'The old lady called her *Miss* Shaw.'

'Have it your own way, then.'

'I'm going to ask her and she's going to say, "Yes." Nothing and nobody is going to stop me. I'll do whatever it takes.'

Early the following morning, Hester was deemed fit to return to her cabin. There had been no sickness and the headache had cleared.

'Go carefully,' the doctor warned. 'The seas are lessening a little, but are still high. We're not going to make a record run, I'm afraid, after that business with the anchor, but we might make it up on the return trip.

That means a few bumps.'

Hester thanked him for the information. It certainly didn't inspire her to walk too far.

'There'll be a fee.' The doctor turned away. 'I'll send an invoice along later.'

Hester hoped it wouldn't be an excessive amount. She might have to ask Mrs Carradine to lend her some money. She made her way back to her own cabin and sat there for ten minutes, collecting her thoughts. Then she went next door. Her employer's first words were not encouraging.

'So, there you are! About time. I have a bone to pick with you. Sit down.'

Hester's heart sank. 'It wasn't entirely my fault,' she began. 'A man fell and knocked me down the stairs...'

'I'm not talking about your accident. You look well enough now. I want to know why you were calling for Alexander while you were delirious. Is that who I think it is? If so, I believe you have some explaining to do.' Mrs Carradine folded her arms and glared at Hester accusingly.

Hester's mind went blank with shock as she stared at Edith Carradine. Had she called for Alexander before she regained consciousness? She supposed it was possible. Her mind spun frantically. Would she be able to lie her way out of this or would it be better to confess?

Nervously she looked at her employer who

sat on the chair, her back like a ramrod, her eyes fixed, hawk-like, on Hester's face. With an effort she forced her mind into action. How much did she know? And, more to the point, how much had she guessed?

Edith continued. 'I may be elderly but I am not stupid and you have, I suspect, been pulling the wool over my eyes. I think I am entitled to an explanation.'

Still Hester hesitated. This was Alexander's fault, she knew, but would Mrs Carradine accept that her favourite nephew had chosen to deceive her? Gathering her courage, she decided to tell the whole truth.

She said, 'Alex and I are lovers. He pays for my flat in Chalker Street and has done for several years. Naturally he didn't want the family to know. He doesn't want to hurt Marcia.' She saw the triumphant gleam in the other woman's eyes.

'I thought as much! Well, I confess he had me fooled. I could have sworn to his integrity, but' – she threw out her hands despairingly – 'my nephew has had a mistress for Lord knows how many years and I knew nothing about it! I trusted that boy. I always have had the highest regard for him. How well do we ever know anyone?'

Hester saw that despite the brave words, the old lady was shaken. 'We have been very discreet,' she began.

'Discreet? You would *have* to be! Certain

standards have to be maintained for his career. Has it occurred to you that you might be jeopardizing his hopes of promotion?'

Hester felt a flash of anger. 'Has it occurred to *you*, Mrs Carradine, that our relationship involves two people? For your information, the original idea was your nephew's and I took some convincing. I could see that by living with him in secret I was ruining my own chances of marriage. My being here with you was not my idea either. Alexander insisted. He wouldn't hear any arguments. As for being his mistress ... I am hardly in an envious position.'

'Indeed? How exactly are you suffering, Miss Shaw?' The tone was colder now.

'I am thirty-one and have always wanted a home, a husband and children. In my present situation I can have none of these and my prospects are poor.'

'You have a home!'

'No. I have a roof over my head. Alexander has *two* homes and I live in one of them. I do not work because he wants me to be available at all times of the day or night – whenever he can steal time from work or home.' She swallowed as the words tumbled out and she realized just how resentful they sounded. 'We cannot go out together in case we are seen. I have few friends.' She became aware that for some time she had tried not to see her situation as a form of house arrest, but suddenly it was becoming horribly clear. She had willingly entered into this relationship without proper regard for the consequences and had been reluctant to face the truth.

Mrs Carradine drew herself up. 'There is no need to take that tone with me, Miss Shaw. You have stayed with him and presumably you were not locked in. Not held prisoner against your will.'

Hester cried, 'I am nothing but a glorified whore!' As she heard the words she had uttered, she was appalled. Not at the utterance, but at the truth behind them. Mistress or whore? Her throat tightened.

Mrs Carradine gave no answer, but turned sharply away. The minutes passed. Hester's headache threatened to return. She felt exhausted from the recent concussion and resentful of her employer's condemnation although she knew it to be deserved. This really was not the best time to have this particular conversation, she thought, putting a shaking hand to her head.

'Have you eaten today, Miss Shaw?'

Hester shook her head. She was starting to feel sorry for herself and was afraid of breaking down. Tears, she was sure, would only incense her employer. Edith Carradine would not tolerate weakness.

With an effort she said, 'Alexander told me that your daughters were both unable to accompany you and that you were having trouble finding someone suitable.

'He seemed to think I would take good care of you. He obviously didn't want you to know that ... that Marcia wasn't the only woman in his life. I didn't fancy the journey so late in the year, but he was insistent and I agreed to please him. It was his idea to pretend I was a dressmaker.'

'Not easy for you, I imagine.'

'No. It's been worrying me.'

'I'm revising my opinion of Alexander.' The old lady pressed her lips together. 'I have always found him perfect in every way and it's almost a relief to know that he does have failings.' To Hester's surprise Mrs Carradine's tone had softened. 'He is human, after all, and as fallible as other men. Well, well! He has a mistress. Wonders will never cease.'

Hester said nothing, hiding her surprise at the change in the old lady's attitude. She seemed on the point of saying something when, quite abruptly, she rang for the stewardess. When she arrived, Edith ordered a pot of tea for two and a round of chicken sandwiches for Hester.

'You must eat,' she said. 'I need you to be fit again. I certainly don't want to be looking after you! As for Alexander, I shall talk to him about this situation. I intend to leave him all my money and he needs an heir before I do. Marcia will never have a child, so he needs to give the problem some serious consideration before it is too late. Perhaps it should be you.'

'Me? But we are hardly in a position to...'

'Then, when Marcia dies, Alexander can legalize your position and that of the child.'

Despite the headache, Hester's head jerked up in astonishment. 'Have a child out of wedlock? You can't mean that.'

'I can and I do. It happens all the time.'

Hester hesitated. 'I think you should save this conversation for your nephew, Mrs Carradine.' The threatening press of tears had receded and she made an effort to compose herself. 'I dislike the feeling that I'm being interrogated. I may have done wrong—'

'You certainly have!'

'But Alexander is also to blame for betraying his wife.' Hester spoke defiantly. Out of the blue, her world was turning upside-down. The secret of their liaison was out and she had no idea what would happen next. She would never agree to have a child out of wedlock. No son or daughter of hers would go through life burdened with such a terrible stigma. It was unlikely Marcia would die while she, Hester, was still young enough to have a baby. Maybe when he knew his secret was out, Alexander would end the affair and start looking for someone younger, secure in the knowledge that his wealthy aunt would eventually approve. Her head throbbed relentlessly now and she wished herself back in the quiet of the hospital room.

A knock at the door brought the tea and sandwiches and they busied themselves with food and drink. Hester found to her surprise that she was both hungry and thirsty.

Her employer was obviously considering every angle of the situation. Her lips were pursed and her brow was furrowed. The lengthening silence was abruptly broken by another knock on the door. Edith indicated that Hester should answer it and she rose carefully to her feet. To her consternation she found Charlie Barnes outside with a small bouquet of flowers.

'Oh, Mr Barnes!'

Edith said, 'Who is it?'

He winked at Hester and said loudly, 'A small token from the crew of *Mauretania*, miss. Our regrets at your accident and our best wishes for your recovery.'

Hester's throat was dry with shock and her heart was racing. Charlie turning up like this completely unnerved her and she was thankful that her back was towards her employer.

'That's ... I mean, this is so ... so kind. I didn't expect...' She stared at the red rosebuds, at once thrilled and terrified. Not for one moment did she believe that the flowers were from the ship's crew. They were from Charlie Barnes and she wondered whether Mrs Carradine would sense that.

Apparently she did not. She said, 'It's the very least they can do. Thank him, Miss Shaw, and close the door.'

Hester studied the flowers, praying that there would be no telltale message. She looked imploringly at Charlie and chanced a quick smile.

'Thank you, er...'

'Charlie Barnes, miss. Glad to be of service. I'm afraid the weather is not likely to improve much so do take care as you move around the ship. Good day to you, ladies.' He gave her an intensely appraising look, turned sharply on his heel, and walked away.

She watched him until he turned the corner and was then filled with a strange sense of loneliness. Shaken, Hester closed the door and tried to calm herself. She felt flushed and excited by the unexpected meeting, but told herself she was being ridiculous. Praying that her face would give nothing away, she turned back from the door.

'Flowers at sea are so inconvenient!' Mrs Carradine tutted irritably. 'You'd better ring for Mrs Pontings and ask her to put them in a vase for you. You'll have to keep them in your own cabin, and you'll have to anchor them in some way. Such a nuisance especially when the ship is being tossed about like a cork!'

To Hester's relief, she showed no interest in the eight roses. *Eight.* Would the old lady read anything into that?

'I'll ring for her from my own cabin,' she said. Then made her exit before Edith could protest.

Eight red roses! One for each letter of 'I love you'! Back in her own cabin she allowed herself a smile. Charlie Barnes was a cool customer, she thought, amused and thrilled by his audacity. No one had ever sent her flowers before. She rang for the stewardess and sat on the edge of the bed to wait for her. Pressing the flowers to her chest, she was overwhelmed by a rush of happiness and, closing her eyes, gave herself up to the pleasure of the moment.

Five

Back in Liverpool, a day later, Maisie Barnes was summoned to the front door by the bell and opened it reluctantly. It was nearly seven in the evening and she was not feeling her best and had only just returned from work at the nearby laundry. Her plump face was still red from the steam, her hair was lank and her back ached from hours bent over tubs full of boiling clothes. It irked her that Ginnie Wenn was still working there. Ginnie had been threatening to leave for weeks now and Maisie had been promised her job in the ironing room which would mean a little more money and better working conditions. It would be a step up in the world and waiting for it filled her with frustration.

She found Annie Green on the doorstep and regarded her without enthusiasm. Charlie's pretty lady friends always made her feel inferior.

'What's up?' She was used to her brother's friends popping in hoping for news of his whereabouts and the dates for his shore leave. Annie, she guessed, would be no

111

different although she had lasted a little longer than most. Blocking the doorway, she tried to convey the idea that she was busy.

Annie said, 'Hello, Maisie. Any news of Charlie? I need to talk to him.'

Maisie held back a sarcastic comment. Annie knew that news from Charlie was impossible, but her interest was aroused. Annie needed to talk to him – or so she claimed. Intriguing. Reluctantly Maisie opened the door to let her in.

'He's halfway to New York!' she reminded her visitor. 'How can I have any news? Unless he's sent a message by carrier pigeon and if so the bird got lost.' She led the way into the kitchen where the stove had gone out during the morning and she had only just relit it. There was a chill in the air, but the small tin kettle, perched above it, was making encouraging noises and a one-eared tabby, by the name of Moggie, had curled hopefully on the rag rug in front of the stove. 'Cuppa?'

'Please.' Annie's glance held the familiar hint of envy before she turned away and began fussing over the cat.

The envy was for Maisie's position as Charlie's brother. No one, Maisie knew, envied her for her youth or beauty – she had no delusions about that. An unkind quirk of fate had decided that Charlie should be the handsome one with a sunny disposition and an easy charm. The same fate had given his sister mousy hair that refused to curl, brown button eyes and a tendency to worry. She was now a shapeless woman of thirty-five with no husband and very little money to spend on herself. This morning, a large, coarse apron was tied round her non-existent waist and the word 'unlovely' fitted her to a T – but Charlie was her baby brother and, as always, that brightened her world enormously.

Annie envied her that, if nothing else, because Annie longed for a similar closeness, but she was simply one of many young women who had come and gone in Charlie's short life.

Annie leaned forward. 'Has he said anything more about ... you know? Wanting to settle down.'

'Getting wed, you mean?' Maisie shook her head. 'No, not to me. But who knows how my brother's mind works.' She fussed with the teapot then glanced up sharply. 'You haven't lent him any more money, I hope, 'cos I can't help you. You know what I told you last time! Say no!'

'It was only a shilling.'

'Only!'

Maisie sucked in her breath with a disapproving hiss. 'You never did! You're mad!'

'I know, but ... Maisie, there's something else. It's about ... you know. Me and Charlie have been ... I mean it's hard to say "No" and he ... I think I'm...' A telling blush was making her prettier than ever.

Maisie's stomach lurched and she clapped a hand to her mouth. 'Don't tell me you're up the spout! I don't want to hear it! Oh Lord! You're not, are you?'

Annie nodded wordlessly and Maisie stared at her in dismay.

'I thought you could talk to him for me.'

Maisie rolled her eyes. Charlie and his women! She had no children and no experience of married life, but they seemed to consider her some kind of expert just because she was his brother. But this particular problem had never cropped up before and she wondered what Charlie would say when he knew.

'Are you quite sure?' she asked. 'You can miss a month without it meaning anything.'

Would Charlie be pleased if there was a child on the way, she wondered. Maybe it would settle him down – if he wanted to settle down. Knowing her brother, it would take a really special person to get him up the aisle! Was that person Annie Green?

'It's two months,' Annie confessed. 'Not one. I tried to tell him the other night when he turned up, but I couldn't find the right moment. You know what he's like.'

Out of her depth, Maisie shrugged and changed the subject. 'I hope he gave you back that shilling!'

Annie shook her head. 'He borrowed some more but...'

'You idiot! What did I tell you?'

'He'll pay it back some time.'

'Like when?' She poured the tea.

'When he has a winning streak – and he's going to take me to Blackpool.'

'Gordon Bennett! That makes it all right then, does it?'

'He can't help it. He'll pay me back out of his wages soon as he gets back.'

Maisie folded her arms. 'But is he going to *wed* you? That's a mite more important than swings and roundabouts and bright lights in Blackpool.'

She regarded Annie moodily. In a way she had been dreading the day when her brother would set up home elsewhere. Not only for his share of the money which helped pay the rent, but for the company. She had never lived alone. When her widowed mother died, twenty-one-year-old Maisie had taken over the tenancy of the flat because Charlie was still at school. Later he had helped keep a roof over their heads. Charlie was fun and he was always cheerful. The men Maisie took a shine to never even noticed her and she was resigned to the fact that she would probably always be single. She lived for Charlie's shore leave and missed him while he was at sea. When he finally moved out she would be forced to take in a lodger, but the prospect held no real appeal.

Maisie said slowly, 'Suppose he won't marry you, then what?'

Annie's face sagged. 'He wouldn't say that, would he? Oh, Maisie, don't say that!'

'Well, how do I know what he'll do? I'm his sister, not his mother!'

'But you wouldn't advise him against me, would you? If he asks for your advice? I mean, wouldn't you like to be an auntie? It would be fun, wouldn't it? I mean, it's going to happen sometime, isn't it, and we could get married before anyone knew? My pa will kill Charlie if he leaves me in the lurch!'

'What about your ma?'

'She's long gone. Left us when I was seven.'

'So why don't you live at home with your pa?'

'Because he's a miserable old devil at the best of times, he's mostly drunk, he hates the sight of me because I'm so like my ma! Is that enough reasons?'

Maisie fought against a frisson of compassion. 'You could always ... You know. There are people ... doctors...'

Annie shuddered, covering her ears with her hands. 'Don't even say the words!'

Maisie hesitated. 'They say that if you jump off a table or something it doesn't hurt that much and ... Or there's something you can drink, but I don't know what.'

Annie uncovered her ears. 'Go to one of those so-called doctors? How could you even think it? How could you tell me to get rid of your own brother's baby?'

Maisie stiffened. 'I didn't say you *should* go to one of them. You were the one who said about your pa killing him if he found out and if you don't get wed. If the worst came to the worst you'd have to think about it. You wouldn't be the first or the last ... but I'm not saying do it.' She stared at Annie with growing dislike. The truth was that she had wanted to give Annie a bit of a fright because Annie had given *her* one – turning up with such news and wanting to take Charlie away. 'So don't you go telling Charlie that I said you *should* do it because I didn't mean it like that and you know I didn't and if you *do* tell him that I shall say you're a liar!' She sat back breathlessly, all her kindly feelings gone. Annie should have been more careful. So should Charlie, but he was her flesh and blood and if she had to take sides it would be with her brother. Did she want this Annie woman for a sister-in-law?

Slowly Annie rose to her feet. 'You haven't even asked me how I feel,' she said, her feelings hurt. 'You don't care, do you?'

'How do you feel? Being sick?'

'No.'

'Then perhaps you aren't. Let's hope not.'

'I am! Not everybody gets to be sick. You an expert all of a sudden?'

Maisie also rose to her feet. She had to be careful, she realized. If Charlie married Annie – and she was beginning to hope he wouldn't – she would want to be a part of it so she shouldn't really antagonize her. In a softer tone, she said, 'Well, let me know how things go. I won't say anything to Charlie when he gets back. I'll let you break the news.' She led the way to the front door. 'And take care of yourself.'

She watched Annie go with a heavy heart. Yesterday everything had been more or less fine. Not wonderful but good enough. She had felt in control. Now everything was spoiled. She closed the door. Back in the kitchen she glared at the cat.

'I hate change, Moggie,' she told her.

Two days later, on the twenty-second of November, the RMS *Mauretania* reached Sandy Hook and her maiden voyage to North America was all but over. The triumphal entry into New York Harbour was impossible due to thick fog and Captain Pritchard insisted that they delay entry on to the berth. The ship waited outside Quarantine until the fog began to disperse, and then made her way cautiously towards the 14th Street pier. Edith was delighted to be in New York, but for Hester it was a heartfelt wrench. In spite of Charlie's insistence that he would see her when they made their return trip, she felt hopelessly bereft. She finally admitted to herself that she had fallen in love with Charles Barnes and had promised to marry him. Their whirlwind romance had left her reeling with shock and dizzy with joy and every moment without him was an agony.

New York was a fascinating and bewildering city, but in the days that followed, Hester was unable to appreciate it. Edith rushed them from pillar to post in the first four days before her appointment with Mr Stafford, the heart specialist whose reputation was solely responsible for their stay in New York. She and Edith Carradine turned up at his lavishly furnished consulting rooms on the fourteenth floor of a skyscraper. Ushered into the waiting room, Edith took one glimpse of the city from the window and sat down hurriedly.

'This is ridiculous,' she told Hester. 'America is a very large country. I see no need to put up buildings at such a height.' She glanced upward. 'How many more floors are there?'

'I believe there are forty in all.'

Hester wished she were with Charlie. Admiring the view together would make sightseeing perfect. She was hoping that Mr Stafford would quickly assess Edith's problem and decide on the best treatment. The sooner the better, in her opinion. The *Mauretania* would make another round trip before Christmas and she was praying they would be on the return voyage. She longed to see Charlie again, every minute was an hour and the intervening hours and days stretched ahead interminably. She hoped the old lady had not noticed her restlessness, but she couldn't be sure. She had said nothing about the promises she and Charlie had made to each other.

First she had to return to Alexander and tell him that she was leaving. It would be hard, but in a strange way she welcomed the challenge. There was nothing she wouldn't do for Charles Barnes. She trusted him utterly. He so obviously adored her and in an intense way, and Hester found this profoundly moving. Once they were together she was determined to make him the happiest man in the world. *The happiest man in the world.* How unoriginal you are, she thought, amused.

'Do sit down, Miss Shaw!' Edith waited, her hands folded neatly in her lap. Raising her voice, she continued. 'He's late! Would you believe that? I come halfway round the world to see him and he's late! It really is unpardonable.'

Hearing this, as she was meant to do, the glamorous receptionist smiled apologetically. 'I'm so sorry, Mrs Garradine. Can I fetch you some refresh—'

'No, no!' Edith fussed with her fur collar. 'And it's Carradine with a "C".'

The receptionist gave a polite nod by way of apology. 'I'm afraid his last patient was ten minutes late, Mrs Carradine. It's hard for Mr Stafford to catch up once that happens. Have you come far?'

'Only from England!'

'Oh!' She was at once interested. 'On the *Mauretania*? How wonderful.'

Edith tossed her head. 'On the contrary. It was a dreadful trip. Ghastly weather and the ship's spare anchor broke free from its moorings and—' She stopped as a tall thin man with silvery hair appeared from another room and beckoned the receptionist. After a whispered conversation, he disappeared again to be followed seconds later by a matronly looking nurse in an immaculate white uniform.

She smiled at Edith. 'Mrs Carradine? Mr Stafford will see you now.'

Edith stood up and turned to Hester. 'I may be some time. Wait for me here.'

Hester watched her go with relief. Now she was free to think about her future. Take as long as you like, Mr Stafford, she told him silently. She reached for a nearby magazine and opened it at random. Staring at a page of garden plants with unfocussed eyes, she thought about Charlie. He was so very different from any man she had ever met or expected to meet. He spoke with an accent she had never heard before and with a freedom she had never known. Words tumbled straight from his heart, warming her with their passion, and instantly brushing away her initial doubts.

Standing at the ship's rail together, at half past eleven on their last night, Charlie's proposal had taken her completely by surprise.

'You do realize...' he had begun nervously. 'I mean, we do have to ... I mean, there's no way you can turn me down. You wouldn't, would you?'

'Turn you down?' She stared at him.

'If I ... when I ask you to marry me.' His expression was hard to see in the light from the nearby companionway, but Hester detected a note of desperation in his voice. It was very different from his usual light-hearted tone, and his body, normally so relaxed, seemed stiff with an unfamiliar tension. Had she heard him correctly? The silence was fraught with uncertainty.

'When you ask me to marry you?'

'Yes, because I will. I am. That's what I'm doing. Asking you ... You may not have noticed that you love me. It's early days. But we have to stay together. I have to know now because you're going away and...'

'Oh, Charlie!' Her voice shook. 'I have

noticed that I love you, but isn't this all too fast? Are we sure?'

'I'm sure. I'm sure enough for both of us because you can't go back to him and we could marry in New York. At least we might be able to...'

'No!' She shook her head. 'I can't do that to him. I have to end it properly. Decently.' She hesitated. 'Do you have anyone to tell, Charlie?'

'No, at least ... yes. I suppose so. It was nothing. I hadn't promised her anything. But ... Are you saying yes?'

Hester held her breath. This was so sudden. It might be a terrible mistake. *Did she love him? Could she bear never to see him again?*

'Yes, Charlie. I am. I will marry you. I can't think of anything I'd rather do!' She laughed shakily as he pulled her towards him and hugged her passionately.

They had remained on deck for another hour and Charlie had made her see that there was another way to live and that her life as Alexander's mistress had been entirely devoid of genuine affection. Through Charlie's eyes, she saw that her relationship with Alexander had been composed of gratitude on her part and convenience on his. She had settled for security in the present with a man who could promise nothing definite for the future except a long wait for the death of his wife – and even then nothing was certain. A younger woman might replace her, leaving her stranded and alone.

Charlie promised her a loving heart, a home and a family. They would never be rich, he warned, but they could be happy and contented.

'My sister Maisie will love you,' he had told her, his eyes shining with anticipation. 'I can't wait to see her face when I take you home. She's certain I'm never going to settle down. You'll get along. She's been more like a mother to me than a sister. We'll get a place nearby so she won't think we've abandoned her – and so she can see her nephews and nieces. They'll be more like her grandchildren because she's older than me – thirty-five or six. Something like that.'

'Not much older than me.' Hester was glad to have the chance to spell it out for him. 'I'm thirty-one.'

He grinned. 'My very favourite age for a woman. Promise me you'll never get any younger!'

'I'll get older.'

'We'll get older together, how's that?'

Now, turning the page of the magazine, Hester smiled at the memory. Charlie was unflappable. In his eyes she was wonderful in every way. He was already planning a wedding and a list of friends who must be there to share the occasion. His delight in her made her feel more lovable and her confidence was growing.

The receptionist leaned forward and coughed to attract Hester's attention. 'Would you like some coffee or tea, Miss Shaw? Mr Stafford may be doing some tests and you may have quite a long wait.'

'Thank you. I would like a cup of tea.'

The tea appeared within minutes, in a small pot with a matching jug full of hot milk. There were three small biscuits on a plate and a dish of brown sugar. As she sipped the tea and nibbled the biscuits, she thought about the best way to break the news to Alexander. She wanted to spare him any pain he might feel at her disloyalty. He had been good to her in many ways, but she didn't think he would try very hard to make her stay with him. Plenty more pebbles on the beach! Younger pebbles, she thought with a smile. But should she tell him face to face or do what Charlie suggested?

'Pack and leave, with a letter propped on the mantelpiece,' he had advised. 'That's what I'd prefer if I was him. I wouldn't want to have to listen to you explaining why you were going off with another man. That'd be hurtful. But make a clean break. It's kinder.'

Was it kinder? Hester wasn't entirely convinced, but she didn't relish the thought of a confrontation either. If Alexander were upset by her betrayal, she would feel guilty and if he were angry she might be frightened of him. He was a proud man and powerful in his sphere of work and used to getting his own way. What would he do? Not that he would do her any physical harm – at least she didn't think so – but he hated to be thwarted. She remembered Drummond and wondered what had happened to him, if anything.

'I don't think I could just vanish,' she told Charlie. 'He might come after me and make a scene. I couldn't bear that. I'd prefer to get it over with in private. Just the two of us. I owe him that much. And there are my clothes...'

His eyes narrowed. 'Don't bring anything he has given you. He might accuse you of stealing. You said he was a policeman. He'd know how to make it stick.'

She regarded him helplessly, then shrugged. 'Why am I fooling myself that he'll care? He'll probably breathe a sigh of relief that he's rid of me. He may have found someone else already.'

Recalling Charlie's immediate rejection of this scenario, Hester smiled and turned another page: *A nourishing family stew. Serves four or five* ... Was she really going to be part of a family, cooking and washing for four or five?

'Please God, yes!' she mouthed.

Wash and scrape your carrots, she read, *and cut into neat cubes. Repeat with the potatoes and parsnips and add to the pan.*

Hester felt a moment of panic. Could she cook? She had never had to try. Alexander had always insisted on eating at home with Marcia or at his club and, before that, when she was a nanny, there had been a part-time cook to prepare the meals. But it couldn't be that difficult, surely. Her glance fell on another recipe – for a lemon tart – which involved making pastry. That looked slightly more daunting, but she would learn. She would learn to sew and mend and cook and plant vegetables and whatever Charlie needed her to learn. Slowly she ate the last biscuit.

As the last biscuit crumb vanished, the door opened and Mrs Carradine reappeared with a face like thunder. She glared at Hester. 'We're leaving and we're not coming back. I never heard such nonsense in all my life.' The receptionist half rose to her feet, looking anxious, but Edith snapped, 'Sit down, woman. I have to write a cheque – apparently I have to pay for Mr Stafford wasting my time!'

Opening her purse, she drew out a cheque book, snatched a pen from the inkstand on the receptionist's desk and filled in the cheque with impatient jerks of the pen and angry snorts of breath. She tore it out and handed it over.

'Mr Stafford hasn't earned a penny of it,'

she told the receptionist. 'It's highway robbery and I told him so. All this way to be told there is nothing wrong with my heart. Telling me it is all in my imagination. He's a disgrace to his profession.'

The young receptionist, embarrassed, was lost for words and Hester thought it was probably for the best. Any conciliatory remarks, efforts to apologize or attempts to support her employer would simply add fuel to the fire of the old lady's wrath.

In the taxi on the way back to the hotel, Edith enlarged on her comments.

'He had the audacity to tell me he could reassure me that there was nothing wrong. *Reassure me?* If I believed that I would never have come to New York. You're a charlatan, I told him, or else you are an incompetent fool. I need to know what is wrong with my heart and I want you to bring about treatment and a cure. But, no, the man tells me to be thankful he could find nothing wrong.'

Hester searched for something appropriate and hopefully safe to say. She decided on, 'Oh, dear! How disappointing!'

Edith fanned herself with a fierce hand. 'Disappointing is an understatement. Disgusting is nearer the truth. He ought to be crossed off the medical register. I shall write to the medical profession.'

A sudden thought brought a hastily hidden smile to Hester's face. Presumably this meant that they would be returning to England sooner than expected and *that* meant she would soon be reunited with her future husband.

Six

Monday, November 25th, 1907 – What a wicked waste of time and money Mr Stafford has proved to be. After various tests he declared that there was nothing wrong with me and I should stop worrying about my health. The man's a fool and I told him so. He actually had the cheek to say I was 'as strong as a horse' and would outlive him. Well, I certainly hope I do. I shall hope to dance at his funeral! As soon as I get home I shall search out a new specialist – someone with something between his ears apart from American fluff!

As for Miss Shaw, I am still wondering what to make of her. I have to confess that, in spite of all that I have learned recently about her duplicity, I rather like the woman. She is efficient and mostly dutiful and has a pleasant manner. I tried to discover how she and Alexander met, but she was discreet without being evasive so I thought it better not to pry for fear she tells my nephew and he takes it badly. Will I ever see her again, I wonder, when she is no longer my travelling companion? I have decided we shall travel back on the Mauretania *as soon as possible.*

I shall make enquiries as to her next sailing.

* * *

Ten days later, on Thursday the fifth of December, while Hester and her employer were still travelling back from New York, the telephone rang in an upper office at Scotland Yard and the call was passed to Alexander.

He listened, frowning, while his housekeeper, Mrs Rice, gabbled incoherently about Mrs Waring and the hospital.

'Stop crying, for God's sake,' he told her. 'Start again and don't mumble!'

'It's Mrs Waring, your wife, Mr Waring. She didn't wake up when I went in with her breakfast and, you know how heavily she sleeps, I shook her and then screamed because, you know, I thought she was dead, Mr Waring, and...'

As she continued piecemeal with her hysterical account, Alexander extracted the basic facts. His wife was still alive. Relieved, he rolled his eyes.

'So what you're saying is that Marcia was taken ill and is now in hospital. Give me the telephone number and—'

'The number? Oh, no! I mean, I don't know because I called her doctor and he called the police and they arranged everything, that is to say I was in no state to ... Well, it was such a shock, Mr Waring, and I was on my own, and it's not every day you find a dead body which was what I

131

thought...' She began to cry again. 'I feel all of a bother.'

'For heaven's sake, pull yourself together, Mrs Rice. She's not dead so why are you crying? Get on with your work and I'll get in touch with the doctor and I'll take a taxi to the hospital as soon as I can rearrange my appointments. Make yourself a cup of tea and carry on as usual. She might be sent home later and she won't want to find the house in a mess.'

Forty-five minutes later he was sitting by his wife's bed. Marcia was unconscious and the young doctor was explaining the position.

'She was unconscious when they brought her in and has remained so ever since. When Mr Barrac comes in, we'll have a better idea of what happened. We've just...'

'Mr Barrac is the consultant, I assume?' The man looked too young to be a doctor, Alexander thought, surprised. But perhaps that was a sign that he was getting old. His thoughts reverted to his wife's condition. Thinking rationally, it would almost be a mercy if Marcia were to die – she had no real life and would never recover from whatever ailed her.

'Yes. A very senior consultant,' the doctor agreed. 'He's due in ten minutes for his rounds, but he does have another private practice and is sometimes late. Can you tell me what medication your wife has been taking – for our notes?' He tapped his notebook with his pencil and tried to look experienced. 'Your wife's pupils are dilated and—'

'I'm afraid not. I don't understand it. I leave it to her doctor to prescribe what she needs. When I left for work she seemed to be sleeping normally and I always try not to wake her. Didn't you ask her doctor for these details?'

'Ah!' He looked somewhat discomfited. 'The truth is there was a bit of a muddle at the time. We had a patient back from theatre and another elderly patient who came in vomiting blood and with one nurse absent ... in the confusion...' Leaving the rest to Alexander's imagination, he shrugged apologetically.

Alexander nodded, his mind elsewhere. If Marcia died he would keep her death from Hester for as long as possible. She would be back in England shortly and he wanted time to decide what to do about her. If he were free to marry again, he must make a sensible judgement and not choose Hester from a sense of misguided loyalty. She might soon be too old to have a child and he needed a family. On the other hand, she had been good for him and he bore her no ill-will. Perhaps he should settle a small sum of money on her so that she could survive until she found another man to take care of her.

Perhaps he could find her a job as a house-keeper. He could write her a reference. That would please her...

But he would miss her. And suppose she found another protector – someone better off who could do better by her than he had done? The thought of Hester in another man's bed hurt him more than he expected.

She might compare him with the next man. Might even *discuss* him with the next man! That thought really did trouble him. Damnation. There must be a way out of the situation. If Marcia were going to die, he would have to give it some serious thought. And quickly.

He took out his watch and frowned. Inter-rupting the young doctor, he said, 'I have an important meeting shortly. Regretfully I shall have to return to my office. But I'll keep in touch and hopefully be back later in the day.'

There was no point in hanging about at the bedside of an unconscious wife who may or may not recover.

In his absence another secretary had entered his office brandishing *The Times*.

'Have you seen this?' she asked.

The two secretaries bent their heads over the short news item on the front page although it was not the main headline.

Scotland Yard officers have arrested a senior figure in the Home Office and he has been detained while further enquiries are made. Mr Francis J. Drummond has been accused of obtaining information by illegal methods. It is understood that an anonymous phone call precipitated the arrest.

That same evening, after midnight, Hester and Charlie sat together in her cabin, making plans. They were also sharing a bottle of wine and some biscuits which he had brought with him.

'So it's all settled, then,' he asked hopefully. 'You will find the right time to tell your chap that you are leaving him to get married. I'll find a vicar to call the banns and get a licence. I'll break it to Maisie and Annie.'

'Who's Annie?' Hester asked drowsily, her head against his shoulder.

'Annie? Oh, she's just a woman I know. Got to tell her I'm spoken for, haven't I? Like you and your bloke, I'll tell her to her face.'

'Was she someone special?' Hester sat up. 'Will she mind? How special is she?'

'Special in that I've known her some time, but not so special I ever wanted to marry her! Don't worry, Hes. She'll be fine. She knew it would happen some day.' He slipped an arm round her shoulder by way of reassurance. 'So then, you'll get in touch –

you've got our address – and you'll come up. Maybe by Christmas. Then we'll get ourselves down to the church. And don't bring anything with you that *he* bought you. I'll send you a bit of cash from my next wages to tide you over.'

Hester relaxed again. 'And we'll find somewhere to live,' she prompted, smiling.

'Chalky knows a place that might do us nicely. And we'll buy furniture.'

Hester sighed with contentment. 'I can hardly believe this is happening,' she told him. 'Tell me nothing will go wrong. I won't wake up, will I, and find it's all a dream?'

'Course you won't. What could go wrong? It is a dream, but it's a dream coming true. Trust Charlie Barnes.' He hugged her so hard she cried out in protest. 'Sorry, I just love you so much! I can't wait to show you off to all my mates back home. They'll be so jealous. Sick as parrots.' He laughed.

'Ssh! Remember Mrs Carradine's next door,' Hester reminded him, pointing at the wall which separated the two cabins.

'Sorry again!'

Hester said, 'I'll have my wages from this trip. I'll buy myself some clothes. And I'll always love the *Mauretania* for bringing us together. Oh, Charlie! Whenever I dared to wonder about my future it was never as wonderful as you and me!'

Charlie kissed her. 'The same goes for me

with knobs on! I do love you. You're stuck with me, you know, because whatever happens, I'll never leave you.'

Early snowflakes were falling on Saturday as Alexander hurried up the steps to the front entrance of the hospital and made his way to the ward where he would find his wife. Once there he received his first shock. Marcia's bed was empty and he glanced round. Perhaps they had had to operate on her. Maybe, God forbid, she had been felled by a stroke or a heart attack – or maybe she had recovered and they had moved her to another ward to make way for more urgent cases. If she had had a stroke, it would mean months of home nursing with a live-in nurse and the house smelling of antiseptics and disinfectants. Ugh! An appalling thought. Frowning, he went in search of the ward sister.

The sister's expression changed when she recognized Alexander. Without a word she drew him aside where they could not be overheard. 'Mr Waring, I'm so sorry to give you sad news, but your wife...'

His stomach churned with apprehension. 'She's not ... Oh, no!'

'I'm afraid so. She slipped away quite painlessly. One minute she was breathing and the next ... We were actually standing beside her bed at the moment she died. It may be a mercy in one way.' She eyed him anxiously.

'She may have remained in a coma for weeks or months and then died. It happens quite often and that's terrible for the relatives. I'm so sorry, Mr Waring. I can assure you...'

Alexander had stopped listening, overcome with feelings of guilt that overwhelmed any sense of loss. That would come later. He had been plotting her demise, he thought, and had somehow spoiled her chances of recovery. And he should have stayed longer yesterday, to talk to Barrac about Marcia's condition. Forgive me, Marcia, he begged silently. You were a good wife. She had supported him through the difficult times and was always...

The sister interrupted his thoughts. 'There will be a few official things to attend to and the Lady Almoner will be happy to advise you.'

He felt dazed by the speed of Marcia's departure. He had not had time to fully consider his future. Nodding, he tried to gather his thoughts. Hester would be home before long and it might look odd if she wasn't informed.

'Would you like to see your wife's body? To say goodbye? I can arrange that for you.'

A young nurse was hovering close by. Bright red curls were held back by the white headdress and he noticed that her eyes were a dark green. Possibly Irish. But did he want to see Marcia's body?

'I'm not sure. Maybe I should remember her as she was yesterday. Sleeping peacefully in the bed.'

The sister looked surprised so maybe he had said the wrong thing. He began to feel pressurized. He was used to being in control and this situation was unfamiliar and put him at a disadvantage.

The nurse said, 'Most people like to say something to the dear departed.' She gave him a gentle smile.

The sister nodded. 'Let Nurse take you down. You may regret it if you don't.'

Alexander found himself glancing down at the nurse's left hand. No ring. He at once felt ashamed of himself for the interest and hoped neither woman had noticed the glance. What on earth was happening to him? He closed his eyes. *Pull yourself together. It will only take a moment.* In his position, at this time in his career, he should behave with the utmost propriety. Opening his eyes he said, 'Thank you, Nurse. I'd like to see my wife.'

He followed her from the ward and they walked side by side along the corridor and down the stairs. She spoke once or twice, the usual platitudes that people feel are suitable for the newly bereaved. She had a pleasant voice and as he stole a sideways glance at the trim young figure beside him, he was startled to see that she was smiling up at him in a way that spoke volumes about the living, and nothing about the dead. Presumably she was unmarried, he thought, and available. In the present circumstances Alexander was afraid to return her obvious interest, but he thought he might remember it for future use. Her figure beneath the uniform was nicely rounded. Perhaps he would send her some flowers to thank her for her care of his wife prior to her death. He must find out her name...

As soon as the doorbell rang, Maisie smiled. Quarter to eight in the morning meant Charlie had left the ship at the earliest possible moment. He loved his home. But as she hurried to the door, the smile faded. She always looked forward to his shore leave, but this time was different. This time she would have to tell him about the baby Annie was carrying and that meant he would marry her and everything would change. Still, she mustn't greet him with a gloomy face. She would wait for the right moment to tell him the news. Restoring a smile to her face, she hurried to the front door. Charlie refused to take the front-door key with him when he was at sea because he loved to stand on the doorstep, waiting to be let in. He was funny that way.

She opened the door, but, before she could greet him, he grabbed her round the waist

140

and lifted her up, crying, 'Wait 'til I tell you my news, Mais! You're going to love it.' He kissed her, released her and charged past her into the kitchen.

Wait until you hear *mine*, she thought, closing the door and following him along the narrow passage. You might not be so thrilled.

He looked radiant, she thought, puzzled, so the news must be great. 'You've been promoted!' she cried. If so she would send him out to bring back a large chicken and she would stuff it with slices of lemon and cook it with bacon and tiny sausages. They would celebrate. Hands on hips, she waited, watching him with affection as he prowled around the small kitchen, his face one big smile, his eyes gleaming with excitement.

'I'm going to be married!' he told her. 'You will have a sister-in-law and then you will have some nephews and nieces to fuss over. What do you think of that?'

Maisie froze. He knew. He had come home on leave and had gone straight round to Annie. Why? She was hurt by his disloyalty. He *always* came home to her first. Always had done, saying that home was the most important place in the world. The home she had created for him all those years ago. 'You went round to Annie's!' she said dully. 'Why?'

That meant that Annie had told him about the baby so at least she was spared that dubious task.

He stared at her. 'What are you talking about? I'm getting *married*! I've met this wonderful girl – at least she's not a girl. She's a bit older than me so I suppose you'd call her a woman. Hester Shaw.' Her name brought another smile to his face. 'She was on the ship. The one I told you about in my letter.'

Maisie sat down under the weight of this revelation. 'The one in the Verandah Café? That woman?'

'Yes!'

'But you've only known her a few weeks!'

Maisie's criticism washed over him like water off a duck's back. If anything, his smile broadened and he continued to prowl around the kitchen, opening the larder door for no reason and admiring the new teapot that stood upturned on the draining board. Wait 'til you meet her, Mais. Honestly, you'll love her. You'll love each other! She'll be coming up to Liverpool as soon as she's sorted things out in London. She's ... . Well, she's living with this man and he's married.' He snatched a glance at her face.

'Oh, Charlie! Do please sit down,' she implored. 'You're making me dizzy. I need to think.'

'What about? Aren't you pleased? I thought you'd be excited for me.' Now it was his turn to look hurt. 'Don't you want me to be happy? We're going to have a proper wedding – she's that sort of person. We're—'

'Wait a minute!' She held up her hand. 'I thought you said she was living with a married man? Where's his wife living? I can't make head or tail of all this.' She was stalling, giving herself time to decide whether or not she should tell him about Annie's child.

His smile faded. 'He lives with his wife who's dying of something or other but he pays for a flat where they spend time together. She's not happy with him. He sounds a real bully and...'

'So he's rich, this man?'

'I suppose so. He's some sort of policeman, but high up. A detective superintendent maybe. Or an inspector. I forget. I don't want to think about him. I just want Hester to tell him about us and get out of there. She can stay here, can't she, until we find a place of our own? I can kip on the floor with some cushions. We're going to live very near you so...' He stopped, disappointment written large over his face. 'What is it, Mais? I never expected you to be like this. Such a wet blanket. Don't you see? I *love* her. I've never felt like this before. Never.'

'Not even for Annie?' Annie was the better bet, Maisie decided suddenly. Annie was one of them and she and Maisie got along. Sort of. This posh woman from London was

143

much more of a threat. Maisie began to prejudge her with what little she knew. 'Has this Hester woman said she'll marry you? Do you trust her?'

He stared at her, astonished. 'Do I trust her? What a ridiculous question! Course I trust her – with my life! She'd never do anything to hurt me.'

'I think Annie trusts you.' She held her breath.

Charlie threw out his hands in a gesture of helplessness. 'Trusts me to do what? I never promised her anything. You ask her. We never talked about getting married. Nothing like that. She'll tell you herself. We had fun, that's all. Now it's over.'

He sat down, watching for her reaction.

'She might have hoped to marry you.'

He shrugged. 'The word never came up. She knows what I am. A girl in every port.' He tried to laugh, but it was more of a grimace.

'Until now?'

He nodded. 'I'm not good with words, Mais, you know that. I can't tell you how much I love Hester, but if I don't wed her, I won't wed anyone.'

Maisie hesitated, her stomach churning with anxiety. Whatever happened, she must not turn him against her. If he married this awful Hester woman, they might move away. They might go back to London! The woman might turn Charlie against his own sister. 'If this married man's wife is dying,' she said slowly, 'he might want to marry Hester.'

Charlie snorted. 'Fat chance. She's in love with me. Honestly, Mais, she adores me and I can't live without her.' His expression darkened and his voice changed. 'If I thought I couldn't marry her I'd ... I'd do something terrible! I just couldn't bear it. I'll go mad if anything comes between us.'

'Don't talk like that!' Maisie was frightened. She had never seen her brother in this state of mind and it set alarm bells ringing. Would he really do something terrible? 'Do something terrible? Such as...?' she asked, dreading his answer.

His face showed his anguish. 'Chuck myself overboard,' he whispered hoarsely.

That was the moment when Maisie knew she could *not* tell him about Annie. Whatever happened, she couldn't be the one to break the news. She had never seen him so taken with a woman so perhaps this *was* the one. There was no way she could ruin his chance of happiness – but Annie could definitely put a large dent in it!

With an effort she thrust Annie to the back of her mind. For the moment she and Charlie must be happy together. He must never think that she was less than enthusiastic about Hester.

'Right then, Charlie!' she cried, forcing a

bright smile. 'Today it's going to be your favourite – a big fat chicken and all the trimmings! Get along to the butcher's while I start on the rest of the meal.'

To her relief, his mood brightened. Jumping up he hugged her so that she cried out, kissed her hard on the cheek and obediently rushed off on his errand. Please, she thought, don't let Annie turn up with her news. Not today of all days. Today must be a celebration. If Hester *was* the apple of Charlie's eye, she would play along. She would make herself love the woman. If Charlie loves her, I'll love her, she vowed. Annie Green was a wild card, however, and she and Charlie must work it out between them, although Maisie couldn't see how it could be done. Sighing deeply, she crossed her fingers. She was used to being important in Charlie's life and prided herself on having guided him through various crises when he was younger, but events, she now realized, were spiralling out of her control. Charlie's future seemed to hang in the balance and for once she had no idea what would happen next.

Marcia's funeral took place on the twelfth of December in pouring rain. Refreshments for the mourners were offered at Hilsomer House, but nobody lingered too long after they had eaten. As the last mourners had left, only Edith remained. She had endured the funeral, not because Marcia had been a favourite of hers, but because she needed to talk to her nephew alone. She had found it hard to mourn the dead woman, and trying to project an air of grief had been a struggle. In her eyes, Marcia had been a weak woman and had not deserved Alexander. Her only asset had been the money and fortunately that now belonged to her nephew.

He gave her a tired smile as he sat back in the armchair with his legs sprawled in front of him. 'I'm glad that's over,' he told her. 'At least she went peacefully and didn't suffer.'

Sitting upright on a hard chair, Edith narrowed her eyes. She would not beat about the bush, she decided. 'I think you should now make an honest woman of Hester Shaw!' She watched with satisfaction as his mouth fell open with shock. That would teach him to make a fool of her. 'Did you really think I wouldn't find out? You must take me for a fool.'

'But how...' he gasped, too shocked to hide his discomfiture. 'Did she tell you?'

' "She" being the cat's mother!' she snapped. '*Miss Shaw* did not tell me because obviously you had instructed her to keep your nasty little secret! I'm surprised at you, Alexander. Leading a double life is not what I expected from you.' She explained briefly how the truth had come to light. 'You can hardly blame the poor woman for rambling when she was concussed. You are the deceiver, Alexander, not Miss Shaw. All my sympathies are with her, if you must know. You have treated her very shabbily.'

He was struggling to regain the high ground, she thought. It served him right. It irked her that she had been deceived for so long.

'I suppose you kept her locked away in a cupboard somewhere!'

'It was a neat little flat!'

'Ah, yes. Chalker Street. And you never took her out anywhere. How could you if you were constantly afraid you would be seen together? Not much of a life for an intelligent and attractive woman.'

'She didn't have to stay,' he protested, flushing with annoyance. 'She could have walked out at any time.' He sat up and drew in his legs.

Edith relished his difficulties. Recovering from the shock, he had obviously resigned himself to the discovery, but he had no real idea what pressure his aunt could bring to bear. He knew he had always been the favourite, but he would be wondering if she was about to disown him. Poor Alexander. Edith held back a smile. She was enjoying herself.

Leaning forward, he tried to justify the past. 'You don't know the state she was in when we met. She was walking along the pavement in Euston Road. Yes, *Euston Road*! You know what that means. She was hoping to find a client. Do I need to spell it out for you? She was at her wits' end. Thrown out of her position as a nanny because the husband wanted to share her bed! Did she tell you that?'

'No. I didn't press her. The past is the past.' She would not allow him to see that she was shocked. So Miss Shaw had a shady past.

'She wasn't a prost—' He bit off the word. 'She wasn't a fallen woman, but she was hovering on the brink.'

'And you rescued her. How very noble of you.' She spoke with a touch of sarcasm in her voice, but she did admire him for rescuing Miss Shaw. However, what had Alexander been doing in Euston Road? She preferred not to dwell on that aspect.

'I took pity on her – she looked so out of place and it was raining hard. She was bedraggled and miserable. When I stopped the cab to speak to her she nearly died of fright, but I would have been the first of many. She said that had been her plan. Eventually she would have fallen very low. You might say I found her in the nick of time. Ask her. She'll tell you that's how it happened.'

Edith's curiosity was aroused. She found it impossible to imagine Miss Shaw tramping

149

the streets around Euston Station, competing with an assortment of street women, who were all in search of wayward men who were looking for ... for what Edith could only call 'gratification'.

'Did she take you back to her room?' she asked, intrigued. This was a side of life that had never interested her before.

'Back to her room? For heaven's sake, Aunt Edith! How could she? She didn't have a room! Hester had no room, no money, nothing and nowhere. I took her to a cheap hotel where I thought I would go unrecognized. There she burst into tears and I felt sorry for her. She was desperate,' he protested, 'and I've been good to her. If she pretends otherwise, she's lying – and I don't think she would lie.'

'Unless you tell her to! She's been sharing your lie for weeks. Friend of a friend cum travelling companion cum dressmaker! Hah!'

A spiky silence lengthened uncomfortably. Edith hesitated. She had to ask a very personal question and it might be that she had gone too far. Alexander might tell her to mind her own business and he would have a right to do so. She took a deep breath. It was harder than she expected.

'You could marry her and have a family, couldn't you? She's not too old, surely.'

'Presumably.' He stood up and crossed to

the window.

'She's a good woman. I like her. She has spirit and you know her well enough. She owes you a great deal. That's my suggestion. You may have other ideas.'

'I have thought about it,' he said slowly, 'and I know she'd agree but...' He turned to her. 'Maybe I need a younger wife.'

Edith shook her head. 'Young women are scatter-brained and cannot be trusted. A younger wife would not have Miss Shaw's presence. Can you imagine attending an important function with a young and foolish girl clinging to your arm? I fear for today's young women – they have no idea of how to behave in a formal setting, and would be of no use to you as a responsible adult. I fear that the modern generation is restless and unreliable. You would regret it, Alexander. Mark my words.' She thought he looked disappointed.

'You're being a little harsh,' he said, resuming his seat. He eased his shoulders with a small groan. 'I feel so tense. I ache all over.'

'It's been a trying time for you, these last few days. Try to snatch some rest. Let Miss Shaw look after you.'

'I shan't move her in at home just yet – that's if I decide to marry her,' he amended hastily. 'I think a few months would be discreet, don't you?'

'Certainly.' She was suddenly hopeful. He

151

seemed to have agreed with her. A few words from her from time to time would probably convince him. 'But you should marry her before she moves in and not after. There must be nothing at which people can point the finger. I want to hear no whispers. Nor do I want to see any sly glances. We have never had a scandal in the family and I don't want one now. You must make an honest woman of her. I imagine that that's what you promised her.'

'I dare say.' *Had he said any such thing?* It was possible, he supposed.

'Good. It must all be above board from now on. Remember you have a career and a reputation to think about.' She frowned. 'That fellow that's been arrested. Drummond, isn't it? Isn't he one of your colleagues? I read about it yesterday. Monkey business of some kind, wasn't it?'

'I knew him, yes. Odd fellow. I never did like him. Something not quite right there.'

'Avoid him like the plague. He could contaminate you.' Edith stood up, having neatly changed the subject. She had said enough about Miss Shaw, she told herself. Let the advice simmer in his brain. He had almost certainly understood the unspoken message. She wanted him to marry Hester. If he did, Edith's money would follow.

Alexander sat for a long time after his aunt

had left. Their conversation had left a sour taste in his mouth. It was clear what Edith Carradine wanted, and she was rarely refused. So much for easing out Hester and trying his luck with the young nurse at the hospital. She was a perfect example of the modern young woman his aunt had been describing. He had thought about her a great deal and recognized that she had signalled her interest in him. She was pretty and flirtatious and young – and very desirable, but his aunt had pointed out a flaw. She would find it difficult to move into his middle-aged way of life – and she might even leave him at some stage for a younger man. The point his aunt had made about his professional life was also valid. Would Della know how to behave at a formal dinner? Would she be able to give a dinner party for business associates and their sensible wives? In other words, would she embarrass him and spoil his chances of promotion? The police force did not suffer fools gladly. Damn.

He glanced up as the housekeeper knocked and entered.

'The washing-up is done, Mr Waring, and I've sent Rosie home. I said not to bother you right now, but said you'd give her the money next week.'

'Thank you.'

'And I know this might not be the right

time, Mr Waring, but are you keeping on all the staff now that your wife ... that is, Mrs Waring has gone to a better place? God rest her soul.'

He nodded. 'I doubt I'll be making any changes for a while, if ever. Is Cook still here?'

'No sir. She slipped away as soon as the refreshments were served because she came in two hours early because of the funeral and with her bad leg. But she left you some of yesterday's mutton pie and I'll put the vegetables on before I go. Will seven o'clock be all right with you?'

He nodded.

'And I'm to say how sorry we are about poor Mrs Waring. You'll miss her.'

Alexander watched her retreat and wondered if he would miss Marcia. He knew he ought to, but that was another matter. Rousing himself, he went upstairs and into the bedroom where his wife had slept beside him for so many years. The room smelled of her perfumes and face powders and when he looked into her wardrobe the racks of clothes seemed to reproach him for the fact that they would never be worn again. Perhaps he could give some to Hester, he thought. She could have them altered to fit. Waste not, want not. Marcia had been a spendthrift in her younger days and had enjoyed shopping in Bond Street and frequent visits to the dressmakers. On second thoughts he would give the clothes away. Even on Hester, they would remind him of his wife and he would rather forget her.

Marcia had not been the ideal wife and had failed to give him children. Her doctor had considered her too frail to risk her health. He recalled his aunt's words about Hester. Would she give him children – and did he still want a family?

'Hell and damnation!' he cried and turning on his heel, strode out of the bedroom and slammed the door. He could not face a night on his own while his mind struggled with so many problems. He needed sympathy and understanding, he thought in a rare moment of self-pity. He would eat his mutton pie and vegetables and then spend the night with Hester. And this time he would stay until morning.

Seven

Hester had not seen Alexander since her return. A note from him about Marcia's death and the coming funeral had taken her by surprise. Her first reaction had been guilt that for so long she and Alexander had been deceiving the poor woman. Then curiosity filled her and she wondered whether she dare attend the funeral. Discarding that idea – Mrs Carradine would spot her – she had tried to concentrate on the words she would use to convince Alexander that he would be better off without her. Unfortunately she had wasted time by luxuriating in thoughts about Charlie Barnes and the prepared speech she needed had not materialized.

This evening she was hoping Alexander would not come to her because she was still not ready to break the news. More importantly, she was determined not to allow him into her bed and had decided to complain of a sore throat and aching joints. She would say she had contracted something on the ship. Alexander hated ill health and would not want to risk catching anything infectious. Trying to think of kind ways to break the news, she had tried to convince herself that he would be relieved at their parting of the ways. Without her tugging at his conscience, Alexander would be free to choose a younger wife and make a fresh start, but Hester suspected that he would prefer to be the one who ended the relationship. How, though, to arrange that?

Hester had received some money from Edith – her wages for her duties as travelling companion – and had secretly bought herself a simple tweed skirt and jacket and a warm blouse to wear on her journey to Liverpool. She still needed to find some stout shoes, but planned to go shopping again tomorrow. Her hopes were that she and Alexander would part on reasonable terms and she clung to that idea as he turned the key in the lock and called out a greeting.

'How did the funeral go?' she asked as she helped him off with his wet coat and hung it on the hall stand. She assumed Edith had told him that she knew of their relationship.

'Well enough,' he replied. 'There was quite a crowd in the church, but don't ask me who they were. Friends of Marcia's, I suppose. I didn't know she still had any. She's been ill so long and they soon lose interest. You could have come, actually.'

'But why should I? I've never set eyes on her. What excuse could there be for my attendance?' She gave a slight cough and grimaced, putting a hand to her throat, but he seemed not to notice.

'The vicar spoke well, but the hymns went on and on.' He threw himself down on the chaise longue and yawned.

'Who chose the hymns?'

'I left that to the vicar. What does it matter? Poor Marcia wasn't going to hear them.'

'Sometimes people write down the hymns they want for their funeral.'

'Well, if she did, I didn't find the list. Don't I get a kiss?'

'I have a sore throat. I was keeping my distance.'

'Oh, God! You sound just like Marcia!' He stretched out his legs and surveyed his shoes. 'I had to wear these old things. The others were ruined by the wet grass. I do hate rain-sodden funerals.'

Hester poured him a glass of brandy.

He sipped it gratefully. 'I shall see the lawyer on Tuesday next.' He held out his hand. 'Come and sit with me. I have to tell you that something odd happened after-wards. It will make you smile. Don't look like that! I won't bite you.' As she settled beside him, he put an arm round her shoulder.

'Someone has recommended you as a replacement for Marcia!'

'Oh, no!' Unguarded, the words slipped out.

'Oh, yes. You'll never guess who it was?'

'Not Mrs Carradine.'

'The same!'

'But why should she? How can she think me at all suitable?'

'She obviously does.' He grinned suddenly. 'Why didn't you warn me that she knew about us? It gave me a terrific shock. Why didn't you tell me she'd discovered our secret?'

'I haven't seen you since I arrived back. You were busy with the funeral arrangements. I would have told you tonight. I'm sorry, Alex. I was going to tell you.' His attitude confused her.

'She thinks I should make an honest woman of you!' He actually laughed. 'I thought you'd be surprised. My stuffy, prim old aunt is urging me to marry my mistress, settle down and raise a family! Wonders will never cease.'

For a moment or two Hester was seized by panic. She went hot and cold with shock. His arm around her shoulder made her feel disloyal towards Charlie so she coughed again to remind him that she was infectious.

Ignoring the cough, he turned to look at her. 'Nothing to say, Hester? I thought you'd be pleased to have a champion. She seems to have formed a very favourable opinion of you.'

'But she doesn't know about ... I mean, she doesn't know the full story.'

'Yes, she does. That's what is so amazing. She insisted on knowing how we met and why we set up home together. She was taken aback, but quickly recovered, and still thinks you're the woman for me! You're fortunate that she and Marcia never did get along. Almost any woman would be preferable to Marcia according to my aunt.'

Hester looked at him. Was that meant to be a compliment? If so it was somewhat dubious. She tried to concentrate. The conversation was leading in the wrong direction and she didn't know how to deal with it. The fates seemed to be conspiring to make it difficult for her to tell Alexander that she was leaving him for another man. Did she dare tell him now, she wondered, before he actually proposed to her? How ironic that Edith Carradine had decided that she liked Hester enough to push her name to the top of any list of suitable future Mrs Warings. Ironic and a little dangerous because Hester had no wish to humiliate Alexander. There was no need to make an enemy of him. Far better to pre-empt a proposal which she would have to refuse. She would tell him immediately, she decided, and took a deep breath.

She said instead, 'Have you had some supper?'

Coward! What was the matter with her? He wasn't going to bite her! And she had promised Charlie that she would tell her lover what was happening.

'Yes, thanks.' Alexander stretched and rubbed his eyes. 'What about you?'

'I'm not hungry ... My throat's rather sore,' she repeated. 'I feel full of aches today.'

'A sore throat?' At last it registered and he leaned away from her.

She tried again. 'Alex, there's something I must tell you...'

'I got Drummond, by the way.' His eyes shone. 'He's under investigation. He won't thwart me again. It even made the front page!'

Distracted, she asked, 'What happened to him? What did he do?'

'You mean what did *I* do!' He grinned.

Suddenly she did not want to know. She took another deep breath. 'There's something I have to tell you. It's about you and me.' She felt his arm stiffen around her shoulder and rushed on before she lost her nerve. 'I do think we've been happy together and I'm glad you're free to marry again but ... I don't think it should be me.'

He drew back and turned so that he could face her and she saw the surprise in his eyes. Tell him now, she told herself, while you still can. 'It's not that I'm not very fond of you or that I don't appreciate what you're offering but...'

He raised his eyebrows. 'What do you

161

think I'm offering?'

'I thought you were suggesting that we marry. Am I wrong?' Hope flared. How stupid it would be to tell him about Charlie if Alexander were not intending to propose. Flustered she hesitated.

'I'm thinking about it.' His expression was enigmatic.

'Ah! Well, so am I and...' She had a flash of inspiration. 'And you will want a family and I am probably too old.' She felt weak with relief. Of course, she could persuade him that she would be a disappointment. That way Alexander could reject her without losing face.

'You're not too old, Hester.' He kissed her lightly. 'I have it on the best authority. Aunt Edith tells me so!'

'She can't know how I feel. It's not simply *having* the children, I would have to care for them for years and I'll be forty-one in ten years' time.'

Please, she prayed, be swayed by this argument and then you need never know about Charlie Barnes. You can get rid of me and not face any criticism.

He shook his head. 'You're not getting cold feet, are you? You will have help, Hester. A nanny, a children's nurse – whoever you need. You can choose them yourself.'

Hester closed her eyes and conceded defeat. They were going round in circles and he was going to propose. She had promised Charlie she would tell him and then leave. Come what may, she would have to tell Alexander.

'There's someone else,' she said. 'It's only fair to tell you. If you want me to go I'll...'

He stood up abruptly and stared down at her in disbelief. Hester thought of the address she had in her purse. If he threw her out she would make no protest. She had enough money for the fare and she would go north on the next train and find Charlie's house. The idea frightened her, but she would do it.

The silence lengthened as Alexander towered over her, a strange expression on his face. An expression she could not read.

She said, 'I'm sorry if it upsets you.'

Deliberately Alexander sat down opposite her and leaned forward. He seemed very calm and that worried her.

'Someone else?' He shook his head. 'What on earth are you talking about? It's settled between us, Hester. We've had an understanding for a long time. You and I will be married and...'

'I can't marry you! Please listen to me, Alexander. I have promised to marry someone else.'

He laughed. 'I don't believe you! You don't *know* anyone else.'

'A man I met recently. We met on the ship.

He asked me and I said "Yes." '

'Nonsense! That's impossible. You were travelling with Aunt Edith. She would know if...'

'We kept it from her. She was indisposed most of the time. It all happened very quickly and it took us both by surprise.' She could see by his eyes that perhaps he was starting to believe her. 'I'm truly sorry if you're ... distressed in any way, but I have never promised to marry you because you have never asked me.'

'Now you listen to *me*, Hester.' He sat back in the chair, eyeing her steadily, and she felt a shiver of fear run through her. 'You are going to marry me because I say so. There will be no discussion about any other man so don't speak of him again. We had an understanding which you are trying to ignore. Marcia is dead and buried. You will marry me.' He gave a thin laugh. 'We can't disappoint Aunt Edith, can we?'

Secretly annoyed by Hester's refusal, Alexander collected his coat and without another word, slammed out of the flat before his temper got the better of him. How dare she find someone else!

'Cheap little whore!' he muttered, striding rapidly through the dark streets, dodging the puddles. He turned up the collar of his overcoat and tried to think calmly. Who the hell was this 'other man'? And why hadn't his aunt kept an eye on Hester? Perhaps with hindsight it had been a mistake to send Hester along on the trip, but it had seemed perfectly reasonable at the time. He could hardly have guessed this would happen. It was enough to try the patience of a saint – and he was no saint. He thought of Drummond and his eyes narrowed.

'You got what you deserved!' he told his absent colleague.

The London streets were eerie at night and heavy cloud made this particular night gloomier than usual, but Alexander strode purposely ahead, his walking stick striking the pavement sharply with every second step. He passed few people – a drunken man weaving his way along the middle of the road and a woman slumped in a doorway. Destitute, sick or drunk?

'This is the twentieth century, for God's sake!' he said aloud. 'This country is going to the dogs!' He glared around the empty street. 'Where the hell are the constables?' Tomorrow he would write a sharply worded memo.

He walked on towards his home, but abruptly, as he reached a corner, he changed direction. Talk to Aunt Edith, he advised himself. She never went to bed until midnight. His aunt would help him find out more about this wretched man who had so impressed Hester. How old was he? Was he a passenger or a member of the crew? An officer, maybe? His breath came rapidly and his heart rate had quickened. Where did he live? What sort of man had Hester fallen in love with? God, what a fool she was.

Unless he was wealthier, younger and better-looking than he was. For a moment his self-confidence wavered, but he quickly straightened his back. Whoever and whatever the man was, Hester was going to remain with him, Alexander – the man who had protected her for years. He would see to it that she regretted her disloyalty and he would eventually convince her of her stupidity. Hester was his property and he was keeping her.

Ten minutes later he was sitting opposite his aunt, perched on the edge of the chair with a glass of malt whisky in his hand. Edith was wearing a voluminous plaid wrap over a pink flannelette nightgown and her thinning hair was hidden beneath an old-fashioned mob-cap made of frilled cotton. If she found it embarrassing to be found in her bizarre nightwear, she gave no sign but gave her nephew all her attention, listening in a disbelieving silence to his revelation. Now it was her turn to be shocked, he reflected grimly.

Edith tossed her head. 'Miss Shaw with an admirer? I can assure you that was quite impossible. I would have known. Really, Alexander, you must think me very dense to have allowed a romance to blossom under my very nose!'

'So, you didn't know.' He forced himself to sip his drink, trying to hide his agitation, aware of his aunt's beady eyes watching his every move.

'There was nothing to know! Perhaps she is pretending.'

'Lying you mean? Why should she lie about such a thing? I'm offering her marriage. Surely that is what she's been waiting for.' He made a determined effort to slow down his rapid breathing. 'I don't think she was making it up. She seemed very nervous, but she was convincing.'

Alexander suddenly hoped she *had* invented this man, but if so, why? Was she trying to make him jealous, perhaps? Women could be devious creatures, in his experience. He recalled the occasion when he had discovered a much younger Marcia burning a letter which she claimed came from a male acquaintance, but which she later confessed she had written to herself to try and reawaken his interest. Contrite, feeling partly to blame, he had forgiven her, uncomfortably aware that he would never be able to discover the truth of it.

If Hester was also inventing an admirer she would soon admit it. Yes, that was it. She was trying to make him jealous.

'You may be right.' He grasped at the idea with relief, relaxed a little and leaned back in the chair. 'Really, Hester is a little old for those girlish tricks!'

Edith was frowning. 'There was one thing ... I do remember one thing that happened which seemed a trifle odd. After she had fallen down the stairs – or been knocked down, whatever it was – the crew sent some flowers. They said it was by way of an apology or some such. A nice gesture, I thought, but the young man was positively beaming at her and I remember thinking about it later and wondering if it were some kind of joke they were playing on her. Or a way of sweetening her, in case she was considering making a claim for compensation for the accident. Something other than a genuine goodwill gesture.'

'What sort of flowers?' he asked slowly.

'They were roses. Red roses.' Her eyes widened as she replayed the scene in her mind. 'You don't think it was ... Oh, no! Not *eight* red roses! Do you?' Appalled, she stared at him.

'Eight? I don't see the significance of eight.'

'I didn't count them, obviously, because she at once took them back to her own cabin – to send for Mrs Pontings, the stewardess. They always have suitable vases.'

'But eight?'

'One for each letter of "I love you"!' She stared at her nephew. 'He would never dare! Would he?'

'It depends what sort of man he is. How did Hester react?'

'I don't know. I daresay she was pleased. Flattered. She mostly had her back to me. I hardly saw the young man because Hester was between us, facing the cabin door.'

'You said "young man" so presumably you saw him.'

'Not really unless – maybe just a glimpse. He had a young voice and a young way of speaking. You know what I mean.' She let out a long sigh and drew her shoulders together, hunching into her plaid wrap.

He said, 'If it's true, all our plans are flying out of the window!'

Alexander felt unable to blame his aunt to her face, although he did hold her responsible for the situation. But he needed her on his side. There was no way he could alienate her without suffering the financial consequences. Somehow he must find out the man's identity. How he hated to be put on the defensive. The wretched girl had made him look a fool.

Finishing his drink in one large gulp, he studied the empty glass until his aunt took the hint and offered to refill it.

'I have an idea,' he told her.

* * *

Hours later, in Garth Street in Liverpool, Maisie and her brother ate their boiled bacon and onion and mopped up the juices with slices of thick brown bread. The atmosphere was tense. Charlie was tetchy and saying very little, while Maisie watched him with a stony expression. When at last he sat back in his chair, Maisie braced herself.

'So when are you going to tell Annie?' she demanded. 'I don't want her turning up here when you're at sea so that I'm the one that has to tell her. It's not fair, Charlie. If you're set on this other girl you have to tell Annie – and the sooner the better. Especially if your girl is coming up here.'

He looked at her unhappily. 'Couldn't you break it to her, Mais? You're good at...'

Her voice rose. 'No I couldn't! I mean I could, but I won't. You've got yourself into this mess, so you can jolly well get yourself out! She won't take it well and you can see why. She must have thought you would settle down with her or she wouldn't keep lending you money.'

He brightened. 'That reminds me, I'll be late tonight. There's a game at Mick's place and they've counted me in. I'm feeling lucky today!' He gave her the boyish grin that always touched her sisterly heart, but she was not about to be distracted from her line of argument.

'Don't talk to me about poker,' she said crossly. 'I'd like a penny for every time you've felt lucky. I'd be a millionaire by now.'

His face fell. 'Look, Mais, I must get a bit of cash together. I've got responsibilities. I've heard of a flat, but it'll most likely be a month's rent in advance.'

'You've been out looking for a place to live? You never said! That's not like you.'

'Chalky told me about it.'

Her eyes widened as a new thought struck her. 'Suppose Annie gets to hear about it – the flat – and you making enquiries at the church and everything. She'll think it's for you and her!'

'Jesus wept!' Charlie was shocked.

He looked, Maisie thought, the way he had looked when he was caught scrumping apples in someone's back garden when he was ten years old. She had to resist the urge to hug him. At the time she had pleaded with the constable who led him home by one ear, persuading him to give Charlie another chance. Now she could do nothing to help him. He was on his own.

The front-door bell made them jump.

'That'll be her!' cried Maisie, jumping to her feet. 'I bet it'll be Annie! If it is I'm off to do some shopping.' She rushed into the passage and struggled into her coat.

'Don't go!' cried Charlie. 'Mais, please!'

He doesn't know what's coming to him,

thought Maisie, determined not to be dragged into the coming row. Ignoring her brother, she snatched up her shopping basket and purse and headed for the front door. As expected Annie waited on the step, her expression a mixture of hope and apprehension.

'Hello, Annie!' Maisie said loudly. 'I'm just off shopping, but Charlie'll give you a cuppa.' She flashed her a smile and hurried out, leaving the door ajar so that Annie could let herself in.

Annie called after her. 'Did you tell him?' Maisie pretended not to hear.

'Hester Shaw!' Maisie grumbled as she distanced herself from the inevitable conflict. 'I'd like to ring your blinking neck!'

Charlie stumbled to his feet as Annie came into the kitchen and in doing so, jerked the table and the milk jug shook enough to spill some of its contents. He was mopping it up with a tea towel when Annie threw her arms round his neck in a clumsy embrace.

'Hang on!' he told her gruffly.

She at once drew back, eyeing him nervously. 'So you're home, Charlie.'

'Looks like it!' He forced a smile. 'I suppose you've come for your money. Well, there's a poker game...'

'No I haven't, Charlie. I've just come to see you – because you didn't come to see me and you always do. First thing when you get your shore leave.'

He cursed his sister for rushing off. She should have stayed to help him. Telling Annie about Hester was going to be very tricky. 'Sit down, Annie. Cup of tea?'

'No, thanks – I mean, yes, please.' She sat down on the chair Maisie had recently vacated and folded her hands over her stomach.

She was giving him a funny look, he thought, but she couldn't have heard. He'd made Maisie a promise – he would tell Annie face to face. He took a deep breath. He would brazen it out. Make it clear that marriage between him and her had never entered his head. He would say, 'Wish me luck, Annie. I'm getting married.' Annie was a good sort. She'd understand.

He said cheerfully, 'Well, how's things?'

'I'm not sure,' she said. 'It's up to you.'

Wrong question and wrong answer. He shook his head as if to clear it.

'Thought you was giving me a cup of tea,' she prompted.

'Sorry. Yes.' He busied himself with tea and milk and handed a cup to her. 'Annie, I've got some great news!' That sounded OK, he thought. 'Yes. Exciting news. I'm...'

'So have I.'

'What?' The interruption distracted him and he frowned. 'Seems I'm getting married!' He closed his eyes, unable to bear the

173

look on her face.

'Oh, Charlie. Maisie told you. Oh, so you are pleased? I mean. I did wonder but ...You know.'

Whatever was she talking about? He opened his eyes and saw that she was beaming at him over the tea cup.

'I thought I'd never get round to it,' he said. 'I said I wouldn't – I never expected to feel like this but ... I just know it's the right thing to do. As soon as I set eyes on her, I couldn't think of anything else. Like a bolt from the blue!'

Poor Annie. She looked totally confused. He wasn't doing this very well. He frowned. 'Mais told me what?'

'About...' Annie frowned. 'Set eyes on who? What are you on about, Charlie? What bolt from the blue? Have you been drinking? You're talking in riddles.'

She lowered the cup and settled it in the saucer and he noticed that she was no longer beaming at him.

'Set eyes on who?' she repeated.

'Hester.' His mind refused to work, but as she continued to stare at him a few of her words came back to him. 'What am I supposed to be pleased about?'

'The baby, of course. Didn't Maisie tell you?'

'Hester Shaw,' he said, determined not to stop now that he had made a start. 'I met her on the ship. We're going to be married.'

As they each grasped the significance of what the other had been saying, shock settled heavily on Charlie's shoulders. He slumped in his chair. A baby. She was telling *him* so it must be his child. A trickle of fear ran down his back and his throat felt dry. He said again, 'I'm going to marry her. I asked her already and she said "Yes".' Did that create some prior claim, he wondered desperately. 'A few weeks ago. I met her on the ship.'

'You've said that already.'

She swallowed hard and he saw the misery in her eyes.

'Look, I'm sorry,' he muttered, feeling his face grow hot. 'I didn't know about ... you having a baby.'

'*Us* having a baby,' she corrected him. 'It's yours as well. I was hoping you'd be pleased. That we could...'

'No! I'm marrying Hester. It's already been arranged. She's coming up here any day now.' Annie must understand, he thought, that there was no way he was going to give up Hester. 'You'd like her.'

'No, Charlie, I won't like her. I'll hate her – because you ought by rights to be marrying me.' Her fear and shock were turning into anger – he could hear it by the tone of her voice.

'Annie, I'm truly sorry,' he told her. 'If I'd known earlier...'

He left the rest unsaid because it wasn't true. Nothing would have stopped him. Or would it? Could he have fallen in love with Hester if he had known Annie was carrying his child? Probably not, because by then he'd have been set to marry Annie and he would never have gone back on his promise. He'd have married Annie and mourned the loss of Hester for the rest of his life.

Annie said, 'I wonder what she'll say when you tell her about me and the baby.'

'She doesn't have to know. I won't tell her.'

'Maisie might. Maisie knew, but she must have been too scared to tell you. She said I had to do it – so I have.' She slid from the stool and faced him, her face pale. 'So you're going to abandon me, is that it? Me and your baby? That's definite?'

'Yes.' He could hardly speak, his throat was so dry.

'Just like that! You're not even going to think about it? Not even for a minute or two?'

'No. At least, I'll help you with the money. I promise.'

'What – with the money you win at poker? You already owe *me* money. Thanks very much!'

'I'll provide what I can, Annie.'

'You don't understand, do you?' she accused him. 'It's not just about the money. It's about us being a family and the baby having a father.'

He felt breathless, paralysed. Couldn't think of any words that would lessen the blow. What would Hester think of him? Would Maisie tell her? Maybe Maisie and Annie would gang up on him. Try to make him do the decent thing by Annie and the baby. How much time had he got before the child would be born, he wondered.

'When's it due?' he asked.

Her eyes brightened. 'July. A summer baby. They say they're the best because of the warm weather and you can put the pram outside in the fresh air.' She was suddenly hopeful and he cursed his stupidity.

'Want to change your mind, Charlie? It might be a little boy. You can play footie with him. It'd be fun.'

He shook his head. If he said any more he would only make it worse. Better to keep quiet. He tried to imagine himself showing a toddler how to kick a ball. Yes, it would be fun, but he would give Hester a child.

Annie put a hand out to him, but he ignored it.

She said, 'Don't you love me any more? You did love me. You said so.'

'I never said I wanted to marry you, Annie.' His heart was heavy and he wanted to cry for Annie's grief. 'I never wanted to marry anyone. You know that. Look, I'm truly sorry but ... It's impossible, Annie. You wouldn't want to marry me, would you, knowing I'm in love with Hester? We'd end up hating each other. I'd hate you because you made me give up Hester and you'd hate me because I couldn't love you ... Oh, Annie, please. I can't!' He put his head in his hands. 'I don't want to hurt you, I never wanted that, but what am I to do?'

'It's really what am *I* to do!' she snapped. 'Your own child and you don't care tuppence about it! You're a selfish pig, Charlie. What happens when I'm out with your kid and I pass you and her with your other kids? How are you going to feel then? How am *I* going to feel – or the kid when it's old enough to understand? How's it going to feel, eh? So much for the great Charlie Barnes!'

Her voice had risen and she was suddenly furiously, wordlessly at the mercy of her emotions. With a cry, she leaned over the table and swept everything on to the floor. 'Damn you, Charlie! You and your blooming Hester!'

Turning in search of something else to throw, Annie snatched up the teapot and hurled it at him. He ducked and she burst into tears as it smashed against the window and fell into the sink. A large crack spread across the window as she ran sobbing from the house. Charlie bent his head, clutching at his chest, as though a similar crack had opened in his heart.

Eight

Two days passed while Hester waited anxiously in London, waiting for the letter from Charlie, wondering whether to go or stay. This was not because she had any doubts about Charlie, but because Alexander and Edith Carradine were making it so difficult for her. Alexander had pointed out that it was almost Christmas and that Edith was spending Christmas with him and wanted Hester to be there to share it. That, Edith had told Hester, would give her time to be certain in her own mind that she was doing the right thing by throwing away a secure and happy future with a wealthy God-fearing man for someone she hardly knew. Edith had added her own particular line of reasoning, saying that with Marcia gone to her eternal rest, Alexander would face a lonely and miserable Christmas if Hester and Edith did not keep him company.

'Surely you owe him that much,' she said. 'You can leave when the Christmas period is over. A few more days cannot make that much difference if you are going to spend the rest of your life with Mr Barnes. I cannot believe you would be so selfish, Miss Shaw.'

When Hester tried to argue, Edith spoke more sharply. 'I think Alexander and I have behaved very well towards you, considering the way you have treated us. I have interceded with my nephew on your behalf and he has forgiven you for your deceit. The least you can do is spare him a few more days.'

Hester's protests that she and Charlie wanted to spend Christmas together fell on deaf ears. There always seemed to be one or other of them present in the flat and Hester wondered uneasily if this was deliberate. She presumed she was free to leave at any moment, but a new nagging doubt had taken hold of her. There had been no letter from either Charlie or his sister. He had promised to write, trusting her to leave London and travel to Liverpool when she felt the time was right – so why was there no letter, she asked herself desperately. Perhaps his sister had talked him out of it, had convinced him that he had a duty towards Annie. Hester would not believe that Charlie had willingly changed his mind. She knew he loved her and she had no doubts about her feelings for him. Was he ill, perhaps? Would anyone let her know if he were sick? Or had his sister been taken ill?

She forced herself to consider what she would do if Charlie had changed his mind –

or had it changed for him by Annie or Maisie. Could she go on living with Alexander? No. That would be impossible, but she had nightmares about travelling to Liverpool only to discover that Charlie had been forced into an alternative relationship.

Edith did her best, whenever the chance arose, to undermine Hester's faith in Charlie.

'You really know nothing about him, Miss Shaw. Compared with Alexander he is an unknown quantity. What do you know about him except what he has told you? He might be a practised liar or ... or a fantasist who believes what he says. He might have a prison record!' She rolled her eyes.

'He would hardly tell you if he had,' she went on. 'Oh, I know you don't want to consider these possibilities but you should at least listen to me and think carefully before you throw yourself into his world. Marriage to Mr Barnes may not be at all what you expect.'

Her other frequent argument was the wonderful picture she drew of her nephew. 'Alexander is a thoroughly upright man and he has been good to you. I can assure you, life with Alexander would suit you very well, my dear. I can honestly say that my nephew has never had an unkind thought in his life. He is highly respected in the force and will no doubt rise to even higher office in time.

Marcia never did appreciate him. One should never speak ill of the dead, I know, but the truth is she was a silly, shallow woman.'

Wednesday morning brought yet another visit from Edith Carradine who breezed in with an armful of holly and a determinedly cheerful smile.

'I don't think Christmas begins until the holly is up!' she told Hester. 'Alexander thinks me an old fool – oh, yes he does! But I don't take any notice of him. I want his house to be wonderfully festive for the first time for years. The three of us will have a happy time – he deserves it. I've watched him over the past five years as his wife went steadily downhill. Christmas was only a shadow of what it should be. She was useless, you see. Poor Marcia.'

'But she was ill, wasn't she?' Hester said. She was beginning to feel sorry for the much maligned Marcia.

Edith tossed her head. 'She wanted to be ill,' she said. 'It gave her an excuse to show no interest in anything. That woman lived from day to day in a world of her own, and nothing I could say would inspire her. I nagged her, flattered her, coaxed her – nothing made any difference. Alexander spent one Christmas Day at his club because she had given the cook the day off! Would you credit such a thing? I was always with my daughters so I could do nothing to help him.'

'That must have been rather sad for him,' Hester agreed. 'I was always alone over the Christmas period so I know exactly how that feels. Alexander never felt it was right to leave his wife Marcia alone at such a time, but he always had a special meal sent round to me from Harrods.'

'Did he? That was very thoughtful of him.' She brightened. 'Well, now, put on your coat. The taxi is waiting outside.'

Hester stared at her. 'Where are we going?'

'To Alexander's home, of course. Hilsomer House. You and I will decorate it and he'll get a big surprise when he gets back from the office. From now on, things are going to change, Miss Shaw – or may I call you Hester?'

The question took Hester by surprise and she hesitated. Somehow she knew that once they were on first names the situation would be subtly changed.

Without answering the question, she asked, 'Should I be seen in Alexander's home? So soon after the funeral it might appear rather ... inappropriate.'

'Nonsense. If anyone asks you are my travelling companion whom I have befriended. Do hurry, dear.'

The 'dear' was obviously going to replace the first name, thought Hester, but, not knowing how to deal with it without seeming rude, she allowed it to slip past. Minutes later they were in the taxi, on their way to Hilsomer House.

Alexander's home was a gracious, three-storey house – one of a row of expensive houses in a desirable street in Chelsea. The front door was reached by steps which meant there was a basement where she supposed the kitchen would be found. The area below ground level was neatly swept and boasted two large pots, each containing a small but well-clipped bay tree which stood each side of a dark green door.

The woman who answered the bell to the door at the top of the steps was a Mrs Rice and she greeted them with enthusiasm. Hester was introduced as Miss Hester Shaw and then Edith swept past the housekeeper saying, 'Ask the taxi driver to bring in the holly, please, Mrs Rice. He can leave it in the hall. And give him this.' She pressed a coin into the housekeeper's hand and hurried along the wide passage towards the rear of the house.

'Do come along, dear,' she urged Hester. 'I'll show you the garden and then we'll have a quick tour of the house. The garden is quite remarkable. As you probably know Alexander hates gardening, but a man comes in twice a week and Alexander does have an eye for colour and design.'

She had not exaggerated, thought Hester, impressed. A smooth lawn curved between neat flowerbeds and small shrubs. She was aware that Edith was watching for her reaction.

'It's lovely,' she agreed politely. This was their plan then, she thought. They would make her see just how much she would be giving up if she turned down Alexander's proposal. It was all rather obvious, but she tried not to be flattered. No amount of grandeur, she told herself, would persuade her to give up her life with Charlie. She knew she was being reckless, but she didn't care. For the first time in many years she felt totally alive and in spite of any doubts, she was eager to start her new life.

Upstairs, the house was spacious and elegantly furnished. She looked at the double bed and found it strange to imagine Alexander sleeping there with his unfortunate wife. No, she thought, firmly, I could never live here. Everywhere they went there were reminders of Marcia – her portrait on the wall, a scarf tossed over a chair, delicate satin slippers still beside the bed.

Edith turned suddenly. 'My nephew has bought you a very special present. I'm not supposed to say anything, but imagine how disappointed he will be if you are not here on Christmas Day! I hope you will bear that in mind.'

To avoid answering, Hester said, 'What beautiful curtains! Marcia obviously had very good taste.'

Edith shrugged. 'She did her best, I daresay, before she gave in to this stupid illness.'

It seemed there were four servants. There was a gardener; the cook; Mrs Rice, the housekeeper, who lived in, and Rosie, a young housemaid who came in most days and worked extra hours from time to time when required.

'Marcia had all the help she needed,' Edith informed Hester. 'She wanted for nothing. Although, I say it myself, Alexander is a very good provider.'

'I'm sure he is.' Charlie will be, too, she reminded herself.

Edith sat down suddenly and indicated that Hester should do the same. They were in a large reception room where the December sunshine filtered in through delicate lace curtains.

'I want you to know that if you decide to marry Alexander, I shall settle some money on you myself.' Ignoring Hester's shocked expression, she continued. 'He will provide for you, as I've said already, but I do feel a wife should have some money of her own. I know nothing has been decided yet...'

'Oh, but it has! I thought I'd made that clear.' Agitated, Hester sat forward in her chair.

'But I thought you should know. Now I don't want to discuss it. We have work to do. If you look in the chest in the passage you will find some Christmas baubles and coloured ribbons. Christmas decorations take time if you intend to do it properly and I do.' Fitting actions to words, she hurried from the room and after a moment's uncertainty, Hester followed.

Saying nothing was safer than saying anything, she reflected. For the time being she would allow herself to be swept along in the Christmas atmosphere. Time to break the spell when Charlie's letter arrived.

Meanwhile a telephone was ringing in Bearsley Police Station. On the outskirts of the village on the edge of Dartmoor, the building was a single storey with a large shed to one side, which housed two stretchers in case of accidents, various boxes of equipment, much of it outdated, plus a lawnmower for use on the small square of grass which filled the space between the building and the stone wall which surrounded it.

Some of these items should have been inside an office in the building, but in a rush of belated enthusiasm some refurbishment was being undertaken and two local men were scraping paintwork and whistling loudly.

Police sergeant Jon Harrow, much to his

187

annoyance, found himself banished to the small reception area with nothing but a chair, a card table and a telephone. Feeling thoroughly disgruntled, he snatched up the phone when it rang and barked, 'Bearsley Police Station.'

'Is that you, Harrow?'

The voice was familiar. Responding instinctively to the voice of a superior officer, Sergeant Harrow sat up a little straighter and fastened the top button of his tunic. 'Is that who I think it is? Is that Alexander Waring?'

'It is. How is life treating you?'

'I can't complain.' The sergeant spoke cautiously as the years rolled back along memory lane. He and Waring had been posted to the same nick in the wilds of Hampshire – it must have been nearly twenty years ago. He grinned at the memory. In those days he had been keen as mustard, eager to put away the villains and determined on promotion. Now he was more interested in keeping his nose clean, but at that time they were both sergeants – before Waring started moving up the ladder. He married the right woman and met the right people. Jon recalled the wedding – a very posh affair. Marcia! That was her name. Snooty name for a snooty woman, he'd said at the time – but not to Waring. Her old man had forked out for a big wedding reception.

188

Poor old Jon was left behind to rot and he'd given up hope of promotion years ago. He knew he had only himself to blame, but it didn't make him less bitter. He'd heard on the grapevine that Waring had been made a superintendent. No surprise there, then. Still, better watch his p's and q's, he thought.

'I have a little job for you – a couple of questions,' Waring told him.

'Ask away. Anything I can do!' He tried to sound eager. During his six years in Hampshire, Jon Harrow had well and truly blotted his copybook over a stupid bribe and Alexander Waring had saved him from suspension by lying on his behalf. Was this pay-back time? He felt a prickle of apprehension. 'Anything within reason,' he amended.

'I've had an enquiry,' Waring said. 'I'm working on something that needn't interest you, but I don't want to go through official channels until I'm sure of the facts. At present it's just a hunch – you know what I mean?'

Harrow tapped his nose. 'I know.'

'D'you recall the Seaforth case? I think it was '98 or '99. We sent a nasty thug down for three years. Battered a chap half to death while drunk! Can't remember his name, but I can see him clear as day. One eye was blue and one was brown.'

'Assault and battery? I remember. Bit of a bruiser, meaty hands. A bit dim, as I recall.

189

Hadn't he been a boxer at some time? He was called...' He closed his eyes to help him concentrate. 'Something beginning with F. Short name. Fish or ... Fitch, was it, or Finch? Tried to pin it on his mate, didn't he? Sang like a canary!'

'Fitch! That's him. Well done. Any idea where he is right now?'

'None at all. What's he done? Killed someone? Never did know his own strength, that man.'

'He hasn't done anything yet ... At least, he's possibly implicated. Just a rumour at the moment. We need evidence and I need to find him. I'm putting feelers out. Can't say more than that, but I need to finger him and it's urgent. But you've no idea where he is?'

'Lord no! Might even be dead. His sort die young and he wasn't exactly popular!' The silence from Waring's end suggested that this was the wrong answer. Harrow said hastily, 'But I could do a bit of snooping if that's what's wanted. See what I can dig up. Can't promise anything, mind. These chaps have a habit of falling through the net. Could be anywhere. Six feet under if I had my way!'

'But you'd know if he was incarcerated somewhere?'

'I could try and find out, but if he's not on record it'll be like looking for a needle in the proverbial!'

'Do your best. You always had your ear to

the ground as I recall. I'll ring tomorrow after lunch. Thanks.' The line went dead.

Sergeant Harrow stared at the silent telephone. 'Tomorrow after lunch? Christ! Who does he think I am? Sherlock bloody Holmes!'

Wednesday, 18th December, 1907 – It seems that Alexander's little plan may be working. I don't know whether to be pleased or sorry. We are both keeping a close eye on Hester and trying to involve her in Christmas at Hilsomer House. She must surely fall in love with the place and see the possibilities of life as Alexander's wife. So far she has made no effort to leave her flat and I have promised to settle some money on her which surely must be a big inducement for her to stay. I suspect she is wavering about her feelings for this other man. Alexander believes that the longer she stays here, the more likely she is to come to her senses and give up the idea of going to Liverpool. I hope he is right.

I am prepared to overlook her foolish behaviour while we were at sea – she was under the man's influence. The entanglement with this ridiculous Charlie person can be considered just a silly fling. Sadly we women are always vulnerable to the excitement of a new admirer. I thank the Lord that I came to my senses before I left Mr Carradine for charming Archie Spicer. (He went on, years later, to be involved in a sordid little fraud and earned himself some very unpleasant publicity. That scandal would have crucified me.)

In retrospect the trip on the Mauretania *was unfortunate for both of us. I wasted time and money on that fool Stafford and poor Hester fell under the spell of a very smooth operator! I shall never refer to him again if she comes to her senses and agrees to marry my nephew.*

My dearest wish is to see him wed again and to someone who will be prepared to take my advice when necessary. Hester is the one. I am never wrong on these matters and I have taken a strong liking to her, and I believe she is warming to me. She is mature, looks the part and will give Alexander handsome children. I will not be thwarted in this matter.

The following day Edith Carradine reappeared in Chalker Street, this time to discuss the Christmas Day menus with Hester, who was in the middle of writing to Charlie. Seizing the opportunity, Hester tried to clarify the situation as she saw it.

'Do sit down,' she said. 'I won't keep you more than a minute or two. I'm writing to Charlie and I want to catch the early post. Please excuse me.'

She returned to her small writing desk and searched for the right words to finish the letter. She had tried to explain to him how awkward the situation was becoming for her and ask him to confirm that everything was in order in Garth Street for her to move in with them temporarily.

My hope is that your sister is willing for me to live with you both for a short period and that the banns have been called. Once we are man and wife everyone, hopefully, will accept us and there will be no unpleasantness from any quarter. Mrs Carradine's pressure on me is mounting and Christmas is only a week away. Are you ready for me to travel up? I am longing to be free of my connections here.

I love you so much, Charlie, but your promised letter has so far not arrived which is beginning to alarm me.

All my love, dearest Charlie, from Hester

PS You can rest assured that there has been no physical contact between me and Alexander as he now knows about you.

Edith was watching her through narrowed eyes. As calmly as she could, Hester folded the letter and slid it into the envelope. She addressed it and added the stamp. 'It will only take me two minutes to the pillar box and back.'

Edith pursed her lips disapprovingly. 'Writing to Mr Barnes, I presume.'

Hester nodded. 'He'll get it when he comes ashore.'

'Have you told him you'll probably be spending Christmas here in London?'

'I've told him you've suggested it.'

'Does he know you are still accepting Alexander's hospitality?'

'He knows I have nowhere else to go – but he trusts me with regard to your nephew.'

The old lady tutted impatiently. 'And I suppose you trust him.'

'I certainly do!'

Annoyed by the direction of Edith's comments, Hester went into the hall and pulled on her coat. She threw a shawl over her head and round her shoulders, then hurried from the flat before the old lady could make further comment.

When she returned Edith was apparently busy with a list. She glanced up and her manner had changed. The disapproving expression was gone.

'I need some help with the menus,' she told Hester. 'I'll read out what I have planned and you can give me your opinion.'

Hester steeled herself. If this was going to be a battle of wills, she would play her part. She sat down and folded her hands in her lap.

'That sounds fun,' she said lightly. 'Even if I am no longer in London I shall be able to think of you and Alexander enjoying good food and opening your Christmas presents.'

Edith ignored her comment and referred to her list. 'I'm catering for three, just in case, and for two days. I shall be with my daughter Dorcas on Christmas Eve. Evelyn may or may not join us. So we start with Christmas Day. A reasonably light breakfast, I thought, with scrambled eggs and smoked salmon with perhaps some melba toast. What do you think?'

'I think it sounds perfect.'

'For the main meal do you think we should have a goose? They are rather fatty, but the flavour is good and Alexander is fond of it. He likes all the trimmings.'

'I personally prefer duck, but I'm quite happy to compromise. When I was working as a nanny, my employer used to stuff duck with orange sections.'

'Did she?' Edith hesitated then wrote again. 'Goose, medium size,' she murmured. 'And a savoy cabbage. Dark green vegetables are very underrated in my opinion. Which vegetables do you like, dear?'

'Parsnips and peas.'

'Parsnips and peas,' she repeated carefully as she wrote them down. Then she glanced up. 'Just in case you may still be with us.'

By the look on her face, Hester knew something more important was coming.

'I've been thinking, dear,' Edith began, 'that the present circumstances must be very difficult for you. Living in Alexander's flat while you are in love ... while you are *involved* with another man must make you feel rather uncomfortable. Taking but giving nothing in return, if you understand my meaning.'

'I do and you are right – except that Alexander isn't asking for anything in return. He quite rightly stays away from any form of closeness and sleeps at Hilsomer House.'

'Does he? I see. What I wanted to suggest...'

'I really don't think you are in any position to suggest anything,' Hester cried, her face colouring with annoyance. 'What happens between me and your nephew is—'

'Wait, wait!' Edith held up her hands. 'I'm only thinking of what's best for the two of you.'

'But we aren't a twosome, Mrs Carradine. I am in love with Charlie, not Alexander. Any day now I shall be leaving London for Liverpool and you will both be rid of me! I won't be causing either of you any anxiety at all.'

Edith shook her head resignedly. 'You young people are so quick to take offence,' she said. 'What I was going to suggest is that you might prefer to come and live with me for a few days, before you leave London. Then you need not feel you owe Alexander anything. My house is quite large and you would have your own room. I should enjoy the company. If you *are* still here over the Christmas period you could come to Dorcas with me on Christmas Eve and then we could travel to and from Hilsomer House together on Christmas Day and Boxing Day.'

Hester was completely taken aback. On the face of it, the suggestion appeared well-intentioned, even generous. 'Thank you, that's most kind. I can't ... that is, I'll think about it – but I doubt very much I shall still be here.'

'If he answers the letter you've just posted, you mean.'

'Yes.' Hester was mortified. Edith had obviously realized just how desperately she wanted to hear from Charlie.

'Right, then we must return to the menus. I don't care for rich puddings so I usually have a light lemon custard on a pastry base. What do you think? Alexander always has a plum pudding – Cook made it weeks ago. Suet, dark sugar, dates, plums and all sorts of rich ingredients. I don't object to a small mince pie, but my digestion suffers if I am careless with my diet.' Waiting in vain for a comment from Hester, she changed the subject abruptly. 'You do know that Alexander is fond of you, don't you? I would go as far as to say he loves you. Most men find it difficult to speak about their finer feelings, but I can assure you that, if you stay with him, he will do his best to forget all this nonsense and make you happy.'

Hester nodded. 'I appreciate what you've

said, but it would be so unkind for me to pretend. Charlie is—'

'Don't! I don't even want to hear the fellow's name. You deserve a decent life for your children when you have them. I hate to think of you scratching a living as the wife of a ship's steward.'

Hester's face was suddenly illuminated by a radiant smile. 'While I cannot wait to be Mrs Charlie Barnes!'

They regarded each other in silence and Hester felt that they had ruined the mood. Before she could think of something to say, Edith took a deep breath.

'I shall leave the choice of wines to Alexander. I am perfectly capable of selecting suitable wines, but Alexander imagines he can do it better. I will allow him that pleasure.'

Snow fell during the night and the people of Liverpool woke up to find two inches of snow transforming the landscape. Grimy houses towered over white streets, children ran wild, screeching with excitement, and the sound of the traffic was strangely muffled. Dogs chased each other up and down the street, cats perched moodily on snow-capped fences, and horses waited with less patience than usual for the comforting contents of their nosebags.

Maisie woke up and was immediately filled

with guilt. She now regretted that she had not posted her brother's letter to Hester Shaw. If he ever found out – and the postmark would be a giveaway – he would be furious with her. For the first time she felt stirrings of anger towards Annie who had talked her into these delaying tactics. Faced with Annie's tears, she had agreed, in the hope they both shared, that Hester would think he had changed his mind about her and decide to stay with her rich lover.

But suppose Hester had grown tired of waiting? She might take matters into her own hands and travel up without waiting for the letter. She might appear suddenly at Maisie's front door. What was Maisie supposed to do then?

'Blooming typical!' she grumbled, climbing out of bed with the beginnings of a headache. She unwound her curling rags and surveyed the result in the mirror, wondering if Hester Shaw was really as beautiful as Charlie had claimed. Just in case she turned up unexpectedly, Maisie wanted to look presentable. She would iron her best blouse, she decided, and give her shoes a polish. And she would bake a few scones.

In the kitchen she made some tea and raked up the embers in the stove. As she sipped her tea she thought of scathing things to say to Annie while a growing curiosity about Hester began to establish itself in her mind.

True, she was older than Charlie, but Maisie wouldn't let that influence her. Thirty-one wasn't *that* old. And her brother must have seen something in her that attracted him. Charlie, she knew, was head-over-heels in love with her. In two days' time Charlie would be back on shore leave and if Hester hadn't arrived he would probably go to London and bring her back with him. She refilled her cup and cut herself a thick slice of bread which she smothered with honey and folded into a rough sandwich.

Perhaps she would stop fighting and give in gracefully. There was no way she wanted to fall foul of her brother. Hester Shaw must not come between them.

'I will like her. I *will*,' she declared. 'Hester and I will be friends!'

She realized that they would certainly not be friends if Hester ever discovered that Maisie had deliberately delayed her letter from Charlie. In it he had told her to come up immediately so they could all be together over Christmas. Now there were only five days to go and if she posted the letter Hester might read it tomorrow and catch the train in time.

'Right. First things first. Tidy through,' she told herself and, swallowing the last of the honey sandwich, she jumped to her feet and prepared to make a start.

An hour later Annie arrived with Charlie's

Christmas present. As Maisie let her in, her heart sank.

Annie glanced at the mantelpiece and her face fell. 'You've posted it!' she cried. 'When? When will she get it?' She was clutching a parcel tied with thin red ribbon.

'Sit down,' Maisie suggested, setting an example by settling herself on the kitchen stool. 'Is that for Charlie?'

'Yes – but the letter. You promised!'

'I changed my mind this morning and dashed to the post box. She won't get it until tomorrow. What did you expect me to do with him coming home on Sunday? It's the first thing he'd see!'

'Not if you'd hidden it like I said! Suppose she turns up here – she'll ruin everything! I wanted Christmas to be wonderful – just the three of us. I've made a cake.' Her mouth trembled. 'You've ruined everything, Maisie!'

'There's not much to ruin, Annie, is there? If she doesn't come up, he'll go and fetch her. I don't want to get the blame for what happens. I wish to God I'd never let you talk me into it and that's the truth – and don't start with your tears, Annie! I've had about all I can stand.'

Annie glared at her. 'So, what about Christmas, then?' She tightened her grip on the parcel. 'I'm not leaving the waistcoat here. If I'm not invited he can come and get it. If he wants it, that is. Maybe she'll be giving him a waistcoat made of gold thread with real pearl buttons and mine won't be good enough! You're a selfish pig, Maisie!'

Maisie sighed. *Here we go again*, she thought. *I'm getting the blame, as usual.*

'You must do what you think best,' she said. 'As far as I can see, Hester Shaw will be here by Christmas. I can't sort out your life for you, Annie. I'm sorry, but you'll have to go. I'm busy.'

Annie stood up slowly, her face hardening. 'So now you're throwing me out. Well, thanks!' She stood up. 'I might as well get rid of the baby. And myself! No one is going to miss us, are they? Certainly not your brother!'

Maisie flushed angrily. 'Don't talk such rubbish, Annie. Charlie's not the only man in the world. You'll find someone else. You're a very pretty girl.'

'A very pretty girl *with a baby*? No man's going to look at me!'

'It's happened before, to other girls. You'll sort something out.'

'Well, for your information, I won't! I daren't tell my family – you don't know them like I do! If Charlie won't do the right thing by me, I ... I don't want to live. Tell him that from me.'

'Why didn't you tell him? You had the chance.'

'Because I didn't really believe he'd leave me in the lurch,' she snapped.

Maisie gazed at her. 'Well, I'm sorry, but it's not up to me.'

It was so unfair, she thought, that even when she was in a temper, Annie looked beautiful. You and Hester Shaw. And me as plain as a pikestaff!

'Can't you see how it is for me?' Maisie grumbled. 'Stuck between you and him and this Hester Shaw? I feel like a piggy in the middle! Hester could arrive at any minute even without the letter. If the man throws her out she has nowhere else to go.'

The bright curls clung round Annie's flushed face and her blue eyes shone with anger. Maisie could see what Charlie had seen in her. Why did life have to be so difficult? 'Hester Shaw might be on the train right now!' The thought frightened her. Suppose she was on the train and the house was still in a mess. She must find the spare sheets and give the windows a bit of a clean.

'I've got to get on, Annie.'

Annie regarded her with disgust. 'Thinking about yourself again! That's so like you, Maisie Barnes. No thought about me.'

'I didn't get you pregnant, Annie.'

The challenge hung between them, but before Maisie could wish her words unsaid, Annie seemed suddenly to run out of anger. Her eyes lost their hard glint and her mouth drooped. She said quietly, 'You'll be sorry when they find my body! Your brother won't care, but you will! I'll be on your conscience for the rest of your life.'

Maisie sighed resignedly. 'Don't threaten me, Annie. I've got enough on my plate already. Just go, please. Talk to your mother or your aunt or your cousin. You've got family. They'll help you.' As she spoke she was leading the way to the front door, thankful that Annie was following.

As she hesitated on the doorstep, Annie said, 'If he wants his present, tell him to come and get it!'

With a furious toss of her head, she turned and walked quickly away without a backward glance.

Maisie watched her for a moment and then slowly and quietly closed the door.

'Happy Christmas, Annie!' she said sadly and went back to her housework.

Nine

Alexander arrived at Hester's flat very early the next day and said he would like to talk to her. She was still wearing a dressing gown over her nightdress and, pleased that he had wrong-footed her, he refused her request to wait for her to wash and dress.

'I can't stay too long,' he told her. 'I have to be in the office in an hour for an important meeting, but I wanted to talk to you about my aunt's offer of accommodation.'

They both sat down and he thought she eyed him warily. *As well you might*, he thought grimly. *You have no idea, my dear, how much havoc I can create for you.*

She waited for him to speak, clutching her dressing gown round herself protectively as though suddenly reluctant to let him glimpse her nightwear.

'I think it might be a good idea,' he began, keeping his voice low and reasonable. 'This awkward period in our relationship is difficult to say the least. For both of us. Edith thinks that we should no longer be seen together here.'

'I'll be leaving any day now,' she protested.

'We don't know for certain, do we? I understand you are waiting for a letter before you leave London. Has it come yet?'

'No, but I'm sure it—'

'Nothing is sure in this world, Hester.' He checked his tone as her expression changed. He must not sound as though he were threatening or bullying her. She must assume his concern was genuine. 'If the letter doesn't come – for whatever reason – you should be seen to be quite separate from me in the eyes of my friends. It should appear, as Edith suggests, that you are *her* friend and that you and I are simply acquaintances of long standing who are then drawn to each other once I am a widower. Are we in agreement over this so far?'

Was he earning her trust, he wondered, watching her closely. Was his kindly approach working? If he was honest, he would admit that what he really wanted to do was slap her and give her a severe shaking, but he must play out his role as planned. He could wait for his moment of triumph.

Unhappily she said, 'I don't want you to think so far ahead, Alexander. You seem determined to believe that Charlie will desert me. He won't. I know he won't. He may not be rich or powerful, but he is a very decent man.'

She leaned forward, her expression earnest

and if Alexander hadn't been so angry, he might have been amused. What an innocent she was, he thought.

She said, 'Alexander, I would like to leave you knowing that we both remember the happiness we once shared. You are a wealthy, attractive man – you will easily marry again and make a much better match. You'll find happiness again and you don't have to consider me any more because I shall be happy with Charlie.'

Not if I have anything to do with it, he thought. I think you can forget that glorious scenario.

Instead, he said, 'But I want you to stay with me, Hester. I owe it to you after all these years and Edith is confident that we will make each other happy. She also worries about you. She has become quite fond of you in fact. Her own daughters have been such a disappointment to her, but...'

Hester stood up abruptly and crossed to the window. Once there she turned.

'May I be brutally honest with you, Alexander?' she asked. He noticed that her voice was shaking. 'I don't love you any more, Alexander. I don't know how to convince you of that. Even before I met Charlie ... I'm truly sorry, but my feelings were already changing. We can't choose who we love.'

He kept his face straight with an effort. Silly little fool. Did she think he had ever loved her? *Loved* her? Of course not. It had been convenient for both of them, that was all.

You are an attractive woman, he thought, and I had needs which my wife could not or would not satisfy. That is all it was. If you chose to have romantic notions that is your problem...

But Alexander knew he had to handle this carefully. He had made arrangements to change Barnes's mind for him, but if scrutiny were ever brought to bear, it must appear that he, Alexander, had truly loved Hester.

He said heavily, 'Is that your last word?'

'Yes, it is. Please let me go, Alexander, without any bitterness.'

He covered his face with his hands and let a minute or two pass. She must think he was finally bowing to the inevitable. When he looked up, he tried to look crestfallen. 'Then I accept your decision, but with this proviso that if your letter doesn't come and Mr Barnes has let you down...'

'He won't let me down!' she cried.

'I am thinking of you, Hester. I – I can't let you go without a struggle. If you change your mind ... There's still time.' She nodded and he shrugged. 'I shall talk with my aunt. Poor soul. She has set her heart on our marriage.'

Hester opened her mouth to speak, hesitated and changed her mind. She stayed silent, staring down at her hands.

Alexander watched her, fighting down the jealousy and humiliation. Hester actually preferred this cheap young steward who could give her so little, to Alexander Waring, a respected man of position and power. When she discovered her mistake it would be too late – and his aunt would have to make do with his young nurse, Della Telson. He had sent some roses with a note promising to meet as soon as it would be considered suitable. He liked to imagine her face when the flowers arrived. How thrilled she would be when they met. The old lady would come round in time, he assured himself.

He returned his attention to Hester. 'Would you like me to take you round to my aunt's house later?' he offered. 'I could collect you in a hansom cab at midday if you could have your things ready.'

She struggled to hide her shock at the abrupt plan for her departure.

'Thank you, Alexander, but is she expecting me?'

'She is. In the circumstances, we have agreed that this flat is not your home any more. I shall put it back on the market.'

In other words she was homeless, he thought, and relying on Edith Carradine for a roof over her head. The thought gave him great satisfaction.

He felt even more satisfied as, on his way downstairs, he patted his coat pocket and heard the rustle of the letter from Liverpool which he had intercepted from the postman on the doorstep when he arrived. His fourth early morning wait on the draughty steps below had been well rewarded.

It was Saturday the twenty-first – four days to go before Christmas. Fitch sat at the bar nursing a pint of ale, oblivious to the mistletoe hanging from the centre ceiling-fitting and the grubby red and gold ribbons draped over one or two pictures. Around him the lunchtime trade was trickling in. Deep in thought, he didn't hear his name until it was repeated.

'Wake up, Fitch!'

Sam sat down beside him and Fitch ordered another pint for his friend. They were very different: Sam lean and wiry with thin features, Fitch stocky with a broken nose, short arms and fingers like sausages.

Sam regarded him quizzically. 'What's up with you, Fitch?'

'Me? Nothing. Why d'you ask?'

''Cos I know that look! You're up to something.' He appealed to the potman. 'Hasn't he got that look? Smug, I call it.'

The potman looked at him. 'Yeah. Smug!'

'Well, you're wrong,' Fitch bluffed. 'I'm not smug. Anyway, it's none of your business if I am.'

'That means you are.' Sam drank deeply, eyeing his friend. He and Fitch had been friends since before they shared a cell together at His Majesty's pleasure for burning down a warehouse for a friend – an insurance scam that went wrong. Sam grinned. 'Come into some money, have you? Rich old grandmother left you a fortune?' He and the potman laughed.

Fitch said, 'You'd be the last to know, mate, I tell you straight 'cos you'd be on the borrow!'

'You've got a fight lined up! That it?'

'No.' Fitch was not averse to the occasional illegal backstreet fight. He could always use the extra money. 'Nothing like that.'

The potman lost interest and wandered to the other end of the bar where three roustabouts were getting noisy. Not that he cared but the governor would be coming downstairs before long and the old man prided himself on keeping an orderly house, much to the amusement of his punters who knew he'd failed long ago.

Sam lowered his voice. 'It's something shady.'

'Exactly.'

'But you're not telling?'

'Right again.'

Sam lowered his voice to a whisper. 'I know it's something.'

211

Finally Fitch could no longer resist. He tapped his nose. 'Interesting orders from above.'

'Above? What, you mean someone high up?'

'Exactly. Who says you're daft! A whisper from a friend of a friend. Starts with a W.'

'A W?' Sam frowned. 'Who the hell...?'

'Think, Sam. You know what I mean. A dark alley, a few minutes' work and...' He rubbed his fingers and thumbs together.

Sam's eyes opened. 'A good earner?'

'Not half!' He drained his glass. 'Drink up, Sam, while I'm still feeling generous.'

Sam frowned. 'Paid up front, was you?'

'Half now, half later.'

Sam held up a clenched fist and raised his eyebrows. Fitch nodded.

'Starts with a W. Friend of a friend. Anyone I know?'

'Maybe, maybe not.' Fitch shook his head. 'Enough said! Hush-hush.'

Sam's eyes opened wider. 'Not...!' He drew an imaginary line round his throat.

'No! Course not. Keep your voice down.' He glanced round nervously.

'A beating?' Sam's voice rose.

Fitch nodded. 'Keep it down, I said.'

'What is it? A debt?'

'No. Woman trouble. Don't ask.'

'Ah! Need any help?' Sam looked hopeful. 'I mean, two of us ... You could slip me a bit of cash.'

'I can handle it.' As two fresh pints were placed in front of them, he said, 'It'll be just like old times.'

In London, Hester was finding it difficult. There had been no letter from Charlie, and Alexander had manoeuvred her from the flat she knew as home and had deposited her at the spacious and elegant flat in Tessingham Terrace where she lived in considerable comfort. The shock of finding herself dependent on Edith Carradine's hospitality had been more traumatic than Hester had expected. She had woken this morning in an unfamiliar bed to unfamiliar sounds as the butcher's boy arrived whistling on his bicycle and the housekeeper clattered cutlery in the dining room. Now she sat in nervous anticipation. Edith had decided that, since Hester might still be in London over Christmas, she should meet Dorcas where they would spend Christmas Eve. To this end, she had invited Dorcas to have some lunch with them the following day. Saturday arrived and Alexander dropped by to assure her, with apparent regret, that there had been no letter at the flat postmarked Liverpool.

There would not be another post until Monday. If it came Hester could still be in Liverpool by Christmas Eve and all the doubts and fears would be swept away, but if it didn't ... In the meantime Hester had spent the empty hours tormented by the unthinkable idea that there never would be a letter. She had begun to suspect that there was an ulterior motive to the kindness Edith Carradine was showing her, as well as the reasonable manner Alexander had adopted towards her. Now that she had been eased out of her home, she found herself entirely vulnerable and this made the letter from Charlie even more desirable.

'Have you been crying, dear?' Edith demanded, peering across the room at her.

They were awaiting the arrival of Dorcas and Hester was beginning to feel hopelessly outnumbered. Had Dorcas also been primed to add her persuasions to Hester on the suitability of Alexander as a husband?

'Crying? No, at least, maybe just a few tears,' Hester admitted. 'I feel rather adrift and I'm not used to the feeling.' Was it her imagination or did she see a brief glint of triumph in Edith's eyes?

'I can understand that, in a way,' Edith told her, 'although I never allow myself to be overcome by emotion. It gets in the way of reasoned thought, and is also a great drain on the body's resources. You need to develop a thicker skin, dear. My mother used to drum it into us that circumstances can only defeat us if we allow them to. If we choose to remain unaffected by ... Oh! There's the bell.

This will be Dorcas.'

Hester stiffened, preparing for the worst. Don't lose your temper, Hester, she advised herself, and don't let either of them rile you.

'So, you're Hester Shaw!'

A middle-aged woman bustled into the room, her hand outstretched. The likeness to Edith was clear, thought Hester, but Dorcas was much heavier. She wore tweeds and heavy shoes and her thick hair had been carelessly arranged.

Hester shook the proffered hand and returned the smile as Edith introduced them.

'You're not quite how I imagined, Miss Shaw,' Dorcas told her, her voice less authoritative than her mother's. They both sat down, eyeing each other cautiously.

Edith remained standing. 'I'll have a word with the housekeeper about lunch. I shan't be long. I feel sure you two will get along splendidly.'

The two younger women regarded each other politely, barely hiding their curiosity.

As soon as Edith had left the room, Dorcas said, 'She doesn't think that at all. She has taken a liking to you, but has never liked me. Alexander has always been her "darling boy" and her own daughters have never been able to compete for her affection. I thought you should understand the position just in case you are foolish enough to remain in London.'

Shocked that Dorcas knew so much and had spoken so frankly, Hester wondered what to say.

Lowering her voice, Dorcas spoke urgently. 'You have a young man in Liverpool. You should go to him.' She glanced towards the door, listening for returning footsteps. 'I don't know what they're up to, but they've had their heads together for days. My mother has always been very manipulative and Evelyn and I had to struggle to free ourselves. We've learned to keep a safe distance.'

Hester thought this rather overdramatic. 'Your mother has offered me a few days here while—'

Dorcas leaned forward. 'Don't trust them, Miss Shaw. My cousin is a very powerful man and can make things happen. Believe me.'

'He's been very fair to me,' Hester protested. 'I do owe him a lot and ... His wife's death has made matters rather complicated. I can understand how he feels.'

'No you can't! You have no idea how his mind works. Poor Marcia. She had a wretched time with him.' She crossed to the door, stepped into the hall and listened. Coming back, she sat down again. 'They are discussing the shopping. We have a few more minutes, I think.'

Hester felt a frisson of alarm at the turn of the conversation. 'Alexander would never do anything to harm me.'

'Don't count on it, Miss Shaw. Ask Evelyn. He's devious and I don't say that from jealousy. Even as a boy he was deceitful. We learned not to trust him as children and he hasn't changed. He's a bad loser. Always has been.'

Hester was becoming distinctly nervous, disturbed not only by these odd revelations but by the obvious sincerity with which Dorcas confided them.

'But now I hear that you have fallen in love,' Dorcas continued.

Hester stared at her. What else did she know, she wondered.

'Lucky you,' Dorcas went on. 'Don't let them spoil things for you. Mother says you owe it to Alexander to marry him, but that's because she feels she can control you. If he marries someone else, she may not be so fortunate. She ... oh—' She put a finger to her lips and sat back in the chair.

As Edith entered, Dorcas said, 'I don't envy you the trip. Mother told us about the rough weather and the trouble with the spare anchor – and the man who knocked you unconscious.'

The housekeeper followed with a tray of tea and biscuits which she set down on a small table before withdrawing.

Hester pulled herself together. 'That was bad luck,' she agreed, 'but we did admire the ship. It was beautiful, wasn't it?' She turned to Edith who was pouring tea through the strainer into the cups.

'It was very attractive, dear,' said Edith, 'but I don't feel any desire to sail on her again. It was a wasted journey. That ridiculous Stafford. What a charlatan! What he knows about the heart could be written on the back of a postage stamp!'

Dorcas said, 'But at least Miss Shaw met a very charming young man which is wonderful, so it wasn't entirely wasted. She has just been telling me about him.' She smiled warmly at Hester. 'Soon you will be Mrs Charles Barnes. How exciting! I imagine it more than compensates for the bang on the head when that man fell on top of you.'

Hester quickly joined in Dorcas's laughter.

Edith gave her daughter a sharp look. 'Nothing in this world is ever certain, Dorcas. It may be that Hester will change her mind. Alexander is very fond of her. We shall see.' She handed Hester a cup of tea. 'I'm sorry to say that only Dorcas married well. Her sister made a wrong decision and now regrets it.'

Dorcas said, 'By "married well" my mother means I married money.'

'You've been very happy, Dorcas. Ian is a good husband.'

'By that, Mother means "a good provider"!'

'He has given you two lovely children.'

'No, Mama, I gave *him* two lovely children.'

'Really, Dorcas, you are quite impossible. Whatever will Miss Shaw think of you?'

Hester took a biscuit from the plate Edith offered, not because she was hungry but because it gave her something to do. The conversation was unsettling and the prospect of spending Christmas Eve here set alarm bells ringing. She bit into a sultana biscuit and came to a sudden decision. She would not wait for Charlie's letter which presumably had gone astray in the post. He might at that very moment be wondering where she was. The *Mauretania* was expected to dock in Liverpool tomorrow. Drawing on reserves of courage she came to a decision. This was a turning point. As soon as an opportunity presented itself she would make her escape from the net which she now realized was closing inexorably around her.

Her chance came when Edith settled on her bed at three o'clock and prepared to take a nap. Dorcas was no longer with them. She wrote a hurried note.

Dear Mrs Carradine,

Please forgive this hasty exit but I am becoming desperate to be with Mr Barnes and can wait no longer for his letter. Suppose he is ill? I have to go to him. I feel sure you will understand and forgive me. I hope so. Thank you for your past kindness.

In haste, your friend, Hester Shaw.
PS I shall write to Alexander shortly.

She hailed a taxi and went straight to the station where she boarded the next train to Liverpool. It was very full and she had to stand but, heady with excitement and happy anticipation, she cared nothing for the discomfort. Soon she would see Charlie again and would start her new life. As the train gathered speed and rattled out of London and into the suburbs, Hester recalled her conversation with Dorcas. There was time to reflect on the surprising direction the conversation had taken and Hester searched her memory carefully to check whether it really had been as worrying as she had imagined. In retrospect the woman's warnings sounded melodramatic and slightly sinister and had certainly galvanized Hester into making her move. Was that the intention and if so, was there an ulterior motive? At the time, Dorcas had made Alexander and his aunt appear as conspirators, but that, Hester told herself, was surely ridiculous ... although Dorcas's manner had seemed genuine and her advice had sounded heartfelt and kindly meant. Perhaps she was prejudiced against her own family – it certainly looked that way. Or did she actually believe that her mother and cousin were trying to control Hester?

She drew in a long breath and let it out slowly. A stout man squeezed past her as he made his way unsteadily along the narrow corridor and she wondered what the time was and how long it would be before she and Charlie were together again. Was he still at sea? If the ship had docked on time perhaps he was already on leave. How would he seem when they met? Would he still love her – and how would she feel about him? She told herself to calm down and think sensibly. With an effort she forced her thoughts away from the future and back to the present. Her back was beginning to ache from standing in the cramped conditions and she was thirsty. Perhaps, if the train paused somewhere, she would join the rush for some refreshment at the station buffet. She had no luggage with her except a small valise containing a night-dress and clean underwear for the next day.

Everyone else seemed to be heading home for a family reunion over the festive period and the excited chatter all around her, plus squeals and giggles from innumerable child-ren, made it difficult to concentrate on her own problems. Better, perhaps, to think only about the future. She pushed the past few days from her mind and tried to focus on Charlie, but in her present emotional state, she was unable even to summon his cheerful image and her uneasiness deepened as the train clattered on, taking her closer and closer to an uncertain future.

On board the *Mauretania*, Charlie whistled cheerfully as he stuffed clothes into a carpet bag and prepared to disembark. He met up with Chalky as they headed for the gangway and terra firma. Chalky punched him playfully on the arm.

'So by the time we next meet you'll be a married man like me.'

'Can't wait,' Charlie told him. 'I've fixed the time at the church and I've found a flat. Not as nice as the one you mentioned, but it'll do until my luck changes. I've paid four weeks in advance.' He beamed at his friend. 'Know what? I feel married already.'

'So will she be waiting for you on the dockside?'

'Most likely. But your missus won't.'

'Nor will yours when she's got kids to look after! Mine will be in the kitchen knocking up some grub to welcome me back. A mutton pie most likely.' He patted his stomach.

As they went down the gangway, Charlie stared hopefully at the small crowd waiting to greet the crew members but there was no sign of Hester Shaw.

Disappointed, he shrugged. 'Probably still chatting with Maisie. Women have no idea of time – have you noticed that? No idea at all, bless them.' He was trying to sound non-chalant, but his heart was beating fast with excitement at the prospect of seeing Hester again.

At the end of the dock they separated. Charlie set off on his own, wending his way through the back streets, taking a well-known short cut. As he reached a corner and crossed the road, he was unaware that someone had moved out of the shadows and had begun to follow him. Someone who was keeping pace with him fifteen yards back. If he *had* been aware, Charlie would not have troubled himself. Born in the area, the narrow streets and hidden alleys were as familiar to him as the lines on the palms of his hands and there was nowhere in the world he felt safer.

Behind him Fitch moved warily, waiting for the right place to launch his attack. It had to be free of prying eyes, preferably in the shadows and somewhere where his running footsteps would not be noticed. Nothing he did must arouse the slightest suspicion in anyone he chanced to meet. He was relying on the element of surprise. *'Get in, do the business and get out!'* They were his orders. The beating was to be a warning, nothing more. He was to leave the victim on the ground after removing all forms of identification. To the police, if they were involved, it should seem like a robbery. Watching the unsuspecting Barnes he refined his plan of action. He would empty the man's pockets and take the bag. That should do it. Once a safe distance from the crime, he would make his way to the room he had rented and see what he had in the bag. He had been told to burn whatever he took but who was to know? He would keep anything he fancied and sell the rest. He assumed the man had papers and he would burn them in the grate in his room. Tomorrow he would catch the first train out of Liverpool and make his way home.

In his pocket he had a small cosh, but he didn't expect to need it. He was handy with his fists and the man would be unprepared. A few quick blows and he'd be on the ground and a few kicks would be enough. They turned into a narrow alley and Fitch narrowed his eyes. There was no one else in sight and this might be the best chance he would get. Barnes was whistling, swaggering along, on top of the world. He, Fitch, would soon change all that! Fitch had no idea why he was being paid to attack the man and he didn't care. He liked the fact that his victim was in a cheerful mood, but that would not last much longer.

Glancing behind him, Fitch saw that the alley was still empty and decided this was the moment. Breaking into a run, he covered the space between them and had his hand raised before the man turned. Fitch's fist crashed into his victim's face and he dropped his bag and staggered back. Another blow sent him reeling against the wall and he began to fight back. Barnes managed to land two blows to Fitch's stomach which made him gasp with shock and gulp for air. Barnes was shouting now, yelling for help and Fitch knew it wouldn't be long before his shouts were heard and some busybody would be fetching the nearest copper. He took the cosh from his pocket and swung it at Barnes who dodged it and smashed a fist against Fitch's nose. With a cry of pain and rage Fitch retaliated with a stream of curses and another swipe to the side of Barnes's head. He felt it land and was aware of deep satisfaction. That would show the bastard!

With a groan, Barnes slid slowly to the floor and Fitch began to kick him.

'That's a warning,' he grunted. 'Whatever you done to upset his nibs, don't do it again! My boss don't like it, see!' He stood panting, watching his victim to make sure he was not going to get up again.

'You just lie there,' he said, dabbing at his nose which was bleeding profusely, 'and suffer! Christ! He's broke my bloody nose!' The pain made him angry and he landed a further flurry of kicks on his victim.

A shout from the end of the alley behind him alerted him to the presence of a woman who peered through the gloom. She started towards him. Damn. He had intended to retrace his footsteps.

'You,' she shouted. 'What you up to! Get off him!'

'Mind your own damn business!' he yelled but she had reminded him of his orders. *Get in and get out!* He rifled the man's pockets, snatched up the bag then turned and ran down the alley away from the direction of the woman who was hurrying forward towards the still figure on the cobbles. God help me if there's someone waiting for me at this end, he thought. This could get messy.

He'd hidden the money in his overnight lodgings. He'd put it in a small bag and hung it behind the wall mirror. There was no reason why the landlady would expect him to have that sort of money. At sixpence a night she didn't expect her lodgers to have plenty of cash.

Glancing back he saw that the woman had been joined by a man who now yelled, 'Stop, thief!' Doubling his efforts, Fitch put on a spurt and broke free from the alley where, to his dismay, he saw a constable running towards him from the right. Abruptly Fitch veered to the left and, ignoring the constable's whistle, ran faster than he had ever run in his life.

Three hours later, just after seven that evening, Maisie hurried to answer the front-door bell. She was smiling, expecting Charlie, but the smile faded when she found a strange woman on the doorstep.

'I'm Hester.'

She was beautiful, thought Maisie resignedly, but she was also obviously tired and anxious. She carried almost no luggage.

Maisie tried a welcoming smile. 'So you got the letter!'

Thank the Lord for that, she thought. Charlie would never know about the small attempted sabotage.

'No. I've heard nothing, but I ... I couldn't wait any longer. They were trying to ... they wanted me to stay for Christmas, but I just left everything and walked out. Is he here?' She glanced past Maisie with such a desperate expression that Maisie's guilt returned. She had said 'I will like her!' and here she was, keeping the poor woman on the doorstep. Opening the door, she said, 'Please come in. He's not back yet, but he will be soon. His ship just docked.'

As they settled in the front room she saw Hester glance at the decorations. A candle surrounded by holly and a scene of the nativity which had been carefully arranged on a small piece of green baize. It consisted of small wooden figures dressed in token robes, and rather shapeless animals made from clay.

Seeing them through fresh eyes, Maisie rushed to defend them. 'Pa made them for Charlie when he was a kid. He loved it. Called it his "Tivity"!' She smiled. 'It's years old, but he still won't part with it. He says it wouldn't be Christmas without it. I offered to redress the figures because their clothes have faded, but Charlie wouldn't hear of it.' She glanced round the room over which she had slaved earlier, busy with polish, dustpan and brush. 'I don't expect it's the sort of thing you're used to.'

'It's lovely! Truly!' There were tears in her eyes which she blinked back, but Maisie felt no need to offer sympathy. She felt shabby beside Charlie's bride-to-be. Although not richly dressed there was a whiff of London fashion in the cut of Hester's suit and she wore it with a certain poise. There was a long and awkward silence.

Hester broke the silence. 'Snow already,' she said, with forced enthusiasm. 'I think it's going to be a white Christmas. I do love snow, but I must buy some suitable shoes.'

'It gets cold up here,' said Maisie.

She's struggling, thought Maisie, with sudden and unwilling compassion. All she wants to do is be in Charlie's arms and she has to sit here making polite conversation with me, knowing that I think Charlie should marry Annie. Or maybe she doesn't know that. Does she know about the baby

228

Annie's expecting? Maybe Charlie hasn't told her everything. She wished, not for the first time, that she had had the courage to steam open her brother's letter, but she had drawn the line there. In the past she had occasionally opened a letter *to* Charlie but never *from* him to someone else. In her role as 'mother' she had felt she had the right to know if his girlfriends were worthy of him and had actively discouraged two of his relationships. Now, instinctively she realized that this time she dare not meddle. Many young women had wanted Charlie, but this time it was different. Charlie wanted Hester.

'He won't be long,' she said. 'He'll come straight here. He says he doesn't feel he's really home until he sets foot in our hall! This is where he was born.'

'There's so much I don't know about him,' Hester said wistfully. 'I've almost forgotten what he looks like! It seems so long since I last saw him.' Her voice trembled.

Maisie jumped to her feet. 'I know. Let's celebrate. Let's have a glass of sherry while we're waiting for him. Then we'll all have another one when he arrives.' Seeing Hester hesitate, she said, 'It'll perk you up. All that travelling. I hate trains – not that I've ever been on one.' She laughed. 'While I get them, you take off your jacket and put a bit more coal on the fire. I can lend you a shawl if you want one.'

In the kitchen she found a bottle of cooking sherry and poured two glasses. She had made a currant cake and cut two thick slices. She wanted Charlie to see that she was looking after his beloved Hester. Hopefully he wouldn't ask about the letter she had posted. Hester, she admitted to herself, was not at all how she had imagined her. She was beautiful but not at all haughty. As the mistress of a wealthy man, she might, Maisie thought, have been rather snooty but she seemed normal enough. The London accent grated a bit but the poor woman couldn't be blamed for that. Born in London, it was to be expected. She longed to ask the question that had tormented her from the start – what was it like being a mistress? It sounded at once mysterious and exciting – but a little dubious. Not quite a lady but not quite a fallen woman either. Almost but not exactly. Intriguing. Maisie knew she would never have the courage to ask but, if she and Charlie's wife ever became good friends, Hester might confide in her.

She carried the refreshments on a small tray and bustled back into the front room. She had never expected to utter the following words, but she now took a deep breath and held up her glass. 'This is a private toast between the two of us. Here's to a long, happy marriage for you and Charlie!'

Ten

Detective Constable Blewitt stared across the table at Fitch and then down at the sheet of paper in front of him on the table that divided the two men. This was a statement given by the suspect but written down by the detective constable. He read it aloud.

I was walking through this alley, minding me own business, when a man in front of me turned and started into me, knocking me around something frightful. He broke my nose and then tried to stab me with a knife, but I was too quick for him and run off.

'And this is it, is it?' he asked sarcastically. 'This is your version of what happened? A full account?'

'Exactly.'

'So how come he's in the hospital and you're not?'

'Picked on the wrong man, didn't he?' Fitch nodded. 'I never done nothing wrong. I'm innocent and he broke my nose. Second

231

time, this is, my nose got broke.'

'So you didn't even know the man. You can't give me any reason why he should attack you.'

'Exactly. Never set eyes on him before.' That was almost true, he thought. 'He could have killed me!' He held up both forefingers. 'This long the knife was. Blooming carving knife.' He shook his head at the fictional near escape he had had.

'We found no knife at the scene, Mr Fitch, and you have no visible wounds except your nose which was punched. How do you explain that?'

'I fought him off, that's how! I can look after meself.' He punched the air by way of demonstration, thinking hard. 'She probably picked up the knife – the old woman, I mean. Saw that it was a good one. It's probably in a pawn shop by now.'

'So why did he attack you, Mr Fitch? Why pick on you, particularly?'

'Dunno. Probably wanted to rob me.'

'Rob you? You look wealthy, do you?' He raised his eyebrows in disbelief.

Fitch had put on his oldest trousers, a frayed jacket and a skimpy muffler – an outfit he had thought would attract no unwanted attention. 'No-o,' he agreed reluctantly, 'but he might have been a bit, you know, touched in the head. It could have been anybody, but he picked on me. I might have been the first

232

man he saw. My unlucky day, you might say.' He nodded. 'Yes, most likely touched in the head. Not making any sense really.'

The policeman sighed dramatically. 'And you're not making any sense either, Mr Fitch. According to the witness, Mrs Wragg, *you* were doing the attacking.'

'What does she know? Probably blind as a bat.' Fitch looked pained. 'He pinched me watch! Gold it was, an' all!'

'What make was it?'

'Dunno. It was just a watch.' He frowned unhappily. Perhaps the watch was a mistake. Fitch knew he had to be careful. These detectives were sometimes cleverer than they looked – and the blasted man was still scribbling down every blessed word he said.

'What did you do with the bag?'

'Nothing. What bag?'

'The witness, Mrs Wragg, saw you running off with a bag.'

'She's lying. There wasn't no bag.' He felt sweat break out on his skin. There would have to be a witness. Silly old cow. Just his luck.

'So if you were being attacked, why did you run away when help was at hand?' He leaned across the table. 'A constable tells me that you saw him coming towards you and you turned and ran the other way. Why would you do that? If you were the victim you'd surely have greeted him with open arms and reported the attack.'

'I was confused. Dazed by the hiding he'd given me.' It didn't sound convincing but it was the best he could do.

'Your statement doesn't tie in with what we know, Mr Fitch. Your victim is lying unconscious in the hospital, but he did recover for a few moments and he repeated something you said to him.'

Now Fitch's hands became clammy and he rubbed the palms on his trouser-legs. He didn't believe for a moment that the detective was telling the truth. It was a favourite trick and he was a bit old in the tooth to be fooled.

'Something I said? Oh, yes? What was that then?'

'So you accept he is the victim?' The detective smiled.

Damn! He'd walked right into that one. 'I didn't say that.'

'He quoted you as saying...' He produced a notebook and flipped through it. 'Let's see ... Ah, yes! According to the victim you said to him, "Whatever you done to upset his nibs, don't do it again. My boss don't like it, see!" So who is "his nibs" and what doesn't he like? I can assure you, you *will* tell me, so why not be smart and get it over with? Prove that you're not as stupid as you look.'

Fitch's stomach clenched with shock. He had never said anything so stupid – had he?

'He's lying,' he declared. 'All lies. I never said that. Why should I? *He* was having a go at *me*, as I recall. So why...?' He sank back in the chair and rubbed the back of his neck. He'd lost track of the argument. It was all unravelling. He should have kept his mouth shut. He'd been told not to say a word, but in the excitement ... Perhaps he could still bluff it out. 'If he said that, *if* he did, then he's a liar and he's trying to set me up.'

The detective said, 'Listen carefully, Mr Fitch. The man you attacked in the alley is in a critical condition and if he dies you will be up on a murder charge. You'll hang, Mr Fitch. I hope you understand your position.'

Murder? Coldness swept through Fitch. 'Hanged. Gawd! Don't even say such a thing!'

'If someone put you up to this, you'd better tell us his name – unless you want him to get off scot-free while you dangle on the end of a rope.'

Fitch drew in a long, quivering breath and tried to pull himself together while he considered his options. There was no way Barnes was going to die – they were trying to frighten him.

'Murder, Mr Fitch! Think about it.'

Fitch shivered. He recalled the final kick to the head. How hard was that, he wondered uneasily. If only he'd run back past the old woman. He could have pushed past her easily. And turning left at the end of the alley had been a mistake because he had quickly run into a second constable. It had all gone horribly wrong.

He said, 'Gimme a chance to think, can't you?'

If he could bluff his way out while Barnes was still alive, he could scarper down to London, collect the rest of his money and disappear. In the circumstances, he might even get a bit more from the boss. Or he could spill the beans right now – but then he'd serve time for the assault and lose the rest of the money. Was it worth a try? If it didn't work he could still do the dirty on Waring. He folded his arms and tried to look unconcerned.

'You're trying to frame me,' he insisted. 'I can't tell you nothing 'cos I never done nothing. My nose is broke and I gotta see a doctor.'

The detective gave a long, slow smile then got up, crossed to the door and opened it. He called, 'Get us both a cup of tea, constable, will you? It's going to be a very long night!'

By eight o'clock Maisie was beginning to worry. She thought that Charlie might have gone round to see Annie, but she didn't want to suggest that to Hester. Had he had second thoughts, she wondered. When the doorbell rang she jumped to her feet.

'That'll be him!' she cried and rushed along to open the door.

Disappointment. A young lad stood outside. Maisie guessed he was around nine years old.

'Ma says Annie's bleeding and you'd best come.' He held out his hand. 'She said you'd give me a penny.'

'Bleeding? Oh my Lord! What's happened to her?'

He shrugged. 'Don't know. Ma never said.'

Maisie saw the way he avoided her gaze and a horrid suspicion began to grow. 'Has there been an accident? Was Annie knocked down?' Or was this what she thought it was? 'What else did your ma say?'

'She's bleeding ... more than most. That's all.'

Maisie hesitated. What on earth should she say to Hester?

'And who is your ma?' She fished in a pocket and found a penny.

'They call her Auntie. Everyone calls her that.' He watched the penny.

Maisie groaned as her worst fears were confirmed. She said, 'Where is Annie?'

'She's still at our house. She's very poorly.'

'Wait there for me.' Maisie went back into the front room. 'I'm sorry, but ... but a friend's been taken ill. I have to go, but I shan't be long and Charlie will be back at any moment. There's food in the larder. Make yourselves a sandwich. I'll be back as soon as I can.'

Hester said, 'Is there anything I can do to help?'

'No! That is, I'm sure I can manage.' She fled before Hester could ask any more awkward questions and followed the boy at a half-run. She rarely chose to be out at nights especially in winter. Tonight the gaslight reflected brightly on the snow and there were other people in the street, some carrying shopping, others pulling small children on home-made sledges. Three boys threw snowballs at anything that passed and an elderly woman, grumbling under her breath, scattered salt over her doorstep. There was a chill in the air, but Maisie was oblivious to everything but the urgency of her visit.

The boy finally stopped at a small terraced house and knocked on the door saying, 'This is it.'

His task finished, he held out his hand for the reward, then darted off, swooping, hollering and kicking snow in all directions, like a dog released from its lead. A woman, presumably Auntie, opened the door. She was small and shapeless and looked tired and dishevelled. Her apron was stained with blood and Maisie's heart fell. She stepped inside the hall which was littered with boxes and baskets on to which clothes had been tossed at random. There was a strong smell of disinfectant and something worse which Maisie failed to recognize. Was it blood? Her stomach churned.

Auntie said, 'Don't you go blaming me now, for I won't have it. They come to me in tears, wanting to be rid of the child and won't take no for an answer. She may be your friend but she brought it on herself and no one can say otherwise. She's in here.' Pushing open the door to a small back room, she stood back to let Maisie pass.

'Annie!' Maisie rushed to the bed where Annie, pale and drawn with pain, was lying flat on the bed with her feet raised on a pillow. She still wore her day clothes, but these had been pulled up to allow Auntie to attend to her.

On seeing Maisie, Annie gave a heartfelt cry and began to sob hysterically.

'I'm sorry, Maisie! I'm sorry. I didn't know how it would be ... and now she says it has gone wrong and it's my fault.'

' 'Tis your fault, you wicked creature.' Auntie stepped closer, glaring indignantly. 'Who else can you blame? Unless it's your fancy man.' She sniffed.

Maisie said soothingly, 'It's nobody's fault. Things happen, Annie.'

Auntie turned on her. 'Young people these days have no idea how to behave. None at all. I see it all around me. I see the results of their wanton behaviour.'

Annie cried, 'We didn't mean any harm.'

'Well, harm's what you've got!'

Maisie wanted to pick Annie up and take her away from there, but she didn't understand exactly what had happened or whether it was safe to move her. Somehow the beginnings of the child had been removed – that much she knew. Or thought she knew. How had this 'gone wrong'? Was Annie still pregnant? She glared at Auntie. 'How bad is it? Has she lost a lot of blood?'

'A fair amount. I've stuck the sheets out in the yard. What a mess!' She planted her hands on her hips and glared at Maisie. 'And what a hullabaloo she made. Sobbing and screaming. I thought we'd have the neighbours round, hammering on the door. "D'you want the child or not?" I asked her. "Yes or no?" ' She shook her head in disgust. 'I've had women younger than her make half the fuss she made!' She rolled her eyes. 'I'll be glad to see the back of her and that's the truth.'

Maisie eyed Annie doubtfully, turned back to Auntie and lowered her voice. 'Is she fit to be moved? I mean, could she walk home or would she start to bleed again?'

'Course she can't walk. Not for an hour or more I reckon, but then she might manage it.' She flung out a hand. 'She's all yours. I've done my part. You find a way to get her out of here, that's all I want.'

Looking at Annie, Maisie's worries multiplied. Suppose her brother found out the truth – he might blame her for not keeping an eye on Annie – not that it was her responsibility and she would tell him so. Suppose Hester found out – what would she think? Would she think less of Charlie? Suppose Charlie blamed himself. Suppose he was mad with Annie.

She said tentatively, 'Could you make her a cup of tea, please? It might—'

'Cup of tea? No I couldn't!' Auntie glared at them, her voice full of righteous indignation. 'What do you think this is, a tea shop? She can have a glass of water – like it or lump it!'

Auntie flounced out of the room. Within seconds she was back again with the promised water which Annie drank eagerly.

Auntie folded her arms over her chest and added, 'And don't even think of going to the police because I'll deny it. Oh, yes! That's the thanks I get from some folk! They come here begging for help, saying their husbands will duff them up, and when I do my best by them what do they do but turn round and accuse me of all sorts of things.' She shook her head, despairing of mankind and young women in particular. 'I don't know why I bother and that's the truth.' She glared at Maisie who seemed to wither under the look. 'Well, I can't stay here all day. I've got more important things to do!'

When she'd disappeared for the second time Maisie remained at the side of the bed holding Annie's hands.

Annie whimpered and her face crumpled. 'What's Charlie going to say?' she asked desperately. 'He'll never forgive me. I know he won't.'

'He doesn't have to know,' Maisie said, her face grim. 'We'll say ... We could say it happened naturally. D'you think it's possible?'

'I suppose so – but then what does Charlie know about these things anyway? Oh, Maisie, I'm sorry I got you into this. I didn't mean it to go wrong.'

'I know.' She was thinking desperately. 'You just lie there and calm down while I work out a way to get you back to your room.'

Hester sat alone in Maisie's front room and watched the hands of the clock tick round. An hour passed, then five minutes, then ten minutes more. What had happened to the sick friend, she wondered. Perhaps she had been rushed to hospital. A thought struck her. Maybe Maisie's friend was male. She might well have an admirer although she hadn't said so and neither had Charlie.

She shrugged. It was none of her business. Once she and Charlie were married it would be, because then the 'admirer' might become her brother-in-law. There would be other relatives and friends and they would all be part of Hester's new life. More time passed and she became restless. Tired of the relentless clock, she went upstairs to the room Maisie had said would be hers. She sat on the edge of the narrow bed and stared round her, vaguely aware of the scent of polish. There was a home-made rug beside the bed, a chamber pot underneath the bed. She turned back the covers and discovered clean but thin sheets and well-worn blankets. The chair beside the bed had a clean towel draped over the back of it and there was a wash stand with a jug, a bowl, and a piece of soap in a saucer. It was a far cry from her rooms in Chalker Street, but she sensed that Maisie had done her best and made a point to remember to praise the little room as soon as Maisie returned.

'Where are you, Charlie?' she cried aloud. She felt tired, lonely and unloved, and was tempted to throw herself down and give way to tears of self-pity. That, however, would be the very worst thing she could do. She remembered the first time they had arranged to meet in the Verandah Café and she had turned up too late. She had let him down on that occasion, but he had never reproached her. Now he was letting *her* down, but she was sure he would have a very good reason.

She had to trust him – and she must not give way to her emotions. It would be too unkind to greet Charlie with red eyes.

Maybe she would make herself a sandwich. Forcing herself to her feet again, she went downstairs and found the kitchen. It was neat as a pin, she thought with approval. The table was scrubbed clean, a kettle simmered on the stove, the window shone and the floral curtains appeared newly ironed. Had Maisie done all this for Charlie or for her? Oh, dear! Now she was flattering herself.

The walk-in larder was lined with shelves and that brought a smile to her lips. Had Charlie made them? She tried to imagine him at some time in the future, putting up shelves in their own flat and that cheered her up immensely.

The bread was in a wooden bin and she found a lump of cheese. Butter was available but it was cold and unspreadable. It all seemed too difficult. Hester lost her appetite and closed the larder door. She would wait for Charlie and Maisie to return. Seeing Charlie would make everything all right. Her appetite would return and the vague headache that now lingered would vanish at the sight of him.

Lost in happy dreams, she was startled by a ring at the front door. Flying down the passage she fumbled with the lock. 'Charlie!' she exclaimed, all her doubts and insecurities disappearing like mist as she opened the door.

'Miss Barnes?'

Shocked, she stared at a policeman. 'No. That is, she does live here, but she's gone to see a sick friend. I'm expecting her back at any moment. Would you like to wait?'

He hesitated then removed his hat and followed her inside. 'It's about her brother,' he confided, removing his helmet.

Hester froze. 'Her brother Charlie? What's happened to him? Is he all right?' She sat down heavily, one hand on her heart.

He hesitated. 'I should speak to a relative.'

'I'm his fiancée. Does that count? I've just come up from London for the wedding. Where is Mr Barnes?'

'His fiancée? Is that so?' He gave her an appraising look.

'Yes. The banns have been called already. Surely you can tell me.'

After a short hesitation, he said, 'I'm afraid Mr Barnes was set upon, miss. He's in the hospital. Now, now!' he added, seeing her jump to her feet. 'There's no cause for alarm. He's not dead.'

For a moment, cold with shock, Hester could only stare at him fearfully. 'But his injuries,' she stammered. 'How serious are they? And who would set upon him? That is, he lives here, he was born here, everybody knows him! Are you sure it's him?'

'Quite sure, miss.'

'Oh, dear! When can I see him? When can *we* see him?'

If only Maisie had not been called away. Hester felt that she needed someone to share the problem.

The policeman frowned. 'You'll have to speak to the doctor or the sister. They'll tell you all about it. But don't you worry – we've got the man who did it. Not a local man, that we do know because he wasn't known to the victim. Robbery gone wrong – that's what I heard.'

Hester sat down as the ominous words repeated themselves in her head. *Robbery gone wrong.* 'What do you mean, gone wrong?'

'Well, that's what we call it when there's a bit of a bashing instead of just the robbery. Like the victim fights back and gets a mauling.'

'Oh God! A mauling. Poor Charlie. Is he badly hurt?'

'It was rather nasty, miss. But...'

They both turned as they heard a key turn in the lock of the front door.

Maisie was a pitiful sight, pale and drawn, her hair dishevelled and with blood on her clothes.

Hester began to feel as if she were in a nightmare. 'Maisie, what's happened?'

Maisie was staring at the policeman in

horror. 'It wasn't what you think,' she stammered. 'The woman was ... that is, she is a qualified doctor but something ... Annie's going to be all right so there's no need to...'

The policeman turned enquiringly towards Hester, who said, 'This is Maisie Barnes, Charlie's sister. A friend of hers had an accident.' To Maisie she said, 'Charlie was set upon and hurt and he's in the hospital and we need to speak with the doctor.'

Maisie's eyes widened. 'Charlie? I thought this was about ... Charlie's *hurt*? Oh, no!' For a moment she stood in a dazed confusion then made a huge effort to pull her wits together. 'Let's go then.'

Without a word Hester and the policeman followed her out of the house, where Hester asked the policeman for directions to the hospital. They thanked him for his help, he left them, and the two women were on their way. There were no convenient buses so they were forced to walk and Hester found it difficult to keep up with Maisie, partly because she was unused to walking any distance and partly because Maisie's stride was longer than hers. As they hurried through the streets, Maisie told her about Annie's hopes of an abortion.

'It went wrong, but don't ask me how,' she said angrily, making no attempt to choose her words carefully or soften the blow for Hester's benefit. 'I suppose you realize that if you hadn't come on the scene, like you did, the banns would have been called for Annie and she'd be marrying him instead of you. She'd have had no need to do anything so stupid!'

Hester, out of breath and stunned by the revelations, reacted angrily.

'So it's all my fault, is it?' she demanded. 'Let's not blame Charlie or Annie. I'm the stranger so it has to be *my* fault.' Already terrified by the attack on Charlie and shocked by the knowledge that he had made Annie pregnant, Hester was in no mood to suffer Maisie's accusation. 'I suppose if I had been a local woman or a friend of yours, it would be different.' She was falling behind and had to raise her voice. A woman passing by on the other side of the street, turned to stare and Maisie turned long enough to hiss, 'Keep your voice down, can't you?'

Hester ran to catch up with her and grabbed her unceremoniously by the arm and swung her round until they eyed each other furiously. 'I'll have you know,' cried Hester, 'that I came up here to marry Charlie because he wouldn't consider anything else. And if you don't approve then that's unfortunate but marry him I will – regardless of you or Annie!'

Maisie wrenched her arm free, her eyes glittering furiously. 'He might think you're wonderful, but I don't and I like Annie and she's been faithful to him and ... and now look what's happened to her!'

Stung by the unfairness of Maisie's attitude, Hester refused to back down. 'And look what's happened to me,' she shouted. 'I've given up a wealthy lifestyle with a big house and servants, not to mention a generous financial settlement by his aunt – and all because I love your brother above everything else.' She snatched a quick breath. 'He's head over heels in love with me! And all I get is abuse from you. All I can say is, if this is the way you treat people, you must make a lot of enemies, Maisie Barnes!'

Appalled by this unexpected attack, Maisie burst into tears. For a moment Hester regarded her dispassionately, but then her anger slowly faded. She reminded herself that Maisie was Charlie's sister and she had no wish to come between them. Charlie loved Maisie and she, Hester, would do well to love her also. For better or for worse, this was Charlie's world and she had promised herself she would fit in. Gently she pulled the other woman into her arms and Maisie didn't resist.

'Hush, Maisie. Tears won't help. I'm here now and we'll do this together.'

'I'm sorry,' Maisie said, sobbing. 'I'm so sorry. I shouldn't have said all that. Please don't tell Charlie. I'm just so tired and frightened and nothing's going right.' She found a handkerchief and wiped her eyes. 'I didn't mean any of it ... at least not all of it, it wasn't fair on you. I don't want to like you, but you seem very nice.'

Hester said, 'Let's get to the hospital and see Charlie. Everything else can wait.'

Maisie nodded. 'And you won't say anything?'

'No. We've plenty of time to talk ... and get to know each other. Let's just go and see Charlie now.'

They both hurried on and by the time they reached the hospital Maisie seemed more together.

The doctor, a Doctor Peterson, was not exactly forthcoming. 'Not because I'm holding anything back, but because the outcome, I'm afraid, is very uncertain.'

'In what way? What are you saying?' Maisie looked baffled.

From the moment she entered the hospital, her confidence had waned again. 'I hate these places,' she had confided to Hester under her breath.

Hester decided to take a firm line. 'But Mr Barnes will make a good recovery?'

Doctor Peterson hesitated. 'We are hopeful, but it's difficult to be sure at present.'

'Why is that?'

'Mr Barnes is not always fully conscious. He drifts in and out. That's because he received a blow to the back of the head and until he recovers fully and can talk to us properly he—'

Maisie cried out, 'You mean he can't *talk*!'

She glanced at Hester who was equally shocked.

Hester said, 'He spoke to the police.'

'A few words, that's all. A few lucid flashes.' The doctor gave them an encouraging smile. 'I have seen patients recover from worse injuries. Mr Barnes was punched and kicked and he has broken ribs and a fracture to his lower left leg.'

Hester was grateful that they were sitting down. Somehow, against all the odds, she had expected Charlie to be out of hospital in a few days. It was now looking increasingly unlikely. 'Can we see him, please?' she asked.

'I'm afraid that isn't a good idea.'

'I won't leave until we've seen him.' Aware that Maisie glanced at her, she amended, 'We both need to see him. Just a glimpse. We won't disturb him.'

Reluctantly he nodded. 'But be prepared for a worrying sight. He is in a bad condition.'

Hester forced back sudden tears. This was not how she had imagined their reunion. She must remain strong, she told herself.

Abruptly she stood up and reached out a hand for Maisie, who said shakily, 'We'd like to see him, whatever he looks like.' Hester knew she had already suffered much anxiety over Annie.

Dr Peterson shrugged, rose from his chair and led the way from his office to the ward. Their first glimpse of Charlie was worse than either had expected.

'Oh, Charlie!' cried Maisie, appalled by what they saw.

Charlie was stretched out in the bed with his arms straight by his side outside the blankets. His broken leg, hidden by splints and bandages, was raised on a wire contraption and bandages hid much of his head and face. He lay with his eyes shut, white and still. His face was puffy and his split lip had been carefully stitched.

Hester stared at him and felt the tears press against her eyelids. 'Is he asleep or unconscious?' She hardly recognized her own quivering voice.

'Unconscious.' To prove this the doctor leaned forward and said loudly, 'Your sister is here, Mr Barnes, with your fiancée.'

Charlie gave not a flicker of comprehension. Hester felt her hopes shrivel. Would he ever recover? Would they ever marry? Tears filled her eyes as she stared at him. This was the ruin of all their plans. Echoing Maisie's earlier words, she whispered, 'Oh, Charlie!'

But Hester's shock suddenly gave way to anger, which deepened so fast that her tears dried before they could be shed. Turning to

Maisie, she said grimly, 'Whoever did this to him is going to pay a dreadful price!'

Mrs Carradine was intrigued to receive a letter from Hester.

I am writing to apologize for my abrupt departure a few days ago. I was beginning to feel drawn towards Hilsomer House, and was losing confidence in my ability to find my way to Charlie's home in Liverpool. I suddenly realized that if I didn't leave, I might never make the move and I was determined to be with Charlie.

'Oh, you foolish girl!' Edith exclaimed. 'You will live to regret that decision.' She sighed. What on earth have you let yourself in for, Hester? she thought. Struggling on the pay of a ship's steward with Lord knows how many children!

She read on, her mouth pursed in disapproval.

However, I hated leaving you without a goodbye as you have been very kind to me and I will always remember that with gratitude.

Now however, I write with very sad news for my fiancé was attacked on the day I arrived here. He suffered a severe beating and is seriously ill in hospital.

Attacked? Heavens! What is the world coming to? Edith had only a vague memory of the steward, but the thought of him being assaulted disturbed her sense of fair play. She had always been disgusted by mindless violence. 'Poor Hester,' she murmured. What a sad beginning to their relationship.

You would be shocked if you could see the terrible injuries that he received. He is still drifting in and out of consciousness and the doctor fears he may yet lapse into a coma. The police have arrested the man who did it, but he claims he was paid to do it by someone who had a grudge against Charlie. The police are still questioning the attacker and are determined to find the person behind it and bring them both to trial. The motive is a total mystery as Charlie's sister says he has no enemies. Meanwhile, Charlie remains seriously ill. I would be grateful if you would remember him in your prayers.

I would be grateful too, if you do not discuss this with Alexander until he has heard about it from me. I shall be writing to him shortly to ask for his understanding. I wish you both a happy Christmas – your daughters also – and hope for a happier New Year for all of us.

Yours faithfully,
Hester Shaw

Edith read it through again and then clasped her hands, closed her eyes and whispered a quick prayer for the young man's recovery. Not that she wanted Hester to marry him but no doubt the young woman had taken it badly and was deeply unhappy and bitterly disappointed by the unexpected turn of events. If Barnes died, of course, Hester might reconsider and ... but no. She mustn't think like that. Most unchristian, she reproached herself sternly.

After a few moments' further thought she decided to do as Hester Shaw requested. She would not speak of Mr Barnes to her nephew until he had heard the news from Hester herself. For one thing, she had no wish to spoil Christmas by the sharing of bad news and – if she was honest – she was secretly afraid that her nephew might gloat. With an effort she decided to put aside all thoughts of Hester Shaw and her young man. Tomorrow was Christmas Eve and she would be with Dorcas who would also remain in ignorance of the assault. With enough goodwill, they could still enjoy the festive period. What a strange Christmas it was turning out to be.

Later that evening, however, when Alexander called in on her unexpectedly, he caught sight of a letter on the mantelpiece and recognized Hester's handwriting on the envelope. Taken by surprise, his aunt handed it to him with a shrug. As he read it he felt as if he had been punched in the stomach. For a moment, as panic enveloped him, his aunt's elegant sitting room swam before his eyes and he sat down heavily on the ottoman. He had heard nothing from Hester. The news of the beating was expected, but the details of Fitch's arrest shook him to the core. He felt a sweat break out on his skin as the significance of the disaster struck home.

Aware that his aunt was watching for his reaction, he forced himself to calm down and drew several deep breaths before glancing up at her. 'If she has written to me, the letter hasn't arrived,' he said. 'Probably lost for suitable words. Excusing a betrayal can never be easy, can it?'

Edith looked at her nephew in surprise, disappointed by his reaction. 'But isn't it dreadful? Mr Barnes being set upon like that! Like him or loathe him, one cannot help but sympathize with the man. It was a most reprehensible act.'

'Very unpleasant,' he agreed, 'but bear in mind Hester does exaggerate. It was probably nothing more than a disagreement. Men of his type are prone to fisticuffs at the slightest provocation. Probably fell out over a game of cards or got drunk!' His heart was pounding and he brushed a hand across his forehead to remove some of the perspiration before his aunt noticed it. 'Probably deserved it.'

'But Hester says Mr Barnes is not fully conscious and may slip into a coma! And that it was *deliberate*. Surely, in your line of business, you find that quite alarming.'

Alexander shrugged. 'Barnes has obviously made enemies. It sounds as though poor Hester has chosen what is known as "a wrong 'un".'

Would Fitch talk? That was the question that echoed through his mind. If he did he would never see the rest of his money. If he didn't, he would serve his time and then come calling for it. That Alexander could just about bear although he had counted on the matter being dealt with quickly and then forgotten. Being implicated in any way would ruin him. He would be arrested, accused of conspiracy to commit a crime, tried and sent down. A senior policeman in prison. The scandal would make headlines in all the newspapers. Utterly humiliating. And life in prison would be dangerous. He would not live long. He handed back the letter and noticed that his hand was trembling.

Edith said, 'At least they have the man who did it. If Mr Barnes dies he'll hang for murder and serve him right! Nasty little thug!'

Alexander felt like throttling her. Stupid old fool! She was twisting the knife with a vengeance – but then she didn't know the true facts. Calm yourself, he told himself again. There was no need to panic at this stage. There may yet be a way out of it. If Fitch was going to cave in he would have done so already and he, Alexander, would have heard about it. It was small comfort but Alexander was clutching at straws. 'How on earth did they catch him?' he asked aloud, trying to speak normally.

'Does it matter? The good news is that they have him in custody. I must write back at once and say how sorry we are.'

Sorry that Fitch went too far but that's all, thought Alexander. Or perhaps he should have told Fitch to kill him and done with it. Then there'd be no comeback at all. He drew a deep breath and then another and composed his features. His aunt was very sharp and he mustn't allow her to suspect anything.

'Are you all right, dear?' she asked. 'You look rather pale.'

'I don't feel too well. Maybe a touch of flu. There's a lot about.'

'Is there?' Edith shook her head. 'Poor Hester. What a calamity.'

'She has only herself to blame.' The spiteful words slipped out and he instantly regretted them. He should sound more sympathetic.

'Oh, Alexander! That's not at all like you.'

At least he had the satisfaction of knowing that Barnes was suffering. Hester, too. Fitch had earned his money on that score but how had the fool allowed himself to be caught? Hester hadn't explained that part of it.

'I doubt they'll have a very happy Christmas,' he said, softening his tone slightly. 'She should have stayed here with us.' He shrugged again. 'I really thought Hester had more sense.'

'That's because you're a man,' his aunt said tartly. 'Only women understand matters of the heart. Poor Hester. If he dies she'll be alone in a strange town.' She glanced up at him. 'Do you think she'd come back to you?'

'Do you think I'd take her back?' Stung, he was once again scornful. 'No, I wouldn't! She's shown herself to be superficial and heartless and I want no more to do with her.' He felt it was safer to talk about Hester and let the details of the attack fade.

They fell silent. Alexander crossed to the sideboard and poured himself a large brandy. He must be on his own to think this through, he thought. He needed time to cover his tracks and limit the damage that the fool Fitch had caused. He'd survived some tough times and taken some serious risks to reach his present position and he certainly didn't intend to let Fitch bring him down.

'I must go,' he told her. 'I've some catching

up to do. A bit of work that can't wait.'

'Oh, poor Alexander!' She tutted. 'You work too hard. You should take a break. It's Christmas Eve tomorrow. Will you join me at Dorcas's? You know you'd be welcome – your first Christmas without poor Marcia. You don't want to be on your own.'

'She hasn't actually invited me, Aunt Edith, so I don't imagine she'd welcome me with open arms!'

'She's jealous, that's all. She and Evelyn are both a bit jealous of our rather special affection for each other.' She smiled. 'But Evelyn will be going to her mother-in-law's as usual and you shouldn't be all alone. Think about it, dear.'

But that is exactly what he did want, he thought irritably. He wanted to be alone with his problems, without interference from well-intentioned women. There would be other Christmases and he would be happy to miss this one although he could see there was no chance of that happening.

Ten minutes later he was back at Hilsomer House, where he let himself in and breathed a sigh of relief. At last Hester's letter to his aunt had given him some advance warning of possible difficulties and for that he was immensely grateful. He was also determined, for some reason he didn't comprehend, that Hester should never understand his part in Barnes's downfall.

Leaning back against the closed front door he considered possible ways to divert attention from himself. Obviously if accused – if named by that rat Fitch – he would emphatically deny any connection with him and would swear on the Holy Bible to that effect if necessary. He allowed himself a thin smile. Rank gave him power. He could beat this threat if that is what this affair was to become. He could bluff his way through, for God's sake! He was not inexperienced in these matters.

He had, however, forgotten about Sergeant Harrow.

Eleven

Next morning, Christmas Eve, it was decided that Maisie would go round to see how Annie was while Hester visited Charlie. Wrapped warmly against a light fall of wispy snow, and with one of Maisie's shawls lending extra protection to her head and shoulders, Hester crunched her way towards the hospital, studying the surroundings with interest, aware that these streets and these people were part of her new life.

It was a far cry from London, she admitted. The streets were meaner, the people less fashionably dressed. There were fewer hansom cabs and more men pushing barrows. Her ear was gradually becoming accustomed to the Liverpool dialect which reminded her of Charlie. It seemed to her that the people were cheerful – there was laughter and good-natured 'ribbing' – and she sensed a feeling of solidarity that she had never experienced in London.

When she reached the hospital and made her way up the stairs to the men's ward, she found a few last touches being made to the

262

Christmas decorations. A cheerful young nurse was laying holly along the windowsills. Three children from another ward were helping one of the ward orderlies to hang small baubles on a large Christmas tree. With a rapidly beating heart, Hester made her way past the other beds, wondering what she would find when she reached Charlie. No doubt he would be wondering about her – she must be cheerful and very positive with no mention of the worrying time she had spent waiting for his letter or the anxious train journey and subsequent disappointments. And not a word about Annie! However, before she reached the bed where she had last seen Charlie, she was waylaid by the sister.

'Very good news, Miss Shaw!' she cried. 'Mr Barnes has regained consciousness and is asking to see you.'

'Asking for me? Oh! That's wonderful.' Hester's relief was huge and she smiled radiantly. 'I can hardly believe it!'

'Your prayers have been answered, Miss Shaw.'

'So it seems.'

'But a word of warning. Your fiancé will tire easily and too much excitement will not be good for him. The doctor wants you to stay no longer than five minutes and to try and keep him calm. Is that understood?'

'I'll do my best!'

She found Charlie propped up against the pillows, and he smiled when he saw her. Despite the stitches in his lip, the darkening bruises, the swollen jaw and the bandages round his head, the love in his eyes shone through. He still loved her, she thought, weak with relief.

'Charlie,' she whispered. 'Oh, my darling Charlie!'

Drawing up a chair, she sat down. There was nowhere on his poor battered face where she could plant a kiss without the risk of hurting him so she picked up one of his hands and kissed it long and hard.

'You came,' he said. His voice was husky and faint and she leaned nearer to hear him properly. 'Sorry ... didn't ... meet you.' He looked at her with such delight in his eyes that it made her laugh.

'You look terrible and happy at the same time,' she told him. 'It's bizarre but ... dearest Charlie, I was so afraid. I thought you were going to die! That beast of a man! But we mustn't talk about that. The sister says you have to stay calm. And I am only allowed five minutes when I can hardly bear to let you out of my sight!'

He squeezed her hand. 'You're ... all I need! You got my letter?'

She shook her head. 'It didn't arrive, but I expect it was the Christmas rush – but I came anyway. And here I am – and I'm here to stay!'

'Still love me?'

'Of course I do! Do you love me?'

He nodded but she could see that even that small movement was an effort.

He said, 'Will we still ... be married?'

'Oh, yes, Charlie! As soon as possible. I'll talk to the vicar and explain what has happened.'

Charlie was staring at her with such a rapt expression and Hester realized that the same expression must be visible on her own face.

He closed his eyes tiredly, but kept a tight hold on her hand.

Hester said, 'I'd love to kiss your mouth, but you're so swollen and bruised it would hurt you. But your hand is just as dear to me.' She kissed it again.

The sister hurried past and mouthed, 'Time's up.'

Hester groaned. 'I have to leave you to rest,' she said, 'but I'll come back tomorrow.'

'Promise.'

'I promise.' Slowly and reluctantly she stood up. It was agony to leave him – such a short reunion – but she was terrified of doing anything that would slow his recovery. 'Don't go away,' she teased.

'No ... chance!' He tried to smile but the damaged mouth made him grimace instead.

As she turned to go the doctor entered the ward and, catching her eye, beckoned her over. Outside the ward he told her that a detective was waiting to speak with Charlie, but they had refused to allow it yet. 'When he is stronger,' he said. 'They do need to know as much as he can tell them, but we have to put the patient's well-being first. It was a vicious attack and it seems they want to make further arrests. I gather there was another man involved. They may well wish to speak with you.'

'I don't know anything about it,' she said, surprised.

'I'm just warning you. They insist that sometimes people know more than they think they do and can recall certain things under judicious questioning.' He smiled suddenly. 'But as for your young man, he must have a strong constitution. It was a very close call and we were not at all sure he would survive.'

Hester's expression hardened. 'I'd like to find the man who did it – and do the same to him! Not very Christian, maybe, but that's how I feel. The last time I saw Charlie he was a normal, cheerful soul...' She bit her lip, unable to go on.

The doctor smiled. 'The moment he regained consciousness he spoke to the nurse, trying to discuss your wedding. He was half delirious and in some pain, but he was asking if you could be married in the hospital. He's so impatient.'

'And could we?'

He shrugged. 'It's most unusual but it might be possible at a later stage. His leg is the biggest problem – it was a bad break.'

'I'm very grateful for all that you are doing for him, doctor.' She hesitated. 'Do you have *any* idea when he can come home?'

He grinned. 'I was waiting for that question, Miss Shaw. The answer is it will be several weeks and may even be months – and he may never totally recover.' He was considering his words carefully, she noticed. 'His head injuries are quite severe and to tell you the truth, we are amazed at his progress so far. He will almost certainly limp, but thankfully there seems to be no paralysis despite the bruising along the spine. Keep praying for him, Miss Shaw, and we will do our best. You know what they say – time is a great healer. Now you must excuse me.'

Hester walked home, her feelings very mixed by what she had learned. The hospital staff were being positive, but Charlie was certainly not out of the woods yet. The doctor seemed to be hinting that the man she loved might never be the same Charlie Barnes! Not that she cared for herself, she would marry him whatever happened – it was impossible to think about life without him, but for Charlie...? Suppose he could never return to his job on the *Mauretania*. She wondered just how much it meant to him to be at sea and it dawned on her that although she adored him and always would, she knew very little about him. But then Charlie knew very little about *her*.

It doesn't matter, she said to herself. We've got all our lives ahead of us in which to find out!

Christmas morning dawned bright and clear, but as Alexander awoke he groaned with frustration. His aunt would be putting in an appearance later in the morning, intent on supervising the cook who wasn't looking forward to what she deemed 'needless interference'.

'Young Mrs Waring always left everything to me,' she had protested in an uncharacteristic outburst, when Alexander broke the news. 'I've cooked here for I don't know how many Christmases without a word of complaint from anyone. And she'll be here to supervise breakfast? What does Mrs Carradine think she can teach me about cooking scrambled eggs? As for the main meal I could cook it with my eyes shut! Your wife, Mr Waring, understood that the kitchen is *my* place and left me to my own devices, but your aunt seems to think...'

Mercifully, at that point, she had run out of breath and Alexander had muttered something suitably soothing and had promised to try and keep his aunt busy elsewhere. He had decided to ask her to go through the linen for him, to see if anything needed mending or to be replaced. He would say that poor Marcia hadn't been up to it during the last months of her illness and he didn't feel the housekeeper would make such a good job of it. He was hoping this subtle flattery would do the trick.

He got out of bed and did his exercises while his thoughts turned towards Fitch and Charlie Barnes and the possible consequences. He would refuse to discuss it with his aunt insisting that this was Christmas Day and they must put all their problems aside and enjoy it. After his initial shock his confidence had returned.

'Look on the bright side,' he told himself, as he searched for a suitable tie – preferably one that his aunt had given him. 'You're a free man.'

He would sort out the Fitch business and then he could relax. Marcia was dead and Hester had fled into the arms of a worthless man. She would eventually see the error of her ways, but by then she could plead on bended knees for a second chance – without any chance of success. He would be making advances to a pretty little nurse, with or without his aunt's approval. Young Della Telson was ripe for the picking, he thought, as he took a last look at himself in the large swing mirror.

'Happy Christmas, Alexander!' he said to his reflection, pleased with himself and the world. He felt cautiously sure that he would soon be in control of his future and he awaited the start of the New Year with a growing sense of excitement.

At half past nine his aunt arrived, fluttering and cooing with festive good wishes and an armful of presents which she placed on the table in the sitting room.

'I do hope you sent Hester a card,' she said. 'I left the address for you.'

'I tore it up. I want to forget her. Whatever hopes you may have harboured I must disappoint you.' He bent to kiss her, thus delaying her reply.

'Tore it up? Oh, really, dear, that is so like you! Ever since you were a child you have never learned to deal with disappointment.' Patting his arm, she smiled. 'But we won't talk about it any more. Let's concentrate on enjoying Christmas Day. Marcia would have wanted us to be cheerful, wouldn't she?'

'I doubt it, Aunt Edith! She would want me to be punished for my liaison with Hester! Oh, didn't you know? She was aware of her existence and took pleasure in trying to make me feel a cad.' He exulted inwardly at the expression on her face. 'For the past few years our marriage was somewhat of a sham!'

For once his aunt was lost for words, he

thought, as he settled her on the ottoman.

'Well, she hid it very well. So she knew. How dreadful.' She gave him a deeply reproachful glance.

He said, 'Marcia the martyr.'

The cook knocked and entered. 'Good morning, Mrs Carradine. Happy Christmas.' She turned quickly to Alexander. 'The dinner's underway, Mr Waring, sir, and should be ready by two o'clock as planned. Breakfast is on the sideboard, but the scrambled eggs won't be moist if you leave them too long. Is there anything else?'

'No, thank you, Cook.'

In the dining room Alexander sat down, his spiteful mood giving way to one of resignation. Somehow he would get through the day. He had had his revenge and it was undeniably sweet. There had been nothing between him and Fitch in writing so there was no chance of problems in the future. Not that he expected any. Fights were common enough and no one was safe on the streets. It was a fact of life. Who was going to worry about a ship's steward?

Urged on by his aunt, he opened the presents. 'Leather gloves? My word, Aunt Edith, they're smart. Thank you. And what's this? A box of handkerchiefs. Splendid!'

'Handkerchiefs are always useful.' She waited hopefully.

'Oh, good gracious!' he exclaimed. 'I

haven't given you your gift. Do forgive me. This has been such a difficult Christmas...' He faltered and tried to look woebegone and thought that Edith's face softened a little. He regretted tormenting her. She was always so determined to think well of him and he had made it almost impossible.

He fetched a large box from behind the ottoman and placed it carefully in her lap. 'Happy Christmas, dear!' He leaned down and kissed the top of her head.

'This looks intriguing!' Her elderly fingers struggled with the large ribbon bow and then began to tear at the paper. It always touched him to see how impatient she was when she was excited – just like a child. He had spent a lot of money on her and saw it as an investment. He needed to be in her 'good books' because he wanted her to approve of Della. There was a lot of money at stake after all. As his aunt folded back the tissue paper the telephone rang. Edith lifted out a wonderfully soft cashmere cardigan in delphinium blue.

'To match your eyes!' he told her.

Before she could utter a word of thanks, Alexander excused himself and hurried into the hall to answer the telephone.

A voice he wasn't expecting said, 'Is that you?'

A wrong number! 'Who is this?'

'It's me, Harrow! I have to speak to you.'

Anger fired up within Alexander. 'I thought I told you...'

'Are you alone? It's rather delicate, if you know what I mean. Rather private.'

Alexander's eyes narrowed and he felt a jolt of unease. He would have to brazen it out. 'Private? What are you talking about? We have nothing to say to each other.'

'It's important.' The sergeant's voice was very low. 'Are you alone?'

'As good as. Look, we have nothing to say to each other. Do you understand?' After a disconcerting silence Alexander asked, 'How did you get this number?'

There was a long pause. 'Ways and means! You'd know about that.'

A knot of real anxiety now throbbed in Alexander's temple. 'If you've something to say, say it – or get off the line! It's Christmas Day, for God's sake!'

A long pause drove Alexander almost to the point of frustration. Surely the fool wasn't drunk?

'It's about that little job. Know what I mean? Seems it didn't go to plan and our lot have got Fitch and they smell blood. Talking to his drinking pals, searching his place. You know the drill.'

'Searching his...!' Now he was thoroughly frightened. The money! The first payment! Where had Fitch hidden it? Alexander closed his eyes and a wave of nausea swept through him. He had to know the worst or he was going to be vulnerable.

Before he could decide how to play it, Harrow spoke again, his voice stronger. 'It's like this – I reckon I'm going to get reporters sniffing round – like blooming bloodhounds they are. Gentlemen of the press! Gentlemen. Hah! You know what they're like. Offering money for information they can use in their newspapers.'

Oh God! Worse and worse! The little sod was blackmailing him. Alexander tried desperately to think, but his brain seemed numb and his heart was racing uncomfortably in his chest. What did one do when faced with a blackmailer? Go to the police, of course – but he *was* the police! What should he do? Think! *Think!*

'You still there?' The voice was relentless. 'I mean, I don't want to tell them anything. You know me, but ... my memory could be a bit weak. That would be convenient, wouldn't it? Know what I'm getting at?'

Alexander ground his teeth with fury. Bitterly he regretted using Sergeant Harrow to get to Fitch, but that was in the past and couldn't be undone.

'Listen to me!' he snapped as forcefully as he could. 'Do not mention my name on the telephone. Not ever! Have you got that?' He raised his voice. 'Do not mention my name! Ever! To anyone!' He took a deep breath and tried to calm himself. 'And never phone me again. If you do I promise you'll regret it.'

Harrow went on as if he hadn't spoken. 'I mean, you're a wealthy man but I'm just a sergeant and a bit of extra cash would be very handy.'

There was now a distinct whine in the sergeant's voice and Alexander swore under his breath. What he wanted with all his heart was to strangle the greedy little blighter and silence him for ever, but that seemed un-likely to happen. So what *was* to be done, he wondered. Suddenly Alexander saw his whole career crumbling – and all because of Charles Barnes. And Hester, of course, be-cause it was Hester who had brought Barnes into the equation.

A timid cough made him turn and he found his aunt standing in the doorway look-ing at him nervously. Hell! He had forgotten all about her. Covering the mouthpiece of the telephone, he said, 'It's nothing, dear. I won't be long.'

'Who is it? Is something wrong?'

'Nothing's wrong. Go back in there.' He jerked his head towards the sitting room. 'I'll be with you in a minute.' As she hesitated he added her to the list of people with whom he would like to deal harshly, but, to his relief, his aunt withdrew as instructed.

Alexander drew another deep breath to steady himself. He would have to deal with this later. He uncovered the mouthpiece. 'I'll see to it. Do you understand me? It's Christmas and this is most inconvenient. I can't talk now. We ... I have visitors. My wife died recently and I still have arrangements to make. The funeral and so on. I'll contact you. Do you understand me?'

He waited in vain for an answer and then the line went dead. Before rejoining his aunt, Alexander sat down on the stairs and put his head in his hands. He tried to recall his side of the conversation. How much had his aunt overheard? He would have to bluff it out. Forcing a smile, he stood up and glanced in the mirror. Yes, he looked as bad as he felt. Badly shaken and furiously angry. He would never have expected Harrow to turn on him. But then he had trusted Fitch to give Barnes a beating, not half kill him! He smoothed his hair, tugged down his waistcoat and eased his collar.

Walking back to the crumpled wrapping papers and presents he said cheerily, 'So sorry, dear! Would you believe it? I'm off duty, it's Christmas Day and some blithering idiot decides to land me with all his insecurities. If he can't do the job he should leave the force and become a greengrocer or a milkman.' He laughed. 'I'll have his guts for garters when I get back into the office!'

'So it's nothing serious? I thought...'

'Serious? Only for him! Now, hold the

cardigan up, dear, and let me see how it suits you.' She was still regarding him anxiously and he ploughed on. 'I thought it the same colour as your eyes. A lovely cornflower blue.'

'You said you were busy with Marcia's funeral.' She looked puzzled.

'Oh! That was just to shut the man up. He isn't to know it's been and gone. I think Marcia would forgive me for that small lie.' He smiled as she held the cardigan against herself. 'Yes! A perfect match.' He leaned forward and kissed her. 'Happy Christmas, dear.'

She laid it reverently over the arm of the ottoman. 'It must have been very expensive. You do spoil me, Alexander.'

He crossed the room to pour himself a brandy. While his back was towards her he took a large gulp and then topped it up. He needed to be alone with his thoughts. Turning back he said, 'Will you excuse me for a few moments. I have to make a few notes before I forget. It will only take about ten minutes.' He pointed to a small present as yet unwrapped. Smiling he said, 'It's a small extra for you. It will give you something uplifting to sustain you while I'm upstairs.'

The book contained biblical quotations – one for each day of the year. It was the sort of thing his aunt professed to like. As she picked it up, he hurried from the room with his brandy and almost ran upstairs and into his study. He was trembling as he threw himself into the familiar leather-backed chair and closed his eyes. The familiar surroundings gave him a sense of security, but he knew it to be false. He was in deep trouble, he acknowledged, and had behaved in an ill-restrained fashion. He had forgotten his mantra which was 'Pause first, act later'. His feelings against Barnes had led him to act first and he was going to regret it later. He should have thrown Hester out when he first learned of her obsession with the young steward. Trying to punish her lover had been a mistake, but he had done it because he thought he could get away with it. He had the power and the connections and the nerve to take revenge. But he had been too confident and that meant he had misjudged Fitch. The fool had gone too far and if Barnes died, he, Alexander, could be found guilty of conspiracy to murder. How could he have been so careless?

Now the worst scenario had happened and he would need all his skill to evade the retribution he deserved. No point in relying on Fitch or Harrow. They would both finger him. He would need all his cunning, skill and courage to fight off the threat. If he couldn't find a way through this, the rest of his life would not be worth living.

★　★　★

278

Wednesday, 25th December – What a dreadful day this has been. A Christmas Day to forget. Thank heavens Hester Shaw was not involved. I hardly know how to write down my suspicions, but I feel sure poor Alexander is in some kind of trouble. When he was a boy he would bring his troubles to me, but now he is politely resisting my efforts to help him. He had a weird telephone call this morning while we were unwrapping our presents and whoever it was upset him quite dreadfully. I think he was bullying him because Alexander sounded very worried and then angry, and when he saw me at the door he tried to pretend it was nothing important but I know it was. He was lying to me!

He went upstairs for ten minutes to finish a report but didn't come down again until Cook announced lunch. He had been drinking and was in a hateful mood. He hardly spoke to me and snapped at Mrs Rice, saying she had ruined the meal which wasn't true. Poor Mrs Rice ran out in tears. When I made to follow her out and comfort her, Alexander screamed at me to sit down and mind my own damned business! I was glad that Marcia wasn't alive to see him in such an emotional state. I wish he would confide in me because as things stand, I don't know how to help him. I shall keep my eyes and ears open. He may think me

*an old fool but I shall make it my business
to know what is going on.*

*I don't think I shall ever want to wear the
beautiful cardigan he gave me – it would
bring back too many unhappy memories.*

Three days later Hester returned from the
hospital looking serious and at once sat
Maisie down.

'We have to talk,' she said. 'We have to
make some plans for the future and Charlie
has to be at the centre of them.'

Maisie nodded. 'I've been thinking the
same thing, but I didn't like to bring it up
over Christmas. We both know the main
problem is going to be...?'

'Money!'

'Exactly. You and I have to face facts. You
kept house for your brother who was earning
a weekly wage. I was keeping house for Alex
and he was keeping me financially. Now
neither of us has anyone to earn for us.'

Maisie sighed. 'We have no idea when
Charlie will go back to work – if he ever can
– so I've been thinking I'll get a job. There's
bound to be something. There's always work
at the laundry where Annie works. Her
friend Ginnie has just left and they've said
she can have her job in the ironing room. So
if Annie takes that job I could have her present job. It's hot and steamy work but it's
regular and it would pay the rent of this

280

place and a bit over.'

'I used to be a children's nanny,' Hester told her, 'until my employer forced his way into my bedroom and then lied about it, blaming me! I could try for something similar. I can also play the piano a little and could give lessons to beginners – if we had a piano.'

'And we haven't!'

They both laughed.

Hester frowned. 'D'you know any rich people with young children I could teach privately? Maybe I could advertise somewhere.' She brightened. 'If a family had a piano I could go to the house and teach there.'

Maisie said, 'The big snag is – who's going to look after Charlie when he comes home? If we're both out at work...'

'I spoke to the doctor again and he still won't commit himself about when Charlie can come home, but he did say in a few weeks we might be able to marry in the hospital.'

Maisie stared at her. 'And you didn't think to tell me! Hester Shaw, you amaze me. That's wonderful news.'

'I'm sorry. I was more concerned about our day-to-day living expenses. I have ten pounds left from the money which Edith Carradine paid me to be her travelling companion. I shall put all that towards whatever expenses you have with this house and our food – and there's the coal! Oh, dear! I realize now how spoiled I was when I was with Alexander. He paid for everything. I'm not really used to dealing with money, but it's high time I learned.'

Maisie steepled her hands. 'There's something else. Annie's not much good at writing, but she's determined to write a letter to Charlie to tell him about the baby and what she did, to say sorry. She's not expecting a reply and she's not expecting him to go back to her, but she says she wants to "wipe the slate clean". That's how she put it – but she doesn't want to upset you. You wouldn't mind, would you, Hester? She's been through a lot and she's very unhappy. I said I thought you'd understand.'

'I don't mind, Maisie. I feel very sorry for her. She's never going to want me as a friend, but I don't see her as an enemy. I can see why she loves Charlie.' She smiled. 'I can't see why anyone *wouldn't* love him.'

A knock at the front door interrupted the discussion and Maisie went to answer it.

A policeman said, 'Miss Shaw?'

'No. I'll ... It's not about my brother, is it? Charlie Barnes? He's...'

'Indirectly. I need to speak with Miss Shaw. In private.'

'You'd better come in.' She sent him into the front room and called Hester.

As soon as the two of them were seated, the policeman introduced himself as Detective Constable Blewitt who was making some enquiries into the attack on Charlie Barnes. 'I understand from the hospital,' he began, 'that you and Mr Barnes are engaged to be married if he recovers.'

'*When* he recovers,' she corrected him. 'That's right. We are.' She regarded him warily.

'We also understand from an informant that you recently lived with Alexander Waring of Scotland Yard.'

Hester frowned. His manner was beginning to alarm her. Why was it any business of the police who she had or had not lived with?

'I don't see what right you have to question me about Mr Waring. And who is your informant?' In an attempt to hide her nervousness she was sounding uncooperative and realized, with a sinking heart, that she was making a mistake.

'You will see, Miss Shaw. I'm sorry to have to tell you this but we have information to suggest that the attack upon Mr Barnes was not random but was in fact *ordered* by Mr Waring.'

Now Hester stared at him blankly. 'I don't quite understand,' she began. 'How could he...? Why would he? None of this makes sense. I thought you'd already caught the man who did it.'

'We have, Miss Shaw, but we now understand that he was merely the hired assassin, so to speak. It certainly does look that way. Could jealousy be a motive, do you think?'

'I don't understand,' Hester stammered. 'At least ... Are you saying someone paid this man to attack Charlie?'

He nodded.

'And you think that man was Alexander? Oh, that can't be right.' She shook her head. 'Mr Waring is a very civilized man. He would never...' She swallowed. Her throat was uncomfortably dry. 'He would never do such a thing! Who says he did?'

'The man who attacked your young man. The man we have in custody who admits to the crime. A certain Matt Fitch. He claims that he was paid by Waring to give Charlie Barnes a beating and—'

'Wait!' she cried incredulously. 'You think Alexander *paid* a man to hurt Charlie? I don't believe it. I know him. He wouldn't do such a thing.'

'Miss Shaw, we need to know if you can think of anything to corroborate Fitch's statement. A telephone conversation, perhaps? A letter he tried to hide? Any slip of the tongue that gave you cause to suspect any wrongdoing?'

'No! Never! That is, I can't recall a single thing that worried me.'

'His wife might have had doubts. She

might have been able to help us but I under-stand she died recently.'

Hester nodded. 'She'd been ill for a long time. I never met her.' Tuning out the man's voice, she stopped listening to him as she tried to reassure herself that Alexander was the man she knew; the man she had once hoped to marry. Surely she knew him better than they did. Alexander had his faults, but at heart he was honourable, she told herself. She had trusted him. Lived with him. *Slept* with him. 'There must be some mistake,' she said at last. Wild-eyed she looked at the detective for a hint that this wasn't happen-ing. 'This man Fitch must be lying!' she said firmly. 'He's trying to pin the blame on to...' She faltered to a stop, chilled by the look of pity on the detective's face.

'I'm afraid not. Matt Fitch has the money to prove it. I'm sorry, Miss Shaw. We found it when we searched his room and have now been forced to widen our investigation.' He sighed heavily. 'The case now has all the hallmarks of a major scandal. Firstly Mr Waring is a highly respected police officer and secondly the victim might have died from his injuries. We understand Mr Barnes's health is not entirely stable. If he should take a turn for the worse then it would be murder. It may be attempted murder. Or conspiracy to murder. You do see the need for great discretion here.'

Hester nodded but her mind was reeling with terrible possibilities. Suppose for a moment that this *was* true and Alexander had decided to punish Charlie. A terrible idea was forming in her mind – that if Alexander had done this to Charlie, then indirectly, that made it her fault. Charlie falling in love with her had brought on the attack and his terrible injuries! That unbearable thought overwhelmed her and, as she cried out in protest, a weakness overtook her and she felt herself sway forward into a welcome darkness...

When she opened her eyes again, Maisie was waving a small bottle of sal volatile under her nose and Hester came round to find herself lying on the floor with a cushion tucked under her head. She was coughing and spluttering with tears running down her face. As her memory returned, she cried out again.

'Come on, love,' Maisie urged. 'It's going to be all right.' She put an arm round her and helped her on to a chair. 'You had a shock, that's all. I'll make us a cup of tea.'

Hester looked round. 'Where's the policeman? He said such terrible things about Alexander. It can't be true ... can it?'

Maisie shrugged. 'Don't ask me. I daresay we'll know all in good time. I sent the policeman packing. Said you'd had enough for one day and was in no state to carry on. He's coming back first thing tomorrow, but we're to say nothing to anyone. He was determined. Very hush-hush, he said. We have to be discreet. That was his word. Discreet. Now sit up and lean back – that's the way. I'll make the tea and then you can tell me everything. Or whatever you can tell me. It all sounds very dramatic.' She paused. 'Cheer up, Hester! Whatever it is we can beat it. We're tougher than we look.'

She bustled out leaving Hester sick at heart and trembling. She would share everything she knew, she decided. She and Maisie and Charlie were in this nightmare together. Somehow they would have to learn how to survive.

Twelve

Edith woke up at ten to five on the morning of Sunday, the twenty-ninth of December. Immediately all her fears came rushing back and she lay awake weighing up what she ought to do about her nephew. She knew he was a grown man and that she had no influence on him any more, but she still loved him like a son and felt that somehow she might be able to help him. Who else could he turn to for support? Marcia was gone – not that she would have been much use.

'Weak as water!' Edith sniffed disparagingly.

Marcia had always taken the line of least resistance and would have been no help at all. Struggling into a sitting position, Edith stared round her bedroom which was familiar but full of night shadows. The moon still shone fitfully but Edith lit her bedside candle, put on her spectacles and reached for her diary. Carefully she reread the last few entries, trying to glean any clue from what had happened over the last few weeks. She knew that before her abortive trip to the doctor in New York all had seemed as usual. It was just around Christmas that matters had turned rather sour and difficult.

Perhaps something had happened while she and Hester were on the *Mauretania*. She had always worried about Alexander's chosen profession. It was dangerous and he must have made enemies along the way. Maybe a villain from his past was threatening him. Possibly a man he had put away had re-emerged from prison vowing revenge. Was her nephew's life in danger? The thought sent a cold shiver through her. Surely he could arrange protection for himself, if that were the case. Unless he was too proud to ask for help. That was probably it. He thought he would look weak if he asked for help and was trying to deal with the problem alone.

Unless he was romantically involved. She gasped. Suppose he had met another woman. But then he'd have no problem because Marcia was dead and Hester had found someone else. She shook her head and ruled out that idea. Unless the woman was married and the husband had found out and was threatening to give him a hiding or report his behaviour to his superiors. She considered the scenario carefully but rejected it. Alexander was a very attractive man, but he had more sense than to risk his career over another man's wife. He was no fool.

She closed the diary, annoyed at her inability to discover the truth. And then another notion took hold of her – Alexander was seriously ill and was secretly fighting for his life!

Oh Lord! she thought. Was that it? He'd be reluctant to upset her and would keep the bad news to himself, but naturally he'd be edgy and moody. But how would that explain the telephone call he had received on Christmas morning? She frowned, trying to recall any words or phrases she had overheard. He'd been speaking to someone – Sergeant Somebody – and he'd shouted at him not to mention his name to anybody. Later he'd said he'd 'see to it'.

She was now wide awake and it was too late to try and go back to sleep so she decided to get up. She would make herself a cup of Bovril – that was always heartening. Later she would go round to Hilsomer House and demand to know what was troubling him. Somehow she would coax or bully the truth out of him. In all probability he would be glad to get it off his chest. Feeling somewhat happier, she climbed out of bed and made her way to the kitchen. She smiled as she filled the kettle. Only a few more hours then she would know the worst and they would both be feeling a lot better.

The hansom cab dropped Edith at the door

just after ten and she marched up the steps, gathering herself for the coming storm. She would tell him that she would not leave the premises until he had told her the truth. Straightening her back she listened for the maid's footsteps, but it was Mrs Rice who opened the door. Not with her normal smile of welcome but with a distraught expression.

'Oh, Mrs Carradine, thank goodness. Come in, do. We're all at sixes and sevens! Such dreadful goings on!' Ignoring Edith's demand to be more explicit, she headed back to the kitchen where Rosie, the maid, pale and upset, was sitting at the kitchen table sipping a mug of tea. Mrs Rice, by comparison, was red-faced and distinctly flustered.

'What on earth is happening here?' Edith snapped, her tone sharpened in apprehension. She was right. Alexander had been hiding something from her.

She looked at Rosie and asked, 'Why aren't you working? You're not paid to sip tea.'

'Because I've got the sack!' Her mouth trembled and she looked to Mrs Rice for help.

'Well, if my nephew has sacked you, you obviously deserved it.' Edith sat on the chair Mrs Rice provided for her and said, 'I'll have a cup of tea, please, and a biscuit. I didn't have any appetite for breakfast.' Perhaps, since Marcia's death, her nephew had been having trouble with the staff. Too strict, maybe, or not strict enough. Maybe the sergeant he had been talking to on the telephone was Rosie's father and they were arguing about her being dismissed. Edith felt marginally more composed. If that was all it was, she had worried for no good reason. Turning to Rosie she said, 'What have you done, you silly girl?'

Rosie's eyes widened. 'Me? I haven't done nothing! Mrs Rice knows. Nor has she. We've both got the sack.' She began to cry.

Edith accepted her tea, added sugar and stirred it relentlessly. She made no attempt to drink it as she sat silent, trying to hide her dismay at this new revelation. So this was it, she thought dully. Either Alexander was not coping without Marcia or he had suddenly taken leave of his senses. She stood up.

'I'll speak with Mr Waring. Where is he? In his study, I daresay.'

As she moved towards the door Mrs Rice said, 'He's nowhere, Mrs Carradine. That's the trouble. He's gone. Packed a few things, called a cab and walked out on us.' Taking pity on Edith, she said, 'Come back and sit down. It's not good news, is it? Sit down and take a few sips of your tea.'

Edith wasn't used to taking orders from a servant, but suddenly her legs felt weak and she made her way unsteadily to her chair and sat down. 'This is most ... You say my nephew has *gone*?' She frowned. 'There must be a simple explanation. You must have misunderstood the situation.' Please tell me you have, she begged inwardly. Aloud she said, 'I can assure you Mr Waring has not walked out. That is utter nonsense. Where would he go? He would have told me.' She was annoyed to hear a shake in her voice. Show no weakness in front of the servants, she reminded herself. Her mother had drummed that into her when she was a very young woman about to be married. 'Take your time, Mrs Rice, and tell me what has happened.' She sipped her tea, watching the housekeeper over the top of the cup.

Mrs Rice glanced at Rosie who said, 'I went up to make the bed as usual and he wouldn't open the bedroom door even though he's usually in his study by the time I go up and—'

Edith said, 'I want to hear it from Mrs Rice. Your turn will come, Rosie.' She knew it made no difference who told her, but she had spoken to Mrs Rice and the girl must not be allowed to take liberties, whatever the circumstances.

Mrs Rice tutted and began her version. 'When Rosie came down and said where should she start because Mr Waring would not let her in I thought it odd but sent her to do the bathroom instead. I was cooking breakfast – you know, ma'am, how Mr

Waring likes his Sunday breakfast. Always two fried eggs and three rashers of best back bacon done crispy—'

'Please! I'm not interested in his breakfast.' Edith added another spoonful of sugar to her tea and began to stir it furiously.

The housekeeper continued. 'Then he came hurrying downstairs and I thought better get the bacon – oh, sorry! He came into the kitchen and said, "No breakfast, thank you. I have to go away in rather a hurry. Something unexpected." ' She raised her eyes to the ceiling as if to improve her memory. 'Oh, yes, then he said, "I've left a note for my aunt. I shall be away indefinitely so here is your pay. A little extra in lieu of notice and because you'll have to find new employment." '

'Did he explain the circumstances?'

'No, ma'am, he didn't. I was so shook up I never thought to ask him and anyway he was off out the door. I followed him along the passage to ask him what was going on, but he must have telephoned for a cab because it was waiting for him and he turned back and saw me at the front door and he didn't even wave goodbye.'

Still sniffling into her handkerchief, Rosie saw her chance. 'I got on with the bathroom like I was told and then I wondered whether to strip the bed and—'

'What's that?' Edith turned to her.

Mrs Rice said, 'Forget the bed, Rosie. Forget all of it.' Her voice rose with a hint of hysteria. 'After all these years devoted to the family, we're not needed here any more.' She, too, appeared to be on the verge of tears.

Edith wished she could join them but tears were far from her eyes. She sat, dry-eyed, her throat tight with fear. Something terrible was happening to Alexander and she was too late to help him. Perhaps he had become mentally ill under the pressure of work at his office or had suffered a breakdown because of Marcia's prolonged illness and recent death. He had gone. Indefinitely, he'd said.

'He must have said why or where,' Edith said desperately. 'He must have said something. Try and remember anything else he said.'

'He left you a note. Maybe that will—'

'Oh, yes! The note.' Edith seized upon the idea. 'Rosie, run up to the study and find the note and bring it down – and hurry.'

When Rosie had gone, Mrs Rice said, 'Mr Waring gave us each three weeks' wages but we'll have to start looking for work elsewhere. It's a good thing you came round because we were wondering what to do.' She hesitated. 'I live here, Mrs Carradine, so I'll have to find another live-in position. I don't suppose you know of anyone.'

'Not at the moment, but I'll think about it

and ask my friends and my daughters. In the meantime, if you've been paid for three weeks you can go on living here and keep an eye on the house. Do a bit of cleaning ... I can't believe Mr Waring has gone for good. But by all means look for another post in case he doesn't return.' Did that sound reasonable, Edith wondered. Was it likely? In her heart she didn't think so but better to 'keep a lid on things'. No point in alerting the neighbours. Certainly no point in starting unsavoury gossip.

Mrs Rice asked, 'What will you do? Call the police? They find missing persons, don't they?'

Edith smiled. 'My nephew is not missing, Mrs Rice. He has chosen to leave Hilsomer House and ... Ah! Here is the note. Thank you, Rosie. I suggest you remake Mr Waring's bed with clean sheets before you do anything else.'

The note was short but for a moment her eyes misted over at the sight of the familiar handwriting.

Dear Aunt Edith,

Do please forgive me for what I have done. I know it will hurt you. The police will almost certainly call at Hilsomer House in the near future and they will explain what has happened. I have to try and start a new life somewhere else –

hopefully abroad. I've been such a fool but I hope you can find it in your heart to remember me with at least a small measure of your earlier fondness.

Sadly, your loving nephew,
Alexander

Through her deep confusion and fear, Edith heard Rosie leave the room, shooed out by Mrs Rice. She read the letter again, searching for clues but there were so few. With a sudden clenching of her fist, she screwed up the letter.

Mrs Rice eyed her hopefully. 'Well? Does he explain what's happened?'

Edith thought rapidly. It would be best to tell the servants as little as possible without actually deceiving them. How little would satisfy them, she wondered.

'No,' she said at last. 'He says only that he is going abroad for a few years. He ... he's given up his job and ... and plans to make a fresh start. And that he's sorry he didn't tell me but it was a sudden decision.' Avoiding Mrs Rice's eyes, she tried to smile as she tucked the offending letter into her pocket.

'Make a fresh life doing what, I wonder?'

Mrs Rice has put her finger on it, thought Edith. The letter raised more questions and answered none. And the police might call. She would have to warn her.

'Alexander says the police might call

during the coming days. If they do … you must say you know nothing about it and send them round to my flat. I don't want you to have to worry about any of that. Just say he left hurriedly and you don't know when he's coming back. What's the matter?'

Mrs Rice was shaking her head. 'I couldn't pretend I don't know anything. I couldn't lie to the police – I'd get into serious trouble.'

The poor woman was right, of course. Edith sighed. 'I have it. I'll move in here for a few days then I can deal with them. That seems sensible, don't you think?'

Mrs Rice's frown faded. 'Oh, yes! That would be wonderful. I mean, you'll know what to say to them. I wouldn't – and he's your nephew.'

Edith decided not to take offence at what seemed like a slur on Alexander.

'Finish the breakfast,' she said. 'I'll eat it and then I'll go home for a few clothes and personal items.'

Her face cleared. She was going to need help to survive whatever lay ahead and it suddenly seemed a good idea to get in touch with someone else who knew Alexander well. After church she would write to Hester Shaw.

Eleven o'clock found Edith Carradine kneeling in prayer at her usual church, praying for Alexander to come to his senses and return

298

to Hilsomer House. She had recovered from her initial shock and her natural resilience had returned. She now felt reasonably confident that whatever the problem was, she could help him. As the congregation rose to sing the final hymn, she slipped from her seat near the rear of the church and tiptoed out. The good Lord would understand, she knew, that she had important things to do. She had made Him aware of the difficulty and would now expect Him to offer her strength of purpose and clarity of thought.

Entering Hilsomer House twenty minutes later, she was pleased to see that Mrs Rice looked more her usual self and that Rosie had stopped crying.

Calling them both into the kitchen, she said, 'I shall make all efforts to find my nephew, but if I don't succeed you may both rely on the fact that I shall write each of you an excellent reference on behalf of Mr Waring. That will make it much easier for you both to find alternative positions.'

She then went upstairs to the study and sat at Alexander's large desk to write to Hester Shaw. After much soul-searching she decided to be completely honest.

My dear Miss Shaw,
I write with a heavy heart to acquaint you of certain facts concerning Alexander. For reasons I do not understand, he has left

Hilsomer House abruptly and has given the servants three weeks' money in lieu of notice. Naturally I am shocked but not yet despairing. With God's help he may eventually return – depending, no doubt, on his reasons for leaving.

He left me a note which explains nothing but I suspect some kind of breakdown. He told the servants to expect a call from the police. I find that horribly ironic. When I know more I will contact you again, but I think you should possibly be prepared for a similar visit, depending on how far-reaching their enquiries prove to be. I hope everything goes well for you with Mr Barnes. When you marry, if you wish to invite me to the wedding, I shall be pleased to accept.

In haste, your friend,
Mrs Edith Carradine

She found a stamp and sent Rosie to the nearest pillar box but before she returned, the police arrived in the shape of a constable and a detective inspector.

Ten minutes later the three of them sat in the study where the constable was searching through the various drawers and cupboards, having been given permission to do so by Edith. Detective Inspector Raffey was asking questions and writing in his notebook while issuing instructions to his constable.

Edith was recovering from the shock of

what she had been told – that her nephew was wanted by the police for incitement to a crime and that his victim was none other than Hester's young steward from the *Mauretania*.

'Is Mr Barnes going to live?' she asked, her voice querulous.

'They think he'll live, but there may be permanent damage.'

'And his broken leg?'

'He'll always limp. That's what the doctors say.' He spoke in a matter-of-fact tone, as though nothing would ever surprise him. She found that irritating. DI Raffey studied his notes, frowning at what he had written. He was tall and thin with frizzy hair and small eyes. He spoke quietly but appeared wrapped up in his note taking and rarely gave Edith a direct look. 'So you do not think Waring has another home anywhere where he might have gone?'

'Not to my knowledge.'

'Any friends or relatives who might be harbouring him?'

Edith stiffened. 'He has friends and relatives and he might be *visiting* them, but as for *harbouring* – the answer's no.'

They were already treating him as a criminal, she thought resentfully, even before he had been charged or tried. What had happened to the democratic way – innocent until proved guilty?

The constable closed the final drawer and shook his head.

DI Raffey said, 'Talk to the housekeeper.' The constable left the room.

'What are you looking for?' Edith asked.

Without bothering to answer, DI Raffey asked, 'Does your nephew own a boat?'

'Good Lord, no!'

'Does he have friends or relatives abroad? France, perhaps?'

'Not to my knowledge.'

She wanted to say that even if she knew she wouldn't tell him but that would be pointless. If this silly business ever came to a trial she would offer herself as a character witness and they would never accept her if she had antagonized the investigating officer. Instead she tried to hold herself together and maintain her dignity.

The detective picked up a diary the constable had found earlier and gave it his full attention.

'What do you know of this Hester he refers to?'

'Hester Shaw lived in a flat belonging to my nephew for several years.'

'So he has another house or flat? When I asked you earlier, you denied it.'

It was true. She felt a moment's panic. 'I always thought of the flat as hers, not his. He lived here with his wife and ... and visited Miss Shaw.'

'But he paid the rent?'

'I suppose so. It was none of my business.'

Edith was asked to give the address and did so. 'But she isn't there now. She is in Liverpool.'

'You do see, Mrs Carradine, how this looks. Waring keeps a mistress, the mistress finds another man and Waring is overcome with jealousy and wants revenge – on both of them. He arranges to have the other man beaten up. He does it because he can. He's a senior policeman and thinks he's above the law – a fatal mistake. He thinks he can get away with it, but it blows up in his face.' He smiled for the first time. 'That's what comes of relying on scum like Fitch. You'd think a man in Waring's position would have had more sense.'

The same thought had occurred to Edith, but she had resisted it as disloyal in the extreme. She said nothing, her lips pursed, her expression giving nothing away. In his note Alexander had wanted her to forgive him but she didn't think she could. If this were all true, what he had done was a most terrible thing and Mr Barnes, an innocent man, had suffered for her nephew's wickedness. Because that's what it was – a vile and wicked act. She wanted to believe that Alexander had somehow been framed by his enemies, but part of her found the facts plausible. The question in her mind was – if

Alexander had hated Barnes that much, could he have done this? If this Fitch character had *killed* Mr Barnes it would be even more serious because then it would be a hanging matter. And poor Hester! Edith wanted to cry but she had been brought up to show self-restraint and now she was denied the release that tears would have brought.

The constable returned. 'The housekeeper says he kept a gun in a box beside his bed but it's not there. Only the box.'

'A *gun!*' Edith's hand flew to her mouth as she choked back a cry. Alexander had kept a gun. How had she not known that? And why had he taken it with him? Who was he going to shoot? Not Fitch, surely. He was already in custody. Would he shoot at the police if they tried to arrest him? How desperate was he?

The two policemen exchanged meaningful glances and suddenly Edith wanted them both out of the house. The strain of trying to remain composed was becoming too much for her. She abandoned her upright stance on the edge of the armchair and allowed herself to lean back against the cushion. She felt smaller and more vulnerable as she did so, but somehow she must convince these men that there was no way they could intimidate her into admitting anything that might incriminate Alexander.

Rosie knocked and was admitted. To Edith she said, 'I usually go home at this time and Mrs Rice doesn't need me so...?'

DI Raffey said, 'You can go for now. Thank you for your help.'

What had Rosie told them? Edith wondered nervously. It seemed the servants knew more than she did.

'Take this back to the station.' He tore a page from his notebook and handed it to the constable. 'They'll need to search this address, too, and the sooner the better – and talk to the landlady if there is one, or the neighbours. We can't afford to miss anything. This case is going to be very big!'

Turning his attention back to Edith, the detective inspector towered over her. 'So you last saw him when?'

'Christmas morning.'

'And why did you come to his home yesterday?'

'Because he seemed upset by a phone call he received Christmas morning. I wanted him to confide in me. I thought he might be ill or ... or having a breakdown. His wife had only just died. He seemed worried. Not himself.' She was aware of a great weariness. 'I've told you all this before, when you first arrived.'

To her relief he snapped shut the notebook. 'I think that'll be all for today, but we may need to contact you again. If your nephew should contact you, you are duty bound to report it directly to me at the police station. Failure to do so means you are interfering in a police investigation and that is a serious matter. Are you clear about that?'

She nodded.

'I'll see myself out. Oh! Do I have your home address?'

'I gave it to the constable.'

'Thank you, Mrs Carradine, for your cooperation.'

After he'd gone Edith still sat in the chair, waiting for the churning in her stomach to stop, but before it did so Mrs Rice came in with a brandy. Neither woman spoke until the door was almost closed. Then Edith said, 'Pour one for yourself, Mrs Rice!'

Edith closed her eyes. It finally occurred to her to wonder what Hester Shaw would think about it all. An unhappy smile twisted her mouth. An invitation to her wedding to Mr Barnes now seemed extremely unlikely.

Three days later Hester sat beside Charlie's bed and broke the news of Alexander's disappearance and the alleged reason behind it. The doctor had agreed that she might safely pass on the information as his occasional lapses into confusion were becoming rarer.

The police were waiting to be admitted so

that they could speak with him and Hester felt that their interrogation would come as less of a shock if he already understood the main points of the conspiracy. As she spoke to him she couldn't avoid making the comparison between the Charlie she had first seen in the bar of the *Mauretania* and the man she saw before her. His curly brown hair was completely hidden beneath white bandages, the alert grey eyes were dulled by the medication he had been given and his cheerful voice with its Liverpool twang was painfully slow, allowing little of his cheeky talk and sweet compliments. But, she reminded herself, he was still alive and for that she thanked God daily in her prayers.

Hester had made the account of Alexander's involvement as simple as possible and Charlie appeared to have understood her.

'So, Charlie,' she said, 'will you ever forgive me? I can see how it looks – that it's because of me and you that you were attacked. Well, actually it's because of me. Alexander didn't really want me, but he didn't like me falling in love with you. I had no idea he could be so violent – or that he cared for me enough. No, it isn't even that he cared. You stole something he believed he owned. He could not bear it.' She stopped, searching his face for his reaction.

Charlie squeezed her hand. 'Not ... your ...

fault,' he insisted. 'Don't … blame you … falling … love … me!' He managed a grin. He still had difficulty speaking, but the doctor believed that it would improve with time. 'The leg's mending,' the doctor had told her. 'He'll soon be up and about.'

They both knew this was an exaggeration, but Charlie was thinking very positively, refusing to think that he might not make a complete recovery. Nobody disillusioned him although the long-term prognosis was not entirely encouraging. As soon as the leg bone had healed they would allow him up for a short time each day and the doctors would design exercises which would strengthen the leg muscles. The trauma to his brain was what worried the doctor.

Hester showed Charlie the cutting from *The Times* newspaper, outlining the case and describing Alexander who was 'on the run and believed to be carrying a firearm'.

'A gun! I can't believe it,' Hester repeated. 'I knew him all those years and trusted him completely.'

'You … were … wrong.'

'And Marcia, his wife! Thank goodness she isn't alive to be caught up in the scandal. I wonder where Alexander has gone … and poor Mrs Carradine! She's a funny old thing and can be difficult at times but she adored him.'

The bell was rung to announce the end of

visiting time, and Hester kissed Charlie's hand by way of goodbye. She longed to fling her arms around him, hold him close and smother his face with kisses, but that was out of the question and would remain so for some time.

'Don't forget I love you,' she told him, her throat tight with the familiar sorrow of leaving him again.

He smiled. 'You ... only ... one ... me.'

'And you're the only one for me. Aren't we lucky?'

He nodded as Hester blinked away tears. Lucky they had found each other and lucky that so far no one had been able to tear them apart.

She said, 'Is it all right if Maisie comes in tomorrow instead of me? She is longing to see you and has been so patient. I feel unkind, keeping you all to myself.'

He nodded and she could see that he was tiring. A nurse appeared beside her with a thermometer in her hand.

'Isn't he doing well, Miss Shaw? A model patient.'

She popped the thermometer into his mouth and prepared to update the notes which hung at the end of his bed.

'I must go,' Hester told him. 'Happy New Year, Charlie!'

As Hester made her way along the now familiar corridors, she thought of the people caught up in the events of the past weeks. Edith Carradine, Alexander – even Annie Green. Especially Annie Green. Why, she wondered, had the price for her happiness with Charlie come at so high a price?

Charlie watched her go for as long as he could, because it was difficult and painful to turn his head. He lived for her visits, but he hated to see her so worried. It was Waring's fault, and that made him hate Waring with a deep passion. He had prayed every night that something bad would happen to him and he was pleasantly surprised that the Lord had heard his prayers and had set the might of the law on him. Serve him damned well right! The man was evil. While in a hating mood, Charlie hated the knowledge that his beautiful Hester had lived with the brute, but there was no way of undoing the past. He hated the fact that Annie had suffered because of him and that presumably she must hate him. Charlie was sad, too, about the baby she had 'lost' and had searched his mind for a way to put that right. The solution still evaded him. He hadn't shown the letter to Hester because he knew she'd be unhappy about it.

The nurse removed the thermometer and glanced at it. 'Still doing well,' she told him. 'So, when's the wedding? Going to hold it here in the hospital, I hear.'

'No ... better ... church. Do it ... properly.'

'Well, wherever you hold the wedding, Miss Shaw will be a very pretty bride!'

Beaming, he gave a small nod, and she moved on to her next patient.

Yes, Hester would make a wonderful bride, he reflected, immediately cheered by the prospect. And she would be a wonderful wife and mother. Three children? Maybe four. His smile disappeared.

In his bedside cupboard there was a letter he had decided not to show to Hester. It was from Chalky and he knew the contents by heart. Chalky had spoken to the boss about when Charlie was well enough to resume work. A steward with a limp and a possible speech problem would have no place on the *Mauretania*, but, as he was well-liked, they would find him another position if he wanted to resume working on board the ship. Perhaps a job in Stores. It was a blow to Charlie's hopes of a decent career. Stores led nowhere and had none of the buzz and glamour of work in the bar – and it would pay less. So maybe four children would be too many on his pitiful wage as a store hand. The prospect dismayed him but he forced aside his doubts. There were compensations. He had survived the revenge Waring had planned for him and would live to see the man brought to justice. Ruined, in fact! And although Charlie was gentle at heart, he was looking forward to watching Waring go through hell while he, Charlie Barnes, shared the rest of his life with his beloved Hester.

Thirteen

The hansom cab rattled along at a sluggish pace, drawn by a tired horse. The cab driver was also tired and reckoned it was long past his bedtime. He often worked until the early hours, but he had started earlier than usual and the day had been busy and his chest was playing him up again. His lungs had never taken to cold, damp weather and he had often thought of moving to Australia or California but never could get the fare together.

'Not a star in the sky tonight, guvnor,' he remarked, hoping for a response from his fare. He'd picked him up at Waterloo station thinking it would be a short and sweet fare and he'd get off home with a bit of extra cash because his passenger had offered to pay double the normal price and that was not to be sniffed at.

'No. Too cloudy,' the passenger replied.

Encouraged, the cabby pressed on. 'I like a bit of moonlight myself.'

No answer. Miserable sod, thought the cabby, resigned. A bit of chat never hurt anyone and it passed the time. Still, they were nearly there. He'd heard half-past eleven strike so maybe he'd be home by one. It was New Year's Day and his wife would nag – until she knew about the bit of extra money. That'd bring a smile to her face. He grinned and whipped up the horse. 'Get up there!' he shouted, to impress his fare. The horse ignored him as usual.

'Ten more minutes and we'll be there,' he promised cheerily. 'Soon be tucked up in a nice warm bed.' He chuckled to show it was a joke but the gentleman remained silent.

True to his word, ten minutes later, he reined in outside a large house and jumped down to assist his gentleman fare who handed over the promised money and bade him a terse, 'Goodnight.'

'Goodnight, guvnor, and a happy New Year!'

Alexander watched the cab disappear into the darkness then turned and walked up the steps to the front door. Taking out his key he turned it carefully in the lock, opened the door slowly, then stepped inside and closed it quietly behind him. Why was he bothering? he thought, with a shake of his head. There was no one here. Mrs Rice and Rosie were gone. They would find other work, he reassured himself. His aunt would help them. He stood in the hallway, waiting for his eyes to acclimatize themselves to the dim light which filtered through the glass fanlight over the front door. He was pleasantly surprised that the house still had that lived-in feel. A certain warmth remained despite the inclement weather. He toyed with the idea of removing his overcoat but decided against it. He stood for a moment with his eyes closed then slipped his right hand into his pocket and fingered the pistol.

Alexander went up the stairs thinking about Marcia and wishing he had been more patient with her during her various spells of ill health. As he walked along the landing towards his study he remembered Hester and regretted that she must now thoroughly despise him. Once inside the familiar study that he had always thought of as his sanctuary, he recalled his aunt and her many kindnesses and wished he could thank her instead of inflicting more anguish. Lastly he thought with relish of the expression of horror on Harrow's face the previous night, just before Alexander shot him.

He sat down at the empty desk, put the pistol to his right temple and, for some reason he didn't understand, waited patiently for the clock in the hall to start striking midnight. After the third stroke he whispered 'Oh God!' as he pulled the trigger.

Seven hours later Mrs Rice splashed cold water over her face and neck and dried herself with the towel. 'It is 1908!' she said with amazement. She had always lived each year in the fearful belief that it might be her last so that each New Year came as a pleasant surprise. Crossing to her calendar she put a line through the first of January and stared at the second. 'Thursday, the second of January! Well, well! Thank goodness last year is over.' She sighed. It seemed that in the blink of an eye her life had changed.

She struggled into her clothes and went downstairs to relight the stove and begin preparations for Mrs Carradine's breakfast.

Outside there was a rough wind blowing, but much of the snow had melted and the slush had been cleared away. From behind the kitchen door, Mrs Rice took down Marcia's apron and put it on with a brief whispered prayer for her ex-mistress's soul. She had taken to wearing it 'in memory of' her departed mistress and liked to think that, should Marcia Waring glance down, she would approve. Not that Mrs Waring often ventured into the kitchen, but in the early days she had sometimes decided to try out a recipe given to her by a friend. Mrs Rice had convinced herself that, now that Marcia Waring was dead, someone else might as well get some wear out of the apron. It would be a pity to waste it.

'Poor woman,' she said, tutting at the wasted life. No children and an unfaithful

316

husband. What good had all that money done Marcia Waring? Kneeling in front of the stove she arranged paper and kindling wood, piled on small coals and lit it.

Upstairs she could hear the old aunt pottering about in her bedroom. Mrs Carradine would soon be downstairs, poking her nose in everywhere – but at least she, Mrs Rice, didn't have to sleep alone in the house. She had also seen a marked difference in the old lady's attitude. It seemed as though her nephew's shame had reduced his aunt in some way. Mrs Rice occasionally felt sorry for her.

Steps sounded on the stairs and Mrs Carradine appeared in the kitchen. She said, 'Happy New Year, Mrs Rice. A new day, a new year.'

'That was yesterday, ma'am. Today's the second.'

'Really? I'm beginning to think my mind is wandering.' She sat down.

'Hardly surprising, Mrs Carradine. You've had a lot on your plate recently. But now we've got a brand new year! Something to look forward to.' She smiled cheerfully.

'Just a few stewed apples, Mrs Rice. I'm not very hungry.'

'Should I serve it in the dining room? Mr Waring ... oh, sorry! That is, he liked to eat there...'

'Yes, yes. The dining room.' She sighed

deeply. 'I didn't sleep well. Something woke me from a deep sleep – I was dreaming about Alexander when he was a boy.' She smiled faintly. 'We were so close. When he went off to his prep school. I went with him on the train because his parents couldn't take him. They led such busy lives. He was only nine and trying hard to be brave...' Swallowing, she frowned at another memory then rubbed her eyes. 'What was I saying, Mrs Rice?'

'You didn't sleep well, ma'am.'

'Oh, yes! Something woke me and I sat straight up in the bed, wide awake. I listened but didn't hear anything. When I looked at the clock it was exactly midnight. Did you hear anything?'

'No, ma'am, nothing, but I do sleep heavy. Like a log, my ma used to say.'

The old lady shrugged. 'Some time I have to speak with the family lawyer, but not just yet. Too many unanswered questions ... I shall start going through the house later today. There is so much to sort out. I hardly know where to begin. All Mrs Waring's clothes, for a start – and Alexander's desk.'

Mrs Rice hesitated. 'I think most of his stuff's gone from the study. The police took a lot away when they searched the house. I do know they cleared his desk and...'

'Yes, yes!' Mrs Carradine interrupted her. 'I take your point. No need to go on like

318

that. We all know what's happened. God knows we do!'

There was an awkward silence. Mrs Rice went to the larder and produced stewed apples, sugar and cream and put them on a tray which she carried through into the dining room.

Mrs Carradine said, 'Where's Rosie?'

'You gave her the day off. Her mother's having a baby.'

'Did I?' She shrugged. 'A baby, did you say? How many's that?'

'There are six children. Rosie's the eldest. All girls.'

'I hope the police didn't take the photographs as well. They can be so heavy-handed. There were some photographs I value. Some taken while Alexander was at school – one on sports day, I recall. He had just won the hundred yards race and he was so proud!'She smiled. 'Beaming and holding up the cup. And another, one of my favourites, taken sitting on my lap at a picnic. He was only four, bless him, and still had his curls. He was such a lovable little chap. I'll try and find them. You might like to see one or two.'

Mrs Rice tried to look enthusiastic. 'That would be nice.'

Stifling a yawn behind her hand, Mrs Carradine stood up. 'Breakfast calls,' she said. Halfway to the door she turned back. 'There is one photograph of the three cousins,

Dorcas, Evelyn and Alexander. Sitting together on the beach at Ramsgate. They all had buckets and spades, but Alexander had a larger size than the girls because, as he insisted, he was a boy! He pleaded so sweetly that I couldn't resist him although it didn't please my daughters. I knew why it was important to him – he wanted to build a bigger sandcastle, you see.' She laughed. 'Method in his madness, you might say!'

Devious little devil, Mrs Rice thought, but simply smiled. She watched Mrs Carradine as she left the kitchen and thought how quickly the spring had gone from her step. The past few weeks had done the old lady no favours.

After a simple lunch of soused mackerel, Edith remembered her promise to Mrs Rice and began to look for the photograph album. With an effort she recalled that it was red leather and somewhat faded from years of handling. It wasn't in the sideboard where she expected to find it, nor was it in the cupboard under the stairs where some of Alexander's things were kept with a few of Marcia's. She found tennis racquets, a pair of hiking boots, a box of Christmas decorations which Marcia had made, several board games, a croquet set and various other odds and ends – but no album.

Perhaps it was in Alexander's bedroom – or

the study. With a sigh she made her way upstairs, trying to visualize exactly where it might be. The study had plenty of shelves and cupboards plus the old trunk in which he had taken his school things to and fro. She smiled. He had been so proud of the new trunk with its brass locks and leather straps...

Opening the door she stood for a moment totally unaffected by the scene that met her eyes. Her sight registered her nephew, but her mind was unable to grasp how he came to be where he was. He was leaning forward, his head on his desk, seemingly asleep, but when she spoke to him he failed to answer. For an awful moment the scene was entirely unreal and she suspected she was losing her mind. Alexander had left days ago so how...

'Alexander!' she repeated. If only he would lift his head and smile the way he did ... then everything would be all right. But deep inside she was being forced to accept that this was not going to happen and that something was terribly wrong. She began to tremble then took a small step forward and then another.

'Oh, my dear!' she whispered.

The blood had spread out across the desk and had dripped off on to the carpet.

'Blood,' she whispered and her legs almost gave way. Could she believe what she saw, she wondered. Her nephew rested there so peacefully, it seemed a shame to disturb him by prying further. But, of course, she must.

Softly, tremulously, she walked round the desk and saw the pistol which had fallen from Alexander's dangling hand.

'Oh, darling! What have you done?' she asked. 'My dearest boy!' She shook her head slowly from side to side, while her hands, overlapping, were spread across her chest. 'What *have* you done?' She laid a hand on his head but withdrew it quickly and stared in horror at the sticky red mess on her fingers. Lifting her gaze she noticed small red spatters on the wall behind his chair.

Shocked into a cold stillness, Edith watched Alexander for what seemed for ever – until the world began again and she was able to draw a long shuddering breath and then another. Still gasping for air, she turned and stumbled from the study on to the landing where she clutched at the balustrade to support herself.

'Mrs Rice! Please come!' Her voice was hoarse and very weak. She tried again. '*Mrs Rice! Please!*'

'What is it, ma'am?' Mrs Rice appeared, holding up floury hands. 'I'm just rolling a bit of pastry for...'

'Leave it! It doesn't matter.' Nothing would ever matter again, Edith thought, a sob rising in her throat. 'You have to come up.' As Mrs Rice came up the stairs, wiping her hands on a damp cloth, Edith warned her, 'I'm afraid ... It's not very pleasant but ... There has been a bit of an accident.'

Within half an hour of the telephone call to the police, the street outside Hilsomer House was full of policemen and newspaper reporters who were augmented by a crowd of interested bystanders who refused to be dispersed. Harried by frustrated constables, the crowd simply moved to another vantage point. Edith and Mrs Rice had been seen by a police doctor and allowed to leave. They had been taken to Dorcas's home where she made them as comfortable as she could and provided warm sweet tea and small lemon cakes by way of light but nourishing refreshment.

For a long time Edith said nothing, reliving the moment when she finally accepted that Alexander was lost to her, but suddenly she recovered enough to tell her daughter a few details. Talking about it brought home the dreadful reality, but she felt that keeping it all inside her head would drive her insane.

'Thank heavens for Mrs Rice,' she said generously. 'She was such a comfort. So calm and...'

Mrs Rice said, 'After my first scream, maybe. I was that shaken up I'm afraid I couldn't stop myself.'

Dorcas nodded. 'It must have been a

terrible shock for both of you. I'm so sorry. Poor Alexander.'

Edith nodded. 'My first thought was to call a doctor, but I knew it was much too late. He must have come into the house after we went to bed and I did hear that noise that woke me up. It must have been the gunshot. I didn't think Alexander would want the police around with all that mess, but Mrs Rice insisted we had to notify them. I thought we should clean up a bit before they arrived but Mrs Rice...'

'I thought we had to leave it as it was because they call it a crime scene and have to take fingerprints and things like that because there might have been another person involved and not suicide and...'

Dorcas said, 'It seems so unkind to call suicide a crime. I mean, it's a very personal thing and I'm sure Alexander isn't a criminal.'

Edith closed her eyes. 'In fact that's exactly what he is, dear. Or was, God rest his soul. The police say he killed a man down in Devon somewhere. He was blackmailing him – the man, not Alexander. It sounded rather complicated but it's all to do with poor Mr Barnes in Liverpool.'

Dorcas looked puzzled. 'But how on earth could that be? It doesn't make sense.'

'I know that, Dorcas, but there were two men involved...' She shook her head. 'Don't ask me to explain. It's making my head spin.'

Mrs Rice said, 'Then perhaps Mr Waring did the sensible thing by ... by what he's just done. Better than hang—' She stopped abruptly in mid word and glanced apologetically at Edith. 'Sorry, ma'am. I don't know what I'm saying. I'm that upset.'

Edith was clasping and unclasping her hands. 'The policeman – the senior man – said Alexander did the decent thing in the end. He's hoping to hush it all up. It would look so bad for the force. One of their own senior men.'

'Not much chance,' said Dorcas, 'with all those reporters outside. I know we never thought Alexander was capable of such bad things but ... but he has killed a man and sent a thug to injure another man. I wonder what poor Hester will make of all this when she hears. She must have loved Alexander once.'

'Of course she did.' Edith glared at her. 'He was charming, considerate, well-respected ... until now. You talk as though your cousin is – *was* – some kind of monster. He was a very good man but for some reason he snapped. Maybe something went wrong inside his head.' She sat up a little straighter in the chair.

'Maybe he had a tumour like that opera singer that went mad and had to be committed. We'll probably never know.' She looked at her companions hopefully, to see if they would accept this version of events.

Dorcas said, 'We *will* know, Mother, because there'll be a post-mortem and they can find out about tumours and suchlike.'

'Well, there you are. Poor Alexander!' Edith embraced the possibility.

'Let's hope so,' said Dorcas, but she sounded unconvinced.

Mrs Rice said, 'Mrs Waring was always on to him to get a new carpet for the study. Good job they didn't with all that ... Oh!' She clapped a hand over her mouth and, afraid to look at Edith, glanced apologetically at Dorcas.

Edith gave her a withering glance which the housekeeper missed and Dorcas said quickly, 'I'll make another pot of tea.'

Weeks passed and Alexander's body was finally released for burial by his family on the second of February, after most of the publicity had been forgotten. To avoid the press, the family had decided to bury him in the Hampshire village where he was born. Hester had been invited and had discussed the matter with Charlie who said generously that she should go 'for the good times'. By this time, Charlie had been allowed to leave the hospital after reassuring his doctor that between Hester and Maisie, he would be well looked after.

Very few local people realized that the funeral arranged for that particular day was that of *the* Alexander Waring who had featured in most of the country's newspapers throughout the first week of January.

The temperature had dropped suddenly during the previous night and the few mourners left their footprints in two inches of crisp white snow as they made their way to the newly dug grave in a remote and untidy corner of the churchyard. The service had been very short with no music and the vicar made it clear by his attitude that he resented the family's choice of Alexander's final resting place. Dorcas, Evelyn, Edith and Hester were the only mourners. Mrs Rice had refused to return to Hilsomer House and Edith had helped her to find a new position. Rosie had returned to her parents to help look after her mother and the new baby.

As they watched the coffin being lowered into the icy ground, Hester ignored the vicar's rushed prayer and uttered one of her own, asking God to forgive Alexander for the wrong he had done and to bear in mind the good things also.

Afterwards they hurried to the small public house nearby where they had arranged for hot tea and sandwiches before the family set off on their return train journey to London, and Hester made her way back to Liverpool.

Hester and Edith parted with a shy kiss.

Edith said, 'I shall think of you often, Hester. Perhaps I could be kept informed as to Mr Barnes's progress.'

'Most certainly,' Hester agreed. 'I want the two of you to be properly introduced one day. Better still, you must come to the wedding. You could book into a nice hotel and enjoy yourself. Charlie remembers you from the ship and sends his regards. He did ask that you should be invited to the wedding.'

'He did?'

'Because, if it were not for you making the journey on the *Mauretania* and taking me as your travelling companion, I should never have met him. We owe you a great deal.'

It seemed to Hester, as she waved them off at the station, that the worst must be over. She was to discover in the weeks that followed, that indeed it was.

Wednesday, 3rd June, 1908 – I received an invitation today to Hester and Charlie's wedding and will be delighted to write and accept.

At last, the solicitors have decided how they will settle Alexander's estate, but we still have no idea when it will be finalized. These things take months if not years. It seems that Alexander did not update his original will. He has left Hilsomer House to Marcia, but since she has predeceased him the house will be sold and the value of the property will be added to the estate and dealt with accordingly. It seems that Dorcas, Evelyn and I are the sole beneficiaries except for Hester. Alexander had very generously left her the flat they shared and I shall suggest to her that she allows me to find a suitable tenant so that the rent will supplement her income until she decides to sell the property – which may be sooner rather than later. Who knows? If Mr Barnes is unable to earn as much as he would have done in his former employment, this will prove to be a very suitable form of compensation (albeit by a circuitous route!) and hopefully Mr Barnes will not discourage his wife from accepting it. I shall write to her on the subject as soon as I have more details from the solicitor and can be more precise.

The more I learn about Charlie Barnes, the more I like him. He made no fuss about allowing Hester to attend Alexander's funeral and I was very touched by that.

On Saturday, the eighth of May, 1909, almost a year later, Edith stepped down from the train and was immediately hailed by Hester who was waiting on the platform with a small baby in her arms – the large perambulator which Edith had insisted on giving to them as a present for their first child waited at home for another occasion. Young Adam Charles Barnes was two weeks old and a lively, healthy boy, with Hester's red hair and what Maisie proudly called 'the Barnes lungs'.

As soon as the two women had greeted each other, Edith took her first look at the new arrival, who was sleeping peacefully inside his blanket.

'Oh, my! He's wonderful,' she told Hester. 'It's a long time since I've seen such a young child and I feel quite privileged.'

'I'm sorry Charlie isn't here to carry your bag, but the ship docks tomorrow,' Hester explained as they made their way along the platform towards the barrier. 'He's getting the hang of Stores and is so thrilled to be back at sea again. It was his greatest worry. Of course he misses being with Chalky and the other stewards, but at least he's on the *Mauretania* and that's what matters to him.'

Outside the station they joined the queue for a cab and were eventually rattling through the streets at a smart pace. Hester stole a glance at the old lady and thought she looked tired but doubtless the journey had fatigued her. Edith had made the journey so that she could attend Adam's christening, but there was another reason, and this had worried Hester. Ignoring Edith's advice to retain the London flat, Hester and Charlie had decided to sell it and buy a home for themselves in Liverpool. The price of houses was much lower there and they had bought a very nice three-storey house, near to Maisie. With no rent to pay, they were also able to let out the top floor as a separate flat and thus add to Charlie's wages.

Edith had made no attempt to hide her disappointment at their decision, but now she was to see the house for the first time.

'Are you sure you want to stay in the hotel?' Hester asked her. 'You know we have a spare bedroom.'

Edith shook her head. 'I love hotels,' she admitted. 'I always have, ever since I was a child. It's the anonymity. No one knows anything about you. It's a wonderfully secret feeling.'

'Maisie is looking forward to seeing you again,' Hester told her, 'although we're both a bit tired. We went to a friend's wedding on Saturday – Annie Green became Mrs Stanley Holler, and Maisie and I made all the refreshments. Forty guests!'

'Forty guests! Good heavens!'

'We made vol-au-vents, sandwiches, sausage rolls, a large cake, jam tarts ... oh, yes, and also cheese straws and salmon patties.'

Edith turned to look at her. 'So, you have a nice life, dear – your beloved Charlie, a home, friends and family – and now your baby son. Who could have foreseen all this eighteen months ago?'

Hester smiled. 'And we have you – a very dear friend.'

Edith blinked back tears and Hester guessed they were for her nephew – she would never recover from his shameful death. Hester searched for the words of comfort that could never be enough, but before she could speak the cab was slowing down outside her house. At once, the past, with all its joys and woes, faded from her mind. With Adam in her arms, she stepped carefully down on to the dusty pavement where future joys and woes now beckoned.